FIC  Alexander, David.

My real name is
Lisa.

$21.00

| DATE | | | |
|---|---|---|---|
| | | | |
| | | | |
| | | | |
| | | | |
| | | | |
| | | | |
| | | | |
| | | | |
| | | | |
| | | | |
| | | | |
| | | | |

# MY REAL NAME IS LISA

# MY REAL NAME IS LISA

## David Alexander

CARROLL & GRAF PUBLISHERS, INC.
NEW YORK

First edition 1996.

Carroll & Graf Publishers, Inc.
260 Fifth Avenue
New York, NY 10001

ISBN 0-7867-0310-5

Library of Congress Cataloging-in-Publication Data is available.

Manufactured in the United States of America.

For Ralph Vicinanza and Joel Gotler,
the best agents a writer could ask for.

# MY REAL NAME IS LISA

# ONE

Though almost four-thirty in the afternoon, the advent of daylight saving time almost two weeks before afforded the children at least another hour to play. The sky was clear and the breeze carried the scent of fresh grass and spring flowers as the girls brought out their dolls. Earlier they had been playing on the swing hanging from the maple tree in the Taylor's front yard but they soon tired of sharing one swing among the three of them and decided that a doll party would be much more fun.

Lisa seated her Christmas Barbie astride a pink motor scooter while Carla and Susan pranced and walked their own creations. The girls were still busily weaving stories of magic and excitement when an old brown Buick made its way down Avery Road and quietly pulled to a stop in front of Lisa's house at number 749.

The girls looked up just as a man dressed in sneakers, jeans, and a black T-shirt jumped from the passenger side and ran into the Taylor's front yard. Without saying a word, he grabbed Carla. He had barely lifted her from the ground when he suffered two unexpected injuries. The first was a stabbing pain in his right shin as Lisa kicked him. The kidnapper uttered a startled "ow" and swung his right leg out of the way of a second blow.

At almost the same instant Carla twisted, bent her head close to his right hand, and bit down on the top of the man's middle finger. As a child might release a cat who has scratched him, the kidnapper involuntarily loosened his grasp and Carla tumbled to the ground. Almost immediately the man spun around to grab her again and instead saw Lisa barely two feet behind him as she struggled to retrieve her Barbie and make her own escape.

When the man looked back over his shoulder Carla was already crawling, stumbling in the opposite direction. After only a split second's hesitation, the kidnapper seized Lisa instead. A moment later he was through the gate and, with Lisa's writhing form still clutched to his chest, he jumped back through the Buick's open passenger door.

Five seconds later the Buick was around the corner and out of sight. Barely a minute and a half after that the Buick was hidden in the underbrush a hundred yards off the highway outside of town and the kidnappers and their victim were already back on the road in a red '75 Mustang and headed for the county line.

At the same time that the Mustang pulled onto the two-lane the first hysterical phone call reached the Oakdale Police Department, it having taken that long for an almost incoherent Susan and Carla to return to Mrs. Fisher's house and make themselves understood.

In spite of the police's best efforts, it was too late. The roads were watched but no car matching the Buick's description was seen. Posters were printed and distributed, announcements made hourly on the AM radio station forty miles to the east, but it was as if Lisa Taylor had been swallowed by the earth.

Oakdale's sole police detective, Carlos Ramirez, spent almost every waking moment for the next two months trying to turn up some trace, some lead to Lisa's whereabouts. And he failed. Every call, every report was pursued and they all led nowhere. Still Carlos and Bill and Peggy Taylor persisted. Summer came and went. Then Halloween. Then Christmas. The phone calls dwindled, leads dried up and finally stopped. How could a six-and-a-half-year-old child be stolen from her own front yard and simply vanish? Hadn't anyone seen her? If she was still alive wouldn't someone notice her? Pictures had been printed, flyers distributed.

She could talk. She could call for help. Wouldn't someone notice her? If she was still alive.

January came and went and with the approaching spring almost a year had passed since Lisa was kidnaped but she had disappeared as completely as if she had never existed.


She was only about three-and-a-half-feet tall, not big enough to clear the tops of the shelves filled with pretzels and bottles of taco sauce and bags of sourdough dinner rolls. I noticed her at the last instant and pulled to my left just in time to miss her. She was around seven or eight years old, blonde hair turning to brown, almost long enough to touch her shoulders. I looked down and smiled.

"Sorry, miss, I didn't see you there," I apologized. "Are you okay?"

I don't know what I expected—a grimace, a laugh, a polite "I'm fine." Whatever it was, I didn't get it. Instead her face bore an expression that I had never personally witnessed before: it was the look of someone who has been hit so many times and expects to be abused so regularly in the future that nothing registers any more, nothing shows beyond the thin appearance of pain and hopelessness.

I stared at her, transfixed by her wide gray eyes. She wore faded blue jeans, red tennis shoes, and an oversize brown T-shirt imprinted with the name of a Mexican beer. Although it was perhaps fifty degrees outside, she didn't have a coat or a sweater. After a second she lowered her eyes and said dully, "You didn't hit me."

It was a voice that I would not have expected from a child—an even, emotionless monotone, not whispered, but set so low that the words barely reached me only a foot in front of her.

"What you doin', Alice?" a man called from behind me. I turned and saw a pudgy man, about five feet ten, with heavy black-rimmed glasses. He was standing at the far end of the aisle that ran in front of the frozen foods.

"She's okay," I told him. "I didn't see her. I almost knocked her down."

"She'll do that. Sneak up on you. Won't you, Alice?"

"I'm sorry," the girl piped from behind me.

"What?" the man asked. His face was puffy and its color was what we used to call "refrigerator white." Maybe thirty-five or forty years old, he had very short hair which reflected the fluorescents as if it had been stroked with Vaseline.

"I'm sorry, Daddy," the little girl repeated.

"You'd best get your stuff and pay attention to business if you know what's good for you."

"Yes, Daddy."

"She won't cause you no more trouble," he said to me.

"There's no trouble. It was—" but he had already turned away, back up the aisle toward the magazines at the front of the store.

The little girl, Alice, turned away too, and wandered over to the next row which was filled with canned fruits and vegetables and bottles of cooking oil. I watched her for a moment as I searched my memory trying to recall where I had previously encountered an expression like hers. I knew that I had seen it somewhere before, in a photo or a movie. I stood there trying to remember, then peered over the shelves to try to catch another glimpse of her face but her back was to me. After a moment's hesitation I shook my head and turned away. The day was ending, I thought, as badly as it had begun.

That Thursday had started as one of those bleak late February days when the sun is little more than a vague glow behind a gray overcast that neither dissipates nor brings the relief of rain. I had spent the last half of the morning and most of the afternoon meeting with Bill Mansell, the Oasis Project Supervisor. Finally, after nonstop arguing and no lunch I began to fight my way through the afternoon traffic in a vain attempt to reach the only available software genius who had a prayer of salvaging something from Oasis' shattered development schedule.

Just because I had sold Orayis Corporation to NowSoft for a pile of cash and stock options didn't mean that I was going to sit on my butt and watch TV all day. I had started Orayis with a $25,000 loan from my dad, a BS from U.C. Berkeley, an MBA from Stanford, and about a million hours of my heart and soul. I was still the CEO, even though we were technically a division of NowSoft, and nothing was going to keep the Oasis product from shipping on time and bug free. If it took a big check and personal plea to a reclusive software wizard ensconsed in the wilds of eastern Contra Costa County, then that's what I would do.

By the time I put the San Francisco Bay behind me and was heading east on Highway 24 through the Caldecott Tunnel and out into the Rheem Valley, the nagging headache that had begun almost two hours before was well on its way to becoming a real skull breaker.

There is something about men and driving, I don't know what it is, but we hate to stop, as if asking for directions or pulling in for gas or a bathroom break is a personal failure, a signal of our inability to persevere until our goal is accomplished, our destination achieved. Just a few more miles and we'll be home; a little longer and we can stop for the night; just one more bend in the road and we'll find the signpost we've been looking for. At least that's the way it is with me.

I've been accused more than once of being stubborn to the point of intransigence. I like to think that I am just determined. I look upon perseverance as a virtue. I certainly hadn't gotten to where I was by giving up when things got difficult. As they say in the military, see the hill, take the hill.

On that dreary Thursday afternoon the little man inside me kept telling me: "You can make it. Only half an hour more and you'll be there. Baumbach must have a whole bottle of aspirin right there in his medicine cabinet. Besides, you're already late. Tough it out," and all the while my head was pounding and my shoulders had begun to feel as if the tendons were made of coiled steel.

Finally, when the vibration from each seam in the road began to resonate in my brain, I reluctantly cut across two lanes of traffic and took the next exit, determined to find a drug store, a 7-11, a supermarket, anyplace that could sell me some pills.

It turned out that I had picked a particularly bad time to abandon determination in favor of logic. The off-ramp ended at an intersection with a two-lane road. To the left the road passed under the freeway, down a gray little valley and curved away, out of sight. To the right it climbed a low hill and disappeared over the top of the rise. Below and ahead of me, bordering the far side of the highway, was a small creek, clogged with bracken and manzanita bushes. A few houses dotted the two-lane, all of them dark, empty in the fading afternoon light. I mentally flipped a coin and turned right.

The road was edged with houses built for the most part in the 1950s and early '60s before the advent of strict building codes and subdivision regulations—all two-by-fours and sheetrock and clapboard siding, strung out on both sides of the highway, some clinging to the hillside to my right, others on the far side of a creek to the left.

After going a mile or so with no sign of what passes in the suburbs for civilization I began to take random turnings at crossroads, often peering toward the darkening horizon as I tried to detect the glow of a Safeway or an ARCO or a 7-11 sign. I'm not sure how far I traveled in that disjointed fashion.

Finally, more through luck than planning, as I was pretty thoroughly lost by now, I came upon a dilapidated store set back from the road on a flat dirt oval whose gravel surface had long since disappeared into the adobe topsoil. At the first hint of rain the ground would puddle up and assume the consistency of overworked pie crust, gritty and sticky. Two or three inches down, the almost waterproof earth would stay dry and hard while the inch or so on top became a soupy-bottomed lake. Many an early settler had built his home with adobe bricks, a testament to the structural properties of this particular soil.

Luckily, the rain had not yet started. I would be here just long enough to get a traveler's tin of Excedrin and a can of Coke to wash it down with, and, I reminded myself, a map so I could find my way to Baumbach's house. By now all I knew was that I was somewhere east of 680 and south of Concord.

There was only one other vehicle in the lot, a faded tan VW Vanagon with a small dent behind the driver's door. The wheel covers were missing, which made the van seem especially aged and ill-treated. I went inside and spotted the refrigerated milk and soft drink cases along the back wall. I nodded briefly to the woman behind the counter and edged through a narrow aisle crowded with cans of soup, wire racks of Twinkies, bags of corn chips, and six-packs of beer.

My head was pounding when I reached the end of the row. I

took a quick step toward the refrigerator door and that's when I almost knocked her over.

Maybe I should have done something about my suspicions right then and there, but what? What could I prove? Being a bad parent isn't a crime. I tried to put the little girl out of my mind.

I grabbed a cold Pepsi and then went to the drugs and cosmetics section that lined the far wall to my right. The store had a small tin box of twelve Excedrin for $3.47, but I was past caring about the price. I opened the box with the nail file that I keep in my key case and downed two of the pills with a swallow of cola on the spot. Then, I thought about the little girl again.

Sometimes you do things that you can't consciously justify, can't explain, but you have a reason for doing them, you know you do— you just don't want to admit it to yourself. I could have walked up the drug aisle, past the allergy pills and the toothpaste and hair spray and shampoo and up to the cash register at the front of the store. But I didn't. For some reason I couldn't turn my back on her. Maybe it was the look in her eyes. So, instead of leaving, I turned around, walked past the near end of the aisle and then up the row holding the canned goods, the aisle where Alice was diligently matching pictures of peaches and creamed corn with the items on her list.

When I got near her, I pretended to examine the labels on the cans of sauerkraut, the prices on the jars of pickles. I had no conscious idea of what I was doing, but I knew, somewhere, some part of me knew what I was after, because just about the time that I was swallowing the Excedrin I remembered where I had seen the expression on Alice's face before.

It was in a book in my high school civics class. A book the teacher, Mr. Ida, a Japanese-American who had been locked up in an American detention camp during the first part of World War II, had shown us. He passed it around and tried to explain things that were unexplainable to fifteen-year-old middle-class children, events which we had not yet seen enough evil to be able to comprehend.

The book contained pictures taken from the Nazi archives at Dachau, pictures of people waiting to die, people not sure anymore if dying was, for them, such a bad thing. Their images had that same hollow-eyed hopelessness, that look of desolation beyond pain that I thought I had seen in Alice's face. I knew that the smart thing to do was to mind my own business. But sometimes when you think something is wrong, you can't just turn your back on it and walk away. At least that day I couldn't.

"Are you all right?" I asked softly as I stood next to her. "Are you in trouble? Do you need help?"

Furtively, she looked to her right over her shoulder. The top of the fat man's head was visible at the front of the store.

"I'll get in trouble if I talk to you," she said softly without looking up at me.

"If you need help, tell me. I could call the police."

"No one can help me," she whispered as she moved a few feet away from me to her right, toward the front counter.

I put down the pickles and grabbed a jar of olives from the shelf next to her elbow.

"Is he hurting you? Does he hit you?" She made no answer. "What's your name?" I asked, thinking that I could call Child Protective Services and that we could track her down if I had her full name. Maybe if I could get her full name and the license number from the van that would be enough to have someone start an investigation.

"Please," I whispered, "tell me your name."

"My real name?" she asked softly.

Real name? I turned to stare at her. For a moment longer she looked at the shelf, then turned her head and peered up at me.

"My real name is Lisa, Lisa—"

"What you doin', girl? You botherin' this man? You telling stories again?" The fat man, I could not think of him as her father, had crept around the end of the aisle and approached us with long strides.

"I'm sorry," I said, trying to smile but not succeeding very well. "I was telling your daughter about my goddaughter, Kristin. I'm afraid that I distracted her," I said making the story up as I went along. There was no need for a confrontation. I would pay for my aspirin, get out the door, and call the police from the pay phone in front. They would sort it all out. Something was wrong here, but what? After all, I told myself, what else could I do? I couldn't hit him. I could be arrested or sued. Her real name? What if she was just telling stories? This was a situation for the police. It was their job, not mine. I nodded to the man, slipped by him, and headed for the front counter.

The clerk was a woman in her late fifties. When she punched up the charges on her Japanese cash register I noticed the nicotine stains that had yellowed the tips of her fingers. Her eyes held the half-vacant, half-bored expression of someone who is waiting for each minute to slip by in hopes that the next one will be better while knowing that it won't.

I rushed outside, took a ballpoint pen from my shirt pocket, wrote the VW's license number on the back of one of my business cards, then crossed to the phone. It had started to rain. I had kept a quarter in my hand from the change when I paid for the cola and aspirin and I shoved it into the pay phone slot. It made one dull clank, then two more as it bounced through the mechanism and into the coin return. I tapped the hook twice and fished out the quarter. A splash of light illuminated the booth as the door to the store opened and the fat man and Alice, no, Lisa, came out.

He walked with his heavy right hand pinching the back of her neck. "What'd I tell you about talking to people? What'd I tell you!" he demanded. At first, she didn't answer, she just looked straight ahead while he squeezed her neck. Angrily, he spun her around, grabbed her shoulders in his pudgy fists and began to shake her, all the time shouting: "What'd I tell you? What'd I tell you?" Suddenly, he released her, slapped her her across the side of her face for emphasis and pushed her to the ground. Lisa's shoulder splashed softly in a shallow puddle that had just begun to form in the lot's rutted adobe surface.

"I'm sorry," she said plaintively as she cautiously crawled to her feet. "He just asked me stuff. I didn't talk to him. I didn't!" She was terribly frightened, but trying, I could tell, not to cry.

"I'll show you to mind me! Just wait till we get home."

I stood there in the phone booth and watched him drag her into the van, the useless telephone receiver still clutched in my right hand. I wanted to run over there and punch him in the face. I was a boxer in college, not all programmers are nerds. I mentally rehearsed the combination of blows. But that was insanity. My emotions were running away with me. Thoughts whirled in my head, none of them coalescing into any plan or decision. There had to be a phone in the store. I could still call the police, give them the fat man's license number.

But what if it wasn't his van? Maybe he had borrowed or had bought it from someone and not given them his right address. What if he had moved and not told the Department of Motor Vehicles? Jesus, he could have stolen the van for all I knew.

It was now about five-thirty and almost fully dark. A car passed on the two-lane and, for a moment, its headlights illuminated the VW. For an instant I glimpsed Lisa's face pressed against the passenger door window, and was struck again by how much she looked like those black-and-white images staring out from the pages of Mr. Ida's book.

But now there was also terror in her eyes. And I had caused it. God only knew what he was going to do to her, but whatever happened, it was my fault. I had talked to her. I had said that I would help her, but when it came time for me to do something, to keep my word, I had just walked out. No, not this time. I wasn't going to run away.

I dropped the phone and sprinted to my car. In the few minutes that I was inside the store the rain had formed a patchwork of puddles on the lot. By the time I had unlocked the door and started my engine, the van was a hundred yards down the road, its taillights already beginning to fade into the rain-soaked night.

I pulled out after them with my tires slipping and spinning on the slick ground. Finally, a minute or two later I caught up to the van. By that time I had decided to follow them home, then knock on some neighbor's door and use their phone to call the police. Once the police were on their way I would ring the fat man's bell and tell him to leave the little girl alone, warn him that the police were coming and that there would be serious consequences if he hurt her.

With the dark and the rain, God knew where we were. All I saw was the occasional house set back from the road, a closed gas station, then empty stretches of highway bordered by the silhouettes of live oak and eucalyptus. The fat man seemed to know where he was going, however, as he stopped, then turned, first onto one road, then another. I just followed along, making sure not to lose his taillights around some blind curve. I knew that if he got away from me that I would never find him again.

In front of me his brake lights flashed suddenly, then disappeared around a sharp right turn. I accelerated, then turned after them, and almost smashed into the back of his van where it was parked a few feet down a narrow driveway. I saw a torn, only partially legible red decal on the right side of his bumper: "_____ ley Police Reserve." Could a man like this be a cop? Maybe the decal was a relic from one of the van's prior owners. What was I getting myself into?

I had barely halted my car before my door was yanked open. The rain had slackened to little more than a heavy drizzle, and the fat man's skin glistened like wax in the reflected glow of my headlights. I didn't want to be trapped in the front seat and I struggled out of my seat belt and lurched from the car.

"What are you doin' followin' me?" he shouted.

"I was worried about the little girl," I said quickly. Already the adrenalin was singing in my blood and I couldn't seem to get my breath.

"She's none of your business. You stay out of my family's affairs," he ordered.

"I'm not going to let you hurt her."

"Who says I'm going to hurt her?"

"I heard you talking when you came out of the store. I saw you slap her. You told her you were going to teach her a lesson. That sounds threatening to me."

"You've been watching too much television or reading too many books, or something. I'm her Daddy and she's got to learn to mind."

We stood there for a heartbeat, staring at each other. My mind was whirling. I couldn't leave and I didn't want to stay. The night was leaden. The sound of the water dripping from the oak leaves was soft and distant as if heard through cotton wool. Maybe it was sheer stubbornness, I don't know, but I realized I couldn't leave him there with the child.

"We're going to call the police and they're going to have to straighten this all out," I told him almost as if someone else were speaking with my voice.

"Mister, are you crazy? You get back in your car and get the hell out of here while you still can."

"Not without the little girl. Both of you can get in my car and I'll stop at the first house and call the police. I'm not leaving until they arrive."

"This is the last time I'm going to tell you," the fat man said as he reached into the the pocket of his windbreaker. "Stop interfering in my family's business." When the fat man's hand emerged from his jacket pocket his fingers were grasped around the butt of a revolver that seemed so small in his pudgy fist as to be almost a toy. But I knew it wasn't a toy. It was a .25-caliber or perhaps .22-caliber pistol, about the same size as the gun that had killed Senator Robert Kennedy.

"What do you think you're doing?" I shouted.

"You've got five seconds to get back in your fancy car and get out of here. I'm not telling you again." For a heartbeat I stood there frozen, staring at the revolver. Against that silence the click of the van's passenger door being opened was unnaturally loud. The little girl's tennis shoes squeaked against the wet, broken asphalt.

When she emerged from the side of the van, the glare from my headlights caught her almost in profile, her eye sockets dark hollows against her flat white face, a face that seemed, simultaneously, to have lost all fear and all hope. The fat man and I both turned toward her.

"Lisa, go back," I shouted, and knew, instantly, that with the use of her real name a boundary had been crossed. Now he knew that I had discovered his secret. The fat man snapped his head back to me and his face passed through several stages, like the movie special effect in which an animal shapeshifts from one form to another in the blink of an eye. He first showed surprise, then fear, then anger, then determination, all in the space of a heartbeat.

"You messed in where you don't belong one time too many, mister. I can't have you spreading lies about me and Alice here."

"The police . . ."

"You ain't gonna tell 'em nothing, even if they believed you,

which they probably wouldn't, but I ain't gonna take that chance."
For an instant he turned back to the child, glared at her and
shouted: "Alice, you see! You see what you've gone and made me
do!" Then he looked back at me and I saw his finger begin to
squeeze the trigger. It was mostly reflex, that and my old boxing
training, but I shifted my shoulders, faking a move to my left. He
flinched and jerked the gun to follow my expected movement. In a
split second he recognized his mistake and began to again center
the barrel on my chest, but in that instant I lunged forward and
heard the gun fire.

It made a sound like a small "pop" which was almost swallowed
by the damp night air, instantly followed by a louder crash of metal
against metal behind me as the bullet smashed into the front of my
car. What I did next was not what a gentleman is supposed to do,
but I make no apologies for it. It probably saved my life and Lisa's
too. I kicked him right in the balls, as hard as I could.

He groaned and leaned forward, still holding the gun but not
trying to aim it at me anymore. I kicked him again in the groin,
then a third time in the solar plexus with the toe of my wingtips,
then I kicked him one last time, with the sole of my shoe flat in his
face.

He collapsed prone on the ground, groaning, with blood pouring from his broken nose and on down across his cheek and onto
the asphalt. I stomped on his right hand hard enough to break a
finger, and the gun slipped free. I caught it with the side of my foot
like a soccer-style placekicker and sent it flying off into the dark.

For a moment I stared at the fat man as he lay bleeding and
retching on the ground in front of me, then I shouted:

"Lisa! Lisa! Hurry, get in the car. We're getting out of here.
Hurry!"

For a moment she hesitated, just stood there in the glare of my
headlights, then, as if recovering from a trance, she ran to my
passenger door and tugged on the handle. I got into the car and
pressed the button to release the locks. Lisa pulled the door open
and as soon as she was inside, I backed onto the highway and took
off. It didn't matter which way I drove, just so long as it was away
from there.

It was surreal, a scene out of nightmare. As soon as the adrenalin stopped pumping I began to shake. I had almost been shot. I turned at the first crossroad, then turned again at the next one. After a mile or two more, when I was sure we were not being followed, I pulled over and doused the lights.

"Are you all right?" I asked.

"Is he going to find us?"

"No, Lisa, he won't find us. I promise, I'll take care of you. I won't let him hurt you." She said nothing, just sat there, a dark form next to me, her silhouette barely visible in the glow from the instrument panel.

"Let's get our seat belts on," I said as if that was the most important thing in the world. I heard her belt unroll and then click as the buckle slid into the connector. I waited a moment, not wanting to ask too many questions, not wanting to upset her, but I knew that I couldn't pretend that nothing had happened.

"He called you 'Alice'," I began, "but you said your name was 'Lisa.' Is Lisa your real name?"

"He told me that now my name was Alice but it's not."

"Was he your father?"

She was quiet for a moment, then a soft whimper escaped her lips.

"Is 'Lisa' the first name you ever had?" I asked.

"Yes," she said after a moment.

"Did your real father, your first father, give you that name?"

"Uh-uh," she whispered, paused for a second, then said: "My Mommy."

"Your mother gave you that name?"

"Uh-huh."

"What was her name?"

"Peggy. Daddy called her 'Peggy.' I called her 'Mommy.' "

"That's the way it's supposed to be. I called my mother 'Mommy' too when I was your age. What about your Daddy, your real Daddy? What's his name?"

" 'Bill.' Mommy and Uncle Jack called him 'Bill.' "

"What's your last name? Everyone has two names. My name is Peter Howard. Your name is Lisa . . . ?"

For a moment it seemed that all her strength had evaporated. She hunched down in the corner between the seat and the passenger door and hugged herself as if she believed that if she could make herself small enough all her problems would disappear and that when she opened her eyes she would find herself at home and safe with Mommy and Daddy and that all this would be just a bad dream. The rain had let up and the only sound now was the low throbbing of the engine. Finally, she opened her eyes and turned toward me.

"He said that if I told, if I told that he wasn't really my daddy. . . ." and her voice caught in her throat. Not since my father died when I was thirteen had I seen anyone grieve that way, silently, as if the sound of their tears would make the pain real, as if you might be able to turn back time if only you didn't cry out loud.

I waited until her little gasps had subsided, then told her: "Everything that man said was a lie. Don't believe anything he told you. I said I would help you and I will. I promise I'll get you home. I promise. But you have to help me. I can't get you home if I don't know where you live. You want to go back to your real Mommy and Daddy, don't you?"

"Yes, but he said that if I told, they would kill Mommy and Daddy. That I could never tell."

"Lisa, he's a very bad man, and bad people lie to get their way. No one will hurt your parents. I'm sure they're looking for you and that they want you to come home more than anything. Your Mommy and Daddy would do anything to have you back. That man doesn't scare them or me. You saw how I knocked him down and got you away from him, didn't you?"

I was rewarded by a sniffle and then a nod.

"So don't give a thought to what he said. You leave him to me. What's your second name?"

I held my breath. Lisa twisted the fabric of her T-shirt and finally said "Taylor."

"That's great! Your name is Lisa Taylor. Now, we need your address. I bet your parents taught you your whole address. I know you're a smart girl and I bet you memorized it, didn't you?"

"Uh-huh."

I already had my ballpoint poised above the back of one of my two remaining business cards.

"So, your full name and address is: Lisa Taylor . . . ?" There
was another long pause, then she completed the sentence:

"Lisa Taylor, 749 Avery Road, Oakdale."

I knew Oakdale. It was a small town down near the edge of the
Central Valley, maybe a three or four hour drive from here, if I
could find out exactly where "here" was. Yes, I know. I could have
driven up to some house, pounded on the door and borrowed their
phone to call the police. But what if the police didn't believe her?
What if they just sent her back to the fat man? What if he had
friends here? He had that decal on his car about the Police Reserve. What if he was a cop?

Jesus, the way he talked, it sounded like he at least had some
friends on the force. If he was molesting this kid, maybe some of
the cops were in it with him. Or at least they might believe him
and not me. It wouldn't be the first time something like that had
happened.

Hell, the cops might arrest me for assault and give her back to
him. You think I was foolish, paranoid? Maybe being shot at had
something to do with it. And I remembered Jeffrey Dahmer. The
police gave one of his victims back to him. I heard the tape of the
911 call. The cops thought it was a big joke. They grabbed the kid,
he was fifteen years old and naked when they found him on a
public street, and just gave him back to Jeffrey Dahmer.

If the police in a major city could do that, what would some
small town cop do with a seven or eight year old? They might well
decide that she was just making up stories and give her back to her
supposed father. When the police gave the boy back to Jeffrey
Dahmer, the young man was killed and eaten. How could I take
that chance with Lisa?

Besides, even if the cops believed her, we would be tied up in
paperwork for hours. Reports would have to be filled out, interviews undertaken. Certainly Lisa would end up spending the night
in Juvenile Hall. Her parents would be called. They would be
frantic. They would drive here like lunatics, maybe get into a
wreck, and then, even if they arrived safe and sound, they would
still not be able to take her home until more reports were completed.

The newspapers and TV stations would find out. The media

would make a circus out of it. After everything that must have happened to her, the child didn't deserve to have twenty reporters screaming at her, asking her how it felt to be kidnaped and molested. It wasn't fair. I couldn't let that happen to her.

On the other hand, all I had to do was put the car into Drive and find the freeway. By nine or ten o'clock tonight she would be home, safe and sound. Clearly, logically, the best thing to do was just to take her home myself. Besides, I had made her a promise. I had taken on a responsibility. Start a job, finish a job. And beyond that, somewhere along the way, maybe when that gun was pointed at me, maybe when I saw the look on the fat man's face, the look that told me he was going to kill us both, in that one split second this had become personal.

I had decided in that instant that no matter what, I would not rest until I, personally, had placed her safely into her parents' arms. Maybe you think that's silly. I don't care. Yes, it was an emotional decision, I know. But that's how people are sometimes. That's how I was that night.

It's only a short drive, I reassured myself. I was sure that I would have her home in only three or four hours.

# TWO

I finally formulated a simple plan for getting my bearings: keep driving west until I ran into Highway 680, then use the California state map in my glove compartment to plan things from there. I didn't know what to say to Lisa, or if I should say anything at all, so for a while I just drove. As it turned out, I didn't need the map after all.

Only a few minutes later I encountered signs of life, one of those strip shopping centers with seven or eight small stores and a gas station on the corner.

"It's a long drive to Oakdale, Lisa," I said as I pulled up to the pumps. "Do you have to go to the bathroom?"

"No, I'm fine."

"Okay, you wait here, I'll be right back."

It was a self-serve station but the attendant hadn't cleared the last sale and I couldn't activate the pump. I glanced back at Lisa then walked over to the office. An old Toyota was hoisted on the lube rack; the Corolla's right rear wheel and brake drum had been removed to give the mechanic access to the brake shoes and cylinder.

The mechanic's back was to me and when he turned around I

revised my opinion of his job description. Mechanics were techni-
cians trained in the intricacies of complicated mechanisms. This
was just a kid, about twenty years old, hatchet-faced, and holding a
pair of pliers in his right hand. I looked past him and saw bright
metal where the pliers had rounded off the edges of one of the
nuts, turning its original hexagonal shape into something more
closely resembling a Cheerio.

"I need some gas," I said as he looked me over. "The pump has
to be reset."

"Sure, give me a second." The boy, the name "Charlie" was
monogrammed on his coveralls in red thread, turned back to the
wheel and clamped the pliers down in a two-handed grip. A metal
shaving fell to the floor as the pliers slowly rotated downward
while the nut remained fixed.

"Shoot!" Charlie swore, dropped the pliers to the concrete and
rummaged through a toolbox on the table to his right, finally
emerging with a pair of Vice Grips that he clamped to the recalci-
trant nut. Next he wrapped a foot of electrical tape around the Vice
Grips' handle to hold them closed. One final trip to the toolchest
produced a ballpeen hammer which he whacked against the Vice
Grips' handle with great energy. On the fourth blow the nut broke
loose and the pliers flew off, smashing into the floor only a few
inches from my foot.

"Always works," Charlie said proudly. "Okay, let's get that gas
for you. You want anything else? Check your oil? Need any anti-
freeze?"

"No, just the gas."

We walked back to the island and Charlie inserted his key. The
pump's tumblers spun around to zero. As I grabbed the nozzle and
maneuvered it into the tank I asked Charlie over my shoulder, "I
want to get to 680 south. What's the easiest way?"

When he didn't answer, I looked up and noticed that he was
staring at Lisa.

"680 south," I repeated.

"Huh?—Oh yeah, sure. Okay, first you go down here about a
mile, then turn right on Slawson—"

"What a minute. I better write this down. Do you have a piece of paper in there?" I asked, nodding toward the office next to the bay and hoist.

"Uh, sure. You can use the back of an estimate form." Charlie trotted off and after locking the nozzle open I followed him. He gave me a three-part form that said "We Care About Your Car" at the top and "Payment Due Before Release Of Vehicle" at the bottom. I turned it over and took down Charlie's directions. When I was done I looked back at my car, then at my watch. It was about six-thirty with a three- or four-hour drive ahead of us. It would probably be a good idea to get some dinner before we got onto the highway. "Any restaurants around here?" I asked. I don't subscribe to the mythology that cops, bus drivers, and auto mechanics know a good restaurant from a bad one but at this point I was ready to eat anywhere as long as it was close, clean, and fast.

"What you looking for?"

"I don't care. McDonald's would be fine."

"One of them a couple of miles north up the freeway. Wrong direction for you. There's a nice place just down the road, though. Marty's Rib Pit. Steaks, salads. Real nice place. Little girl ought to like it." Charlie stared at me expectantly. What was I supposed to say?

"Thanks, we'll give it a try," I said after an awkward silence, and then handed him my credit card.

"Where you from?" he asked as he set the digits on the card imprinter.

"Los Altos Hills, near Palo Alto."

"That's a ways off. How'd you hear about this place?"

"What do you mean?"

"Nothing, just an expression," he said quickly. Then he paused and tapped the card machine nervously with his index finger. "Look, nothing personal, but we've had some problems with these cards. If the boss gets one more fraud claim they're going to shut us down, you know what I mean?"

"What? Look that card is fine. You can . . ."

"No, I mean, I have to write down your license number and see some ID. Sorry, but, you know how it is."

Something should have clicked right then. I should have told him to forget it or just paid cash but it didn't register. I was tired and I'd been in business long enough to know that credit card companies have a rule that if a business reports more than a certain percentage of fraudulent transactions in any one month they yank the merchant's credit card privileges and deny him the right to make any further credit card sales. Since credit transactions are anywhere from thirty percent to eighty percent of a small business's sales this can be a sentence of instant bankruptcy.

So I showed him my driver's license and he wrote down my ID and my plate number. I went back to the car, put on the gas cap, and got inside. Lisa was still sitting there quietly, thinking about God knows what. When I pulled into the street I checked the rear view mirror and noticed Charlie standing by the pump and watching me drive away. Did I look that much like a crook? For fourteen dollars worth of gasoline?

"Lisa, are you hungry?" I asked as I followed Charlie's directions and turned right on Slawson Avenue.

"I'm fine," she said quietly without turning her head.

"When was the last time you had something to eat? Did you have lunch?"

"I had cereal, Rice Krispies."

She hadn't eaten all day. I knew she was upset, had to be upset, but enough to have no appetite at all? Then I thought about it for a moment. If every time you asked for something you were hit, you learned not to ask. If every time you said you were hungry, you were hit, you learned not to say you were were hungry. If everything you said or did was wrong, then you learned not to say anything or do anything except what you were told to say and do, when you were told to do it.

Her bladder could be bursting and she wouldn't volunteer that she had to go to the bathroom. She could be starving and she wouldn't admit to being hungry.

"Well, I'm hungry," I told her. "The man at the gas station said there's a good restaurant just down the road. We're going to stop there for some dinner."

"I don't like him."

"Who?"

"The man at the gas station."

"Why not?"

"He looked at me, you know."

"How did he look at you?"

"He looked at me, you know, the way they do. Not like you look at me."

"How do I look at you?"

"You look at me the way Daddy did. Not like them. I don't like it when they look at me that way. I don't like the man at the gas station."

"Lisa,—" I began, then caught myself. What was I going to say? Tell her that she was wrong? That she was being silly? Ignore her? No.

"I don't blame you, Lisa," I said finally. "I don't like him much either. I'll tell you what: I'll buy a big steak and some french fries and a big salad. I'll give you part of it and if you're not hungry, you don't have to eat it. Sometimes we think we're not hungry until the food comes, then we find out that we are. What do you say? Is that okay with you?"

"Sure. I mean, yes."


From the outside, Marty's Rib Pit would not have excited Julia Child. The building was wood, single-story with fake brick trim. Spelled out in neon on the wall to the left of the front door was the motto: "Just Good Eats."

It was dark inside. Fake kerosene lanterns were mounted on the rims of wagon-wheel light fixtures and turned down to a dull orange glow. Tables and vinyl booths in two rows lined the front of the building with the kitchen straight back and the bar to the left. A small dance floor fronted the bar and occupied the leftmost one-quarter of the main room.

The tables were about half filled and a waitress carrying a tray stacked with heavy white platters of beef and baked potatoes called out, "Sit anywhere, Hon," when we entered. I picked a booth along the front wall next to a window. Through the smeared glass I could see a few feet of the parking lot which was partially illuminated by the flickering glow of a neon sign mounted on the crest of the building's shake roof.

Lisa stared nervously around the room, her eyes briefly focusing on the shadowed tables and the vague shapes outlined by the light spilling from behind the bar, then she quickly lowered her head, afraid that by her glances she might draw attention to herself.

Once or twice I started to talk to her, but each time stopped myself, fearing that my questions would only make her more uncomfortable. The waitress had disappeared into the kitchen and I looked around, hoping to catch a glimpse of her.

"Are you cold?" I asked Lisa when I thought I noticed her shiver.

"I'm fine," she answered quietly, her eyes still lowered. I was convinced that she had been taught, through methods that I did not want to imagine, never to ask for anything, never to complain.

A moment later, from behind me, I heard the waitress approaching. Her jeans made a scratchy, rustling sound as they rubbed against the burgundy apron that seemed to be the extent of Marty's employees' uniform.

"What can I get you folks?" she asked brightly. It was still early. In an hour or two, her eyes glazed from the smoke drifting in from the bar and the thousandth step on the uncarpeted pine floor ringing against the soles of her feet, her welcome would become perfunctory, much of her attention diverted to the aching in her shoulders that burned even as the assistant manager of the Wash-N-Spin and his spandex-clad wife pored over the menu and tried to decide between the baked potato and the French fries.

Maybe I'm too jaded, too single-minded someone had once said about me when they didn't know I was within earshot. Maybe before Janet left me. . . . At the end when I, foolishly, wanted reasons from her, explanations, a blueprint for a quick fix, Janet told me that I was stubborn, obsessive, rigid, and unemotional and that I should get professional help.

There it was, the insult of the eighties, "You're no fun. You need a shrink." Sure, I was working eighteen-hour days. I was building a business so that when we were ready to start a family we could afford to spend time with our kids, send them to college, do everything right. I wasn't unemotional, just organized. You have to plan ahead in life if you want things to work out. I did my best for her. I wanted kids. She was the one who—, damn, I was doing it again, still thinking about a failure that was long over. You can't argue someone into staying in love with you. They always have a reason why they don't love you anymore, and they never have a reason. I guess I sort of understand that, but I can't explain it. Damn, let it go. I pushed Janet's image from my mind.

"Would you like a drink while you look over the menu?" the waitress, Candace, according to her name tag, asked us as she handed both Lisa and me huge red cardboard menus with strings down the centers and a tassel at the top.

"I think I know what I want. New York steak, medium; green salad with blue cheese; baked potato; side order of fries; side order of Salisbury steak; lots of bread and butter; a Sprite and a glass of milk." For a moment I thought about asking Lisa if that was all right with her, but I knew that she would just say that it was "fine." "Oh, and bring an extra plate and we'll share everything."

"Sure thing," Candace said, her mind already on her next customers who were just now coming through the door. As she hurried off I looked at Lisa. For a moment her eyes brushed my face then she looked down at the table top and pushed herself into the corner between the wall and the end of the booth.

When our food arrived, I diligently divided it between us. After a bit of prompting Lisa ate the fries and bread and butter but didn't seem to like the beef. And she would eat only those portions of the salad that were untouched by the dressing. I finished before she did and put the remaining food on her plate.

"I've eaten all I want, Lisa. Please try to finish as much as you can. It's a sin for food to go to waste."

"A sin?"

"That's an expression. It means something that's wrong."

"I know what sin is," she said with a hint of determination in her voice. "Sin is when you break God's laws." Lisa paused for a breath, then continued with a catechism that she had obviously labored hard to memorize:

"God's laws are written in the Bible and those who break them are sinners who will be cast down into Hell," she said in a singsong voice. When she ended her recital, she smiled, fleetingly, displaying a flicker of pride that she had successfully completed her lesson.

I hesitated for a moment, unsure of what to say. As an adult, I realized the horror that lay behind that recitation, what the fat man must have put her through to learn it. Confronted with my silence the smile fled from her face.

"That's very good, Lisa," I said hurriedly. "You must have worked hard to learn your lessons, didn't you?"

She raised her head briefly, then nodded. "I'm impressed," I continued. "I didn't realize what a smart little girl you are." I paused for a moment, then, more to change the subject than anything else, asked: "Can you eat any more?"

For the next few minutes Lisa picked at the remnants of our dinner, then announced, "I'm full."

"Okay, you ate a good dinner. Let's go wash up then we'll get out of here and I'll get you home." I left a pile of bills on the table and helped Lisa from the booth.

The restrooms were at the end of a hallway that ran between the kitchen on the right and the bar to my left. I walked Lisa to the door marked "Gals."

"You go in there and go to the bathroom and wash your hands. Stay inside until I knock on the door. Okay?" Taking her silence for assent, I waited until she had closed the door behind her, then, for a moment or two I stared at the pay phone at the end of the corridor. I thought about calling information and getting Lisa's parents' phone number, but then what? What would I say?

"Hi, you don't know me, but I'm out here in the middle of nowhere and I have your kidnapped daughter. I'll bring her home in a few hours. Trust me."

And after they had recovered from their hysterics or accused me of being the worst kind of crank caller, I would be right back to turning her over to the local police. No, in a few hours I would have her home. After all the time she must have been gone, another three hours wouldn't make any difference. I turned my back on the phone and went into the mens' room. The door had a plastic "Guys" plaque in the shape of a cowboy hat.

When I came out a tall man with long gray-black hair was waiting in the hallway. "You all wait for me in the van," he called to two men just leaving the bar, then he pushed past me and into the men's room. I decided to give Lisa an extra minute or two then knocked on the ladies' room door. She emerged just as the tall man opened the "Guys" door. He paused for a moment and looked down at her.

"Did you wash your hands?" I asked her and was rewarded with a nod. "With soap?" This time no reply. "Why don't you go on back in and wash them again real good with soap, okay?" Lisa looked up at the man to my right, paused for a moment, then hurried back into the rest room.

"Cute kid," the gray-haired man said, nodding toward the ladies' room door. "Are you a friend of Ken's?"

Confused, I just stared at him. Jesus, did he know the fat man? Was this guy part of some molestation ring or had he just seen Lisa around town? I listened to myself and decided that I sounded like some loony seeing conspiracies everywhere.

I looked at the stranger carefully. His hair seemed like a net of black and gray threads twisted tight and pulled into a cue. Though in his mid-forties or early fifties, his frame was spare and his skin looked, in that dull light, like old leather stretched over wrought iron bones.

I just stared at him, afraid that whatever I said would make things worse. The door opened and Lisa slipped out, hugging the wall on the far side of the hallway. I nodded to the man then hustled her out the front door. Was there a cop around anywhere? If I found one, what would I tell him?

"Yes, Mr. Howard, that's very interesting," the policeman would say. "But what evidence do you have that this man has committed a crime?"

"He said the child looked familiar."

"Yes, and what crime is that?"

"He's very suspicious."

"Of course. And what crime is that? And by the way, what is this gray-haired man's name? Where does he live? What does he do for a living? How long have you known him? Where can we find him? And what are you doing with that little girl? You say you beat up the man who claimed to be her father, put her in your car and drove off with her. Put your hands behind your back, please."

Yes, calling the police to arrest the gray-haired man made perfect sense! Once in the car, I got Lisa buckled up and we headed for the freeway. She was as talkative and as animated as a rag doll.

"Do you know that man?" I asked her. "The one in the hallway. Have you ever seen him before?" Other than a soft noise like a sniffle she made no response.

"Is he one of the bad men? Is he one of the men who came to the fat man's house? Was the fat man named 'Ken'?" I asked her in a rush.

"He's bad!" Lisa said suddenly, her words already mingled with silent tears. Who was bad, Ken or the gray-haired man, I wondered.

"He did bad things. He told me God said he was supposed to do those things but it's a lie! He hurt me," she said, her voice cracking then her words dissolved into low sobs but without tears and which stopped almost as soon as they had begun. "I'm not supposed to cry," she said sniffling again and wiping her face with the ragged sleeve of her T-shirt.

"It's okay to cry, Lisa. Sometimes it's good for you. I'm sorry, but I have to ask you, it's important. Was the bad man's name 'Ken'?"

"He said to call him Daddy, but other people called him Ken." She paused for a long moment, then added, "The other man, the one who took me, Daddy—Ken, called him 'Eric.' " This last sentence was uttered with a vehemence, an edge of hate of which I would not have thought her capable.

"Did he, Eric, did he hurt you?"

"He told me that he had friends who would kill Mommy and Daddy. I saw them. They're bad men. They scared me."

"Don't be frightened, Lisa. It's going to be all right. I'll have you home soon where he won't be able to hurt you. Was the man in the restaurant Eric?"

Lisa shook her head. "I don't know him," she said finally. "What if they come back again, like the last time?" Lisa asked struggling to hold back her tears.

"The last time? What about the last time?"

"I was in my front yard. We were playing with our dolls. The car stopped in front and a man got out, Eric, and then he grabbed me and pulled me inside. Then he hit me. Maybe he's a friend of that man with the gray hair. Now he's seen me and he'll just come and get me again."

Was the gray-haired man was one of the kidnappers? Lisa didn't recognize him but he sure acted like he knew something. I had let him go. But if they caught Ken, he probably could lead the police to the rest of them. Tomorrow, after she had had a good night's sleep, her parents and I would call the FBI and they would track these guys down. I still had Ken's license number. I could identify both Ken and the guy from the restaurant. Ever since Ken had tried to shoot me, my brain had seemed to have stopped working. Maybe it wasn't too late. Maybe if I stopped, turned around, found a phone. . . . But then, in front of me I saw the on-ramp for 680 south. Hell, surely the guy was gone by now. Anyway, it was too late now to turn around and go back.

Almost of its own volition my car turned right and I accelerated up the grade and into the thinning evening traffic. I pressed harder on the gas. Trees slid past on either side of the highway, gray-black humps in the darkness as we headed toward Lisa's home.

# THREE

---

"Don't get too close to him," Jimmie Devries ordered.

"Relax, Jimmie, he hasn't got a clue. The way he's going, I could drive right up his bumper and he wouldn't notice. Why are we following him anyway? I don't know why we didn't just grab the kid back there."

"In Marty's parking lot? Jump this guy in a public place in a town small enough to have bored cops who are just waiting for something to do? Is that your plan?"

"I've done it before. We'd be long gone before the cops got there."

"Eric, who's this van registered to? Do you have a nice legible license plate on the back? And when the cops come around looking for you, you won't give them my name, right?"

Eric made no reply other than to gun the van's engine and move closer to Howard's Lexus as it headed for the freeway on-ramp.

"He's heading for the freeway. Where's this guy think he's going?"

"That's why we're following him. I checked out the name Charlie got off his driver's license. He's some bigtime high-tech executive. None of this makes any sense. I wish I could get a hold of Ken and find out what this Howard guy's doing with the kid. If he's a citizen, why hasn't he called the cops? If he's a player, where the hell is he taking her?"

"Maybe he's got a secret place out in the boonies somewhere," Ray suggested from the backseat. "You know how those sicko's are. Gacy had that secret room. Maybe Howard's got some cabin or something all set up with video cameras and handcuffs and all that stuff. Maybe he bought her from Ken and he's taking her up there to do her," Ray said, excitement creeping into his voice.

"I hope you're right. If he's a freak, we've got nothing to worry about. In fact—" Jimmie paused while he considered the possibilities. "In fact, that might work out real good. I got a call yesterday from the guy in Texas. He's got a buyer who'll give us $50,000 for a kid like her, some South American freak who's into it big time. This kid would be perfect. It would be a lot safer just to take her from this Howard than to grab a new kid. If this guy's in the game he can't complain to the cops."

"So, when are we gonna do it? I don't want to follow this guy all night."

"Eric, don't try to think, just drive. If he was straight, he would have called the cops, but it doesn't feel right. The freaks give off an odor; I can smell it on them. I don't get that from him. Something doesn't fit. Just follow him. Let's see where he goes. When he stops, I'll call Ken again and find out what the story is."

"Yeah, then what?"

"Then we grab the kid and sell her again."

"What about this Howard guy?" Eric demanded.

"He wouldn't be the first guy to disappear," Jimmie answered. "He won't be the last."

# FOUR

I took 680 south to 580 then headed south and east until we reached Interstate 5. I had forgotten what it was like to drive on I-5, but the cars roaring past me out of the darkness soon jogged my memory. Here the 55-mph speed limit was a fantasy. Years ago, long stretches of I-5 were reclassified as 65-mph zones and even that speed limit was almost universally ignored. It would take an army of CHP cruisers to slow down the traffic on this road, a goal that practically no one wanted to achieve.

I-5 was laid out almost ruler straight along the western edge of California's great San Joaquin Valley. In many places it was only two lanes in each direction. Slow drivers stayed in the right lane and kept their cruise control on seventy. Occasionally these timorous individuals would encounter an aging semi or a cattle truck with a couple of bad cylinders plodding along at sixty or sixty-five.

After a few minutes of cars roaring up behind them, then whipping around and accelerating past, they would cautiously pull into the next opening in the fast lane and scoot by, but God help the driver who perched permanently in the left lane doing anything less than seventy-five.

When that happened a car or a pickup truck would line up a few feet behind them, then another, then another, all the time the gap between the lead car and the slower vehicle shrinking foot by foot until the urge to escape the iron beasts behind would drive the law-abiding motorist back again into the right lane with the other "slow" drivers.

To the left of me, to the east, the flat valley floor stretched to the horizon, its far edge at the foothills of the Sierra Nevadas fully 70 miles away. To my right the ground rolled away in swales to the low hills and on to the coastal mountain chain that separated the interior of California from the ocean.

Driving this road now, in full night, was almost like sailing down a dark tunnel. The pastures and road signs and occasional crossings over the All American Canal were vague shapes that disappeared behind me almost unnoticed in the gloom. With no turns, no structures on the horizon by which to gauge the distance, my speed became illusory, merely a number on the dashboard, a concept devoid of intuitive meaning; seventy-five or forty-five, it was all the same.

For the first twenty minutes or so Lisa didn't speak. She was only a silent shape barely discernible in the glow of the instrument panel and the rhythmic strobing of the oncoming headlights. How much did she understand of what had happened to her? How could a child comprehend the motives of the people who had abducted her, and then, apparently, sold her like a washing machine or a used car? What could she make of Ken who had performed acts upon her body that I refused to allow myself to contemplate?

Did she think she was being punished for something? Did she believe that she had done something bad, that she *was* bad, that she had in some way been the cause of all that had happened to her? And if she did cause it, how could she avoid believing that it must, therefore, happen again?

Children do not think the way we do. Their logic is not intuitively understandable by adults. Cause and effect to them can be mysterious events connected by threads invisible to our grown-up eyes. They are suckers for what Father Dozier used to tell us in parochial school was "post hoc, ergo propter hoc," logic.

I prided myself on remembering that long-ago bit of Latin,

which is liberally translated as: "If a second event occurs after the first one, then the second event was caused by the first one." Every morning the rooster crows, then the sun rises. Therefore, the crowing of the rooster *causes* the sun to rise.

"I made a noise and Daddy yelled at me. Then Daddy yelled at Mommy. Then Daddy hit Mommy. Therefore, when I made the noise, I caused Daddy to hit Mommy."

I remembered an article about a little girl who was raped by one of her mother's friends. She told her mother about it and a few days later the rapist was found shot dead in his apartment. The child's uncle was suspected of the crime but nothing could be proven. When the little girl heard that her attacker had been murdered she was desolated because she decided that by revealing what had happened she had caused the man to be killed. From this she concluded that if she continued to talk to people, she might again, inadvertently, cause other people to be killed as well, and so she resolved never to speak again. It was three years before she uttered another word.

Where was the justice in that? I couldn't find any, couldn't imagine any. Perhaps none was possible. Personally, I do not deal in justice. I deal in rules. Maybe that's why I was in that car that night, speeding across the new Promised Land with a wounded child huddled in the seat beside me. Perhaps I was trying to practice, if not justice, at least a measure of consolation, generosity, compassion, in an indifferent world. Someone had to help this child.

I glanced at the horizon and, without planning, wondered, how old would—well, we never named her, never got the chance to— how old would *she* be now?

Almost against my will my mind had slipped back to that forbidden topic. She'd be six or seven by now I guessed. I could do the math if I tried, but I didn't want to. I had trained myself not to think about her. It had all been over before it even began. By the time I found out it was a *fait accompli*.

I came home that day late, as usual. The bank had turned down the credit line we needed. I had spent hours desperately trying to find some financing that would keep the company out of bankruptcy. All I wanted to do was get something to eat and crawl into bed. It was also a Thursday, strange how I remember that so clearly, about nine o'clock, and Janet was already in bed. She looked awful.

I asked all the usual questions: Are you sick? Is it the flu? Did something happen? All I got were a few monosyllables, but I kept at her. Finally, she shouted, "I had an abortion today. Okay! Are you happy now?"

"But, what . . . I don't under—."

"Look, Peter, it's my body. This isn't the right time for us, for me. I don't want a baby now."

"But, why didn't you tell me? Talk to me. . . ."

"Because I knew what you would do. You'd start making lists, planning options, figuring out budgets. Telling me what we were going to do. I didn't want to argue about it. I had made up my mind. It's my body. It's my decision."

I was stunned. Who was this person who killed our child? Was this my wife, the woman who said that she loved me? We were going to have children. We had talked about it. As soon as the business was going. Soon, maybe next year Janet was going to get pregnant. That's what she had said, had promised. Hadn't she? I didn't know what to say. Then the question slipped out, one that I wish I had never asked.

"What was it? The baby."

"Peter, it's not important. Let's just forget. . . ."

"What was it, God damn it!" I screamed at her. I had never raised my voice to Janet before and she cringed away. I must have looked as if I was ready to hit her.

"A little girl," she whispered, and then she began to cry. I stood there for a minute, two, I don't know, then I left her sobbing in our bedroom. After that we started counseling. Then I tried to fix things with attention, discussions, shrinks, and money. About that time we released Nexus 90 and our stock tripled in value. I bought a million-and-a-half-dollar house in Los Altos Hills figuring that might patch things up. I thought a house would signify security and commitment. Of course none of it worked. She just didn't love me anymore. I don't know, maybe she never did. Maybe what she felt for me was something else. I am sure of one thing. I'm sure why she did it. It wasn't that she didn't want to have a child. The problem was that she didn't want to have a child with me. Janet remarried a year later. Someone told me he raced motorcycles. Janet used her half of the divorce settlement to bankroll his racing team.

If our daughter had lived, little Karen or Jennifer or Christy (or Lisa?), how old would she be now? Six and a half I realized, my mind doing the arithmetic automatically. A year or so younger than the child beside me. What would she have looked like? Would she . . . ? I clenched my teeth and forced all such pointless questions from my head.

I glanced at Lisa as these thoughts chased through my mind and, by some psychic pressure, I felt forced to try to engage her in conversation.

"Lisa, do you know anything about where we are, about this valley?"

"No."

"Did you ever go to Sunday School? Did you ever hear of the Land of Milk and Honey?"

"That's in the Bible. I know the Bible. Ken made me read it every day."

What a fool I had been! The last thing I had wanted to do was to remind her of Ken. I tried to go on, to gloss over my mistake.

"That's right. I remember how well you recited your lesson. Well, the Land of Milk and Honey was the Promised Land, the land where the children of God would find rest and salvation. It was a place from which all good things sprang. In a way, this," I motioned to the darkened landscape around me, "is the Land of Milk and Honey."

"It is? Where?" Lisa asked as she turned in her seat, then pressed her face against the passenger window and peered into the formless darkness beyond.

"Over that way," I said, pointing ahead of us and to our left. "They grow everything here. Your Dad can take you out and show you. They have fruit stands that sell everything. When you drive down old Highway 99 you'll think you're in Galilee."

"What do they have?"

"Milk, of course, and honey. Olives and oranges, dates, walnuts and almonds, peaches and plums, apples, cherries, kiwis, pistachios, grapes, wine. Everything out of the Bible and lots more, all grown within a hundred miles of where we are right now." Lisa stared out of the windows with more interest than she had displayed since I had met her. Had that been only two or three hours ago?

About an hour and a half after we left the restaurant we reached the Highway 152 turnoff that would take us east to U.S. 99 which runs down the center of the valley like a stream bed following the low point in a canyon.

Having at last found something to catch Lisa's interest, I expounded on every fact I knew or imagined I knew about the country through which we were traveling. Rather than being inhibited by the darkness which obscured all details of the land around us, I was, in fact, stimulated by it. I felt that I could paint a picture of the countryside with my words that might be more interesting to Lisa than the real landscape might appear in the harsh light of day.

When we turned east on Highway 152 I remembered that only a few miles behind us on this road, just out of our sight over on the western edge of I-5, was the huge San Luis Reservoir which provided a substantial part of the vast amount of water which was required to make the valley bloom, and I described that lake to Lisa as an expanse of clean water rippling under cloudless skies. I invented fishermen and water-skiers and high-powered motorboats to populate my story.

I thought she enjoyed my ramblings, but who could tell? Perhaps she was just humoring this strange man who seemed to have taken control of her life and appeared to wish her well. I pretended, at least, that making her listen to me was preferable to letting her mind roam back over recent events. I pointed out to her each irrigation canal that we crossed, the San Luis Canal, the Delta Mendota Canal, the Highline Canal, and tried to explain the massive irrigation network which comprised hundreds of miles of such artificial rivers and stretched the length of the Valley. I told her that not even the Romans in their prime had built such a system, then I tried to explain who the Romans were. Anything to keep her interest.

Not once did she let me down. She never nodded off, though

certainly she must have been very tired. She didn't retreat into a welter of "uh-huhs" and phrases like "isn't that interesting?" the way an adult subjected to such a boring monologue would have.

We passed through Los Baños, "A Friendly City," the sign at the edge of town proclaimed, and continued east, toward Highway 99. Here and there I could make out isolated farmsteads scattered across the Valley, each surrounded by a stand of trees, probably eucalyptus or valley oak or bay laurel. Crossroads flashed by, some of whose names I remember: Box Car Road, Turner Island Road, Road 15¾. Who would ever name a street "Road 15¾"?

At one point we passed a sign depicting a sailfish leaping from the sea. Above it were the words, "Red Top Cafe" and below it, "Red Top World Famous Fish Museum." What wonders did it contain, I asked myself. As we approached the overpass for Highway 233 I could see, silhouetted against the night sky, the spindly stalks of hundreds of palm trees marching north and south along the crossroad as if they were giant dandelions that had sprung up at the edges of the concrete. From their height I guessed they were coconut palms. Who could have planted them here, I wondered, and why? In an instant they were behind us, invisible again in the darkness.

Shortly we came to Chowchilla, a small town that everyone who has lived in Northern California for a few years remembers. It was here in the middle 1980s that a couple of rich kids from Portola Valley, a wealthy suburb out behind Stanford University, kidnapped a school bus full of children, then buried the bus with the children still inside while the kidnappers tried to extort ransom for the youngsters' safe return. It felt somehow appropriate that we had to pass through it on our way back to Lisa's home.

Miraculously, the children and their bus driver were eventually able to dig a passageway out through the roof emergency hatch and escape before being suffocated. They made a TV movie about it, I recalled. The kidnappers are still in prison, though not teenagers any more. I seem to recall that they had recently asked for parole on the grounds that they had made a youthful mistake, were sorry, and had learned their lesson. As yet, the California prison system had not seen fit to release them.

Just past Chowchilla we joined Highway 99 south, down past

Madera and Fresno, Kingsburg and Visalia. Farmersville and Go-
shen slipped behind us as well. As we neared Pixley I began to
watch for the cut-off to Oakdale. I had ended my travelogue some
miles before and Lisa was again curled up in her seat, drowsing.
The towns to the east now had names like Woody, Fountain
Springs, and White River.

I remembered Oakdale because of jazz. I had a friend in college,
Bobby Malone, who was crazy about classical jazz and one weekend he talked me into taking a drive with him up to Three Rivers
in the Sierra Nevada foothills to attend a jazz concert. After the
concert we drove over to the Sequoia National Park. I had noticed
Oakdale then, on the map, south of the park on the Kern river. It
was one of the larger towns in the area, maybe three thousand
people, mostly dedicated to the summer tourists attracted by the
Sequoia National Forest and the Kern River itself.

I left Highway 99 for Kings County Road J21 which disappeared into a maze of orange groves. The trees, heavy with fruit,
lined the two-lane like green walls. Signs at roadside stands offered ten-pound bags of navel oranges for three dollars. In the
winter, farmers line up for their burn permits so that they can
dispose of the agricultural detritus that has collected after the fall
harvest but, as I drove deeper into the groves, the scent of smoke
was overpowered by the fragrance of the orange blossoms.

Strangely enough, in February, as the farmers are harvesting
one crop of oranges, the blossoms are already starting to form for
the next cycle. Now, on this late-February evening, the sweetness
of the flowers and the fruit was almost magical.

I passed through a village, barely more than a crossroads, Brier.
Appropriately enough, the cross street was named Orange Belt
Drive. Thirty seconds later Brier was only a memory and fifteen
minutes farther still the orange groves had vanished as suddenly as
they had appeared. Now I entered mile after mile of rolling pasture land interspersed with grass-covered hummocks one to two-
hundred feet high.

Maybe my sense of smell had been stimulated by the groves, or
perhaps I was simply more aware of the odors that drifted in on
the night air, but now I could smell the fresh grass covering the
pastures. In the daytime herds of Holstein cows would crowd the

water troughs at the base of the windmills which dotted the landscape. Palm trees became more and more common, springing out of the night and appearing in my headlights at unpredictable intervals.

It was now almost eleven o'clock and Lisa had fallen into a deep sleep. The pastures gradually grew more crowded with rounded hills and the road became more challenging as it wound its way between them. Ahead of me at a distance that could not be estimated in the dark, the edge of the Sierra Nevada Mountains was suddenly at hand, appearing as a distant, vague black wall. The road turned north and paralleled the Kern River for five miles or so, then became Oakdale's main street.

The majority of the town stretched along the highway, with the balance only a few short blocks on either side. It was the standard sort of small town: a liquor store, video tape rental, gas station, Mexican restaurant, pizza parlor, post office, antique shop, church, school, hamburger stand, City Hall/Police Station, minimart. The minimart alone showed signs of life. I pulled into the lot. The clerk should know where Avery Road was.

The manager was an older Hispanic man, maybe fifty, with luxuriant black hair and a full mustache just beginning to show an edge of gray. When I entered he looked up sharply, sized me up, then seemed to dismiss me as not an immediate threat. I didn't blame him. His was an occupation statistically more dangerous than that of FBI agent or professional soldier.

"Excuse me," I said when I reached the counter, "do you have any local maps for sale?" A quick smile creased his face. By offering to buy a map instead of merely asking for directions I had moved myself from the category of freeloader into that of customer.

"Harmony Realty had these fliers printed up," he said, handing me one. "You can keep it if you want."

The flier was a three-fold brochure showing the river with exaggerated sketches of fish and out-of-proportion buildings representing the principal commercial and civic locations: restaurants, the City Hall, and, of course, Harmony Realty. Four or five streets were labeled, none of them the one I wanted.

"What you looking for?" the clerk, probably the owner, I decided, asked.

"Do you know where Avery Road is?"

The man, Al Guiterez, according to the label pinned to his shirt, thought for a second, then shook his head.

"Never heard of it. You sure it's around here?"

"This is Oakdale isn't it?"

"Sure is, but I don't know any Avery Road. There's an Alvy Road about five miles up the highway. Who you looking for?"

"Bill Taylor. Ring any bells?"

"Hmmmm, no. There's a Jerry Taylor who owns the laundromat."

"Is his wife's name Peggy or Margaret?"

"Sandra. I don't know anyone like that. You sure you want Oakdale?"

"Is there anyone else I could ask? Someone who's lived here longer than you have?"

"Not likely. I was born twenty miles down the road. Been here all my life. Never been out of the state even. Hell, the farthest I've ever gotten is when the wife and I took the kids to Disneyland when they were small. Boy's a senior in high school now," he added proudly.

"No Avery Road?"

Mr. Guiterez shook his head.

"No Bill or William or Will Taylor or Peggy Taylor?"

"Nope."

"Lisa Taylor?" I asked finally after a long pause, then held my breath. If I expected any light of recognition, I was disappointed. Guiterez shook his head and his face showed not a flicker of surprise or interest at her name.

Now what was I going to do? I must have made some simple mistake. I just needed a little time to correct it.

"Maybe I did get the address wrong. Look, is there a motel or something around here? I'll try to figure this out in the morning."

"Sure," Al said, smiling now that I had asked a question that he could answer. "Keep on up the road the way you're going, about a mile. Belair Motel. Nice place. Cable, HBO. Lots of room this time of year."

"Thanks," I said, suddenly tired, as if all of the energy that had kept me going for the last five hours had unexpectedly leaked away. I paid for a couple of bottles of apple juice and a packet of granola cookies for Lisa in case she woke up hungry or thirsty, and then got back into the car. She was still asleep.

A few minutes later I pulled into the Belair Motel, a single story "U" with a very cold-looking swimming pool in the center. The neon "vacancy" light was flickering and most of the units appeared empty. A girl of about twenty watched me through the glass front door. After noting my rumpled suit and loosened tie she reached out and released the deadbolt.

"Help you?"

"Yeah, I need a room—make that two single rooms for tonight."

"Two rooms?" She looked over my shoulder but could not see Lisa slumped down in the front seat.

"Two rooms."

"How many people?"

"One person in each room."

"Two single rooms?"

"Yes, you moron," I wanted to shout, "two single rooms!" Of course I didn't say that. My upbringing succeeded in containing the comment firmly within the confines of my skull.

"Yes, two people, two rooms, one person in each room."

"Okay, fill this out," she said as she handed me a three-by-five registration card.

"How much?" I asked without looking up from the form.

"$31.50 each, but that includes a continental breakfast from eight to ten." She sounded worried that I might decide to argue that such rates in the off-season were barely less than highway robbery. There was no danger of that. I just wanted to get Lisa safely to bed and get eight hours sleep myself. Tomorrow I would figure out where I had gone wrong and straighten things out. I had money in the bank, my credit cards, my Lexus, my education, my position, my organized mind, my determination. I was sure that whatever mistake I had made that I could fix it.

# FIVE

"Now, it starts to make some sense," Jimmie said when he saw the Lexus pull into the convenience store lot.

"I'm glad you understand it," Eric snapped. "The guy drives the kid out here in the middle of nowhere, then leaves her alone in the car while he makes a quick trip to the 7-11. He couldn't get a microwave burrito back in the East Bay?"

"What's the name of this town, Eric?"

"I—"

"Hey, I got it!" Ray broke in. "This town's named Oakdale. He thinks he's taking the kid home!"

"Give the man in the backseat a cigar."

"So he's a citizen after all," Eric concluded.

"Oh no, not just a citizen, Eric, a romantic, a hero in the making. It's not enough for our Mr. Peter Howard to have rescued the damsel in distress; he's planning on taking her home all by himself. He can already hear the applause. Don Quixote had nothing on him."

"Don who? Is that the customer in South America?"

"Jeez, Eric, don't you ever watch TV? He's a Spanish guy who was crazy about windmills. Right Jimmie?"

"I couldn't have said it better myself, Ray."

"Let's just cut the crap. So he's a citizen after all. What are we going to do?"

"We're going to follow him until he stops for the night. We cover up your license plate and wait until we're sure he's asleep. Then we grab him and the girl and we find out how much he knows and who he's told."

"And then?"

"And then we do our magic act."

"What?"

"We make him disappear."

# SIX

---

I followed the gravel drive to the far side of the motel and parked in front of unit 19.

"Wake up, Lisa. We have to get you into your room. Come on, you have to wake up for a moment."

Lisa opened her eyes a crack and muttered sleepily, "Are we home? Are we there?"

"Almost. We're in Oakdale but it's too late to take you home tonight. We'll find your folks first thing in the morning. I've got you a nice motel room all to yourself. Come on now."

I got out of the car and motioned for Lisa to follow me. After what had happened to her, I was afraid to pick her up, to carry her, even to touch her. I didn't want any contact, even of the most innocent sort, to cause her to classify me with the men whom I was sure had abused her. After a moment's hesitation, she cautiously joined me at the door. I went in first, turned on the lights, and checked out the room.

"I'm sorry I don't have any clean clothes for you," I called to her from the bathroom where I unwrapped a bar of soap then unfolded a clean towel and left them on the Formica counter next to the

44

sink. When I returned to the room I saw that Lisa was still stand-ing a few feet inside the doorway and staring fixedly at the bed.

"Look," I said, kneeling down so that our faces were on the same level, "this room is all yours. Why don't you go into the bathroom and wash up, then go to bed and get a good night's sleep."

She just stood there, her expression unreadable.

"It's going to be fine," I told her. "Tomorrow we'll find your parents and this will all be over." She stood there frozen for a moment longer, then walked slowly toward the bed, which, like those in most motels was mounted high off the floor. When she reached it I noticed how small she was next to it, her head less than two feet above its surface. I pulled back the blanket and sheet where they had been tucked in under the mattress.

"After I leave, lock the door," I said, pointing to the deadbolt. "Just twist it to the right. Then get washed up and go to bed. Don't open the door for anyone except me. I'll knock on your door tomorrow morning at eight o'clock." I pointed to the digital clock on the dresser opposite the bed. "Do you need anything before I leave?"

"Where are you going?"

"My room's right next door. If you need anything, just pound on the wall."

"Why are you leaving me alone here?"

"You need your privacy, Lisa. Don't worry. Everything will be fine. I'll only be ten feet away. Just remember, don't open the door for anyone but me." She didn't say anything, just stared at me with an expression that I found unreadable, opaque. I thought for a moment about the man at Marty's Rib Pit.

"So, no matter what anyone says, no matter who it is, you keep the door locked. You only open it for me. Understand?"

"How will I know it's you?"

"I'll knock like this," I said after a moment's pause, and tapped my knuckles on the night table three times, "knock," pause, "knock, knock." "Here, let me show you again. Knock, then knock, knock. Okay?"

"Okay," she answered with a brief, uncertain smile.

I walked to the door and turned to look back at her. She had not moved from her position next to the turned-down bed. She seemed smaller and more vulnerable than she had appeared only a few minutes ago.

"Don't worry, Lisa," I said smiling. "Everything will be fine. You'll see." I held up my hand and waved to her. She hesitated a moment, smiled again, almost painfully, and waved back. Watching her through the narrowing opening, I slowly closed the door.

"Turn the lock, Lisa," I called through the door. I waited five seconds, ten, then heard the deadbolt click home. I let myself into unit 20 next door, an exact duplicate of Lisa's room down to the picture of the rainy Paris street scene on the wall above the bed. I pulled off my rumpled clothes and dropped them onto the orange vinyl chair. Wearing only my underwear I washed my face and then climbed into bed. I was sure that as soon as I turned off the bedside lamp that I would sink into a dreamless sleep like a stone dropped into a deep, still pond, but I didn't.

When I closed my eyes Ken's face floated through my mind. Ken in the minimart; Ken getting into his VW; Ken pulling his gun, his face edged with the glare from my headlights; Ken staring at Lisa with a hungry look in his eyes as he undid his pants. I tried to will the image away and it vanished, for a moment, then reappeared. "Think about something else," I told myself and tried to clear my mind.

I replayed the events of the day and tried to figure out how I had come to find myself here in this deserted motel in the Sierra Nevada foothills with this ravaged child. Step by step each event seemed to make sense, to have a logical connection with the one before it and the one after, but the chain of circumstances, as a whole, was tangled and confused and out of place in my normally well-ordered life.

Why was I here? Why hadn't I just called the police, given them the child, and had done with it? I could have made her someone else's problem. But that would be treating her like she didn't matter, like a thing, like a lost sweater or suitcase, like a lump of flesh to be thrown away.

"Lost and found? Yeah, I found this kid. Here, you take care of her. I'm a busy man. I have things to do." No, I couldn't do that. How could I abandon her that way? Not like Janet had done to our daughter. I kept thinking of the words to "Amazing Grace." "I once was lost, but now I'm found."

Without warning I had found someone who needed me. Someone whose life I had the power to save. And I was determined to do it. I was going to find her parents. I was going to take her home. I was not going to be a bystander, not this time.

I could get her home as well as the police, better, I was sure. I would get her back to her parents as fast as they would. And I wouldn't call in the reporters. I wouldn't ask her a lot of painful questions. I wouldn't frighten her as they surely would. I would protect her from all that. She still needed me and I was not going to give her up just because things hadn't worked out exactly as planned. I could still fix it. I had learned that almost anything could be put right if you just worked hard enough. Besides, it was almost certainly too late for me to call the police.

"If you were only going to take her home, Mr. Howard," I could imagine the detective asking me, "why did you take her to that motel? What did you really have in mind, Mr. Howard?"

"Are you crazy? Do I look like a child molester?"

"What does a child molester look like, Mr. Howard?"

"You said you were taking her home, Mr. Howard, but how is it that you took her somewhere that no one knows her?"

No, it was way too late to call the police. At this point, too many questions would be raised. I would become a suspect. And then what would happen to Lisa?

"Peter, you've got no logical alternative now," I warned myself. "You're stuck. It's too late to call the cops. You're just going to have to take her home, then no one can accuse you of anything."

Yes, that's the logical reason I gave. But the emotional reasons held more sway over my actions. I had found something that needed to be done and about which I had no moral doubts. As contrasted with every other aspect of my life, this was not about rules, this was about justice. I had been given the opportunity to save an innocent's life, to do the Right Thing. Isn't that what Father Dozier would have wanted me to do?

I had faced down a man with a gun, for her. How she had come into my life was unimportant now. I had taken on a job, an important job, one that I believed in completely and one that I was not about to give up—I would not give her up. As foolish as it may sound now, I was determined that I was going to be the one who put her into her parents' arms, not some police officer, not some social worker. Me.

I thought about the gray-haired man. I tried to remember his face, the color of his eyes, the sound of his voice. If he was one of her kidnappers I had let him get away.

I rolled over and opened my eyes. The inch-high red numerals on the digital clock showed 2:14. I must have slept, but I didn't feel like it. I put a pillow over my head and tried to concentrate on some innocuous subject, some restful scene that would wash the events of the past eight hours from my mind. A few moments later I threw off the pillow and looked at the clock again: 3:08. I was exhausted but I couldn't sleep and I realized that I had to use the toilet. I rolled out of bed, stumbled to the bathroom and a minute later made it back to the bed again without tripping over anything.

I was just about to crawl back between the sheets when I heard the crunch of tires on the gravel drive. I eased back the curtain but didn't see any headlights. I pulled the drapes a few more inches apart. The sound of the car drew closer. I rested my forehead against the glass and tried to spot something moving. After a second or two I caught a glimpse of a dark shape, a black or dark blue van, creeping up the drive toward me with its lights off.

Sometimes the thing that frightens us most is the prospect of looking foolish. The urge to conclude that the noise downstairs is just the house settling, that the commotion next door is just the TV, that the "bang" from across the street is just a car backfiring, is overwhelming. When I was a boy we lived next door to an old lady, Mrs. Schlosher. One day while I was watching television I heard her voice, calling. I paused and listened, heard nothing, and assumed that I had been mistaken. I found out later that she had fallen and needed help. She was calling for help and I ignored what I had heard because I didn't want to appear foolish. I learned then that sometimes looking foolish is not the worst thing that can happen to you. Now, I did not hesitate.

I pulled on my pants and slipped my bare feet into my shoes. I heard the van stop directly outside my door. What if it was Ken or maybe the gray-haired man? What if they had followed me from the restaurant?

"You're paranoid, Peter," I told myself. "You've got the middle of the night heebie-jeebies. Tomorrow morning you're going to feel like an idiot."

"Fine," I argued with myself. "I'd rather be a healthy idiot in the morning than a rational victim tonight."

A weapon. I needed some kind of a weapon. I heard the side door on the van unlatch and slide open. I looked around the darkened room. Everything was built in or bolted down except the lamp on the bedside table. Most motels had abandoned freestanding lamps in favor of wall fixtures, which were harder to steal, but not the Belair. Maybe this out-of-the-way place attracted a better class of visitors than the more popular resorts.

The lamp consisted of a ceramic base, perhaps fifteen inches high, topped with a cylindrical shade another ten inches from bottom to top. I reached through the top and unscrewed the wing nut that secured the shade. I heard footsteps on the gravel outside. At first the electric cord refused to come loose, then, finally, I managed to pull the plug from its socket. Hurriedly, I wrapped the wire around the shade support, just below the bulb, then grabbed the lamp at the same place with my hand on top of the coil of wire. The lamp's base was weighted and I held the fixture like a club.

I heard a faint scratching at my lock. In a minute they would be through the door. If I stood behind it, it would slam into me when they threw it open. If I stood anywhere else I would be an easy target. I needed something to keep the door from swinging all the way back. I put down the lamp and placed the chair against the wall near the door. I heard the knob turn, then rattle, but the deadbolt still held.

I picked up the lamp and squeezed my back flat against the wall to the left of the chair and toward the door's hinges. The scratching at the lock had ceased and the night was absolutely still. The lamp dangled from my right hand. For perhaps half a minute nothing happened and I wondered if the deadbolt had defeated them. I let out the breath that I had been holding and, in that instant, the lock shattered under a sudden blow. The door flew back on its hinges, crashed into the chair and rebounded only to be thrust open again as several shapes raced into the room. Still hiding in the pocket between the door and the wall, they could not see me and they ran on past.

It looked as if there were three of them. When the last shape passed me I pushed the door out of the way and clubbed the rearmost intruder with the base of the lamp. I don't know what I expected. I suppose that I thought it would feel like hitting a rock or perhaps the blow would make a dull thud as if I had pounded on a side of beef. But it wasn't like that at all. At first there was resistance, a brittle snap, then a sickening release like that of a spoon breaking through the shell of an egg.

My victim collapsed without uttering a sound although the lamp's base cracked noisily on impact. The second man started to turn, to face me, and I swung at him as well, a poorly aimed blow that bounced off his beefy shoulder. So much for the element of surprise.

Now that there was no more reason for silence, I began shouting at the top of my lungs: "Police! Call the police! Burglars! Help! Call the police!" I backed out of the door, leaving the intruders alone in the room. Once outside, my cries echoed off the stucco face of the motel. Not wanting to be further exposed I backed away from the doorway. Between my shouts I heard voices from my room.

"Grab Ray, we've got to get out of here."

"Jimmie, where's the girl?" the second man called.

"Check the bathroom!"

Suddenly a light showed in the manager's apartment and I heard a man's voice call: "What's going on out there?"

"Burglars!" I shouted again. "Call the police! Call the police!"

"You out there," the manager shouted back. "The deputies are on their way. I've got the cops coming!"

"She's not here!" one of the attackers hissed.

"Grab Ray's shoulder."

"Leave him!"

"If he talks, we're all finished. Now grab him and let's get out of here."

It suddenly occurred to me that I was standing there half naked, holding a broken lamp, and about to confront two men who might well be armed. I ducked past the end of the motel and hid around the corner. They dragged out the man I had hit and threw him into the van through the open side door, the door that Lisa and I would have disappeared through had things gone differently.

The unconscious man's heels dug two furrows in the gravel and he landed on the van's floor like a sack of grain. Had I killed him? Was this one of the men who had abducted Lisa? One of Eric's gang? It had to be, didn't it?

The van's engine roared to life. They had parked it pointing toward the bottom of the "U" so that the side door faced my room. Now they tore through the gravel, across the grass between the motel's two "arms" and then back out onto the highway in a thunder of pistons, gears, and spinning tires.

When the van reached the road its tires screeched against the asphalt and I could smell the stench of burning rubber. Its headlights flickered as it headed north, up the highway, but I could not see the plate.

Once they had gone, the owner, a skinny, balding little man somewhere between fifty and seventy years old, came running over. I reached inside the shattered doorway and flicked on the light. As he approached, the glow spilling from the room painted his features with a pale yellow cast. He wore a reddish-brown wool bathrobe that looked like it had been cut from an old blanket. It was belted over white cotton pajamas which were short above his ankles and baggy at his wrists. Round, steel, wireframed glasses made his eyes seem too large for his head.

"What the hell's going on?" he barked as he reached the gravel drive in front of my room. He strutted past my car and up onto the walkway and stared at me as if I were some vandal who had decided to single-handedly destroy his motel. His gaze focused on my right hand in which I still clutched the fractured table lamp. "What do you think you're doing?" he demanded when he noticed its cracked base. "You know, you're going to have to pay for that!"

I was about to explain that I was the victim here when I heard the wail of an approaching patrol car's siren. "Why don't we wait until the police get here so I don't have to say everything twice," I told him, then leaned back against the unit's stucco wall. The cruiser turned into the drive and headed directly for us. The siren slowly spun down into silence and as soon as the vehicle stopped and the officers got out.

God, where do they get these guys, I asked myself. Are they stamped from some genetic cookie cutter? Caucasian; between twenty-one and thirty; short hair: one blond, almost crew cut, the other's hair medium-length brown; one with blue eyes, one with gray; high school graduates; eight or ten or fifteen weeks, if they were lucky, in a physical fitness based training course, then given a badge, a gun, a club, and told to enforce a set of laws that not even lawyers, judges, or the Supreme Court itself pretended to understand.

"George," the blond one said, nodding to the manager. "What's this all about?"

"Ask him," he said pointing at me. "Sally checked him in. First thing I know I hear a crash and he's shouting for the police. I look out the window and see a van tearing up my lawn, racing out of here like a bat out of hell and him standing there holding a busted-up lamp. Now you know as much as I do," he grumbled and stared at me accusingly.

"What happened is . . . ," I started to say but was cut off immediately.

"Just a minute, sir," the blond one interrupted. He said "sir" the way most people would have said "ax murderer." "Name please."

"Peter Howard."

"Address?"

I gave him my address, my work phone number, my home phone number, my fax number, my driver's license, and then he confirmed that the car in front of unit 20 was, in fact, registered to me. I finally gave him one of my business cards which identified me as the CEO of the Orayis Division of NowSoft Corporation.

"Okay, Mr. Howard, why don't you tell us what happened."

Tell us what happened. And my answer was . . . ? I glanced, briefly, toward Lisa's room. The lights were out. It appeared deserted. If I was going to tell them the whole story, now was the time. I looked up at the deputy and, incongruously, remembered my high school history class. When Caesar had returned to Rome against orders, he became a criminal. Once he crossed the Rubicon River it was too late for him to turn back. When Caesar reached that point of no return, he is supposed to have said, "The die is cast."

"I was in bed," I began. "I woke up. I had to go to the bathroom. When I came back to bed I heard a car out here on the gravel, but I noticed that its headlights weren't on. That seemed strange to me. I heard it stop in front of my room. I got scared. I thought that since I was from out of town that I might be the target for some crime.

"I heard them approach the door and they started fooling with the lock. I unplugged the lamp and stood behind the door. They kicked it open and ran in. I hit one of them with the lamp and knocked him down. Then I swung on the second one, hit him, ran out of the room, and shouted for someone to call the police. They grabbed their friend, the one I knocked down, and drove away. That's all I know."

The blond cop glanced at his partner and turned back to me. I knew that look. It was an expression that said: "Sure, that's all you know. I believe that. Now tell me the one about the Three Bears." The deputy stared at me a moment longer, daring me to tell him what this was really all about. But I didn't. I kept my mouth firmly shut.

If I started talking about kidnappers and lost children, they'd want to put me in the loony bin, until they saw Lisa. Then, likely as not, they would tag me as a child molester. They would just love to arrest some Bay Area executive on a nice juicy felony like that. "A Current Affair" here we come. And what would they do to Lisa?

I knew the answer to that. They would try to make her to confess that I had molested her. They would keep at her and at her, trying to make her tell them what they wanted to hear. That kind of atrocity was perpetrated on children by police and alleged therapists every day. But not this time. Besides, I didn't need the cops to get Lisa home. In the morning I'd track down her parents' phone number and and we'd take care of everything ourselves. In the state I was in it made perfect sense to me. To hell with these wise-ass deputies! I looked away. The die was cast.

"Tell me, Mr. Howard," the blond officer began overly politely, "do you have any drugs in your room or your car?"

"No, I don't."

"Would you mind if we took a look in your room?"

"Help yourself."

"Bob," the blond cop said, turning to his partner, "why don't you check the car. That okay with you, Mr. Howard?"

"Sure."

Yes, I could tell them to go to hell, to get a search warrant, but that would convince them that I was a co-conspirator in a drug deal gone wrong rather than an innocent visitor targeted by a band of thugs. Since I didn't have any drugs it was easier to let them search.

"May I have the keys, please?" the dark-haired officer asked.

"When you finish searching my room," I told him. "One thing at a time. I want to watch you."

"Are you implying that you think we might plant some drugs on you?" the blond asked.

"I'm not implying anything. I don't know you. You don't know me. I've been the victim of a violent assault and you're acting as if I'm the criminal. That makes me very uncomfortable. You mistrust me. That makes me mistrust you. So we'll do this together. You can start with my room. Help yourself. You won't need a key to get in."

Again, one of those looks, those, "Doesn't this guy think he's soooo cute" expressions passed between the two deputies, then they went inside. The search didn't take long.

"Where's your bag?" the blond asked.

"I don't have one."

"Shaving kit?"

"Don't have one."

"Clean underwear?"

"Don't have any."

"Where'd you say you were from?"

"Los Altos Hills, between San Jose and San Francisco."

"That's what, three, four hour drive from here?"

"Something like that."

"And you drove all the way down here and you didn't bother to bring even a razor or a change of clothes?"

"That's right."

"Sounds like a rush trip. What's the emergency?"

"I have to interview someone in connection with a major project for my company. It came up at the last minute."

"Who are you here to see?"

"William Taylor."

"Never heard of him," the blond one said. "How about you, Bob?"

"News to me. Where does he live?"

"Avery Road."

"What city?"

"Oakdale."

The blond cop looked at his partner who shook his head. "George?"

"I don't know what he's talking about."

"You sure it's Avery Road?"

"That's my information."

"Mr. Howard, there is no Avery Road in Oakdale, or anywhere around here."

"Are you sure? Couldn't there . . . ?"

"Mr. Howard," the brown-haired deputy, Bob, cut in, "I've lived here all my life. Jack and I drive these roads eight hours a day, every day. If there were an Avery Road within twenty miles of here, I would know it, or Jack would, or George would."

"But my client was very sure. Avery Road, Oakdale."

"Oakdale, California?"

"What?" I asked. Of course it was California. It had to be California, didn't it? But wait. Lisa hadn't told me the state. She just said "Oakdale." I assumed it was Oakdale, California. How stupid of me! Young children sometimes have a spotty understanding of geography. When I was four or five my parents told me that we were going to Canada for a vacation. They explained that Canada was a foreign country. I remember asking them what the people in Canada looked like. Did they have two heads, four arms? I had no concept of what a country was. Lisa probably didn't know what a state was, leastwise what state Oakdale was in or if it was a different state from where she had been held captive.

"Is there another Oakdale?" I asked, embarrassed.

The deputies looked at each other with an expression that seemed to say: "Boy, you're a real smart executive!"

"You'd have to check with the library on that one, Mr. Howard," Jack said overly politely.

"Hell, there are probably ten or twenty of them," George, the owner said, glaring at me. "Jeanette at the post office told me that she gets mail for one Oakdale or the other all the time. Boys, am I done here? Do you need me anymore?"

"No, George. You can go on back to bed."

He started to leave, then turned back. "You're going to have to pay for that door, you know!" he demanded.

"Why should I pay for it? I didn't kick it in. Those burglars did. Talk to your insurance company."

"It's your room. You're responsible. Besides," he said, looking at the deputies, "there's more to this than you're telling. I think you're mixed up with those guys. It's going to cost a hundred, two hundred dollars to fix up this mess. I'm not going to take the loss! Jack, you see that he pays!"

"George, go on back to bed and let us do our jobs," the blond cop ordered. The manager paused a moment, snorted, and stomped off across the torn-up lawn. Jack stared at me for a moment but I didn't say anything.

"Let's take a look at your car now, Mr. Howard, if that's still all right with you."

"Fine," I said, and walked over and opened the trunk. That search didn't take long either. Except for some CDs, an umbrella, a few tools, six road maps, and the usual odds and ends that collect in a glove compartment, the car was empty. "Satisfied?" I asked when they handed me back the keys. The blond cop pursed his lips in a sour expression and turned away. The brown-haired deputy, Bob, hesitated, then took a step toward me.

"Look, Mr. Howard, let's stop playing games here. We're not idiots. We've been on the job long enough to have learned a few things. Here you are, hundreds of miles from your home, no bag, no change of clothes, the only guy in this whole motel and out of the blue three guys, not one guy or two guys, but three guys kick in your door in the middle of the night?

"If that's not enough, you're waiting for them with a lamp in your hand? You just happened to wake up? You just happened to put on your pants before they broke in? They don't stay to steal anything, even if you had something to steal? And you tell us you're here looking for someone we've never heard of who lives on a street that doesn't exist. Give us a little credit, Mr. Howard. You're no innocent victim here. There's a lot more you're not telling us. Why don't you level with us and we'll see what we can do."

What could I say? What facts, what details did I have? None. Trying to explain this would only make things a hundred times worse. And they would take Lisa away from me.

"I'm sorry you don't believe me. I don't know what else I can tell you."

"Okay, Mr. Howard, have it your way. We'll file a report. If you think of anything else, give me a call. Here's my card. Jack, let's get out of here."

"Right behind you," the blond deputy called as he followed his partner, ignoring me when he walked past me on his way to the patrol car. I pushed the door closed and turned off the light. I put on my socks and shirt and gathered up my coat and tie then sat on the bed. I waited ten minutes until I was sure they were really gone, then I slipped out and knocked softly three times on Lisa's door.

"Lisa, it's me. Open the door," I whispered. There was a pause of a few seconds, then I heard the lock turn. She opened the door a crack and peeked out then pulled it back. I slipped inside and quickly closed the door behind me.

"Don't turn on the light," I said softly.

"What happened? Was it them?" she asked, her voice tight with fear. She's not crying. Why isn't she terrified, sobbing? Because they probably punished her every time she cried, I thought. Because they tried to kill everything alive and normal inside of her. I sat down on the floor about two feet in front of her so that our faces would be on the same level.

"It's all right, Lisa. They're gone. There's no need to be afraid," I told her. "You're lying, Peter," I told myself.

"They said I would never get away," she said, clearly terrified but still not crying. "They said that if I tried to run away that they would catch me and kill me. They'll never let me go."

"They'll have to stop me first."

57

"They said they would kill anyone who helped me."

"They're liars and cowards. You mustn't believe anything they say. They'll say anything to frighten you, but it's just talk."

I didn't know if she understood what I had said, or, if she did, if she believed me.

"It's all right to be afraid," I said softly. "There's nothing wrong with that. But that doesn't mean we have to give in to our fear. Tell me, could you go back to Ken again? Could you?"

Lisa looked down, then after a moment's pause, raised her eyes. "No," she said quietly, and shook her head.

"Then there's no point in getting upset. You can't go back and I won't let them take you back. Look, sometimes the things that frighten us the most, that make life really, really hard, are figuring out what to do. We want to do one thing, but we're afraid to. We could do something else, but we know its wrong. We can't make up our minds.

"But, now, you and I, we don't have that problem. You know that you can't go back to Ken and I know that I have to take you home. That's it. We don't have any decisions to make. So, in a way, it's a lot easier for us. It's okay if you're a little afraid, but only a little."

"You could leave."

"No, I have to take you home."

"Why?"

"I gave you my word. I made a promise. A deal is a deal."

"But they might kill you."

"Lisa, listen to me. They can't have you and that's all there is to it. I don't care what they do. It doesn't matter any more. If you don't go home, I don't go home. That's it. It's both of us, together, no matter what. Do you understand what I am saying?"

"You're not going to leave me?"

"No."

"Never?"

"Not until you're home safe."

She stared at me for long a moment, her eyes clouded and confused. She didn't understand this. How could she? I wasn't sure that I understood it myself. But, in the end, that didn't matter. Understanding is often highly overrated. I had told her that I would not abandon her, no matter what, and that was more important to her than all the logic in the world. She clung to me, then rested her head against my shoulder, and, in a few minutes, was asleep.

# SEVEN

How did I get into this business, Jimmie sometimes asked himself. But not often. He was not a contemplative man. Jimmie Devries rarely thought about the past, leastwise questioned it. He had no regrets and no long-term goals, other than a vague desire to become rich enough to be able to drink Cuba libres beneath palm trees all day and screw compliant women all night. Not that he really planned on ending up that way. The fact is that he never thought about how he would end up at all.

Growing up on the Texas Panhandle Jimmie decided early on that there had to be better places to live than a dried-out truck-stop town surrounded by sand and cactus and fields of creosote bush. He escaped Stone Flats, Texas with a stint in the Army. Jimmie caught the tail end of Viet Nam and didn't know why people complained about it so much. Lots of excitement, money, if you knew the angles, and more women than you could screw in a lifetime. And the Army liked his work.

Jimmie got more information, more "cooperation," from suspected VC sympathizers and agents than anyone else in his unit. It was a good life, until the war ended. Jimmie figured he would make a career out of the Army then he got home and all the bullshit started. Rules, rules, and more rules. It got so you couldn't take a piss without written permission. And nothing to do all day but push papers and salute officers. The stateside Army had become boring, stingy, and offered little chance of advancement or reward for someone with Jimmie's talents.

By '74 Jimmie was looking for a new career and he was still just a kid, if you didn't look too deeply into his flat gray eyes. But the Army had taught him valuable lessons: the benefits of planning, organization, and adopting a sound strategy tailored to your mission's objectives.

For a while Jimmie worked odd jobs, a payroll stickup here, a jewelry store take-down there, but his first arrest cured him of any inclination to remain a hired hand. One of the morons he went into the jewelry store with pistol-whipped the clerk. This encouraged the police to look for them a little bit harder than might otherwise have been the case, which meant paying one of their snitches a hundred bucks for information on who was spending too much money and who was trying to sell women's watches out of the trunk of his car. Jimmie's partner was soon picked up and he instantly fingered Devries.

In spite of dire threats by the detectives coupled with vague promises of "consideration" if he cooperated, Jimmie kept his mouth shut and the case against him was eventually dismissed when the police could find no evidence to corroborate his partner's claims, the testimony of a co-conspirator being legally insufficient, standing alone, to convict.

Jimmie learned his lesson. From then on, he was the boss of his own scores. Just to make sure that he wasn't ratted out again, nine months later Jimmie's former partner was found sitting on the sidewalk outside the Gray Bar Tavern, with his tongue cut out, dead. The police could never prove anything, but the message was clear: it wasn't healthy to roll over on Jimmie Devries.

For quite a while after that Jimmie worked as a "professor," planning jobs for a percentage of the take, but seldom participating directly. His Army training stood him in good stead in organizing the details of the crime and in making sure that he wasn't denied his share of the loot.

As the years went by, Jimmie diversified: occasional drug smuggling, one or two big-score robberies each year, and a growing reputation as a specialist. If the money was right and the target wasn't too hot, Jimmie would get rid of someone for you, permanently. Since he never paid taxes, Jimmie was able to squirrel away a good chunk of cash, until he met Linda.

It was as if he had been saving all of his stupidity for one big jerk binge. By the time it was over, he had lost $150,000, much of which vanished when Linda did. Jimmie often amused himself with thoughts of how he would kill her, exactly how he would do it and how long it would take her to die, if only he could find her. But Linda was now Debbie, living in Maimi, and married to a successful orthopedic surgeon. It was unlikely that their paths would ever cross again.

So, in need of money and too old to be taking down check cashing parlors, Jimmie hit on the child-stealing racket. The right kid would bring twenty-five to fifty thousand dollars, maybe more if you could find a "motivated" buyer. Plus, you could turn them over. When the buyer got bored and wanted a new toy, if he hadn't killed the kid, you could re-sell the child to someone else. If the kid made it until twelve or thirteen, you could get another ten or fifteen thousand from a pimp who would turn them out. Of course, there wasn't much left of them by the time they were nineteen or twenty, if they lived that long, but that wasn't Jimmie's problem.

And, until now, things had worked out. Still, his current problems were solvable. Ray's body would disappear into the woods. No one would miss him. Lisa and Peter Howard were still on the loose, but Jimmie was confident that he and Eric would soon remedy that.

# EIGHT

I awoke stiff and sore and found myself still sitting on the floor in Lisa's room, my back leaning against the side of her bed. She was breathing softly, sleeping deeply the way young children do, sleeping hard, my mother used to say. I looked at the window and saw light filtering through the edges of the curtains. My right arm was asleep where it cradled Lisa to my chest. I opened and closed my hand several times to restore the circulation, then lifted her onto the bed. The clock showed 6:34. I had gotten less than three hours sleep and my back was killing me.

I made sure that Lisa was tucked in then went into the bathroom and washed my face. In the cold light of morning with the adrenalin burned away, I began to have second thoughts about not telling the deputies the whole story last night. That might not have been such a good idea, I decided, but it was too late for second thoughts now. Way, way too late. Like Br'er Rabbit and the Tar Baby, I was well and truly stuck. But, hell, things weren't so bad. I'd find her parents this morning and have Lisa home by nightfall. It would all work out fine, I was sure.

It was pretty clear that I would have to find a store and get a razor, toilet articles, some underwear, a couple of shirts, and a clean pair of pants. There had to be a K-Mart or a Target or a Sears somewhere back toward Bakersfield. Until then a little soap and hot water would have to do.

When I left the bathroom Lisa was still sleeping. I sat in the chair and closed my eyes but I knew it would be impossible for me to get any rest. And the longer I waited the more uneasy I became. There was too much to do and the remaining intruders still out there, somewhere. The sooner I got her home the better. At about twenty after seven I finally made a decision: Lisa could sleep in the car. We had to get out of there.

"Lisa." I shook her gently as I called her name. "Lisa." She awoke slowly, then suddenly her eyelids snapped up. A frightened look crossed her face, then she recognized me and seemed to relax.

"It's time to get up. You should go into the bathroom and wash up. The first thing we're going to do is find a store and I'll buy us both some clean clothes. Then we'll have breakfast."

Lisa stared at me for a moment, wondering why we had to do all that if this was Oakdale and she was almost home, then, without a word, she crawled out of bed and went into the bathroom. When she came out a few minutes later I was faced with the disagreeable task of explaining that I had screwed up.

"I'm ready," she said primly.

"Lisa, sit down for a moment. There's something we need to talk about." A worried expression crossed her face. "Aren't we going home?" she asked, already frightened.

"Sure we are. But there's a problem. How can I explain this? Lisa, sometimes there are two cities with the same name. There's a city in California called Menlo Park. There's also a city in New Jersey called Menlo Park. There's a Rochester, Minnesota and a Rochester, New York. The thing is, we're in Oakdale, California but your parents don't live here. They live in some other Oakdale, another city somewhere else that's got the same name."

As I spoke Lisa's face displayed a range of emotions: fear, worry, confusion, disbelief? Maybe I was just another one of those adults who said and did things she could not comprehend.

"Lisa, when your parents taught you your address, was there another part of it? Was it Oakdale, Nevada or Oakdale, Kansas or

Oakdale, Idaho?" I could see her already starting to shake her head. "Anything? Do you remember anything about the state you lived in?" She lowered her head and stared at the floor.

"Think—anything at all?"

"I don't know," she said reluctantly raising her eyes. "I don't remember." She paused for a moment then brightened a little. "You could tell me the names of all of the states and maybe I would remember it if I heard the one you want."

I took a deep breath and tried to figure out how to explain that that wouldn't work.

"Lisa, there are fifty states. One or maybe several of them could sound familiar to you but that wouldn't mean that's where you lived. It might only mean that you had heard the name before, on TV or something." Her plan rejected, Lisa's eyes turned down again to stare at the floor.

"Don't worry. That doesn't mean I won't get you home. We just have to go to the library and check the telephone books. We'll look for an Oakdale that has a Bill Taylor. Then I'll call your parents on the phone and we'll know we have the right one. Then we'll just get on a plane and you'll be home in nothing flat." Wait a minute, phone number? Could it be that easy?

"Lisa, did your parents ever teach you your phone number?" Lisa closed her eyes for a moment then recited:

"555-1748"

"That's great, but do you remember any other numbers?—three numbers in the beginning?"

"That's what they told me. I remember: 555-1748. Isn't that right?"

"Lisa, there are three more numbers, they're called the 'Area Code.' Different states have different area codes. I can't tell where that is without them."

"I'll never get home," she said softly.

"Sure you will! I promised, didn't I?" Lisa made no reply.

"Look, Lisa, you've got to trust me. I have it all figured out." Famous last words, but I was sure that I had everything almost under control. "Like I said a few minutes ago, we'll find a store and get some clean clothes, then we'll go to the library. By this afternoon we'll have found the right Oakdale. The airport is only a few hours away. It will all be fine." She looked up slowly.

"Are you sure?"

"Of course I'm sure. Now, the sooner we get out of here, the sooner we'll have you home. Are you ready to go?"

"Yes, Peter," she said in a resigned tone, still unsure but trusting me. Once she was in the car I told her to sit down low so that she couldn't be seen until we were out on the highway. The motel office was closed and I slipped the two keys through the mail slot. I decided to worry about any breakage charges when my credit card bill arrived next month. By eight o'clock we were headed west, back toward Highway 99. A low fog had condensed out of the dawn air, Valley Fog it's called. It cloaked the two-lane in a white-gray mist. This was the sort of fog that appears in clumps and billows of unexpected intensity. At times the visibility would be forty or fifty yards. A few seconds later we would round a bend and our vision would suddenly be reduced to forty or fifty feet, a circumstance that had caused numerous multi-car wrecks on Highways 99 and I-5.

Someone would be cruising along at the limit of visibility, or just beyond it, and then would find themselves in a fog bank. For a moment or two they would peer ahead trying to figure out what was in front of them, where the road had gone, then, when the absence of all reference points farther than a few feet in front of them registered, they would slam on their brakes.

Often it would be too late and they would already be only an instant away from colliding with a more cautious driver in front of them, or alternatively, they would be rear-ended by the vehicle behind that was still barreling through the fog. In the next instant another car would pile into the wreck. Then another, then another.

For that reason I was careful to maintain visual contact with some object ahead of me, a car, a tree, a power pole. As the distance to the farthest visible object shortened, I decreased my speed so that I could stop before I reached it. Traveling in this herky-jerky fashion it took almost an hour before we finally reached Highway 65 north of Porterville. A mile or two after we turned north on 65 I spotted a huge sign looming over the orange trees: "Farmland Discount Center."

A half mile ahead and to our right a large flat-roofed, single-story building lay at the back of a two-hundred-car parking lot. The store's name was repeated just below the building's roofline and beneath that was its slogan: "For All Your Farming, Building, & Household Needs." Though only about a quarter to nine, ten or twenty cars were parked in front of the main doors. When I approached the entrance I could see people moving around inside. Next to the glass doors was a plaque announcing the hours:

"Weekdays: 8:30 a.m.–8:30 p.m."

"Lisa, wake up," I said gently as I shook her shoulder. This time she awoke more easily, without the panic that had grasped her at the motel.

"Where are we?" she asked sleepily.

"We're at the store. We're going to get some clean clothes. Then we'll find a restaurant and have breakfast. Do you know what size you wear?"

"Size? Uh-uh."

"That's okay, I'll find someone to help us."

We went inside and I looked around for the children's department. Hardware, housewares, and appliances were grouped in a line near the front wall. To my left in the back I spotted racks of clothing. They had placed the children's and toddler's outfits in the far corner and the men's department next to it on the right. As we approached the clothing section I noticed an older lady, perhaps sixty, manning the cash register at the front of the children's department. I was going to have to give her some explanation for our disheveled state.

"Excuse me," I said when we reached the register. "Could you help us?"

She peered first at me, then looked over the top of her narrow glasses at Lisa and her mouth drew into a tight line. Yes, she would definitely need some kind of a story. The badge pinned to her sweater said: "Hello, my name is:" and below it was a strip of label-maker plastic tape imprinted with the name "Elaine Goodwin."

"We have a bit of a problem," I said. "Our luggage was stolen and we need to get some clothes."

"Yes, of course," she replied but her tone seemed to say: "That's an interesting story, but do I believe it?"

"What kind of clothes do you want?"

I stared at her for a moment, "I'm sorry?"

"I mean, do you want jeans, dresses, blouses, T-shirts?"

What kind of clothes did an eight-year-old girl wear? Something with Mickey Mouse on it? I had no idea.

"That's a good question. Her mother packed everything. Lisa's going to be spending a few days with my parents. Could you pick out what you think she would need?"

"What's she going to be doing?"

"Doing?"

"Is it a farm? Will she be playing outside a lot?"

"Oh, I see. No, they live outside of Bakersfield." I paused for a moment. I didn't like the look in Elaine Goodwin's eyes. She was suspicious as hell.

"Could I talk with you for a moment, please? Lisa, why don't you look around for a minute and see if you find something you like."

I motioned for Ms. Goodwin to join me a few feet away. "This is a little embarrassing, Ms., ah, Goodwin," I began, glancing again at her name badge. "The truth is that my wife and my parents don't get along. You know how it is. We've had this trip down to my folks planned for weeks and last night, Carol, that's my wife, Carol, decided that we weren't going." I could see from her expression that Elaine had had her own in-law problems over the years.

"Well, we had a big fight, shouting, everything. Finally Carol yells, 'I don't care what you say, I'm not going down there and spend three days listening to your mother criticize me!' 'Fine,' I said, 'we'll go without you!' So I grabbed Lisa and got into the car and here we are, no clothes or anything. We can't show up at my parents' house like this. Could you help me? Could you pick out everything that Lisa would need for the weekend?"

Elaine's expression softened and she glanced over her shoulder at Lisa, then turned back to me.

"I know just what you're going through," she said in a hushed voice. "My late husband, Harry, hated my father. You couldn't put the two of them in the same room for five minutes without them getting into a fight. Many's the time I wanted to leave him home when I went to visit my parents." Elaine paused for a moment and shook her head gently, no doubt remembering a particularly unpleasant Christmas or Thanksgiving. "You leave it to me," she said. "I'll get your Lisa fixed up."

"I can't thank you enough, Ms. Goodwin. If you don't mind, I'll go over to the men's department and get some clothes for myself. Oh, can you tell me, is there an ATM in the store? I had better get some extra cash too."

"Oh, yes, right up in front by the lost and found," she said pointing behind me.

"I won't be long. You'll keep a watch on Lisa for me?"

"A pretty little thing like her? Don't worry. I won't take my eyes off her for a second."

"Lisa," I called to her. She turned away from the rack of dresses and ran back to me.

"Lisa, Ms. Goodwin here will help you pick out the clothes you'll need for the weekend with grandma and grandpa. I'm going to get my clothes but I'll be back in a few minutes." Lisa stared at me blankly. I didn't know what she had made of my reference to grandma and grandpa. I just hoped she didn't say anything that would alert Ms. Goodwin to my lie.

"Okay?"

"You'll be right back?"

"Ten minutes, I promise."

"Okay," she said with a hint of fear in her voice. Did she think I would come all this way and then dump her in some discount store? But, why should she trust me? How could she understand my motives, or those of any adult?

"Lisa," I said firmly, staring at her, "I'll be right back."

She paused for a moment; her gaze locked on my eyes. She must have seen something there, determination, concern, love? Then she broke into a smile.

"Okay, I'll be right here."

"And I'll be right back. Thanks again, Ms. Goodwin."

I headed for the front of the store. Not everyone took credit cards and I only had about forty dollars in cash. The ATM was along the front wall and it happily accepted my Bank of America Versateller card. A few moments later it spit out ten twenty-dollar bills, the maximum that I could withdraw in any one day. I folded the bills in half and slipped them into my hip pocket. I was always uneasy about carrying a large amount of cash in my wallet. If I kept the bills in a separate pocket, then if my wallet was stolen, I wouldn't lose all my money.

Next to the ATM was a bank of pay phones. It was now about 9:05 Friday morning and I was already late for work. I picked up one of the phones and made a credit card call to my office.

"Hi, Jenny, it's me," I said when the receptionist answered. "Let me talk to Ann." There was a brief wait, then Ann, my secretary, came on the line.

"Ann, it's Peter," I began as soon as she picked up the receiver. "Look, I've run into a, uh, 'situation' and I won't be in today. Cancel my two o'clock. Call Jack Henry over at Marsden's and tell him the redlines are ready. Fax them to him. Tell him to look them over and I'll call him on Monday for any changes. Reschedule my meeting with Baumbach for Monday too. Tell him an emergency came up. Everything else can wait until next week."

"Are you all right? Do you need anything?"

"I'm fine. I—" I stopped. I didn't know what to say. I started again.

"I ran into someone who needed some help," I began. I was going to explain, was going to tell her that I had found this child, this kidnapped little girl, and I had rescued her and . . . , but I found that I couldn't talk. Without warning I felt tears well up in my eyes. What was wrong with me? Was I some kind of wimp? I scuba-dived. I skied. I had played football in high school. I was in Golden Gloves, then on the UC Boxing Team. I had stood up to an armed man and beaten him to a pulp. Why was I acting like some kind of cream puff? What was wrong with me? I took a deep breath and tried to explain things one more time.

"Ann, you see, I was going to Baumbach's last night, and I stopped at this store for some aspirin, and this man was there. There was this little girl with him and she was in trouble, and I had to. . . ." and I felt my voice begin to go. When I thought about what that man must have done to Lisa, a tide of emotion washed over me. What was wrong with me? I never let myself get emotional. And there was no reason for me to react this way. Janet always said that. . . . well, to hell with Janet too.

"Get a grip on yourself, Peter," I told myself. "Just calm down. It's been a scary night. You're still in shock. You were almost killed, for God's sake. No wonder you're a little upset." I took another deep breath and steadied my voice.

"Look, Ann, it's a long story. I can't explain right now. It's just something I have to do. You hold down the fort and I'll be back on Monday. Anything else we need to talk about, any problems?"

"No, not really. Jeri Wallace from First National called. She said the bank has approved the financing for the new building and they should be able to send us the commitment letter by the middle of next week. Are you sure everything's all right? We got kind of a strange call."

"What kind of a call?"

"Some man, about your car. He said he bumped into it in a parking lot and wanted to confirm that you were the Peter Howard with the silver Lexus. He read me your license number. When I told him you weren't here he wanted your home phone number and address. I told him that I couldn't give out that information. Then *he* read me your address and asked me to confirm that it was correct. When I told him that I couldn't give him any information and asked for his name and phone number, he said, and I wrote this down, 'It doesn't matter. If you talk to Mr. Howard tell him that I have all the information I need and that I'll take care of it.' Then he hung up. Are you sure you're okay?"

"I'm fine. Everything's under control. I'll see you Monday. Bye." I hung up the phone and stared at the wall. They knew my home address. The Department of Motor Vehicles no longer released that information on request. The name of the inquiring party and the reason for the inquiry were required. It was possible that they had filed a request with the DMV but how had they acted so quickly? The man had called shortly after nine this morning, hardly time to get any information from the state.

Then I remembered the kid at the gas station. He had said that he needed to check my driver's license because of credit card problems, but that was after he had seen Lisa in the car. My driver's license had my home address. Had he recognized Lisa? Was he tied into this in some way? Maybe the gray-haired man's appearance at the restaurant had not been a coincidence. Maybe Charlie had called him and told him to look for us at the Rib Pit. How else could they have found us?

I went to the men's department and bought a pair of jeans, a sport shirt, a nylon windbreaker, underwear, socks, and handkerchiefs. Next I picked up a rechargeable electric razor, two toothbrushes, toothpaste, deodorant, and shampoo, then hurried back to the children's department. I charged it all on my credit card and held onto the cash.

I looked around, but didn't see Lisa anywhere. My heart began to race. Could they have grabbed her right here in the store? Frantically, I ran down the aisle until, behind me, I heard Ms. Goodwin say, "I think that looks very nice." I found them on the far side of a circular rack of blouse-pants combinations.

"How are we doing?" I asked as I tried to calm my pounding heart.

"I think we have everything you'll need," Ms. Goodwin answered pleasantly. Apparently Lisa had not said anything to alarm her. If she only knew.

"I can't thank you enough. Here's my credit card. Could Lisa change into some of these clothes while you're ringing this up?"

"Sure, just let me take the tags off." Elaine removed the bar-coded stubs from a pair of blue slacks, a pink-and-white-striped T-shirt, and a package of underwear, then handed them to Lisa. "Right through that doorway, dear," Ms. Goodwin said, pointing to a hallway marked "Changing Rooms" along the back wall.

About the time that I had finished signing the credit card slip Lisa, dressed in her new clothes, returned. I was now acutely aware of my own shabby appearance.

"I just bought these in the Men's Department," I told Elaine showing her the receipt for my purchases. "Would it be possible for me to change too?"

"Well, this is the children's' department, but since no one else is back there, I suppose it will be all right. Lisa, why don't you stay here with me while your father puts on his new clothes."

Lisa's expression didn't change when I was referred to as her "father," though I couldn't help wondering how many times Ken, and perhaps other men, had used the same story. I hurried into the dressing room and slipped on fresh underwear and jeans. It took only a minute to change my shirt and stuff my old clothes into the plastic bag.

When I returned to the cash register I saw that Ms. Goodwin had acquired two new customers, both mothers with little ones in tow. I took Lisa's hand, thanked Ms. Goodwin for her help, and headed for the front of the store.

"What are we going to do now?" Lisa asked as we approached the front door.

That was a good question. I had been so intent on getting us ready to travel that I had forgotten that I still hadn't figured out where we were going. I had no idea where Lisa's parents actually lived. The closest city of any size was Visalia. I guessed that they would have a public library with phone books from around the United States. Lisa and I walked back to the pay phones and I called the Reference Desk at the Visalia Public Library.

"I'm trying to find the phone number for someone," I told the librarian. "I have the name of the city but not the state. Do you have some kind of an index that cross-references names with cities?"

"No, I'm sorry. We do have telephone books for most of the large metropolitan areas if that would help."

"I'm afraid it won't. It's a common city name. There could be twenty of them across the country, and I have no idea which is the one I want."

"I wish I could help you. We've been trying to get the funds for a CD-ROM drive for our computer but the budget hasn't been approved yet. Money is so tight right now. Several companies have compiled all the telephone numbers in the country on CD-ROM disks. If we had the equipment then we could check the whole country all at once."

"Thanks for your help. I'll figure something out."

Our problem was almost solved. Now, if there was only a computer store somewhere around here, we'd be all set. The Yellow Pages listed two possibilities: "Computer World—Everything For Business And Home Computing Needs" in Farmersville and

"DataLand—Your Multimedia Specialists" in Porterville. Multimedia would use CD-ROMs and Porterville was only a few miles south on Highway 65. I called the DataLand number. The phone was answered on the second ring, "DataLand Computers, Barry speaking."

"Barry, this is Peter Howard. I'm down here on business and I need to do some research. I was wondering if you have a CD-ROM disk that has all the phone numbers for the United States?"

"Yes sir, we have a brand new product, PhoneHome. It includes all fifty states, Puerto Rico and the District of Columbia. There are three versions: Residential Only, that's $85; Residential and Business for $195 and Residential, Business, and Yellow Pages for $495. We have both Mac and Windows versions in stock."

Barry sounded like he was about seventeen years old and was already pushing for the Assistant Manager's job. Well, that was fine. He might be more willing to satisfy our needs than an employee who was only killing time until his next coffee break.

"Barry, that's great. Now, I don't want to buy the disk. As I said, I just need to do some research. How about if I pay you fifty dollars to help me find the phone number I need, sort of a service fee?"

"We can't loan the software. I'm sorry. That's store policy."

"I understand that, Barry. All I want you to do is to run the residential listings on one of your computers there in the store and help me look for a number. Think of it as an in-store demo."

"That would be all right. Mr. Jenks is always giving demonstrations. He says, 'They won't buy it if they don't understand it.' "

"That's great, Barry. My name again is Peter Howard and I'll be there in a few minutes. I'm on 65 north of town. Why don't you give me directions?"

I pulled out a Discover credit card application from the rack next to the phone and wrote what he told me. Apparently DataLand was on Porterville's main street in the center of town on the right hand side next to Beverly's Coffee Shop. We were there in ten minutes.

Barry was a tall, skinny kid with glasses, and reddish-blond hair cut short on the sides. Except for the earring in his left ear he could have been the Computer Nerd Poster Boy.

"Barry? I'm Peter Howard. I talked with you a few minutes ago."

"Hi, Mr. Howard. We can use old Horace back here."

"Horace?"

"Oh, we name all the computers. We use Horace mostly for demonstrations. He's pretty old—a 25 meg 386, but he's got lots of room, half a g-byte of disk space. I've already installed the db."

"Was that a problem for you?"

"No, it's just that CD-ROMs are real slow," Barry explained unnecessarily. I let him ramble on. "The access time's about 350 milliseconds. It would take a long time to search the database at that rate. So, when you install a CD-ROM program, it copies its data base index on to the hard disk. The hard disk access time is only about 10 milliseconds. This guy," Barry said, smiling and pointing to a plastic CD-ROM box like the ones that hold music disks, "has an index to his db that's about ten megs. Anyway, it's all copied on to the hard disk now, so we can fire it up any time."

"Okay, let's do it."

Barry punched a few keys and a color menu overlaid on top of a picture of a futuristic telephone appeared on screen.

"Do you want to search by name?"

"Yes, the name's—" I began but Barry had already clicked his mouse on the first item in the menu, "Search By Last Name." Now a question appeared on screen: "Type In Part Or All Of The Last Name Of The Person You Wish To Find. Press ENTER Or Click On The GO Button When You Are Done Typing."

"What's the last name?"

"Taylor."

"I'll bet there'll be a few of those," Barry said smiling. His fingers danced over the keys and half a second later, the screen filled with Taylors. A box at the upper-right corner of the screen said "19,674 Matches Found." Along the bottom of the screen was the message: "Narrow Search By:" followed by several boxes. "Zip;" "First Name;" "City;" "State."

"What's the first name?" Barry asked, the mouse cursor already hovering over the "First Name" box.

"I want to search by city. Search for Oakdale."

"Great, that will narrow it a lot."

Barry clicked the "City" button, typed "Oakdale" into the blank line, then clicked on the "GO" button. The screen cleared, then displayed a new list of names. The box at the top now said "73 Matches Found."

The Taylors were arranged alphabetically by first name, Aimie to Zachary. Each line showed the Taylor last name, then the first name, the city, Oakdale, the state, and the phone number. But no addresses.

There were three William Taylors and one Willard Taylor. The Williams were in Oakdale, New Jersey; Oakdale, Tennessee; and Oakdale, Colorado. The Willard was in Oakdale, Oregon. His number was 555-1748. Bingo!

Now I checked the list for any Peggy Taylors. There were none, but there was one Margaret Taylor. Her number was 555-1748. That had to be them. I gave Barry my Gold Card.

"Look, Barry, while you're writing that up, can I make a credit card call? I want to call this number and see if it's who I'm looking for."

"Sure, help yourself."

I dialed Willard Taylor's number in Oregon then my credit card billing number. After a few seconds the phone began to ring, then a machine answered:

"Hello. This is Bill Taylor. Peggy and I aren't home right now, but your call is very important to us. We check our calls several times a day. We'll call you back as soon as possible. Please leave a message of any length at the tone. Thank you."

I took a breath, but what should I say: "Hello, you don't know me, but did you lose your daughter? By the time you get this message I'll be on a plane, so you can't call me back." Of course not, but I had to say something. A short beep sounded, then a second, a third—beep—beep—beep—beep—it wouldn't stop. The tape must have run out or broken or gotten twisted or something. I hung up the phone. The message said "Bill and Peggy." And the message sounded . . . anxious, almost desperate. This had to be the right Taylors, didn't it? Well, by the time I got to San Francisco they should be home from work or wherever and I would tell them we were coming. With a little luck I would have

Lisa home by dinner time. I signed the credit card receipt and headed for the door.

"Is it really them?" Lisa asked me when we got back inside the car.

How could I explain this to an eight year old? Children instinctively live in a digital world—right, wrong, yes, no, good, bad. Maybe, probably, most likely, possibly, were often unfathomable concepts.

"Lisa," I said, holding her hand, "I found a Bill and Peggy Taylor who live in Oakdale, Oregon. They have the same phone number that you gave me. I'm certain that's them. They're probably just at work right now. But it's okay. There's no reason to worry. Here's what we're going to do.

"We're going to go to the San Francisco Airport. That's only a three- or four-hour drive. By the time we get lunch and then drive there it'll be, oh, three or four this afternoon. By then one of your parents may be home. I'll call them on the phone from the airport. If they are your parents, and I'm sure they are, we'll get on a plane right there and fly up to Oregon."

Lisa stared at me, confused, then looked down. This was all too complicated. "If this then that," "if this other thing, then something else." What did it all mean? She had been sitting forward on the edge of the passenger seat and now began to kick her feet out and back.

"Lisa," I began again, "look, you have to trust me. I promise, I promise, no matter what, I'll get you home."

"Why?" she asked suddenly and turned to face me.

"Why—?"

"Why are you doing this for me? You fought with Ken. You didn't even run away when he tried to shoot you. You drove me all this way and bought me clothes. You paid that man to find out where my parents live. Now you say that you're going to take me to San Francisco and buy plane tickets. I don't understand. Do you want me to do, you know, do something for you, like Ken did? I mean, if you do, if you'll really take me home. . . ."

I can't imagine what expression my face displayed when she said that. Shock? Outrage? Pain? No, sadness, I think. More than anything else, sadness. What had happened to this child that she could not imagine anyone helping her just because she was in trouble and she needed help? What had the last twenty-four hours been like for her, wondering what I was doing and why, afraid that at any moment I might reach for her the way that Ken had?

"Lisa, I want you to listen to me very carefully. What Ken did to you was wrong. I would never, ever, ever do anything like that. Please don't think that about me, ever. I'm not like Ken. He was," I paused, at a loss as to how to describe a pervert in an eight year old's terms, "he was a very bad man. No one will do that to you as long as I'm around. Do you understand that?"

"I guess so."

"Lisa, I don't know if I can explain this to you so that you can understand it, but I'll try. Most people, they want to do the right thing, but most of the time they're asleep inside. They go to work; they watch television; they take a day off and go to the beach or they visit their relatives. And every day, inside, they fall a little more asleep. They never get the chance to really help anyone. And they start to forget how to. If they do get the chance, then, by the time they realize it, it's usually too late. They don't get a second chance. But not me. Not me. When I found you I got the chance to do the right thing, and I decided to take it. I woke up.

"It's all about what kind of a person you think you are. If you think you're not important, then you'll act as if you're not important. If you think you're bad, then you'll do bad things. If you believe that you're a good person, then you have to live up to that, so that you can respect yourself.

"I know that the right thing to do is to help you get home. And that's what I'm going to do, no matter what. Does that make any sense to you?"

"But you're spending all this money, and, and . . . What I mean is, I don't know how to pay you back."

"You can't pay me back with money."

"I don't understand."

"You don't have to give me anything. You don't owe me anything."

"But, if . . ."

"Lisa, you don't have to give me anything, but if you want to, there is something you can do for me, sometime."

"What?" she asked, suspicion again creeping into her voice.

"Someday, help someone else."

"Who?"

"You'll know when the time comes."

"What should I do? How will I help them?"

"You'll know when the time comes."

She stared at me silently for a moment, thinking, then her face suddenly brightened.

"Is that why you're helping me, because someone helped you a long time ago?"

"In a way, yes, I suppose that's right." Was I lying? I don't know, but it was an explanation that finally made sense to her.

"You mean, when you saw me in the store, and you figured out that Ken was hurting me, you knew that I was someone you should help?"

"That's right."

"And when you knocked Ken down and took me away from him, that's when you knew what you had to do?"

"Yes," I said softly, suddenly almost unable to speak. "So, some-day, when the time comes, if I find someone to help, then I'll know what to do, and I can do that for you?"

"If you're really lucky, the way I was really lucky to find you."

"And then they can help someone else?"

"I hope so. Now do you understand why I have to take you home, safe and sound?"

"Yes," Lisa said, at ease, I think, for the first time. She reached out and squeezed my hand, then sat back in her seat and peered over the dashboard.

"Can we eat before we go? I'm really hungry."

"You bet," I said, laughing. "How does Beverly's Coffee Shop there look to you?"

"Do you think they have hamburgers without onions? I hate onions."

"I'm positive they do. Come on, let's eat."

It was almost noon by the time we finished lunch and got back to the car. I had it all figured out. Lisa was happy. I knew, or at least thought I knew where her parents lived. I had bought a map of Oregon in the bookstore next to the coffee shop and I located

Oakdale not too far north of the California-Oregon border. We could fly in to Klamath Falls and rent a car. My Gold Card would open every door. I had traced out the route on the map. I had a plan. In a few hours we would be at SFO and I would be buying plane tickets. I pulled out, back onto Highway 65, feeling better than I had in a long time. And I paid not the slightest attention to the midnight blue van that slipped away from the curb four cars behind us.

# NINE

The trip was Bill's idea. It had been almost a year since Lisa had been kidnapped and he and Peggy had not had a vacation in all that time. Instead, every spare minute was consumed with mailing fliers, calling the Center For Missing and Exploited Children, and waiting for the phone to ring, waiting for the call telling them that Lisa had been found, that she was alive and on her way home. A call that never came. But neither did they get the other call, the one telling them that the body of a young girl had been found.

Bill had become obsessed with never being out of touch. He bought the most expensive answering machine he could find, one with a digital greeting and a one-hour tape cassette message capacity. He put in a new tape just before he and Peggy left for Hawaii. Unfortunately, misreading the instructions, thinking about the call that never came, Bill put the tape in backwards, the empty portion of the spool at the beginning instead of at the end. There was no tape left on the reel on which the machine could record an incoming message.

Blame the engineer, blame the programmer. The device should have been smart enough to say "Tape Full" or at least to rewind itself and record over what it believed were old messages that had already been retrieved, but one of the features of this model was that you could replay your previous calls. So the device steadfastly refused to automatically rewind itself.

Peggy called home every day, often twice a day, and punched in the secret code to retrieve their messages, but each day the machine's digital voice merely gave the same response: "You-have-ZERO-messages."

Bill called home on their third day to test the unit, but he listened only long enough to confirm that it answered the call and issued a beep at the end of the greeting, then he hung up. It never occurred to him to try to leave a test message. Everything seemed to be working. Well, their friends and the police all knew they were trying to get away and put the nightmare behind them for a few days. When he thought about it that way, Bill wasn't surprised that no one had called.

Peggy lay in bed and looked past her toes to watch the sun rise over the Pacific. The sea was dove gray under a lightening, gunmetal blue sky. Tomorrow, Saturday, was the last full day of their vacation. They would leave Sunday morning and arrive home late Sunday night. Bill would be back at work on Monday and she would start the rounds of calls again.

She looked over at Bill. They had wanted another child. Had. Now the thought of beginning again . . . That's not what she would have thought, before. If you had asked her, as a theoretical exercise, if she would want another child under these circumstances, she would have answered immediately, "Yes, of course."

It's not like Bill and I weren't trying before Lisa was . . . lost, not kidnapped, not taken—lost. Because what is lost may be found. Where is Lisa right now, she wondered.

The lower edge of the sun had cleared the horizon and brought color to the palms and bougainvillea and the red and green concrete tennis courts that lay just beyond and below their fifth-floor window. Peggy could hear the "thwock" of the tennis balls from the early risers' first game of the day. How many hours later was it on the mainland, three or four? Was it late enough to call and check their messages? Bill was still asleep. No sense waking him. She could wait a little longer. She had almost a year's practice at waiting. Peggy closed her eyes and tried to return to sleep. Below her, the pool boys adjusted the lounges for another day in paradise.

# TEN

---

Jimmie did not tell Eric what he had done with Ray's body. "Ray who?" was all he said when Eric asked him. Jimmie had a rule, one he often repeated to Eric but one which the younger man seemed to be unable to comprehend: Jimmie called it "need to know." It was simple, really. If Eric knew where Ray was buried, then Eric could deal that information to the police if he ever got into trouble, which Jimmie thought was a one hundred percent certainty. Eric had no need to know.

"Yeah," Eric might tell the cops, "sure, you got me for a penny-ante burglary, but what if I could give you a killer? I was talking to this guy and he told me how he killed this guy. I know where he buried him. I could take you there, if we can make a deal."

Of course, Eric would only implicate himself, dig both their graves, but he couldn't count on Eric to do the smart thing. Quite the reverse. Jimmie realized that he would have to "lose" Eric one of these days, soon.

"Don't get too close to him," Jimmie ordered. "I don't want him to spot us."

"He's no cop. He wouldn't notice me unless I ran into him, which, if you ask me, is what we should have done this morning."

"I didn't ask you."

"You should have. Christ, in all that fog I could have nailed him before he knew what hit him. Crash! and our worries are over."

"And if you wrecked the van and we were stuck there? Then what?"

"I know what I'm doing. I used to do accidents in L.A., for the insurance. Had a crooked lawyer—aren't they all? I'd do the crash and he'd get the bucks out of the insurance company. I took all the risks and that son of a bitch got seventy percent of the money. You want to know why I hate lawyers? But I fixed him. Anyway, like I said, I would have done it right."

"Not all accidents are fatal. That's a new car. It has belts and airbags. They would probably have walked away from it."

"No way. We just pull over, I lean through the window with my knife, zip, zip, and it's all over."

"So someone driving by sees us ram Howard's car, pull over, slit the throats of the passengers, then watches us get back into the van and drive off? That's your plan?"

"There wouldn't be any witnesses. In that fog, who would see us?"

"In that fog, how would you know who was around *to* see us? Eric, just forget it. I stuck a nail in the treads of each of his rear tires. As soon as he started up at least one of them was pushed through the rubber. Three miles, four tops, he'll be pulled over nice and neat, no muss, no fuss. And if anyone sees us stop by Howard's car, they'll think we're just good Samaritans and they'll drive on by. Besides, I told you, I don't want them dead yet. I want to find out what Howard knows. And the kid is still worth a lot of money."

"If you ask me—"

"Get ready, Eric," Jimmie interrupted. "He's pulling over. And remember, I want them alive."

# ELEVEN

---

North of Porterville, Highway 65 narrows from four lanes to two. The fog had long since dissipated and we could see the fertile landscape of the San Joaquin Valley. Orange groves alternated with stands of walnut, almond, and plum trees. At random intervals the trees lining one side of the road or the other would end at a knife-edged boundary to be replaced with acres of Thompson Seedless grape arbors, the vines brown and naked of leaves in the crisp February light. There were no more towns between Porterville and the city of Tulare which sat astride Route 99 a little over twenty miles north and west of us. By now I was watching my gas gauge with some concern. I had put over three hundred and fifty miles on the odometer since filling the tank last night. At constant freeway speeds the V-8 in my Lexus would go about four hundred miles on a tankfull. Well, I would get another twenty out of her I assured myself, while the needle hovered just above empty. There would be plenty of gas stations in Tulare. But there wasn't a lot of traffic, I noted with some uneasiness.

With no other towns between here and the freeway plus the fact that it was lunchtime, the road was almost empty, only the occasional pickup truck or diesel passed us in the opposite direction. If we did run out of gas it might take a while to flag down some help.

I was concentrating so hard on the fuel gauge that I didn't immediately notice the increasing pull in the car's steering. Unconsciously, I gripped the wheel tighter and corrected for the slight drift away from the center line. Finally, about five miles north of Porterville I realized that the front end was pulling decidedly to the right and I noticed a vibration from the rear wheels. Even as I concentrated on it, the rumble became more pronounced.

Was it the pavement? Were there seams in the road? I listened intently then experimentally moved the wheel left and right. The car seemed to wallow a little more with each turn and the vibrations became increasingly severe. A flat tire. Damn! I must have run over a nail or something on the way out of town.

Ahead the highway made a gentle turn to the left and I pulled over into the shelter of a line of orange trees, full with fruit. The bend in the road made it impossible for me to see oncoming traffic. Behind us, the highway was almost empty; I could detect only one indefinable black spot on the horizon a mile or so back. Well, the Lexus was a new car, and I knew how to change a tire.

"What's wrong?" Lisa asked as we drew to a stop almost beneath the trees twenty or so feet away from the edge of the asphalt.

"I think we've got a flat tire. Don't worry. I'll have the spare on in a few minutes." As I released my seat belt and reached for the door handle Lisa looked at me with an expression that showed, if not fear, at least concern.

"Can I come with you?" she asked.

I was about to tell her to stay in the car, but I could see that she was worried, afraid to be alone even for a few minutes.

"Sure, maybe you can give me a hand. Have you ever changed a tire before?" She shook her head. "Well then, you can learn something useful from this. Everyone should know how to do it. You can't depend on finding a gas station right in front of you every time you need one. Come on then, I'll show you how it's done."

Lisa slipped out of the passenger door and automatically depressed the lock before closing it behind her. Probably another of the rules that Ken had beaten into her. No matter. The driver's door was open and in any event I had the keys in my hand.

I opened the trunk and decided that I would make this into a little lesson and perhaps take Lisa's mind off her troubles.

"The first thing you need to remember, Lisa," I pontificated, "is to always remove everything you need from the trunk before you jack up the car. Some people get the tools out first, jack up the car, then have to wrestle with the spare tire while the car's up in the air. If they bounce around enough trying to get the spare out, they might knock the car off the jack. So," I said bending over and reaching into the far end of the trunk for the flashlight that had rolled all the way against the back wall, "get all of the tools first, especially your flashlight, so you can find the right spot under the car, ugh," I grunted and the light slipped from my fingertips and rolled a few more inches to the left, "the right spot," I continued, "to set the jack."

My voice reverberated in my ears and I realized how silly I must sound lecturing an eight year old on the mechanics of flat tire repair while I was stretched out almost full length inside the trunk. My lesson could wait, I decided, until I had retrieved the flash-light, the rest of the tools, and the tire itself.

As soon as I stopped talking, though, I heard other sounds—the crunch of tires against the dirt at the road's shoulder and the hum of an engine winding down to idle. Obviously some good Samari-tan had pulled over to give us a hand. I reached once more for the flashlight, caught it, and slowly levered myself back out of the trunk. As I pushed myself free I heard a car door open behind me followed by footsteps on the dry winter earth.

I began to turn around to thank the other driver for his concern and to explain that we didn't need any help, but when I turned I realized that I had made a terrible mistake. The vehicle behind us on the shoulder was not a battered pickup or a farmer's stakebed truck, but rather the dark blue van I had seen last night and the same two men were running toward me, already almost on top of me. The one on my right was the gray-haired man.

My back was to the Lexus and the car blocked my escape. I yelled, "Lisa, run!" then kicked at the younger man who was passing to my left. He avoided my blow and continued on around toward the right side of the car. I heard Lisa pulling on the door handle. Her instinctive reaction was to get inside and lock the door behind her. But the passenger door was already locked. The man who chased her was about twenty-five, burly, with short-cut brown hair and, as he swung wide around me and headed for Lisa, I saw a greenish-blue tattoo of a snake on his bare left arm. I couldn't let him catch her.

"Run, Lisa! Run into the trees!" I shouted as I dived to my left and tackled the tattooed man around the knees. He tottered for a moment then we both went down. I released my hold and tried to get to my feet but suddenly time seemed to flicker. One moment I was on my knees, struggling to stand, praying that another car would come by and see what was happening, would chase the kidnappers away, and then, the next instant, with no apparent interval in between, I was on the ground, on my back, flailing my arms and attempting to roll onto my side. The man with the tattoo was no longer in my line of sight.

"Lisa!" I tried to shout, but, to my surprise, I barely made a sound. Suddenly a lance of pain exploded in my back, below my left kidney and I fell back down again, flat on the ground. I heard Lisa scream and I managed to roll my head a few inches to my left. The tattooed man emerged from around the side of the car. Lisa, her arms and legs flailing, was clenched in his grasp. She looked down at me and shouted:

"Peter!"

I made one more attempt to roll to my left, but only managed to move my head an inch or so. As a result, the gray-haired man's boot caught my skull above my left ear, merely driving me into unconsciousness instead of crunching into my temple and putting me into a two-day coma. At that instant, as they say in the movies, everything went black.

I have only vague recollections of the next few hours, bits and snatches of sounds and movement, all filtered through shattered nightmares, the kinds of fragmentary and disconnected dreams you half remember the morning after your fever has broken.

The next thing I clearly recall was the sound of the van's side door sliding open. Even today I can't hear that noise without a ribbon of fear coiling inside me.

At first I thought I was blind, then a few blurry shapes began to cross my vision. Was my optic nerve damaged? Did I have a concussion? As I was dragged out of the van I caught a glimpse of two lighted windows, one at the front and one at the side of a small house or cabin on the slope above me. It was night. How long had I been unconscious? Six hours at least. Maybe twice that. I had no way of knowing how much time had passed.

A six-hour drive from Porterville could have taken us anywhere north of Sacramento, south of Los Angeles or even east into Nevada. One of the men dragged me backward away from the van and up the hill. The house spun out of sight. My heels dragged across the earth. I was being pulled along just like the kidnapper I had hit with the lamp, and like him, I left shallow twin furrows in the dirt behind me. Someone was getting a lot of practice in moving inert bodies.

I could not see the moon, but the stars were out in the clear winter sky. There were trees, pines or fir, behind the van. The house was uphill from the driveway and I sensed that the land dropped off beyond the drive to a gully or stream bed in the woods on the far side. I could only see one line of trees silhouetted against the sky as if the trees farther away were lower because of the presence of an intervening depression.

Halfway up the slope I heard the man who was dragging me call out.

"Jimmie, come over here and help me. This son of a bitch is heavy."

"I've got the kid. You're almost to the house anyway."

"You hit him. Why don't you carry him?"

"Because that's your job, Eric. If you don't like it, you can go back to busting into houses for junk jewelry. You want that, you can leave any time."

"Give me a break, will you? I don't know why we didn't just dump this guy somewhere. Why should we treat him any better than we did Ray?" asked the man with the tattoo. At least from the sound of his voice I assumed that's who it was because I recognized the other voice as that of the gray-haired man, Jimmie. We had reached the house's front steps. I felt the tattooed man, Eric, rise up behind me, then my butt hit the edge of the first step.

The gray-haired man, Jimmie, appeared in my line of sight, and I closed my eyes to slits. He had Lisa draped over his right shoulder, her head toward his back so all I could see was her bottom and the backs of her legs. Her ankles were tied together with a strip of cloth. It must have been some light-colored fabric since I could see it in the dim light leaking from the window on the front wall of the house behind me. In his other hand, Jimmie clutched a vague mass of clothing, perhaps the old clothes that Lisa and I had left in the backseat of my car.

"If you ever tried to think, Eric, you'd be dangerous," Jimmie said. "This guy made two phone calls from that store. Who did he call? What did he tell them? Don't you think we should find that out?"

There was a second grunt from behind me and my butt bumped over the edge of another step. The man behind me, Eric, stopped and took several deep breaths.

"What could he know? I say we just kill him now and be done with him. What can they prove?"

"What could he know? You really do frighten me sometimes, Eric. You should get down on your knees and thank me for doing your thinking for you. Who was it thought of wedging that nail in his tire? Hell, Eric, if you were on your own, you'd get yourself caught in a week. Think about it—he could have gotten our license number last night."

"In the dark?"

"Maybe he eats lots of carrots. He took her away from Ken. Maybe he knows where Ken lives. His car's still back on the highway. Suppose that when this guy goes missing and the cops start looking for him they find out that he's told someone about Ken, then they find Ken. He talks—"

"Ken's not saying nothing. He'd be cutting his own throat."

"Ken's a lunatic. Who else would pay us $30,000 for a kid? He's got squirrels in his head. You don't know what a guy like that will do."

"So we take him out. End of problem."

"What about Esther? Do we take her out too?"

"If we have to."

"And his neighbors? Suppose the cops talk to them and find out

<del>90</del>

about the kid? Suppose one of them saw you or got your plate number when you delivered the kid?"

"You told me to deliver her! It's not fair that—"

"Eric, just shut up! Now get the guy into the house. We'll find out what he's said, then we'll handle it. When we find out what we need to, we'll get rid of him where no one will ever find him again. Now come on! The kid's getting heavy."

Eric took another deep breath then dragged me up the remaining steps. When we reached the porch he let go of my shoulders and I fell back against the wooden floor of the porch and on top of my bound arms. I fought to keep from crying out in pain. I heard the rattle of a key, then the sound of a door being pushed open. A patch of light spilled out onto the porch and I closed my eyes completely. Eric grabbed me again, pulled me inside and dropped me on a thinly carpeted wooden floor. Behind me I heard Jimmie's footsteps, heavy now with Lisa's weight across his shoulders, then I heard the door close and latch.

"All right, here he is then," Eric said once Jimmie had bolted the door. "Let's get this over with and go to bed."

"Not tonight."

"What?"

"It's late and I'm tired. I need to be clear-headed when I question him, and he's still out cold."

"So what am I supposed to do with him?"

"Lock him up in the closet. And take off his clothes. I don't want him too comfortable in the morning."

"Why go to all that trouble? I can make him as uncomfortable as you want any time you want."

"Eric, one of the keys to a successful interrogation is to make the subject feel vulnerable, at the mercy of the interrogator."

"Where'd you come up with that?"

"Never mind. I learned it. That's all you need to know."

"What about the kid?"

"Undo her legs, tie her hands together, then tie her to the pipe under the sink in the bathroom. Make sure she won't be able to untie the knots. Give her enough rope to reach the toilet."

"Getting soft in your old age, are you, Jimmie?"

"You're the one who's going to have to clean up after her. Of course, if you enjoy mopping piss off the floor, then suit yourself."

Through my slitted eyes I saw Eric grimace, then I closed them completely as he leaned over and began to untie the cord around my ankles. My jeans were pulled down over my feet and my legs bound again. Next, I was rolled over onto my stomach, my hands released, and my shirt removed.

I continued to let my body go limp, feigning unconsciousness. Now clothed only in a pair of jockey shorts, my hands were retied behind my back and I was dragged into a closet. I heard a thump as a chair was wedged against the outside knob. I leaned my head against the door. Any scrap of information I could overhear might save my life.

"Make sure that's all the stuff I got out of his car," Jimmie ordered.

"What for?"

"We'll know that when we check it out. Now, take a look in the van and make sure we got it all."

I heard the front door slam and then after a few moments' delay the door of the van opened. A few seconds passed and then the door closed again. In the background I heard Jimmie going through my jeans.

"You got it all," Eric said a moment after the front door was opened and closed again. "There any beer left?" Eric called a moment later from the kitchen. I heard a refrigerator door unlatch and the clink of jars being jostled. "Damn it, Jimmie, did you have to drink the last one?"

"Poor baby, you're breaking my heart. Why don't you take a drive to the all-nighter. It's only 25 miles, each way," Jimmie shouted from the living room, then cawed in laughter when Eric slammed the refrigerator door. "Yeah, that's a good idea, Eric, my boy. You drive on down to the market and buy us a six-pack. Oh, and pick up a pizza while you're at it, why don't you! How about a couple of steaks? And I'd like one of those barbecue chickens. And a cake. A nice big birthday cake. That would be nice, wouldn't it?" Jimmie whooped another laugh.

"You're very comical, Jimmie. Very funny. You should go on TV.

Get yourself your own show: 'The Laughing Child Molester' you could call it. You'd get real big ratings."

"You watch your mouth, Eric," Jimmie shouted, suddenly angry. "I'm no chicken hawk! It's just business to me. I'm just a business-man supplying a product. What those sickos do with 'em is nothing to do with me. So you watch your mouth!"

"Sure, sure, whatever you say, Jimmie, but I still want a beer."

"You know what your problem is, Eric? You've never learned to do without. You want something, you run right out and take it, no matter what. You have no patience. You have to learn patience, Eric, or you're going to spend your life in the slammer."

"Look, all I said was—"

"I know. Well, there isn't any beer left. I drank the last one, so you'll have to do without. Do you understand what that means? You can't have what you want right now. So make do. Get yourself a glass of ice water. Take a look through that stuff from the car, then go to bed and forget the beer."

"I already checked it out on the drive up here. Nothin' there, just a pile of dirty clothes. You found his wallet in the jeans, right?"

"Wallet, comb, handkerchief, keys, and, by the way, a business card with Ken's license number on the back. But he doesn't know anything, right?"

"Shit! How'd he get that?"

"Maybe he asked Ken for it real nice when he took the kid. Nothing in the other clothes?"

"That's what I said, isn't it?" Eric shouted. "I'm getting tired of you treating me like I'm one of them kids. Damn, why'd you have to take the last beer?"

"Forget the damn beer! Just shut up and go to bed."

"I'll go to bed all right, but I won't forget the beer. Soon as we finish with these two tomorrow I'm getting me a case, two cases, then I won't have to hear this stupid lecture of yours again."

"Amen to that, Eric. I don't know why I even bother. You take the couch. I'll be in the bedroom. And don't even think about arguing about it."

Other than the sounds of drawers being opened and the rustle of clothing being removed, the house fell silent. I tested my bonds but I knew it was pointless. My hands and feet were tied with

93

some kind of nylon line about the thickness of the cord used in curtain pulls but much stronger. Not only was it far too strong for me to break, but the cord's narrow diameter cut into my flesh each time I strained against it. At least Eric had left me my underwear. Not out of any compassion or decency but most likely from sheer laziness.

The closet was too small for me to lie down. My back was sprawled against the corner near where the hinges were fastened to the wall; my knees were bent and my feet wedged against the far corner. I twisted my shoulders and shuffled my knees in a vain attempt to find a more comfortable position, but soon gave up, realizing that there wasn't one. For a few minutes I cataloged my aches and pains, the throbbing in my skull, the cramping muscles in my thighs and shoulders, the piercing pain in my back where I had been kicked, then gave up the exercise as pointless and depressing.

Surely there had to be a plan, some strategy that would get me out of this mess, but I couldn't think of one. Finally, I decided that the best that I could do would be to pretend to be more injured than I was, wait for them to untie me, then take my chances. Maybe it was the concussion or the hours without food, but somehow I slept, not the healing sleep that Shakespeare wrote about but an exhausted, tormented daze in which I bobbed back and forth between consciousness and the kinds of twisted, unfocused dreams which left no clear memory, just the aftertaste of horror and frustration.

Finally, the fiftieth or sixtieth time I opened my eyes I noticed a line of gray light seeping from beneath the door. I strained my ears but heard nothing. My eyelids slipped down for what seemed like just a moment and then flew open at the sound of Eric's voice in the room outside:

"There any eggs left or did you eat them too?"

"Thanks for offering to make breakfast, Eric. I'll have mine over easy."

"Yeah, right. You want bacon too?"

For what I guessed to be fifteen or twenty minutes I heard the muted sounds of water filling a pot, a frying pan banging against the stove, forks clinking against plates. I was sure that I could smell the grease from the frying bacon though it was probably my imagination. Finally I heard dishes being stacked in the sink. In a moment they would be coming for me. In half an hour I would likely be dead and Lisa worse off than when I had first found her.

I had set out to be the hero and instead had only made things infinitely worse for both of us. Did she hate me, I wondered. I had screwed up everything. Strangely enough I think that bothered me more than what was going to happen to me, that I had failed Lisa.

Was there any way out? Maybe I could get them to untie me. I could say I had to go to the bathroom. Then what? They would watch me twice as carefully. That's when they would expect me to try something, when I was in the bathroom, one on one.

I tried to think it through. These men were criminals. They surely had been locked up themselves at one time or another; certainly Eric had. They must have had these same thoughts about their captors, conjured up their own desperate dreams of escape. They would know what I was thinking. Suppose I got them to let me use the bathroom? One of them would go with me. The other one would stay back, out of the way, with Lisa. Even if I overpowered my escort the other one would kill me when I came out of the bathroom.

I had to think! After I used the toilet, they might tie my hands right away, but they wouldn't tie my feet. They wouldn't want to carry me back to the living room. If I was going to have any chance, I would have to attack them when they were both together and when they had relaxed as much as possible. Then what? I didn't have a clue.

The closet door opened suddenly and my eyes squinted against the light.

"Mr. Howard, you're awake," Jimmie said in a neutral voice. "Good. Come on out here and have a seat. We have a few things we need to get settled."

Eric leaned into the closet, grabbed my right shoulder and hauled me to my feet. Stumbling, half-blinded by the morning sunlight, I staggered forward in Eric's grasp. I had a brief glimpse of a cheap bent-pipe kitchen chair set in the middle of the living room floor, then I was pulled off my feet and pushed down into the chair. That didn't take much effort because I was cramped, aching, and exhausted and also I was trying to look as weak as possible.

"You understand the trouble you're in, don't you, Mr. Howard?" Jimmie began in a reasonable tone. I made no response other than to suck in deep lungfuls of air as if I had just run the length of a football field instead of merely staggering halfway across a small room.

"This can go easy, Mr. Howard, or hard, whichever way you choose. Our nearest neighbor is over a mile away. No one's going to hear anything that happens here."

"I can pay you," I wheezed. I knew that no matter what they promised they would kill me, but I was sure that they expected me to try something. The dumber and weaker they thought I was, the more they underestimated me, the better chance I would have.

"How much?" Eric asked instantly.

"Be quiet, Eric! We're getting ahead of ourselves, Mr. Howard. First you have to answer our questions, then we can talk about alternatives."

"Just let me go. I'll make it worth your while."

"We'll see. We'll see. But first, who did you tell about the girl?"

I dipped my head and breathed noisily. I needed time to think. If I said I had told no one, they might kill me on the spot, or, if they didn't believe me, they would hurt me enough to make sure that I was telling the truth. If I said that I had told my secretary, they might decide she didn't know enough to be dangerous and they would kill me or they might decide to kill her too.

"Trade," I mumbled.

"What?"

Wearily, I raised my head and looked up at Jimmie.

"You want something, I want something. I'm hungry and I have to use the bathroom."

"Spoken like a true businessman, Mr. Howard, but I'm afraid that you're not in a very good bargaining position. Who did you tell?"

Sullenly, I dropped my head to my chest. Jimmie didn't say anything. Perhaps he gave Eric a hand signal, or merely nodded his head, but an instant later Eric slapped me across my face hard enough to knock me off the chair. With my hands still bound I could only lay on the floor on my side while my cheek burned. It was a blow designed more to shock me than anything else, to hurt, but not to injure. It was merely a wake-up call. Eric righted the chair then muscled me back onto it.

"As I said, Mr. Howard, you're not in a very good bargaining position."

"Not talking," I muttered from my already swelling lips.

"Jesus, Jimmie, let's stop fooling around. Give me a few minutes and he'll be telling us his life story."

"Patience, Eric," Jimmie said calmly. This time I saw his chin nod. Eric drew back his right arm then pivoted forward and buried his fist in my stomach while Jimmie's hands on my shoulders held me down in the chair. The pain was numbing and I was unable to breathe.

"We can do this all day, Mr. Howard, can you?" Jimmie asked quietly. I was unable to answer and didn't even try. Instead I merely struggled to breathe. Finally, I caught a breath and wheezed:

"Bathroom. Food. Water."

Eric removed his belt and wrapped the leather around the knuckles of his right hand. I guess it was supposed to scare me, but I was way beyond merely being scared. I was numb. I just stared at him blankly and hunched my head down as close to my chest as possible and waited for the blow.

"Mr. Howard, you're a bit of a surprise, do you know that? A true believer in the principle of negotiation and compromise. All right, I'll give you a chance."

"Jimmie, just let me—"

"Relax a minute, Eric. We'll try it Mr. Howard's way. There'll be plenty of time for more direct measures. You said, food, water, and bathroom?"

"For the girl too."

"You want too much, Mr. Howard. You'll have to earn food and water for yourself and the girl. That will be your reward for answering my questions. But, just to get things started, I'll let you use the bathroom."

"I'd rather bust his mouth, and if that doesn't work, we'll see how he likes watching me play with the kid."

"Mr. Howard, you see what you're up against? Eric doesn't like fat-cat businessmen much. He'd like to knock out a few of your teeth just for fun. I promise you that if you don't cooperate, I'll let him do just that. Then I'll give him the child." I raised my head and glared at Jimmie. "You can't afford to hurt her. She's worth too much money to you."

"Oh, Eric won't break anything. He'll just have a little fun with her. Now that I think about it, things might go better if she was here. I don't think you'll be so stubborn if you have to watch Eric make her pay for your actions. Eric, get the girl."

I turned my head and saw Eric smile before he walked past me toward the bathroom. "Come on, kid," I heard him say. "Time to join the party." Lisa was led past me, her hands tied in front of her, the end of a long leash of nylon cord dangling from Eric's fist. Her eyes were dull, her movements stiff and awkward. When she walked by she turned to look at me and her face clouded with pain and fear. Here was the man who was going to save her, who had promised to take her home, no matter what: almost naked, bound hand and foot, bruised, bleeding, and humiliated. Neither of us spoke. "Tie the line to the chair," Jimmie ordered, nodding at a cheap wooden chair with a pillow strapped to its seat near the wall ahead of me and to my right. Eric looped the line around the armrest.

"Okay, take him to the bathroom," Jimmie ordered nodding at me.

"Why give this guy anything?"

"Because this is going to take a while and I don't want him stinking up the living room. Do you?"

"Come on, smart guy," he said as he pulled me to my feet. "I hope you try something 'cause I'd love an excuse to break your face." I let my body go almost limp and forced Eric to half carry me to the bathroom. When we got there he made me lie on the floor while he untied my hands from behind my back.

"Roll over, real careful," he ordered. When I was on my back, he retied my hands in front of me, then pulled me to my feet.

"Pull down my shorts," I told him.

"You can get it out with your hands tied," he said.

"I gotta do more than pee."

"Too bad."

"It won't smell good if I do it in my pants."

Eric paused a second, grimaced, then pulled my jockeys down and sat me on the toilet. When I was done, I held out my bound hands again.

"Unless you want to do it," I said.

I don't think I had ever seen a more suspicious expression than the one that crossed Eric's face, but in the end he had little choice. I wouldn't smell too good otherwise. He untied my hands and stood back warily. I finished what I needed to do, weakly levered myself to my feet then made an ineffectual attempt to reach my shorts.

"You want 'em on, you pull 'em up," Eric said, smiling. I made as big a production out of it as I could, and finally managed to get my jockeys back into position. Trembling with exhaustion, I held my hands out in front of me. Without thinking twice Eric retied my hands in front of rather than behind me, then marched me out of the room. One small victory.

For better or worse, this was going to be my only chance. Once I was back in that chair and my legs were tied, I was as good as dead. A few paces into the living room I let myself collapse. Eric was instantly suspicious, but I just lay there gasping. Finally, he hauled me to my feet and half carried me back to the chair.

I let my body tumble bonelessly back into the seat while I took in great lungfuls of air like an exhausted track star. My eyes half closed, I lolled my head back and breathed noisily through my mouth. Disgusted with me, Eric knelt on the floor in front of me and bent down to wrap the cord around my ankles. This would be my only chance.

As soon as his head was lowered and he had leaned forward and was off balance, I kicked out with both feet as fast and as hard as I could. My left foot went wide, sliding off Eric's cheek and brushing past his right ear, but the instep of my right foot caught him just below the Adam's apple. Eric went over backward and made a thin gasping sound as he unsuccessfully tried to breathe.

Before he had even landed on his back, I was falling to my right, out of the chair, rolling to my knees then getting first my left foot, then my right under me and turning to face Jimmie even as I stood. When I had struck Eric, Jimmie had lunged toward me, but by the time he reached the chair, I was no longer in it and his leap tumbled both himself and the chair to the floor a bit ahead of me and to my right.

Even as I turned toward him he was starting to rise. Heedless of the risks, I ran at him. If he regained his feet, Lisa and I were both finished. He had put his right hand on the side of the overturned chair and was pushing against it to lever himself up. I kicked at his wrist. The chair bucked and he lost his grip and fell back to the floor. I kicked my heel at the bridge of his nose, but missed and hit his mouth instead. Almost instantly blood stained his teeth and he reached for his mouth with his right hand. His legs were clenched together, but his stomach was exposed and I kicked him there. He doubled up in pain and I kicked again at his face.

Desperately, I looked around for a weapon. The room was sparsely furnished with the kinds of things you would find at a Goodwill store or at an auction of the assets of a bankrupt motel: a couple of wooden chairs, a rattan couch, an end table, nothing of much use as a weapon. Jimmie groaned and started to unclench his legs. In a moment he would be back on his feet. On a TV tray table along the wall next to the couch I saw a beer bottle, the famous last beer about which Eric had complained so bitterly.

I stumbled to my left, grabbed the bottle's neck with both tied hands and then ran back to where Jimmie writhed on the floor. I kicked at his stomach again, but this time he reached out and grabbed my foot. With a burst of adrenalin I wrenched it free then kicked again, catching a glancing blow against his solar plexus. He curled up on his side and grasped his head protecting his face from another kick. I moved behind him, gracelessly fell to my knees and, with an awkward two-handed grip, brought the bottle smashing down on the side of his skull.

The glass shattered and the broken stub in my hand raked his scalp which immediately began to spurt blood. Jimmie lay on the floor rocking back and forth and moaning softly. I was almost ready to breathe easily when Lisa screamed, "Peter!"

Still on my knees, I looked up and saw Eric charging, almost on top of me. He had a knife in his right hand. My hands were still tied together in front of me. There was no way that I could get to my feet before he reached me. Instinctively, I thrust my arms out in front of me to push Eric back, to ward him off. I still held the shattered stub of the beer bottle. Eric ran full into it, impaling himself on the serrated glass before he even realized what had happened to him.

The bottle tore through the seam in his shirt, through his skin and his muscles, and through the wall of his stomach as if there was nothing there. I felt practically no resistance at all. It was almost like stabbing a feather pillow.

An expression of astonishment clouded Eric's features, and for a moment, he paused, still holding his knife, then it slipped from his hand and tumbled to the floor as Eric grasped his stomach in a vain attempt to hold his blood and flesh within his body, and failed. Still wearing an expression of incredulous surprise, Eric gasped once and collapsed to the floor. I still held the broken bottle. It and my hands were covered with his blood.

I threw the glass away from me and it shattered against the wall, then I struggled to my feet. Jimmie was still moaning and rolling on the carpet. I reached down and picked up Eric's knife and staggered over to where Lisa was tied to the chair.

Her face bore an expression beyond terror, a gasping kind of fear and exhaustion for which I had no name. But she didn't cry. It's strange sometimes what we think of, the things we notice at the oddest of moments, but that's the first time I realized that she had never cried out loud, not when I took her away from Ken, not when we couldn't find her parents, not last night when Eric had tied her up on the bathroom floor, and not now. Perhaps she had spent all of her tears weeks or months before. Maybe she was so wounded, so abused, that real crying was no longer possible for her, that bit by bit, that part of her humanity had been ripped away.

"Hold out your wrists so that I can cut the rope," I told her. Her eyes fixed on my bloody hands and she paused for a moment then complied. Eric's knife parted the nylon line effortlessly. "Take the knife and cut me free," I told her. She paused then removed the knife from my still bound hands, its handle slick with Eric's blood.

I watched the way it stained her hands as she sawed at the cord that encircled my wrists. As soon as the line parted she dropped the knife to the floor then looked wonderingly at her own now bloody hands. She started to wipe them on her jeans, then stopped and let them drop to her sides. She would live with the blood a little longer.

I heard a sound behind me. Jimmie still lay moaning on the floor. I looked around for my clothes but saw only the wrinkled suit pants and dress shirt that I had worn Thursday evening when I had first found Lisa. I wiped my hands on my shorts then I grabbed those clothes and pulled them on. My shoes were across the room under a chair, but I didn't see my socks. I slipped my bare feet into the shoes and was about to try to figure out what I was going to do about Jimmie when I heard a crash behind me.

Jimmie, his cheek and neck covered with blood, had crawled to the bookcase near the far corner of the room next to the kitchen and pulled it over in an attempt to get to his feet. I half started to run back to hit him again when I saw what he was reaching for. A revolver had spilled from the rear of one of the shelves and it was only two or three feet from his grasp.

I looked at Jimmie fifteen feet away from me as he crawled toward the gun, then I turned back to Lisa. Could I get to Jimmie before he reached the gun? If I did, could I stop him? Could I knock him down again? The beer bottle was gone. The knife was on the floor, across the room, near Lisa. It was too far away for me to get it and then get back to Jimmie before he got his hands on the gun. Frozen, I looked back and forth: Lisa, knife, front door, Jimmie, Lisa, knife, front door. Jimmie was on his hands and knees, another foot closer to the gun. I decided that it was time, past time, to get the hell out of there.

I ran, more like a fast stumble, across the floor, grabbed Lisa, threw her across my shoulder, and lurched out the front door. Luckily, the van was downhill from the house. If I had had to climb up the driveway, we never would have made it. I threw open the driver's door, more or less tossed Lisa inside, and then climbed in myself. I figured that if I were a couple of vicious criminals using an out-of-the-way cabin as a hide-out, I would leave the keys in the car so that I could escape at a moment's notice. I wouldn't want to hear the cops breaking in the front door in the middle of the night and not be able to slip out the back window because I had forgotten where I had put the car keys. Maybe I have a criminal mind, or maybe I was just lucky, but the keys were in the ignition and Jimmie had obligingly turned the van around so that it faced back down the driveway. I guess that stuff about preparing for a quick getaway made some sense after all.

Just as I started the engine, Jimmie lurched into the doorway. A shot rang out and I heard a hollow "thunk" behind me where the bullet hit the side of the van. I dropped the shift lever into drive and floored the accelerator. Another shot was fired, this one hitting the van near the front of the passenger compartment. We careened down the driveway as two more bullets buried themselves into the van's metal carcass before a bend in the road concealed the house from my sight.

# TWELVE

The van lurched down the driveway barely under my control. Within the first fifty yards I discovered that the road's surface was not hard-packed clay but a treacherous mixture of dry soil on the top and damp earth and pea gravel in the hollows. A couple of times I almost bounded off the drive. Pines and valley oaks bordered each side of the track which threaded its way through a seam between two forested hills. Beyond the hills, on each side, ridges towered several hundred feet above us.

I had driven the last hundred yards of our escape clinging to the steering wheel, my butt bouncing in and out of the driver's seat. About a half mile or so from the cabin we reached a paved road. I slammed on the brakes and brought the van to a jarring halt. The replacement of the sound of the roaring engine and protesting springs with the chirpings of jays and starlings and the sigh of a soft breeze through the pines was startling.

I took two deep breaths and swiveled my head left and right. Lisa had somehow managed to more or less remain in her seat during the wild ride and now, ashen-faced, she clung to the passenger door armrest with both hands.

Though paved, this road looked more like a private drive or, at best, a little-used county highway. About three hundred yards in the distance to the right I could see a sheer forested wall perhaps a thousand feet high rising in front of me. I turned toward it.

After several turns the road emerged from the low hills and crossed a narrow strip of land, through the middle of which gushed a swollen creek. A small steel bridge spanned the stream and after crossing it we found ourselves at the edge of a two-lane blacktop highway which hugged the base of the cliff before us. The highway was empty, without even the hum of distant traffic. We were in the bottom of a narrow canyon, heavily forested on both sides, with the road following the course of the stream as it wove its way through the gorge. The highway bore no route markers or signs of any kind. I paused for a second longer, then arbitrarily decided to turn to the right.

"Lisa, put your seat belt on," I ordered and spared a glance to the side to make sure that she complied. I needn't have bothered. Lisa had been thoroughly trained to follow orders. I realized that I could not remember one instance when she had refused to obey my instructions. I wished I could have thought that was a good thing.

As soon as I heard her buckle snap closed, I reached up and behind me and pulled my own belt across my shoulders, fastened it, then turned right and headed up the highway. I looked at the gas gauge. It showed that we had half a tank. Now, if I only knew where we were and where we were going.

"Lisa, are you all right?" I asked once the emergency items were, for the moment, out of the way.

"I'm fine," she said quietly, her voice tight, almost on the verge of a sniffle, but without tears. So well conditioned, I thought. I said nothing more for a second or two. A hundred thoughts whirled through my head but none paused long enough for me to consider it seriously. Each instant each idea was replaced by another, and another. Decisions and planning were, for once, beyond me. Grimly, I pressed harder on the accelerator, moving faster over the twisting road without the slightest idea of where we were going but assuming that what lay ahead of us could be no worse than what we had just left behind.

"Is he dead?" Lisa asked suddenly.

"What?"

"The man with the snake on his arm. Is he dead? Did you kill him?"

What do you say to an eight-year-old child who has just asked you if you have killed someone? She shouldn't know about death in such intimate detail. She should be concerned with soccer practice or a new dress for school or what she wants for her birthday. She might as well have asked me to explain what the SS did at Dachau.

"I don't know. Maybe. I didn't do it on purpose."

"I hope he's dead!" Lisa said with sudden energy. A little girl sees a man gored before her eyes and says she hopes he's dead. That her life had come to this made me ashamed.

"He's a bad man!" she added when I did not respond.

"Because he helped tie us up and take us to that house?"

"No," she said, then after a pause continued: "He was the one. Him and another man."

"He and this other man, were they the ones who took you away from your home?"

From the corner of my eye I saw Lisa nod. I had never asked what had happened to her. I had been afraid to question her, to force her to relive those painful memories, but now she seemed to want to talk about it. Maybe that was a good thing.

"Would it bother you to tell me what happened, what the man with the snake on his arm did?"

She shook her head then looked down and stared at her shoes. I resolved not to press her. If she wanted to talk about her kidnapping she would. I drove down the empty road still not finding any route markers or signs of habitation.

"We were playing," she said softly a moment later.

"Were you in the park, at school?"

"No, I was home. In the front yard, with Carla and Susan. We had been on my swing. Then we started playing with our dolls. I got a pink scooter for Barbie for Christmas."

"What happened, Lisa?"

"We were playing and Carla said that for her birthday her mother was going to get her a convertible for her Barbie. She said a car was nicer than my pink scooter. I said that Barbie liked her scooter better because it was more fun than an old convertible. Then a car stopped in front of the house and the man with the snake got out. He just jumped out and he ran right up to us. It was a mistake!"

"What do you mean? What kind of a mistake?"

"It wasn't supposed to be me! He didn't want me. It was a mistake!"

"I don't understand, Lisa."

"He ran over to Carla and he grabbed *her*. Susan ran away, but I kicked him in the leg. Carla was crying and trying to get away and when I kicked his leg he sort of dropped her and she ran away. But when I tried to run away too he grabbed me and took me back to the car and the other man drove off. If I had run away like Susan, he would have taken Carla. It wasn't supposed to be me!"

As I listened to Lisa's story, a ball of ice formed in my stomach. This little girl had attacked a grown man to save her friend, and she felt guilty about it. And, without realizing it, she probably felt guilty about feeling guilty. Part of her kept whispering: "You're a fool. It's all your fault. If you had just been smart enough to run away, like Susan, everything would be all right," while another part of her probably whispered, "You're bad because you wish you had run away and they had done all this to your friend instead of to you."

"I admire you, Lisa," I told her warmly, "You were very brave."

"I don't want to be brave. I just want to go home."

"I know. So do I." I thought for a moment and tried a different tack. "You know what a policeman is, don't you?"

"Sure."

"Policemen try to stop bad men like Eric, the man with the snake. Lisa, if a bad man was chasing you, and if a policeman saw him, do you think the policeman would run away and let the bad man catch you or would he try to stop him?"

"You mean the way you stopped Ken?"

"Sort of. Wouldn't the policeman help you? Wouldn't he fight the bad man?"

"I guess so."

"What if the policeman knew he might get hurt if he helped

you? Should he let the bad man catch you? Shouldn't he help you anyway?"

"I guess. That's what you did. Are you a policeman?"

"No. I just happened to see that you were in trouble. Just the way that you saw that Carla was in trouble. I tried to help you the way you tried to help Carla. Do you think that I'm sorry I tried to help you?"

"I don't know."

"I'm not. I would do it again. Do you know why?"

"No."

"Because I think helping you was the right thing to do."

"Do you always do the right thing?"

I thought of Janet. "No, lots of times I don't."

"Then why did you do it this time?"

"Sometimes there are small 'right things' and sometimes there are big 'right things.' Helping you was a big 'right thing.' Would you rather I hadn't helped you? If you could take things back, would you want me not to have taken you away from Ken?"

"No. I hate Ken. I hope he dies like the man with the snake."

"Do you think Carla is happy that you saved her?" Lisa paused and thought for a moment before answering.

"I suppose."

"Lisa, you fought for your friend. You did a very brave thing."

"If I could do it again, like you said, I wouldn't. I don't want to be brave. I wish he had taken Carla and left me alone!" Lisa's eyes were red and she began to sniffle and again lowered her head.

I had no true insights on "Life" or "Human Nature" but I had to say something to make her feel better, to help her live with what had happened, even if it I had no idea if what I was about to tell her was really true.

"You can't help being brave, Lisa," I told her. "That's just the way you are. You know what? If this happened all over again, you would do the same thing."

"No, I wouldn't. I'd run away!"

"You think that now, here, that you would, but you're a brave person and you can't help but act that way. As much as you might want to run away, you wouldn't. You would fight back and you would save your friend. I'm very proud of you. You should be proud of yourself. When we get you home, everyone will tell you that. Not just me."

Lisa was quiet for several minutes, then, without warning, asked, "Will he find us again?"

"Who? The man in the cabin with the gray hair? The one named Jimmie?"

"Uh-huh. Will he? I don't want to be brave anymore."

"He doesn't have a car and he doesn't know where we are or where we're going. Besides, we'll find the police soon and they'll get you home. He won't mess with them. He's going to run away as fast as he can. The last thing he'll do is get anywhere near us again."

Without realizing it, apparently I had made the decision I had been trying so hard to avoid. I had tried to do everything myself and had almost gotten both of us killed.

"Aren't you going to take me home?" Lisa asked fearfully.

"Sure, but the police—"

"Will you be there? Will you go with me?"

"I'm not leaving you. We'll have the police call your parents and they'll come down to get you. I won't leave you until they get here."

"But what if the police can't find them? What then?"

"They'll find them. Don't worry."

"But what if they don't? Can I stay with you? Will the police let me stay with you?"

"Well, that might not be a good idea. They'll find a nice police-woman to take care of you until—"

"No! You promised! You said you would take me home. You said that no matter what you would take me home. You promised!" Lisa shouted.

"I'm not going to leave you. I'll stay there until your parents come for you."

"But the police might not let you; that's what you said. You said I could trust you. You promised. . . ."

"Lisa, listen, this is dangerous. They almost got you back. I don't even know where we are. My wallet's gone. I don't have any money. I can't even buy us any food or get gas for the van."

"What about the money you got from the machine at the store? Don't you have any left?"

The money I had gotten from the ATM? I had put it in the hip pocket of my suit pants. Hadn't I transferred it to my jeans? I slipped my hand under my right buttock and pressed my fingers against the fabric. By God, I could feel the bills under the cloth. The money was still there! Eric had been too lazy to search my pants after all! I didn't have a wallet or a driver's license or credit cards or clean underwear or a pair of socks or even a comb, but I did have two hundred dollars in cash. Would it be enough to get this bucket of bolts to Oakdale, Oregon? I figured that depended on where we were.

But what if that guy did find us again? What if I got stopped for speeding? How was I going to explain my not calling the police? But, of course, it was already too late for that. I had crossed that bridge back at the Belair Motel. If they found me with Lisa before I got her home I would look like a pedophile.

"You promised," Lisa whimpered.

Oh, hell, sometimes you just have to break your promises. But, God, I hated to do that. I prided myself that my word was good. Dad always told me, nothing is more important than keeping your word. A deal is a deal. That's one of the last things he said to me. And he was right.

But wouldn't the intelligent thing be to turn her over to the authorities and face the music? As long as they didn't succeed in browbeating Lisa into saying that I had molested her, which was a substantial risk, it might work out. By calling the police I would be breaking my promise to her but someday, when she was older, Lisa would understand. Damn! How many times when I was a kid had some grown-up said that to me?

"When you're older, Peter, you'll understand."

It was all bullshit, an excuse for taking the easy way out. I knew about that.

When I was eleven a new kid, Mike Levine, came to my school and he took an immediate dislike to me. I don't know why. We were playing soccer in gym class and he used to go out of his way to just nail me whenever he could. He was bigger than me but I told my friend, Terry Dahlberg, that I was going to have it out with him anyway.

"Jeez, Peter," Terry said, "he'll beat the crap out of you!"

"Well, I'm tired of being pushed around. I'm going to stand up to the guy."

"Then what?" Terry asked. "After he breaks your nose, the next day in soccer he'll just stick it to you all over again."

"I've got to do something. I'm tired of taking it."

"Pete, the smart thing to do is just talk to Mr. Hayman. Let him handle it."

"I'm not going to squeal on Levine!"

"You don't have to. Just tell Hayman that somebody's got it in for you and that he's using soccer practice as an excuse to beat you up. It's Hayman's job to take care of stuff like that. Look, he'll either transfer you to Mr. Morressy's class or he'll see what Levine is doing and he'll tell him to cut it out."

"I don't know, Terry. I think I should handle this myself."

"What's the point? Jeez, Peter, use your head. It's like my dad always says, 'Never play to the other guy's strength.' If you play it Levine's way, you're history. Besides, stuff like this is Hayman's job. The smart thing to do is to let him handle it."

And, logically, Terry was right. So that's what I did. I did the smart thing. I will never forget the look Mr. Hayman gave me when I told him "someone" was pushing me around. He might as well have said, "I feel sorry for you, kid. You're just a little tattle-tale coward and you don't know any better." Hayman asked me a couple of things like, "Maybe you're mistaken," and "Have you tried talking to this guy and working the problem out?", stuff like that. I felt like a real jerk and just kept saying, "I don't know, I don't know."

So, anyway, I got my wish. Mr. Hayman sent me to finish the year in Mr. Morressy's class. And everyone knew I had turned tail and run. God, how Levine used to laugh every time he saw me in the halls. I did the logical thing, the "smart" thing. I got out of my problem without taking even one punch, without even an argument, and it was one of the worst decisions I have ever made. The only good that came out of that whole incident was that I got real interested in learning how to box and building up my body.

There's something about knowing that you can flatten a guy with three punches that gives you a terrific level of confidence.

God, I wish I had stood up to Mike Levine. I would rather that he had beat the shit out of me than what I did. And here I was thinking about doing the same thing again. Call the cops. Dump the kid on them. Let them handle it. Go home and avoid all the hassles. Run away. Just like Janet had done.

Wasn't that what I was going to do now, break my promise and run away? I looked over at Lisa. She was curled up in the corner of the seat, still fighting not to cry. Who had ever needed me as much as she did? Who had ever believed in me as much as she did? All I had to do was find a phone. Lisa looked up at me and I realized that I couldn't give her up, not now, not yet.

"Okay, Lisa, I won't call the police."

"You mean it?"

"Sure. A minute ago, I forgot something. I forgot that a deal is a deal. When you make a promise you've got to keep it. I forgot that when you're doing something really important you can't just quit. I'm not going to quit and run away. Not this time.

"We've got two hundred dollars. We'll see how far that will get us. If it runs out I'll have to think of something else. If we get stuck and I can't get you home right away, I will call the police. And I'm going to keep calling your parents. As soon as they answer I'm going to ask them to come down and get you. Do you under-stand?"

"Yes, Peter. How long will it take, you know, to get home?"

"I don't know. Soon, I hope. Real soon."

Did this make any sense? Maybe not, but I felt good about it. Just this once couldn't I allow myself to be emotional? That's what Janet said was wrong with me, that I was all head and no heart. I had always done the logical thing, until now. Maybe Mr. Spock would not understand my decision to take Lisa home, but I did.

I looked over and saw that Lisa had stretched out in her seat, and for only the second time, I saw her really smile. Now that I had no more difficult choices to make I felt as if a great weight had been lifted from my shoulders. The clock on the dashboard said ten minutes to nine. I looked down the highway and pressed harder on the accelerator.

# THIRTEEN

Jimmie fired all five shots and continued to click the trigger impotently on the expended chambers, then he drew back his arm as if to hurl the gun down the empty driveway, but he restrained himself. He might need the gun again. Jimmie went back inside, glanced at Eric's body, briefly, and turned away. At least that was one problem solved. A bungler out of the way and no one left to share the money with. Muscle like Eric was a dime a dozen. He'd find a replacement easily enough. You just had to know where to look. Tim Mathias, for example, always needed money. After he washed off the blood and bandaged his cuts Devries dialed Mathias's number.

Tim answered the phone on the third ring.

"Yeah?"

"Tim, you recognize my voice?"

"Yeah, Jimmie D—"

"Don't say my name, just listen. I need you to get a truck or a van that can't be traced to you. Can you do that?"

"Sure, but it'll cost—."

"There's a grand in it for you if you get it right away. Can you get it to the cabin in an hour?"

"I guess. But I'm going to have expenses."

"Just get here and I'll take care of you. Remember, if they trace it back to you, you're the one who's going to be in trouble, so make sure it's clean."

"Don't worry. I know a guy who can handle it."

"It can't be hot."

"New color. New plates. Never be traced."

"Okay, drive past the road to the cabin, about a hundred yards, then pull over. If no one's following you, I'll get in. You got it?"

"Sure, no problem."

"How soon can you get here?"

"Two hours, maybe a little less."

"Hurry." Jimmie hung up the phone. It was a calculated risk. He could run. If the police had been called they'd be there long before Mathias. So Jimmie would wait in the bushes along the highway, just in case. But Jimmie didn't think Howard would call the cops. The businessman was still on his "hero" trip, he decided. Howard was going to take the kid home himself. He understood people, Jimmie did. He was betting that Howard would just drive the van straight up to Oakdale, that he would just keep right on tilting at that windmill.

What a fool, Jimmie thought. Didn't Howard realize that Devries couldn't afford to leave any witnesses? There was no statute of limitations on murder. Jimmie knew the law. Ray and Eric's deaths occurred during the commission of a crime. That was felony-murder. They would be charged to Jimmie. Lisa and Howard could identify him. He would never be safe unless he got rid of them. Didn't Howard know that Lisa was still worth money, not to mention the fact that Jimmie had a score to settle? Jimmie was very big on settling scores.

But first, he needed to wipe his prints from everything he had touched in the cabin then get rid of Eric's body. No body, no proof that Eric was dead, as long as there weren't any witnesses around to point any fingers.

Jimmie peeled off his clothes and stepped into the shower just long enough to wash off the blood, then he bandaged his wounds. Hastily he pulled on a clean pair of jeans and a fresh shirt then he used the damp bath towel to wipe down all the door knobs, the refrigerator door, the tables, everything he might have touched. With all his clothes and sheets and the bath towel stuffed into the pillowcase he slipped outside.

It was still early. The jays chattered in the trees as Jimmie jogged down to the highway to await Mathias's arrival. If Peter Howard thought Jimmie Devries was going to turn tail and run, he was fatally mistaken.

# FOURTEEN

A mile or two after we entered the highway the road reached the end of the canyon and began to climb. Manzanita and bare-branched acacia filled the spaces between the stands of valley oaks and ponderosa pine which covered the slope above us and to our left. A sheetmetal sign planted at the road's edge announced that we were passing 1800 feet of elevation and we were still climbing.

The highway bore left, hugged the shoulder of the mountain and, as we rounded the next curve, a vista opened before us. As far as we could see, in every direction, was a picture of devastation. Gone were the bushes, the groves of pine and eucalyptus and oak. For miles into the distance there was only ridge after ridge barren of all life save a thin carpet of grass. Blackened stubs of trees protruded from the mountainsides like rotten teeth. The landscape looked like something that had been blasted by a nuclear bomb.

The road continued to climb the left wall of the canyon until, five or six miles after we had turned onto the highway, we reached a little town, barely more than a wide spot in the road, called Round Mountain. The sign said it had a population of 500 and an elevation of 2000 feet. Just inside the town limits a cross street joined the highway from the right in a "T" intersection. Planted in the shoulder to my left was a metal stake bearing an oval California state route symbol with the numbers "299" in the center. A rectangular black-on-white sheetmetal sign next to it announced:

← **Redding 31**
**Burney** → **20**

I thought about that for a moment and realized that I knew where we were. California Highway 299 runs from Eureka on the Pacific Ocean to the Nevada state line in the extreme north-eastern corner of California near Goose Lake in Modoc County. I had taken a year off between college and business school and worked for Hewlett-Packard. There had been some discussion about building a new LED manufacturing facility near Redding and I had been assigned to gather some of the basic data on the area for my boss's report. So I knew a little about the geography of the region.

When I had bought the map in Porterville I spent a few minutes trying to figure out how to get to Oakdale. If my memory was correct, Oakdale, Oregon was north and east of us, perhaps 250 or so miles away. I pulled into a minimart and bought a Shasta-Cascade area map for two dollars and fifty cents. Yes, the geography was as I remembered it. I turned back onto Highway 299 and headed for Burney.

If only the van would hold together for a few hundred miles more, but when he had gone about ten miles I noticed that we had lost almost a quarter of a tank of gas. Apparently, Jimmie hadn't been such a bad shot after all. In this deserted country I had no option but to keep driving and hope that we would reach Burney before all of the gas leaked out. I glanced to my right where Lisa lay back and passively watched the burned and blasted landscape slip by. Occasionally a clump of trees would appear near the highway, sometimes even a small grove, usually around an isolated house or next to the road and you would think, "Oh, finally, we've reached the end of the fire zone," and then you would top a rise or round a bend and another panorama of destruction would be revealed.

Many of the trees had been so blistered by the flames that their bark had cracked and pulled away, leaving a bone-white stem behind. At first, I thought that these white trees had been painted, banded, to mark them for removal, then I realized that their bark had been torn away by the inferno leaving them to stand naked like the exposed bones of the forest.

We continued to climb and the gas gauge continued to fall. We finally reached the crest of the pass, Hatchet Mountain Summit, about six miles to the west of Burney. At about 4,400 feet a sweeping vista opened before us. Below and to our right a carpet of forest returned while to the left and above us the fire's devastation was still clear.

In the those fourteen miles the gas gauge had fallen from a little over a quarter of a tank to just a hair above empty. I hoped that we would make it the next few miles to town before the tank ran completely dry. The needle seemed to hold a fraction of an inch above the "E" and the last six miles were downhill from the summit into the valley perhaps 1500 feet below.

Perhaps the bullet had penetrated the side of the tank allowing the gas to leak only to the level of the hole, leaving a gallon or so of fuel below the point of entry. As we reached the outskirts of the town I felt as if we were running on fumes.

Located just a few miles north of the Lassen National Forest and almost on the southern edge of the Shasta-Trinity National Forest, Burney is one of those quiet little towns that doesn't change much from decade to decade. The summer months would bring fishermen, campers, and day-hikers. Now, in late February, the town was mostly patronized by people taking a meal or gas break on their trip along Highway 299, the occasional local farmer, and the town's own citizens whose shops catered to these needs.

Like most such places, Burney consisted principally of one main street, called, appropriately, Main Street, which was the name within the city limits of Highway 299 itself. As we entered the town we passed a sign announcing, "Burney, Gateway To The Intermountain Area." A prized trout-fishing stream, Burney Creek, crossed the highway at the edge of the business district just past the point where the road widened from two lanes to three. Wide shoulders bordered the highway and provided parking in front of the stores that lined Main Street.

At the far end of town were a few signs of the outside commercial world: a McDonald's, a Safeway, a Round Table pizza franchise. Several motels provided lodging for weary travelers; I noticed one, The Sleepy Hollow Motel, and sort of liked the name. I saw no K-Marts, no Targets, no Home Depots. I guess the citizens drove the fifty miles or so to Redding if they needed an item that the local shops could not supply.

Highway 299 made a bend to the right, dipped down one final hill, then crossed Burney Creek and bore straight ahead through the heart of town. On the left side were auto parts stores, a garage, and a transmission repair specialist; to the right, a cafe, bakery, a sporting goods store, a drugstore, a cleaners, a thrift shop, a glass company, and a bank—all the sorts of establishments that you would see on any main street in any small town anywhere in America.

"Why are we slowing down?" Lisa asked, an edge of concern clear in her voice.

"We're almost out of gas, Lisa. I think one of the bullets hit the tank and it all leaked out."

"Can you fix it?"

Could I get it fixed?

"I don't know," I told her, but even as I said it, I knew it was impossible.

A mechanic couldn't very well weld a patch on a gas tank; there would still be fumes in it. He would have to replace the whole thing. Even if he had one in stock, it would take a day at least and it would cost more money than I had. And I couldn't just sit around this town with Lisa in tow. No, if that was the only option, I would have to turn her over to the police.

"I don't think it can be fixed, Lisa," I told her a moment later.

"Are you sure? Couldn't you put some tape or something on it. Maybe it wouldn't cost that much."

"I don't think so. And the money's not the only problem. After he looked at the tank the mechanic would be sure to notice the other bullet holes. He would know that someone had been shooting at us. He might call the police. He might even know the man who owns the van. We can't take the chance."

"What are we going to do?" she asked in the tone children use when they are afraid and are trying hard not to cry.

I could call the FBI when Lisa wasn't watching and . . . What was wrong with me? Was I going to sneak around behind the back of a seven- or eight-year-old child? I either looked her in the eyes and told her I was calling the police or I forgot about it.

What was the lesser evil: breaking my word to her, frightening her, causing her to be subjected to the inevitable brainwashing by well-meaning therapists and police officers who would try to make her admit that I had done terrible things to her, or keeping her trust and continuing on this insane odyssey? Which would hurt her less? Wouldn't a day's delay in getting her home be worth helping her escape all that pain?

Maybe I didn't give up and call the police because of that stubborn streak that won't let me ask for directions when I'm lost, that voice that won't let me quit any job that's only half done. Maybe, when I looked into her eyes I just couldn't abandon her. Not like Janet—.

Ahead of us, on the far corner at the end of the block I saw a pay phone. As we approached it, I stared at it, but I could not seem to get my foot off the gas pedal and in a few moments we had driven on by.

Well, one thing at a time. We would get some clothes and eat and get cleaned up and then decide what to do next. Maybe some miracle would save me from having to turn her over to a small-town police department and explain why I had waited so long to call in the authorities. They couldn't think I was one of those people, could they? Sure they could. I probably wouldn't even get bail.

And if that happened, by the time the DA's "therapists" got done with her, Lisa probably would believe that I had molested her. That's how she would think of me for the rest of her life. I couldn't let that happen. Besides, I was sure that I could still fix things, make them right.

Lisa looked at me as if to ask, what do we do now? That was a good question. Could we get the van repaired? Should we try? What about clothes and food? I needed time to think. I had seen a coffee shop a few stores back and ahead on the corner of Plumas and Main was the Ponderosa Thrift Center.

With the gas gauge needle now solidly on the big "E," I turned right and pulled the van into the alley behind the thrift store where it would be out of sight from the road. Lisa looked at me anxiously when I turned off the engine.

"Come on," I said, as I opened the door and stepped to the ground. I walked around to the passenger side, helped Lisa out, and took her hand until we were safely on the sidewalk.

"We have to buy some more clothes," I told her brightly. "You should be pretty good at that by now."

Shopping at the Ponderosa Thrift Center was a bit different from my experience at the Farmland Discount Center near Porterville. No acres of merchandise. No sales assistants. This was purely a "help yourself" environment.

Two women combed the children's section along with us, and two more examined women's clothes on the next aisle over. A fifth lady carefully compared two well-used toasters on a shelf against the front wall while a man in his fifties methodically matched combinations of sport coats and dress shirts in front of a small mirror in the far corner.

It didn't take us long to find what we needed and at prices that were way below those you would find in any K-Mart. A pair of child's jeans was three dollars. Two T-shirts were a dollar and a half each. A nylon zipper jacket with a lining cost four dollars. A couple of pairs of underwear and socks for fifty cents each completed Lisa's requirements.

I found a pair of men's cotton slacks for five dollars and a cotton sport shirt for three. A navy sweatshirt cost two dollars and a black windbreaker was six. Socks, underwear, handkerchiefs, and a belt for five dollars more completed my wardrobe. Lastly, I bought a nylon sports bag for seven dollars to hold our new possessions. A trip to the drugstore for a comb, deodorant, toothpaste, a disposable razor and two toothbrushes would meet our immediate needs.

As we shopped I noticed Hathaway cotton dress shirts on sale for five dollars each and a silk Yves St. Laurent tie for four and I wondered what my vice president, Rick Barnes, would think if I showed up for a meeting wearing thrift shop clothes instead of my normal $90 fitted shirts and $50 ties. But then, how would he know?

By the time we had rung up our purchases and paid the tax we had about $150 left. The items from the drugstore one shop down reduced that balance to just over $140.

Jim and Jenny's Cafe a few stores east up Main Street, was running a special that morning: an all-you-can-eat pancake break-fast for $2.99. I ordered the special for myself and a bowl of corn flakes for Lisa. After the waitress took our order I walked Lisa to the ladies' restroom and gave her clean underwear and socks and a clean T-shirt from the bag.

"Wash good and brush your teeth," I told her, "then change into your clean clothes. Put the dirty clothes into this plastic bag and we'll wash them later if we have to."

Lisa took the bag and her toothbrush without comment and, with a bit of effort, pushed through the ladies' room door. I took the nylon bag into the men's room and used the disposable razor and some soap from the hand dispenser to get a much-needed shave. Next I went into one of the stalls, applied some deodorant and changed into a clean sport shirt and cotton slacks. I shoved my old clothes into one of the plastic bags from the thrift shop and in turn stuffed that into the sports bag. When I was done I felt revived. There was a pay phone just outside the mens' room door and I called Lisa's home and was again rewarded with a string of beeps.

A moment later Lisa emerged from the ladies' room, and I hung up the phone. I put her dirty clothes into the bag and zipped it shut. We returned to our table just as our waitress was delivering the food. She had probably been holding our meals, watching for us. I could tell by her smile that she approved of our new, more respectable appearance.

Although she had not complained of being hungry, Lisa quickly finished her corn flakes. I poured some syrup onto the plate that had been beneath her bowl and gave her two of my pancakes, which she happily chopped into dozens of very tiny pieces and covered with more syrup all before taking her first bite. Why do children do that, I wondered, cut everything up into tiny pieces before eating instead of cutting a few pieces and eating those, then cutting up a few more and eating those? When getting dressed should it be both socks then both shoes or one sock, one shoe, second sock, second shoe? I shook my head slightly as if to clear it of my strange musings and returned my attention to my breakfast.

I'm sure the waitress saw Lisa eating some of my pancakes, which was universally against the "all-you-can-eat" rules, but when I asked for a second helping she brought them without complaint, even going so far as to give Lisa a big smile when she placed the heavy oval platter of steaming 'cakes in the center of our table.

"How about another pancake, Lisa?" I asked when the new pile had been reduced to only two remaining.

"I'm full," she said shaking her head.

"Are you sure? We may not get another meal for awhile. You should eat as much as you can."

"I'm really full."

She had finished her cereal and almost three pancakes. That was a lot, I guessed, for a little girl. We would have about a hundred and thirty-five dollars and change left after I paid for breakfast with a long way to go and no sure way to get there. I speared the last two pancakes and dropped them onto my plate. All those years of exercise and low-fat meals and here I was forcing down pancakes covered with syrup as if there were no tomorrow.

Maybe there isn't any tomorrow, I thought suddenly. That was a concept that was completely foreign to my life. Rules and planning and covering the details were the pillars of my existence. What was it Janet had said? "Peter, when you die you'll have scheduled your funeral two months in advance," or something like that. We were shouting at each other at the time and my memory might not be exact, but that was the essence of her charge. Could she have been right about me? I always thought that she was just trying to hurt me, as of course she was. But she might, I suppose, have been right just the same. But not today.

Sitting there that Saturday morning in Jim and Jenny's Cafe, out in the middle of nowhere, dressed in used clothes, no car, without so much as a business card with my name on it, no clear idea of what I was going to do next or how long this odyssey would take, I began to wonder, maybe for the first time in my life, if tomorrow isn't really just a figment of our imagination, a fictitious environment, like cyberspace or virtual reality.

I began to wonder if, in fact, there is only today, only this present fragment of time, second by second, and everything else is an illusion constructed by our need for order and predictability. Could it be that if I just did the best I could, right now, that tomorrow would take care of itself? Subversive thoughts for a CEO. For the moment I put them out of my mind, finished my coffee, then caught Lisa's eye.

"You all set, sweetie?" I asked. I don't know why I called her that. I had always called her Lisa, but "sweetie" just slipped out, unbidden, unplanned. I never had pet names for people. Janet was always Janet, not "honey," not "sweetheart." If Lisa thought my lapse was strange she gave no sign. She just smiled and nodded.

"We don't know when we'll get the chance again so you better use the bathroom now. Even if you don't have to go. And wash the syrup off your face," I added and patted the top of her head as she slid from her seat and headed for the restroom.

A few minutes later I had paid the check and we were out on the sidewalk. It was about ten o'clock on Saturday morning and I hadn't a clue about what to do next, a predicament that I was unwilling to explain to Lisa. Without further discussion I took her hand and led her down the sidewalk back toward the thrift store. I hadn't searched the van. Maybe there was something useful in it.

Crossing Plumas and running behind the Ponderosa Thrift Center was the small alley where I had parked the van. When we reached it I saw that a large truck bearing the Ponderosa Thrift Center name on the "box" above and behind the cab was now parked in the alley, facing out. As we neared it, I heard a "bang" as if a heavy container had been dropped onto the truck's steel bed, immediately followed by a man's voice shouting "Ow! Damn, damn, damn!"

Curious and a little concerned, I led Lisa down the alley past the right side of the truck. When we reached the loading area in the back I saw a small pudgy man of about fifty, mostly bald, sitting on a large crate and furiously rubbing his shin bone below his right knee.

"Are you all right? Are you hurt?" I called to him.

"Damn, damn, dam—, oh, sorry," he said suddenly when he looked up and noticed Lisa. "I didn't mean to curse in front of the child."

"It's all right. You didn't know we were here. What happened?"

"It's that—that darned Billy Harris! He was supposed to load the truck and ten minutes ago he calls in and tells me he's got to help his Uncle Dave pull stumps. Like H—, like heck! He and his friends are going into Redding for the RV Show and I'm stuck here trying to get this *darned* couch into the truck all by myself. It's as heavy as heck and I'm lucky it didn't break my leg."

The bald man glared at the couch which lay partially on the truck's rear hydraulic ramp then he bent over and began again to massage his leg. I looked from the davenport to the pudgy man and back to the couch. It was clear that if he continued to try to manhandle that thing alone that he would break his neck before lunch.

"Would you like some help?" I asked him.

"Do you mean it?"

"Sure, I'll give you a hand. Between us I think we can get it into your truck."

"That's *darned* nice of you, Mr.—?"

"Howard, Peter Howard."

"Sal Gianinni. I sure appreciate this. I'm going to have a few words with Billy Harris next time I see him, let me tell you."

"No problem, Sal," I said and pointed to the rear service door to the thrift shop. "Lisa, why don't you stand over there, way back out of the way. I don't want this thing hitting you if it slips or something." Obediently, Lisa moved close to the building fifteen or twenty feet back from the rear of the truck. Sal smiled at her then got up and limped over to the couch. I put my bag down on the asphalt near the wall and joined him and for a moment we both studied the couch as if it were an engineering problem equivalent to that of designing a skyscraper or assembling a Saturn rocket. "I'll tell you what, Sal," I said after a moment's additional study. "You get on the platform and just lift your end an inch or two. I'll swing the other end around and we'll slide enough of it onto the lift so that it won't fall off when we raise it."

Without waiting for Sal's agreement, I positioned myself behind the end that still sat on the ground. Sal paused a moment, then got up onto the lift.

"Okay, Sal, pick it up and pull it back as close to the end as you can." Sal grunted and lifted his end three or four inches and together we maneuvered about eighty percent of the couch onto the ramp with the remainder protruding from the passenger rear corner at a thirty-degree angle. I told Sal to change places with me. I stood on the ramp and he was on the ground, then I had him activate the lift. In a few seconds my end of the couch was even with the back of the truck.

"We're almost there. Sal, get under your end and just lift it up a couple of inches while I pull mine back into the truck." After more maneuvering the couch finally ended up inside the cargo bay. Sal lowered the lift, then rode it back up and joined me inside. Together, we used bungie cords to secure the sofa to the driver's side wall.

"That's great, Pete," he said as we rode the lift back down. "I couldn't have done it without you. Say, you got any plans for the day? I've got a few more items and I'm going to need help unloading all of this stuff in Adin."

"Adin? Where's that?"

"I didn't think you were from around here. That's my bag, isn't it?" he asked pointing to the sports bag I had bought that morning.

"Yeah, I just bought it. I'm from the Bay Area. I'm taking Lisa back to her relatives," I said, nodding toward her.

"Adin's about, oh, fifty-five miles east of here. That the way you're goin'?"

"East, on 299?"

"Right, a little more than halfway to Alturas."

There went my excuse for calling the police and taking the easy way out. Sal would take us 55 miles in the right direction in exchange for moving a little furniture. And I couldn't have been happier. Maybe it was a sign, a portent that I was doing the right thing after all. That's what I told myself anyway.

"I'll tell you what, Sal. You take Lisa and me to Adin and buy us lunch, burgers are fine, and you've got a deal. We're heading up to Oregon, by the way, so if you've got any friends in Adin who might be able to help us along, we'd appreciate it."

"I can't promise anything, but I'll do what I can. There's a guy—he's got a farm up toward Alturas. Anyway, he comes in my place up there almost every Saturday. I'll call Bella, she runs the shop for me, and tell her to keep an eye out for him. If he shows up, he'll probably give you a ride up that way, maybe all the way into town. No promises, but I'll do what I can."

"Fair enough, Sal, I appreciate it."

"Great, that's great. Taking the little girl home. I like that. That's a fine thing to do. Listen, I'll go inside and call Bella and you can get started on the other stuff," Sal said happily as he waved at a motley collection of chairs, lamps, a barbecue grill, two end tables and a loveseat all jammed into the Thrift Center's storage room.

"How much of this stuff are we taking?" I called to his departing form.

"All of it," he shouted over his shoulder, "all of it." "What a wonderful negotiator you are," I said to myself.

"Lisa, you may as well sit down in one of those chairs," I told her as I began counting items and trying to calculate the interior dimensions of the available space inside the truck. "It looks like we might be here for awhile."

# FIFTEEN

Oakdale had a total of eight uniformed police officers, five on the day shift, two on the night shift, and one on the graveyard. In addition it had a receptionist, Nancy Stern, a chief, Mark Powell, and one plainclothes investigator, Carlos Ramirez, who had worked detectives out of LAPD's Hollenbeck Division and had come to Oregon to escape murders and rapes and drive-by shooting and kidnappings. It was to Carlos, almost a year before, that the Lisa Taylor kidnapping had been assigned.

He had never worked harder on a case in his entire career and never had so little to show for it. He sent out fliers, still, every week. He called the FBI and the Center for Missing and Exploited Children twice a month. He followed up on every tip, pursued every lead, and was not one bit closer to finding Lisa or her kidnappers that Saturday than he had been on the afternoon of her disappearance almost a year before.

Technically, it was his day off. He was supposed to be home, but at one o'clock that Saturday afternoon he had stopped by the station to check on whether anything further had come in from the Cleveland PD. When he arrived the fax from the CPD was already on his desk. Carlos began to reach for the phone, then stopped.

Bill and Peggy were still in Hawaii. There was no point in leaving a message for them on the last day of their vacation. Especially one telling them that a child's body had been found in Ohio but had been identified as someone else's lost little girl.

Carlos methodically scanned the Taylor file in the vain hope that somehow he might find some scrap of evidence, some overlooked clue that would break the case. It was always that way in an important case, the feeling that hiding somewhere in the mountain of reports and interviews was the key that would unravel the mystery. Again Carlos reviewed what he knew.

It was a strange kidnapping. About four-thirty p.m. last April 27th a dark blue, brown, maroon or black early, mid or late eighties GM sedan, or maybe a full-size Ford, had pulled up in front of Lisa Taylor's house where Lisa and her two friends, Susan and Carla, were playing. Mrs. Fisher next door was taking care of the girls that afternoon. A retired lady who doted on Lisa, she had gone into her house to bake a batch of cookies for the girls. After all, what could happen to them in their own front yard? No one else was outside; most of the neighbors were either at work or running last-minute errands before starting dinner.

A man, a big man according to Susan, had gotten out of the car, run into the yard and, without saying a word, had grabbed Carla. Blocked by the fence, Susan ran around the side of the house toward the backyard and she saw nothing further.

Apparently, from the bits and pieces that Carla was able to remember, as she squirmed and tried to get free, Lisa had attacked him, kicking at his legs. When Carla bit the kidnapper he dropped her. She ran away and the kidnapper grabbed Lisa and sprinted for the car.

Mrs. Fisher had heard the girls screaming and for a second or two thought they were just playing a game, then she became concerned. Perhaps they had seen a snake or something. She hobbled to the front door as fast as her arthritis would allow, all the while the children's screams become more frantic, more hysterical. She opened her door just in time to see the back of the departing sedan, which turned the corner at the end of the block and promptly disappeared. She didn't realize what had happened until she managed to get the girls back into her house and calm them down enough to understand what they were trying to tell her.

She had not seen the license plate, if the car had a plate, if it had a valid plate, which she would not have been able to read in any event as she had been studying the directions on the new brand of cookie mix and was still wearing her reading classes when she struggled to make her way to the front door.

Allen Dykstra might have seen the car heading west, out of town, but he wasn't sure. There was nothing remarkable about it, just a dark-colored, ordinary GM sedan, maybe a Buick, maybe a Pontiac, or an Oldsmobile, or a Ford Crown Vic. They never did find the car. If he had planned the crime, Carlos would have switched cars as soon as he was out of sight. Maybe they did. Maybe they parked the sedan on some back road and drove off in a different car they had stashed there. Perhaps one of them came back that night or the next day and retrieved the original vehicle.

Or, maybe they holed up for a few days in a house or a farm in the area. Hell, maybe they flew her out in a helicopter. Oh, Carlos did all the standard things. He called the County Sheriff and all the surrounding police departments. Within half an hour roadblocks went up on the major highways, but the car was not found.

Fliers were prepared and posted. Gas station attendants within a hundred-mile radius were contacted. Had they seen the car? Yes, they had seen twenty such cars. No, they couldn't remember what the drivers looked like, or yes, white, male adult, aged twenty-five to forty, medium height, medium weight, brown hair, no glasses, beard or mustache. Some of the drivers had used credit cards, but which slips matched which car, no one knew; they hadn't kept license numbers on the credit card gas receipts for years.

The police flooded the area with pictures of Lisa and a description of the car and the kidnapper, such as they were. Over the course of the first two weeks they received several hundred calls, all of which were checked out and all of which were dead ends.

Carlos looked at his desk one last time, sighed and began to stand. He was about halfway out of his chair when the phone rang.

"What've you got, Nancy?"

"Detective, it's someone about the Lisa Taylor case. Wants to talk to the officer in charge. Says her name is Linda Blankenship. On one. Do you want me to take a message?"

Carlos paused for a second. Probably another blind alley. Still . . .

"No, I'll take it.— Detective Ramirez," he answered. "How can I help you?"

"Detective, this is Linda Blankenship at the QuickServe Market in Round Mountain. This may be nothing. I'm probably wasting your time, but, well there was a man in here early this morning. I've been thinking and thinking about this all day and I finally decided to call you, even though it's probably nothing."

"That's okay, Ms. Blankenship, just tell me what happened."

"This man, he didn't look right. He was all beat up, his clothes were a mess. He wasn't even wearing any socks. There was definitely something wrong about him."

"Go on, Mrs. Blankenship," Carlos said politely, though inside he was shouting, "Just tell me!"

"Well, anyway, he bought a map, that's all, just a map. I watched him when he left. I was suspicious. You know, in my business you get a feeling when something isn't right. I get all kinds here."

"I'm sure you do. How, particularly, can I help you, Ms. Blankenship?" Carlos asked with forced politeness.

"Well, when he left I walked over to the window and watched him get into his car, well, a van really. A dark blue Ford van. I don't know the year. I saw two letters on the plate, "RG," but I couldn't read the rest of it. You see the store is higher than the parking spaces, it looks down on them, and I could see into the van. There was a little girl in the front seat and she looked an awful lot like that little girl in the poster you sent me. I swear, she looked just like the picture of that Lisa Taylor."

"Did she seem to be in trouble? Did she signal you or try to get away?"

"Oh no, she looked, you know, normal."

"Was there anyone else in the van?"

"Ummmm, no, I don't think so. No, I could see inside. It had that big windshield and it was parked facing my window. No one else."

"Then she could have gotten out while he was in the store and run away if she wanted to?"

"Yes, I hadn't thought of that."

"So, she wasn't tied up or anything?"

"No, in fact, now that you mention it, when he got in the van, the man reached over and helped her with her seat belt, so I remember that her arms were free. She didn't seem to be afraid of him. That's why I didn't call right away. I thought, 'If he had kidnapped her she would be afraid of him' and, well, I could tell by the way she looked at him that she liked him. But I kept thinking about it and looking at her picture and I'm just sure that was her. So, anyway, that's why I called you."

"Did you see which way they turned when they left? Which direction were they going?"

"East on 299, toward Burney."

They're heading my way, Carlos thought. He paused for a moment, then thanked Ms. Blankenship and got her address and phone number. "It looked like Lisa." How many times had he heard that? This lady was looking through two layers of glass from thirty feet away into a vehicle at a downward angle. Any white, female child with light brown or dark blonde hair might have looked like the picture on the flier. And heading back this way? The chance that it was really Lisa was one in a million. Still . . .

After a second's hesitation, Carlos called the Shasta County California Sheriff's Department and asked them to have their cruisers keep an eye out for a blue Ford van with the partial plate RG. Then, just to be sure, he called the Burney PD as well. Wearily, Carlos stood and headed for the door. Just another dead end, he was sure.

# SIXTEEN

The cab of Sal's truck was a tight fit for the three of us, but I wasn't about to complain. Lisa sat in the center and was barely able to see out the windshield. Still, this didn't seem to dampen her interest in the passing landscape. Shasta and Modoc Counties were among the few parts of California where the phrase "sparsely inhabited" was an understatement.

The Bay Area contains millions of people and when you leave it and head north you think you will end up "in the country." But for a long time you don't. If you follow Interstate 80 north and east to Sacramento you realize that you are never out of sight of human habitation. Everywhere are houses, restaurants, gas stations, the detritus of humanity. Then, when you leave Sacramento, you think, "Okay, now I'll find the wide open spaces!" but for a long while you don't.

Just about all the way up Highway 99 from Sacramento to Chico, over 160 miles north of San Francisco, you are almost never out of sight of some building or other. It's only when you finally pass Chico and continue to head north, approaching Red Bluff and Redding, that you can drive for mile after mile and see only natural features. Here, east of Burney, we were really "in the country."

There was little traffic and almost nothing to see other than trees, and rolling vistas with the occasional sight of farmhouses or plowed fields.

I tried to find things to discuss that might interest Lisa, occasionally asking Sal to identify some of the plants or wildlife that slid past the windows of the truck.

"Look, Lisa, a blue jay!" "Are there many deer around here? Do you think we might see one?" "What kind of tree is that?" I prattled on.

My efforts were a dismal failure. Lisa responded to my bird and wildlife identifications with restrained courtesy but no discernible interest. Sal proved to be fundamentally ignorant of the locale's flora and fauna:

"What's that big tree over there?"

"I dunno, just a tree, maybe an elm,"

"I don't think so. It might be a sycamore. Do you have sycamores up here?"

"I don't know. What do they look like?"

Not that Sal was unfriendly or introverted. It turned out that he was an opera buff and made a vain attempt to convince me of the joys of Don Giovanni and Der Miestersinger, though he confided that German composers, Wagner especially, were not his favorites.

"I don't think it's my cup of tea, Sal," I told him finally. "To me it's just so much screeching. And it's all in a foreign language. Maybe if they sang in English. . . ."

"Impossible! That would destroy the whole effect! When Pagliacci sings, 'La commedia il finito,' my heart wants to break. What would he say in English, 'It's all over now'? It would destroy the emotion of the piece."

"I'll take your word for it, but I think I'll stick with Elton John." Sal snorted disdainfully, finding the comparison not worthy of comment. Luckily, none of the local radio stations specialized in Italian operas and Sal had forgotten to bring his cassette player.

"Do you like music, young lady?" Sal asked Lisa.

"I don't know."

"Do you have any favorite songs you sing in school?"

"No."

"What grade are you in?"

"I don't know."

"You don't know?"

"Lisa's been staying with people who taught her at home," I said hurriedly. "Her folks are going to get her back into class." All things considered, the less we said to strangers about Lisa's situation the better. "She'll finish the third grade this year."

"So, what does that make you, Lisa, about eight?"

Lisa looked at me quickly, as if to ask "Is that right?" I nodded slightly.

"Yes."

"That's a great age. What's your birthday?"

I was about to interrupt with the first date that came to mind but Lisa answered:

"August 10th."

"A Leo! My mother, God rest her soul, was a Leo."

"What's that, a Leo?" Lisa asked. I guessed that Sal might have been a teacher in another life because he launched into a detailed explanation of the concept of astrology (he believed in it) and not only made it understandable, but even succeeded in arousing Lisa's interest. He led her in a spirited dialogue about the character and personality traits of people born under the various signs: Aries were flighty; Virgos imaginative; Leos, such as herself, commanding and decisive.

Lisa listened to it all with an intensity that surprised me. Fifteen minutes fled by. I even joined in, to a limited extent. I'm not a believer in astrology. Wouldn't life be simple if it really worked! Only twelve kinds of people in the world, or maybe twenty-four if you counted the ones born "on the cusp." Still, I was able to add a small footnote to the topic.

"In a sense, our jury system is based on astrology," I said when Sal paused in his lecture.

"What do you mean?"

"Have you ever wondered why there are twelve people on a jury? Ten would be a more common number. We all have ten fingers and ten toes and our arithmetic is based on the number ten. But we have twelve jurors. The reason is that when juries were first established, each was supposed to contain one member born in each of the twelve months to give the jury a balanced cross section of the population. Of course, when the courts got into questioning jurors about their background and opinions and the like, they abandoned requiring that each one be born in a different month."

"I never heard that before," Sal said, impressed. "You a lawyer or something?"

"No, I just remember it from an anthropology course in college," I said after a moment's hesitation. There was a moment of awkward silence then Lisa spoke up.

"Can you tell when a person was born by how they act?" she asked.

"That's a good question, Lisa. Sometimes you can. Now Peter here, he's very careful, organized. I would say he's a Capricorn. That's late December and most of January. Am I right?"

"August 29th."

"A Virgo! That was going to be my second choice. See, Lisa, sometimes you can guess, but of course, it's not perfect."

"So," Lisa began hesitantly, "if someone was really mean, and hit you and did bad things, when were they born?"

Sal paused, startled by Lisa's question, but I understood it instantly. I now knew why she had been so interested in Sal's revelations about the "science" of astrology. She was looking for answers. Ken and Eric and Jimmie were a mystery to her. Why had they captured her? Why did they hurt her? Why did they do bad things? Maybe, she thought, it had been because of something she had done, some weakness or failure within her. But now she wondered if there might be another explanation.

Perhaps they were just born at the wrong time! If you happened to be born in March or October or whenever, then you would be a bad person and do bad things and no one could do anything about it. So as long as she wasn't predestined to be a bad person, so long as August 10th was not within the zone of evil, then she would be all right and the behavior of those people who had brutalized and abused her would make some sort of sense. But, of course, that solace was denied her.

"I'm sorry, Lisa," Sal began slowly, "but there's no particular time that good or bad people are born. Astrological signs just deal with personality traits, like being organized or artistic or easygoing. Anybody, no matter when they are born, can be good or bad. Do you understand?"

Lisa's face looked bleak and she hung her head in the gesture of pain that I had come to recognize well over the last two days.

"I understand," she said softly, her head still down.

"Oh, don't worry." Sal replied with forced good humor. "I can promise you from wide personal experience that Leos almost never go bad! Isn't that right, Peter?"

"As an almost-Leo," I said in a joking tone, "I hope not. Lisa, when do you think Sal was born?" But the magic was gone. Lisa's interest in astrology had instantly vanished with the realization that it would not provide the key to understanding what had happened to her. She just continued to stare at the floor and the silence stretched into minutes, broken only by the growl of the engine and the whistle of the truck's passage through the rising February wind.

A wrack of clouds began to pile in from the west and within a few minutes the sun had been blotted out.

"Looks like we're in for some rain," I volunteered.

"That's what the weather guy said on the news last night. Supposed to be a storm coming in. I hope we get this stuff unloaded before it hits." The atmosphere within the cab had cooled with the weather and there was little in the way of conversation for the rest of the drive. It was close to noon when we pulled in to the Adin branch of the Ponderosa Thrift Center and by then the sky was obscured in a blanket of gray clouds, their bases mottled in shades of charcoal and ebony.

Adin was almost at the eastern end of something called the Big Valley, a flat, treeless, upland plain that stretched from Nubeiber, about seventeen miles to the west to a mile or two east of town. As in Burney, Highway 299 turned into Main Street although this time it did not get any wider.

Adin seemed to consist mostly of a line of neat, well landscaped frame houses, an old-fashioned white wooden church with a steeple, which looked like something from a Hallmark Christmas Card, Nelson's Frosty, a minimart, the obligatory volunteer fire department, and across from Chace's General Merchandise and just on the far side of the bridge over Ash Creek, the Ponderosa

Thrift Center, Adin Branch, though God knows there hadn't been many ponderosa pine between here and Burney, the trees on the slopes at the southern edge of the Big Valley being mostly juniper and scrub sugar pine.

Directly ahead of us and towering over the town was a barren hillside, perhaps three or four-hundred feet high, with the word "Adin" spelled out in white rocks about two-thirds of the way up.

Following the "last in, first out" principle, Sal and I unloaded the small items, the lamps, the end tables and the like first. We had just gotten the couch onto the lift when the first fat raindrops began to splatter the tarmac in front of the storage room.

"Lisa, go inside, get out of the rain," I shouted from the back of the truck. Sal looked up at the sky, frowned and grabbed the end of the sofa with renewed energy. In the distance I heard the crack and rumble of thunder. The wind gusted and brought with it the promise of the storm's full force. Sal hurriedly lowered the ramp but no sooner had it reached the ground when a clap of thunder sounded almost directly overhead and was immediately followed by a driving downpour.

My hair was plastered to my scalp before we had the couch halfway to the storage room. By the time we made it inside our heads and shoulders and the cuffs of our pants and the cushions of the couch were all thoroughly soaked.

"Well," I said, wiping the water from my face with my bare hands, "we almost made it. Will it dry out okay?" I asked, pointing to the sofa.

"Yeah, it'll be fine, I think. I should have Scotchgarded it. Hell, sorry, heck, it's too late now." Sal stared at the sodden couch, shook his head, then looked back at Lisa and me. "Come on, let's get dry," he said a moment later after a final appraisal of the sofa. We entered the shop through a door in the far end of the stock room and Sal introduced us to Bella, a cheerful, heavyset black lady of about the same age as Sal.

Bella bustled around and got us towels, then efficiently brought Sal up to date on the week's business. The customer Sal had mentioned, a man named Larkin McCray, had not yet appeared, and she had no idea if he would be by at all. Still, they had some rope, garden tools, and a spare tire of the same size that McCray had on previous occasions purchased all in stock, all items in which McCray had, at one time or another, expressed an interest. Bella carefully checked Lisa's clothing to make sure that she had not also been caught in the storm.

"Where's a good place for lunch?" I asked Sal when we had more or less finished drying ourselves off.

"The Wagon Wheel, across the street and a block to the left is good. Look, Peter, I've got some things I have to do before lunch. Here, let me give you ten dollars to cover the meal I promised you. You all have a good lunch, then come on back and and we'll check on McCray. If he shows up in the meantime, I'll know where to find you." Sal opened the cash register and pulled out two fives that he held out to me.

"Thanks, Sal," I said, taking the bills. "We appreciate it. Are you hungry, Lisa?" Lisa's depression had lifted and she was back to her old self, if not exactly happy, at least not visibly upset.

"Yes, I guess so," she said without enthusiasm.

"Okay, then, let's get something to eat. See you in an hour or so, Sal."

Before we reached the door, Bella stopped us and handed me an umbrella from a bin next to the cash register.

"You go out there in that storm, you'll catch your death," she warned. "You take this and keep that little girl dry. You can bring it back when you're done."

I studied her pleasant features and nodded my thanks. Lisa was quite taken with Bella, I could tell. I happened to glance at Sal and noticed the way that he watched Bella when she wasn't looking. I sensed that their relationship was more than merely employer and employee and was pleased that he had found such a warm-hearted companion.

Lisa and I huddled under the umbrella and made our way against the wind-driven rain a couple of hundred feet up the street to the Wagon Wheel Restaurant. More than half the tables were already filled with farmers, diesel rig drivers, a couple of gas station mechanics, and two town women taking refuge from the storm. In well-worn jeans and cheap windbreakers, no one gave us a second glance. I picked out a booth in the corner, isolated from the other diners by a couple of empty tables and a cigarette machine.

After we ordered I walked back to the pay phone near the entrance to the restrooms and had the operator ring the number for Willard Taylor in Oakdale, Oregon, billing the call to my office number. Again, the malfunctioning machine answered the call and I hung up.

We had a quiet lunch with a minimum of conversation. I was still uneasy about pressing Lisa for details of her captivity. I didn't know if getting her to talk would be doing her good or cause her harm, but I felt that I had to do something to try to relieve her pain. When we had finished our lunch and the waitress had removed the dirty plates, I leaned forward and caught Lisa's eye.

"I understand why you were asking Sal those questions about astrology," I told her quietly. She looked at me, her face almost empty of expression, holding only a hint of what?—fear? concern? hope against hope? I'm not sure, but I saw some faint emotion peeking from the corners of her eyes, in the set of her lips.

"You want to understand why Eric took you, why Ken hurt you the way he did, don't you?" I said. Her fear became more visible now. She was, after all, only a little girl who had not yet learned an adult's tricks of deception.

"Are you afraid, Lisa, that somehow everything that happened to you is your fault?" Her lips quivered slightly but she did not cry, would rather die, I think, than cry out loud. After a moment's pause she nodded her head slightly and continued to stare at me as if I were the only person in the world, as if I alone held her salvation in my two hands. "Lisa, I'm not sure how to explain this so that you can understand it, but I'll try. It's not your fault. You didn't do anything wrong. It just happened. Lots of times things just happen that are no one's fault. There's an expression: 'It's fate.' That means that it's just the way it is. Does that make any sense to you?"

"But why did they pick my house? Why did they pick me?"

"They picked you because you were there. If you weren't in your yard with your friends, they would have picked someone else. And that person would have asked, 'Why did they pick me?' It had to be someone. It just turned out to be you. It was bad luck, that's all."

"But why did they do it? Why did Ken do the things to me? Why did he hurt me? He said I was bad. He said that I had to learn the ways of the Lord."

How was I supposed to explain a pedophile/religious fanatic to an eight-year-old child, or to anyone for that matter? I decided to try a different tack.

"Lisa, people always want to blame someone else for what they do. The more bad things that people do, the more they want to blame them on somebody else. Ken wanted to do bad things to you, but he didn't want to admit they were bad, that he was bad, so he said God told him to do it."

"Why would anyone want to do those things? Why did those men give me to Ken if they knew what he wanted to do to me?"

"Lisa, a long time ago I read a story where the author asked the same question you just did, why do people do bad things? He didn't know the answer, so he made up one. That's what his story was about, his answer. It wasn't true, you understand; it was just a made-up story, but it's a way, sometimes, to make it easier to think about people like Ken. Let me tell you his story.

"Do you know what a professor is? No? Well, he's a teacher. A professor teaches in a college. In this story, there was a professor of geology, that's the study of rocks and minerals. He would often go down into mines and caves and look for mineral deposits."

"What was his name, the professor?"

What was his name? I uttered the first name that came to mind that sounded sort of collegiate.

"Gregory, his name was Gregory." The character now properly identified, Lisa smiled and again gave me her full attention.

"One day Gregory was exploring a new cave, one that he had never entered before. He went deep into the cave and way at the back of one of the last caverns, at what looked like a solid stone wall, he discovered a loose rock. When Gregory pushed the rock it rolled right out of the way and behind it he found a small tunnel. Gregory got down onto his hands and knees and began to crawl through the tunnel. He crawled and crawled and finally he came to a huge room. All around the room were boulders and strange crystals.

"Gregory was particularly interested in one of the crystals, something that he had never seen before. It was light pink and in the shape of a rod about three inches across. When he tried to get a sample of it Gregory found that it was very hard and he finally had to hit the bottom of the crystal rod several times with his hammer in order to break off a piece.

"The professor took the crystal back to the university and tested it in his laboratory. He discovered that although it was very light, the crystal was harder than glass. He thought that it might be a good material to make eyeglasses from, so as an experiment, the professor cut two pieces from the crystal, polished them, and fitted them into a pair of eyeglass frames.

"Gregory put on the glasses and then looked around his laboratory. The glasses were comfortable and he could see through them just fine although everything looked a little pink. It was night now and he decided to wear them for a while and see how he liked them.

"Gregory left the building and walked to a small restaurant at the edge of the campus. From out of the darkness a student approached him on the sidewalk. They exchanged a brief hello and when they passed each other Gregory thought that he saw a shimmering in the air around the student's head, but he decided that it was just a shadow caused by the streetlight.

"The professor reached the restaurant and he went inside. That's when he saw them: around everyone's head was the same sort of shimmering shape that he had seen a few minutes earlier. As Gregory watched them, these shapes changed. Sometimes they would pull back and form a face that whispered into their person's ear. Other times they would constrict into a tight band around someone's head and the band would sparkle with bright red sparks and bolts."

"Like lightning bolts?" Lisa asked, enthralled.

"More like a piece of melted plastic with lights glowing inside it. Anyway, the professor looked into the mirror behind the counter but could see nothing around his own head. He began to wonder if he was going crazy. He blinked his eyes several times but each time he opened them the shapes were still there. For the rest of the evening he sat quietly at a table in the corner of the restaurant and watched the customers and the things around their heads. They all had one of these shapes, except him, and they were all different."

"What were they doing?"

"That's what Gregory wanted to find out so he studied them, but no one could see them except him. One of the men in the restaurant asked Gregory what he was staring at. Gregory pretended that he just wasn't feeling well and he turned away."

"But he could still see them?"

"Yes, he could still see them. Finally, he realized that the glasses might have something to do with his new ability and he took them off. The shapes around people's heads disappeared. Gregory put the glasses back on and the shapes reappeared. He found it fascinating. Carefully he began to study the other customers every chance he got. And he started to notice things.

"One of the men, a construction worker, was loud, shouting at the other men at the table with him. He seemed to be trying to provoke a fight. Gregory noticed that the workman's shape often formed a face that screamed into the man's ear, then it shot bolts of electricity into his head. Every time the man seemed to calm down and begin to relax or to laugh, the face would re-form and again start screaming into the man's ear, trying to get him excited and angry.

"Later that night the chaplain from the college came in. His shape was just the opposite of the ditchdigger's. When someone bumped the minister's elbow and he started to get angry, his shape assumed a placid face and whispered soothing words into the minister's ear.

"At the counter, two of the men were playing a game with a pair of dice to decide who would pay the bill for their dinner. Gregory noticed that one of the men was cheating, switching the dice when he saw that he was going to lose, but each time, just before he cheated, the professor saw that the gambler's shape whispered secretively into his ear, suggesting how he could cheat the other man when he wasn't looking.

"After a while Gregory realized that whatever one of the men did was often caused by these shapes whispering into their ears, goading them, upsetting them, urging them on in ways that none of them even realized, that it was hard for the men to resist doing what these shapes told them to do because they didn't know the things were even there. Gregory found that he couldn't be angry with the laborer or the gambler because he knew that all the mischief they did was really caused by these shapes and that the ditchdigger and the gambler and the rest of them were victims as much as anyone else.

"Lisa, the point of the story is not that we really have these 'ghosts' around our heads. We don't. What the man who wrote the story meant was that each of us has a conscience, an inner voice that tells us right from wrong, good from bad, and in some people this voice is dead or asleep, or sometimes it is evil or crazy.

"Eric and Jimmie don't have an inner voice anymore. They lost it and they don't feel anything for anyone. All they care about is themselves. Ken's voice is crazy. It's like he's got a ghost wrapped around his head, all the time telling him to do crazy things. There's no understanding why he's that way. It's just the way he turned out."

"What about me?"

"What about you?"

"Do I have a little voice?"

"Do you think you know right from wrong?"

"Yes."

"Do you want to hurt people?"

"No—except for Ken and that man, Jimmie. I hope they die. I hope they both die. Does that mean something's wrong with me?"

"No, Lisa. If there were something wrong with you, you wouldn't care if something was right or wrong as long as you got your own way. I know how you feel about those men, but if you got the chance to hurt them, hurt them really badly, you wouldn't do it. You're a good person, Lisa, and I know that you wouldn't do that. So, stop worrying about Ken and Jimmie. They're long gone and they won't find us now. And nothing that has happened is your fault."

"You're sure?" Lisa asked uncertainly.

"I'm sure. Come on. Let's see if Mr. McCray will give us a ride to Alturas."

Lisa paused a moment, trying to comprehend what I had told her, then appearing to come to some decision, she picked up her jacket and slid from the booth. Outside the storm had trailed off and we splashed through the puddles back to Sal and Bella's front door, oblivious to any imminent danger more serious than another sudden burst of rain.

Jimmie was long gone, I had assured myself, probably already three states away. So, we wandered back to the Ponderosa Thrift Center and the hoped-for ride north to Alturas and on to Lisa's home. But instead of heading away from trouble, we were heading right into it.

# SEVENTEEN

Larkin McCray was a bear of a man, barrel-chested, with a great, wild, gray-and-black beard that almost reached the top of his overalls. Lisa and I had just about given up hope of his appearing on that rainy Saturday afternoon when he bustled into the Ponderosa Thrift Center.

"Bella!" he called as soon as he strode through the doorway, "I've come to take you away from all of this."

"Not today, Larkin. Maybe next week."

"That's what you always say. But, I suppose if I can't have you, I'll have to settle for a truckload of shovels."

"You sure know how to flatter a lady."

"That I do. What have you got for me?"

Bella and Larkin recited these lines with the easy familiarity of old friends rehearsing a favorite play. Lisa and I had settled down near the front door next to the shelf of fifty-cent paperback books, and with a glance in our direction, Bella led McCray into the stock room where Sal had assembled the week's load of tools and equipment.

"Is that the man we've been waiting for, Peter?" Lisa asked when the two had disappeared through the rear door. I could tell that she was a bit frightened of McCray. His straggly beard and booming voice were a little overwhelming for an eight year old.

"She called him 'Larkin' so I think it is. He seems like a friendly man. Maybe he'll help us." Lisa didn't respond to my optimistic evaluation. "Don't you like him?"

"He's kind of scary," she said and moved closer to me and took my hand.

"Yes, he's a big man. And that beard makes him look sort of wild, doesn't it?"

"Uh-huh," Lisa mumbled and nodded her head.

"Most of the time what people look like doesn't mean much. Usually you can't tell what they're like that way. Bella seems to like him, doesn't she?"

Lisa paused a moment then said, "I guess."

"I have the feeling that she wouldn't like someone who would do us any harm. I'll tell you what: let's play a game."

"What kind of a game?"

"Let's pretend that Mr. McCray is just dressed up like that because he's an actor in a play. What if he wasn't that big after all? What if he was wearing a special suit with lots of padding that made him look real big? And let's suppose that he really doesn't have that beard, that it's just a play beard like the ones actors wear in the movies. Let's pretend that before he got all dressed up that way, that he looked just like me. You wouldn't be afraid of him then, would you?"

"No," Lisa answered a little uncertainly. "I guess not."

"Okay, then, let's pretend that what he's like inside is different from what he looks like outside and let's try to guess what he's really like without that costume and without that fake beard. Okay? Now, ignoring what he looks like, what can you guess about him?"

"I don't know. He talks real loud."

"Good. Sometimes people who talk really loudly like that do it because they want to be noticed. It would be hard to miss Mr. McCray when he came into a room, wouldn't it?"

Lisa nodded her agreement. "Sometimes people who want to be noticed are kind of show-offs, but they do it because they like people and they want everyone to come over and talk to them. That's okay, isn't it? What else can we guess about him?"

"He likes Bella."

"Yes. I think Bella is a nice lady. So if he likes her, and she likes him, maybe he's a nice man. What else?"

"I don't know."

"Does he seem happy or sad?"

Lisa thought about that for a moment before answering. "He looks kind of happy, the way he smiled and talked to Bella."

"Let me tell you something, Lisa. Lots of people who aren't very nice are unhappy. A lot of them seem, to me at least, to be angry most of the time. Sometimes that's why they're so mean. I bet Ken wasn't very happy, was he?" Lisa nodded her head in agreement.

"There's a song I like. Let me tell you one of the lines. " 'You've got to wake up every morning with a smile on your face and show the world all the love in your heart.' I think that Mr. McCray may wake up with a smile on his face. What do you think?"

"I don't know. Maybe."

"Are you still afraid of him?"

"A little, but I guess it would be okay if he gives us a ride."

"That's my girl," I said and hugged her, then caught myself. She wasn't my girl. She was just someone in trouble whom I was helping. She wasn't, couldn't be, part of my life. She was someone else's little girl. An instant later we heard McCray's booming voice approaching from the stock room door.

"So, does Sal know what a lucky man he is?" he asked Bella, laughing.

"That's what I keep telling him."

"He probably can't hear you over that god-awful howling he listens to. Some time when he's not looking, you slip a little Grateful Dead into that machine of his."

"He'd have a heart attack!"

"Pitiful when a man doesn't appreciate good music. This them?" McCray asked suddenly pointing at us. I took Lisa's hand and we walked to the rear of the store.

"Mr. McCray," I said, holding out my hand, "I'm Peter Howard and this is Lisa."

"Hello, Lisa," McCray said formally, bowing at the waist to shake her hand. "How are you today?"

"I'm fine. Are you going to give us a ride?"

"I don't know. Where do you want to go?"

"We're going home."

"Where's that?"

"Oakdale."

"That's Oakdale, Oregon," I added.

"Yeah, I know. Been up that way once, a long time ago. I've been most everywhere in this part of the country, one time or another. You planning on hitching the whole way?" Larkin asked, fixing me with a hard stare.

"Truthfully, I don't know. I lost my car and wallet a while back. Now we're just taking it one step at a time. Sal told me that you have a farm near Alturas. Could you give us a ride that far?"

McCray's expression retained its flinty edge. It was pretty obvious to him that Lisa and I were in some kind of trouble, and the easiest thing for him to do would be to say "no" and not get involved.

"Lisa, would you do me a favor?" Larkin asked politely. "Would you go and use the little girl's room now. Bella, why don't you show her where it is." Though stated as a request, McCray's suggestion was more of an order. As soon as Lisa was out of earshot, he turned to me.

"You're in some kind of trouble, aren't you?"

"Mr. McCray, it's kind of hard to explain. I'm just—"

"If you're running from the law, I don't want to know about it. I've been there myself, when I was younger and crazier than I am today. The worst thing I did was to get my friends mixed up in it, hiding me out."

"The police aren't looking for me. At least I don't think they are."

"Putting it that way doesn't make me real comfortable—you don't 'think' they are. She your daughter?"

"No."

"Niece, relative of some kind?"

"No, I'm just helping her to get home."

"That doesn't sound good to me. What are you doing out on the road with that little girl?"

Up until that point I had avoided explaining much of anything to anyone, but I had the distinct impression that Larkin McCray would not be an easy man to shine on. One look at his eyes and I knew he wasn't going to be satisfied with a few innocuous answers. I took a deep breath.

"The truth is that I found her in a bad way down in the Bay Area and I promised I would take her home. We've had some problems but I'm going to get her there."

"This doesn't make any sense. What do you do for a living?"

"I run a high-tech company in Santa Clara."

"If that's true then you're the craziest executive I ever met, and at one time or another I've met a lot of them. Hell, I used to *be* an executive, but that's another story. You know better than this. Why didn't you just call the FBI? They'd have her home in nothing flat."

"It started out as a three-hour drive. Then it got out of control, and now it's too late for that. I can't call them now. They'd think, well, it isn't true, but they'd never believe me. Look, we're almost there. It isn't a good alternative, but it's the best one I've got. If I had it to do over—but I don't. I don't have a time machine. I've just got to finish what I started."

"Look, Howard, if you're fooling around with that kid I swear. . . ." The door to the ladies' room banged open and Lisa and Bella emerged from the hallway at the right rear corner of the store. Lisa ran over to me and took my hand. "You all set, Lisa? Do you need something to drink or eat before we go?" She shook her head.

McCray was watching me intently and he didn't miss the way Lisa clutched my hand. Lisa started walking toward the door. McCray followed uncertainly behind. He had not yet made up his mind about what he was going to do. I suspected that he was half a step from turning around, picking up the phone and calling the police.

When we reached the front door Lisa noticed that McCray was hanging back. She turned around and stared up at his massive chest, his bulging arms, his tangled black-and-gray beard, and again became afraid of him. She paused for a moment then, anxiously staring up into McCray's face, said: "Can I ask you a question?"

"Sure, anything you like."

"Do you wake up every morning with a smile on your face?"

"What?"

"Peter told me. It's from a song he knows. He taught me some of the words: 'You've got to wake up every morning with a smile on your face and show the world all the love in your heart.' I was just wondering if you did that."

I had the feeling that McCray was not surprised by much, but that Lisa had stopped him cold. He looked from her to me, then back to her, then squatted down to get as close to level with her face as he could.

"Lisa, it took me forty years to figure that out. You're lucky you've learned it so soon. Yes, most days I do. Any more questions?"

"Can we go now?"

"Yeah, I guess we can," he said after a second's pause. "We should get out of here before the rain starts up again." McCray walked on ahead and opened the back door to the loading area. After I passed through he gave me a fleeting confused glance then led the way to his pickup truck now loaded with farm equipment. We got inside. He started the engine and pulled out into the gray afternoon light.

# EIGHTEEN

Carlos Ramirez and his wife, Jennifer, were in their backyard planning this year's garden when the phone rang. Carlos paused with the hammer in midair above the stake which marked where the row of beans would start, then completed the swing when his wife volunteered to take the call.

"Carlos," she shouted a minute later, "It's for you. It's the station."

"Coming—," he called wearily as he rose and wiped his hands on his jeans.

"Detective, you've got a call from the Burney PD. They found that van you were looking for."

"Van—? Oh, yeah. Do you have their number?"

"He's on hold. A Lieutenant Jamison. I'll transfer him." After two or three clicks, a new voice came on the line.

"Detective Ramirez? This is Lieutenant Bob Jamison of the Burney PD."

"Hi Lieutenant, what's up?"

"We found that van of yours abandoned a block off Main Street."

"Abandoned?"

"We're pretty sure. It's not going anywhere with a bullet hole through the gas tank."

"What?"

"Actually, there are four bullet holes in it. And some blood near the driver's seat, but not much. More like the driver was scratched or cut. Not enough to have been shot. Do you mind my asking why you were looking for this vehicle?" When Jamison mentioned the bullet holes, a shiver had gone up Carlos's spine. Could this really have something to do with Lisa Taylor?

"Lieutenant—"

"Bob."

"Bob, I had a report this morning that a kidnap victim, Lisa Taylor, might have been spotted in that van. I was just following up on it. Could you have your men check around and see if anyone saw a little girl, possibly with a WMA, shabbily dressed, shoes but no socks, sometime this morning. You've got a flier on her with a description and a color picture. If your men could show it around as soon as possible I'd really appreciate it."

"Sure. How old is she?"

"She'll be eight this summer."

"I'll do it myself, right now."

"Take my home number. I'll be waiting for your call." Carlos hung up and nervously returned to the backyard. "Do we have enough stuff in the house for dinner?" he asked his wife.

"I thought we were going out."

"I can't. I have to stay home. I'm expecting a call." Jennifer was about to say something, to ask what had happened, but she saw that Carlos had that faraway look he got when he was thinking about an important case, and she swallowed her question. Since they had left Los Angeles there was only one case Carlos took that seriously. And it was the one she feared would break his heart when it was finally over, when it ended the way they all knew it had to. Silently, she turned back to helping him stake the other end of the row of beans.

# NINETEEN

Jimmie drove through Burney about fifteen minutes before Sal's truck departed. If the van hadn't died he probably would have caught it somewhere on the highway between Burney and Alturas, but he didn't see it parked there in the alley behind the thrift store.

Jimmie figured that Howard would just keep on driving it all the way to Oregon. Jimmie knew, of course, where Lisa's parents lived. And he was sure that Howard was still trying to take her home.

But he missed them, went right on by. But figuring that they couldn't make it all the way to Oakdale on the gas in the tank, he decided to stop at every gas station between Burney and Alturas. By the third station he had his story down pat.

"Hi partner," he would begin. "I'm hoping you can help me out. I'm looking for my granddaughter. Here's her picture," he would say politely, showing them a picture of Lisa that he had cut from a missing child flier he stole from a supermarket bulletin board. "Have you seen her?"

Usually the attendant would stare at the photo for a few seconds then hand it back with a shake of his head.

"My no-good ex-son-in-law's run off with her. My daughter left him and to get back at her, he took the kid."

"That's terrible," the attendant would say and shake his head. "They ought to lock him up."

"Hell, you know how the cops are. They can't be bothered with a domestic problem. I told her not to marry him, but she wouldn't listen to me. Now my granddaughter's gone. Listen, I know that you're a busy man, you've got a business to run, but I sure would appreciate it if you would keep an eye out for her. Here's twenty dollars for your trouble and my phone number. I'll be out driving the highway, looking for them, so just leave a message on my machine. I'll call in and check it every hour. If you help me find them, there's another fifty dollars in it for you. Last I knew he had a blue Ford van but he might have gotten rid of it by now. I sure would appreciate it if you would keep an eye out for them."

"No problem," the attendant would answer, fingering the twenty and thinking about earning fifty more. "Glad to help."

"Oh, one more thing. Whatever you do, don't let on that you've seen me. If he gets wind that I'm on his trail, God knows what he'll do to the little girl. Just let him go on his way. Don't say anything. Remember, he's her father. If the cops get involved they'll just give her to him and then my daughter and I'll never see her again. So, don't let on that you know anything. Okay?"

"Sure, I'll leave it to you."

"That's the ticket! Thanks, partner. You keep a good lookout now."

And with that, Jimmie would speed off to the next gas station ten or fifteen miles down the road. By the end of the day he had established a network of informants. Jimmie was sure that Howard was unaware that he was being pursued. "He probably figures I'm long gone," Jimmie decided, smiling.

# TWENTY

We headed east from Adin just ahead of the rain. The highway soon entered a wide canyon at the edge of the Big Valley. Scrub pine ranging from the size of small Christmas trees to specimens 15 or 20 feet high dotted the mid to upper slopes of the canyon's walls. Rush Creek paced the highway and crossed often from one side to the other. Small farms appeared here and there where the canyon widened enough to support a few head of cattle or a small orchard, though the land appeared rocky and was covered with tufts of mixed olive green and grayish-white scrub grass.

Ten or twelve miles east of Adin the hills closed in and the road began to rise once more. The Big Valley was actually a high prairie about 3,800 feet above sea level and now we were going higher still. When we left the canyon the trees thickened.

Other than comments directed mostly to himself about the state of the road and our impending bout with the storm, McCray didn't say much. The highway was a rain-slicked two-lane that climbed up the west side of the Adin Pass through virgin country crowded with pine and spruce.

The storm held off until we had almost reached the crest then it announced its return with a crack of thunder and a bolt of lightning near the 5,200-foot summit. A few moments later we were engulfed in a downpour that slowed McCray's pace to about 15 miles an hour. We crept over the pass then crossed the Pit River which paralleled the road almost all the way to Alturas. On both sides of the highway mature ponderosa pines towered 75 to 100 feet high. For about six miles we traveled through this forest then we broke out of the trees and descended to the next valley, still about 4,000 feet above sea level. Like the Big Valley behind us, this one was a flat, treeless, high prairie given over mostly to cattle grazing and the cultivation of oats and hay.

On a sunny spring day it would have been a beautiful drive but on that cold and gloomy February afternoon Lisa and I couldn't wait for it to be over. It was after three when we left Adin and it was almost four when we neared the little village of Canby only about 20 or 25 miles to the east.

As we approached the town the rain diminished then sputtered out, leaving a leaden sky which masked a rapidly fading gray afternoon light. As in Sal's truck, Lisa rode in the center between us, though there was even less room for her in Larkin's pickup. We had almost reached the sign announcing the Canby city limit when a raccoon sprang from a clump of bushes on our left and darted across the highway directly in front of the truck. Lisa saw the animal when it was about to disappear under the pickup's wheels and let out a fearsome scream.

More startled by the scream than by the raccoon McCray jerked the wheel hard to the right and slammed on the brakes. For a moment the truck responded then it began a slow speed slide toward the edge of the road. We had almost come to a stop when the passenger side front wheel slipped off the edge of the asphalt and smacked into a half-rotted tree stump almost hidden in the tall grass. There was a momentary resistance, then a snapping release, then silence. Ahead of us the raccoon paused, turned to peer at us, then bounded off into the fields to the right of the highway.

Considering that Lisa's scream was probably the cause of the accident, this was not the time for me to say anything. Silently, McCray and I got out of the truck and took a look at the right front tire. The wheel had been turned hard to the right when it encountered the stump. Now it was bent in at an impossible angle. Mc-

Cray just paced back and forth in front of it as if a more thorough examination might solve the problem. Finally, he shook his head, looked up at the sky, and said in a tight voice, "We'd better get inside."

"Tie rod?" I asked as I opened the passenger door and motioned for Lisa to join us.

"Probably," McCray said flatly, then turned and headed across the road. A few houses, two service stations, a general store, a couple of restaurants, and a hotel comprised the bulk of the town of Canby a hundred yards or so ahead of us. McCray led the way past the Canby Hotel to a gas station that resembled one of those ancient waystations you see in old movies—two narrow old-fashioned pumps on an island outside of a little restaurant with a sheetmetal Coke emblem on the front wall and a glowing Miller's logo over the door. A lighted white plastic sign with black letters identified it as "Lou's Cafe." Pale yellow light seeped through the front windows. A five-year-old Oldsmobile and two well-used pickups were parked in the small asphalt lot to the left of the building. No attendant was in evidence. In front of the building two men in jeans and nylon windbreakers were arguing in half-restrained tones. As we approached I heard a few words:

". . . I've got commitments. You can't just . . ."

"I don't care. I've changed my mind and . . ."

"You can't change your mind. You . . ."

"No, I said, I'm not . . ."

As soon as we drew near, the men noticed us and immediately stopped talking, then the shorter one glanced back at his opponent one last time, said harshly "I'm outta here," and hurried off to one of the pickup trucks in Lou's lot. Angry and upset, the second man stormed after him. We went on inside.

"Why don't you two take a little break for a minute. Old Lou likes to play the cantankerous local character, but he makes a good cup of coffee," McCray said as he headed for the pay phone in the corner. His anger seemed to have dissipated a bit and his tone now was almost normal.

A counter ran the length of the back wall and a line of booths lined the front of the room on both sides of the door. A couple of the tables were occupied and one customer sat at the counter and nursed a cup of coffee. A thin, ancient stick of a man leaned against the wall behind the counter. About five feet four inches tall with thin wisps of white hair pasted across the top of his head, he could have been anywhere from seventy to a hundred and five. He looked like he barely weighed a hundred pounds. Apparently, this was Lou. I led Lisa up to the counter and helped her onto one of the stools.

"How about a glass of milk?" I asked, looking down at her. Though she was wearing her jacket I noticed her shiver in the damp afternoon chill. "Maybe hot chocolate would be better. Do you have any hot chocolate?" I asked, turning my attention to Lou.

"Sure I've got hot chocolate! I got the best hot chocolate in town."

"You've got the only hot chocolate in town!" the man at the end of the counter broke in. It was an old joke but one that still amused Lou, who smiled widely, then finished the exchange.

"Yeah, but mine's still the best," he said and then limped over to the refrigerator to get a carton of milk. Behind me the door rattled open and a gust of damp air blew on our backs. I turned in my seat and saw the second man who had been involved in the argument, the taller of the two, enter the cafe and then swing the door closed behind him.

"Hey, Lou, how about a couple of burgers and a coke to go," he called to the counterman's back as he slid onto the stool next to me. He toyed with a spoon for a moment then turned toward me.

"Where're all from?" he asked and forced a thin smile.

"Down south, just passing through," I answered noncommittally.

"Hell of a day for it."

"You get a ride when you can."

"You're hitching then?"

"Sort of. I moved some furniture in exchange for the ride up from Burney."

"Where you headed?"

"North, Oregon, at least we were. We've had a little car trouble."

"Oh yeah? What happened?"

"We swerved to miss a raccoon. I think we lost a tie rod."

"What kind of car?"

"His truck," I said, nodding toward McCray who was still on the phone in the corner.

"Well, maybe I can help you out. I've had a little bad luck myself." At this point Lou returned with Lisa's hot chocolate and I reached into my pocket for a dollar which I put on the counter. The man paused a moment and when I didn't say anything he started to speak again.

"I guess you saw me arguing with Cliff out there," he said a bit apologetically. "He was supposed to help me out, deliver a load of hay for me. He's left me high and dry so it looks like I'll have to go myself. I wouldn't mind a little company if you don't mind the three of us sharing the truck's cab." I paused a second longer and I took at a careful look at him. "Oh, sorry," he said, holding out his hand, "Name's Ed Doherty."

"Peter Howard," I said, taking his hand. "Where're you going?"

"Up west of Lakeview on 140 toward Klamath Falls. I could drop you off in Lakeview if you like."

I made a quick mental calculation: Lakeview was a few miles north of the Oregon border on U.S. 395. That would get us about two-thirds of the way there, about 35, 40 miles south and east of Oakdale.

"When are you leaving?"

"Right away, I guess. I only came in to get some dinner to take with me. I figured I'd just drive it straight on through and eat in the truck now that Cliff's flaked out on me."

"You're leaving now, in the storm?"

"As soon as Lou brings me the burgers. I'm gonna hit the men's room. You let me know if you want the ride."

Eddie had barely slid off the stool and headed for the bathroom when Larkin stomped over and took Eddie's place at the counter.

"Hey, Lou, how about a cup of coffee, hot."

"My coffee's always hot," Lou called over his shoulder as he flipped Eddie's burgers. "When have I ever served you cold coffee?"

"Never, but I wouldn't want this to be the first time." Did these people script their whole lives, merely replaying the same lines over and over again? Then I thought about the conversations in my office: "What's new?" "Did you see the 49'er game?" "How are you?" Always the same questions, the same answers. And please, please, don't tell me how you really are. The only acceptable answer is "Fine", because I don't really want to know.

Lou put down a heavy white cup to which Larkin added two sugars and a healthy slug of half-and-half.

"Can they fix your truck?" I asked him.

"Can they fix it? Sure. When can they fix it—that's another matter."

"How long?"

"Dave figures he can get over here in his tow truck in an hour or so. Then he has to haul me back to the shop, then find the parts, then do the work. If I'm lucky and I pay extra I might get out of here by noon tomorrow." McCray paused a moment, exhaled, and ran his big right hand through his hair. "There's a hotel a couple of doors down. Clean, not too fancy. I can call you there when she's fixed."

"Thanks, but we may have another option."

"What?"

"Well, . . ." I began, but was interrupted when Eddie emerged from the men's room and walked over to me.

"So?" Eddie asked.

"So what, Eddie?" Larkin said.

"He a friend of yours?" Eddie asked him, pointing at me.

"I was giving him a ride to Alturas. What's it to you?"

"He says he's going to Oregon. Told him he could ride with me if he wants. I've got a load of hay to deliver."

"He's allergic to hay," Larkin replied sharply.

Clearly, there was no love lost between the two men, and I didn't want to get caught between them.

"Larkin, I appreciate your concern, but this gentleman says he can take us all the way to Lakeview tonight. It beats being stuck here. With any luck, I can have Lisa home by lunch tomorrow."

"There're worse things than spending the night in Canby."

"I don't understand. What's the problem?"

"Yeah, McCray, what's the problem?"

"You and I both know you're up to something, Eddie. Leave him out of it."

"I don't know what you're talking about. I'm an honest rancher. I pay my taxes and stay out of trouble. I'd be doing him a favor, taking him and the kid all the way to Lakeview. What's wrong with that?"

Larkin ignored Eddie and instead turned to me.

"Peter, I have a rule: I don't run other people's lives, but if it were me, I'd wait for a better offer." McCray stared at me, his face locked in a determined expression. I got off the stool and led Larkin a few feet away.

"What's wrong with him?" I whispered. "I mean, is he violent? Do you think he'd dump us somewhere?"

McCray's face reflected his frustration and a reluctance to tell anyone what they should do. He paused, looked at Lisa, and decided to make one last attempt to get me to take his advice.

"All I can tell you is that Eddie has a reputation for being a little on the shady side. He says it's a load of hay but maybe it's stolen car parts. He's trouble on two legs." While I was sure McCray was sincere, he didn't seem to have any solid information. It sounded like Eddie had some kind of a reputation but no one had really caught him doing anything wrong. Besides, what choice did I have?

"Larkin, I appreciate what you're saying and the help you've given us, but I've got to get Lisa home as fast as I can. I can't pass up this ride."

"Your funeral," McCray said, scowling and shaking his head, then turned back to the counter. "It was a pleasure meeting you, Lisa," he said formally, extending his hand to her. She took it with equal solemnity. Larkin let it go, smiled at her, then caressed her hair with his huge right hand. He paused a moment, then turned to Eddie.

"You take care of my friends," he said harshly.

"Jeez, McCray, I'm only giving them a ride!"

"I'm going back to check on my truck," McCray said coldly then turned and walked out into the rapidly falling night. I learned later that late the following morning when the truck had been repaired McCray took an unscheduled trip to visit his daughter in Crescent City, either to avoid any further possible involvement with us or, I prefer to believe, because we had started him thinking about her and how much he missed her.

The room was quiet when the door closed behind him, then Eddie broke the silence.

"Don't pay old Larkin too much mind," he said, turning toward me. "He's got himself religion and he can't help preaching. He knows I like to have a few drinks now and then so he's got me on his black list. Hey, don't worry," he said suddenly when he saw the expression on my face. "The strongest thing I've had today is Lou's coffee. I don't drink and drive, never. That's a rule."

"Sure, I understand. Look, I really appreciate the ride."

"That's the kind of guy I am. But hey, tick tock, as they say. You and the kid ready to go?"

"Sure. Lisa, are you finished?"

"Uh-huh," Lisa said quietly, then carefully wiped the chocolate from her lips with one of Lou's paper napkins.

"What do I owe you?" I asked him as Lisa slid off the stool.

"Seventy-five cents ought to do it."

I left the dollar on the counter while Eddie put down a five and picked up his bag of burgers and coke. A moment later Lisa, Eddie and I were outside walking through the light drizzle of the reawakening storm.


Inside, Lou slipped into the kitchen and reached for the phone. He picked up the slip of paper with Jimmie's phone number on it and squinted at the smeared digits. A moment later he pecked out the number and waited for the machine to answer. "I check my calls every hour," the message began. "Leave your number and I'll get back to you as soon as I can."

"Ahh, hello? This is Lou Foster, at Lou's Cafe in Canby. That guy was just in here with your granddaughter. He and Eddie Doherty are heading up to Lakeview. Eddie usually drives a gray Oldsmobile but I expect he'll be taking his fancy new truck. It's a new Ford Ranger, blue. You should be able to catch up to them in Lakeview if you hurry. That's a nice little girl you've got there. It's a sin what some people do to kids. Remember, you promised me another fifty dollars if I found them for you.

Lou stared at the phone for a moment longer as he tried to think of something that he would tell Jimmie he would do if Jimmie didn't pay him the extra fifty, but no stratagems came to mind. Too late he realized that he should have insisted that Jimmie bring him the money before he told him what kind of truck Eddie owned. Too late now. Vaguely frustrated, Lou hung up and hoped that Jimmie was an honorable man.

Eddie led us to the parking area, past the pickup truck and over to the Oldsmobile.

"Where's the truckful of hay?" I asked him, confused.

"At my ranch. No big deal. We'll be there in ten minutes. Hop in." Eddie unlocked the driver's door and, once inside, reached over and worked the latch on the passenger side. I reached in the front door and released the rear lock, then opened the back door for Lisa. The panel resisted at first and the steel made a dull snap when the door cleared the first few inches.

I fumbled around in the back seat until I found the ends of the seat belt and made sure that it was securely fastened around her. The rain had picked up in the time it took us to reach the car. It dripped down my nylon jacket and soaked the backs of my legs. As soon as I closed the passenger door Eddie started the engine and turned on the lights.

"Heck of a day," I said nodding at the beads of rain splashing against the windshield.

"Yeah, but sometimes I like it like this. Good for us farmers," Eddie said, then began to laugh.

"What's so funny?" I asked him.

"Nothing. It's a local joke."

The Olds pulled to the right, out of the lot, and headed west for a block or so on 299. The sedan's lights cut a yellow swath through the streaming rain. In thirty seconds we were almost through Canby and Eddie turned left onto County Road 54, toward Cal Pines. We crossed County Road 175 and off to the left a gently sloping valley spread out below us. A hundred yards to our right rose low hills covered with scrub pine.

The highway seemed deserted. The fence posts along the shoulder were made of dead branches and lumberyard scraps. After a mile or so the yellow line began to disappear from the center of the road as if it had been slowly scraped away. About two miles after we left 299 Eddie turned right on an unmarked road, crossed a cattle guard, and continued south into the Modoc Wildlife Refuge. The road followed a seam between the low hills then broke out into another small, isolated valley.

"I didn't know you could farm here," I said to Eddie and pointed to a sign announcing the refuge.

"Sure, you just can't hunt. I mostly grow oats, raise some pigs, a few alpaca goats, and some ostriches."

"Ostriches?"

"Sure, for the feathers and the skins. Fashion designers buy them. That's my cash crop. There's a big market for ostrich feathers and hides. Have you ever seen an ostrich, little girl?" he called over his shoulder.

"No, sir," Lisa answered politely.

"Well, if we have time, I'll show you one. They're big birds, six, seven feet tall. They come from Africa," Eddie told her as he negotiated the rain-slicked one-and-a-half lane road. Lisa didn't reply. I think she was wondering if Eddie was telling her the truth or just teasing her but she was too polite to accuse him of lying.

It was now almost fully dark and the landscape beyond the road was indiscernible. I had only the impression of tree-shrouded hills interspersed with an occasional pasture. About five minutes after we had left the highway, Eddie took a second turnoff. I guessed that this one was the driveway to his farm and, in fact, about half a mile later the road broke free of the enclosing hills and entered a small compound containing a two-story wooden house and a barn separated by a large fenced corral in which several pigs wandered, oblivious to the rain.

"Home sweet home," Eddie announced happily as we crossed the compound and approached the barn. He left the engine running and fixed the headlights on the front of the building. "Say, what's your name again?"

"Peter."

"Right, Peter. Okay, Pete, you want to jump out and get those doors open for us." Clearly, Eddie intended me to work for my ride. I opened the passenger door and was confronted by a wall of rain. Splashing my way across the compound I grabbed the right side barn door and pulled. It moved half an inch, then stopped. I wedged my fingers into the gap and heaved it again. This time it slid about a foot or two then ground to a halt. I managed to squeeze into the gap between the two doors and pushed with all my strength. Slowly the huge panels scraped and groaned along their tracks until I had created an opening large enough to admit the car but Eddie did not drive inside. Instead he parked with the driver's side of the Olds almost flush with the right side of the open door, then turned off the engine and the lights, jumped out, and ran inside.

"Come on, kid," he shouted at the car and waved for Lisa to follow him. A moment later the rear driver's side door opened slowly and she slipped out, sprinted across the driveway, and joined us inside the barn. Eddie walked over to the wall to the right of the door and fumbled around for the lights.

Outside the wind rose and drove sheets of rain against the side of the barn and several feet inside through the open door. Lisa huddled against me. Her head and shoulders were soaked and I caressed her hair then held her to my side while we watched the rain puddle in the yard. In the distance I heard the muted boom of thunder. A moment later Eddie found the light switch and two naked suspended bulbs glowed to life.

I was a city boy, but the barn looked more or less as I expected: four rough wooden walls, stalls, empty, along the right side, tack and equipment hanging from pegs on the left. Workbenches lined the front walls to the left and right of the sliding doors. The rear third of the building was filled with bales of hay to the width of the structure and piled almost twenty feet high in a stairstep arrangement, like the sides of a Mayan pyramid. Near the edge of the pile, facing toward me, was a battered, rusted-out old Chevy three-quarter-ton pickup. I spotted a fragment of cloth on the bench and I dried Lisa's hair and shoulders as well as I could.

"There she is," Eddie said, pointing to the Chevy. I didn't say anything. I was too busy counting the rust spots and cataloging the dents. "She's seen better days," he admitted after a moment's pause, "but she's got a good motor. She'll get us to Oregon, no problem. Well," Eddie said when I didn't respond, "I guess we better get to work."

"What?"

"Well, not all of the hay is in the truck. I figured you wouldn't mind helping me finish loading it. It won't take long. You don't have a problem with that, Pete, do you?"

And if I did? What could I say? Hell, I had helped Sal load and unload his truck in exchange for a ride. Still, it was the dishonesty of Eddie's approach that bothered me. He waited until we were stranded here before asking us to "pay for our supper" so to speak.

"No," I said after a moment's pause to control my temper at being manipulated, "I don't have a problem with that."

"Great. Let's do it."

I followed Eddie to the back of the barn, positioned myself to the right of the bale nearest the rear of the truck, and waited for him to grab the other end. I paused there, bent over the end of the bale for a few seconds then looked up and saw Eddie 20 feet away and several bales up the pile.

"Come on over here, Pete," he called. "Those are too old. We only use those for the bottom of the stalls. The ones underneath don't dry out as fast; that's what I'm giving my customer."

As I said, I'm a city boy, but that didn't seem right to me. I had a sinking feeling that McCray might have been right after all, but it was too late to do anything about it now. I joined Eddie up on the pile and together we removed the top layer of hay and exposed the bales underneath. They looked no different to me.

We lifted out the first one and Eddie studied it carefully, then nodded to me and grabbed one end. I guessed that it weighed 70 or 80 pounds but we managed to get it over to the truck and into the bed. Eddie had me get up there with it and push it back against the rear wall of the cab. I jumped down and we repeated the process eight more times until the truck was almost down on its rear axle. I leaned against the side of the cab while Eddie looped heavy nylon line through the tie-downs in a zigzag pattern until the load was secured.

"Whooeee," Eddie said, wiping the sweat from his forehead with the cuff of his jacket. "That sure took the starch out of my shorts. Listen, I've got to make a phone call, check on my mama,

see how she's doin'. I'll be right back, then we can get out of here."
Eddie ambled to the open door, stared at the now-slackening rain,
then ran toward the darkened house across the compound.

"Lisa, how are you doing?" I asked as I walked over to the stall
where she huddled out of the wind.

"I'm fine," she said evenly.

"Look, we'll be out of here in a few minutes." I checked my
watch, the only thing besides my underwear that Eric had not
stripped off me when he took my clothes. It was almost five-thirty.
Eddie might have his burgers but Lisa and I would need to stop
for dinner. We should be able to find someplace to eat within the
first hour of the drive. That would only be six-thirty. It looked like
we were more or less on schedule. From behind me I heard the
splash of booted feet and a moment later Eddie ran back into the
barn. I took Lisa's hand and led her toward the passenger side of
the truck.

"Hang on a second, Pete, we've got a problem," Eddie said, out
of breath.

"What's wrong?"

"It's my mom. She fell down. They think she might have broken
her hip. I've got to go over there right away."

"What do you want us to do? Can we stay here for the night? Do
you want to leave in the morning?" Eddie frowned.

"Ahhh, I don't know. If she has to go to the hospital, if she needs
surgery, they would do it right away. It could be days until I can
get loose."

So this was what Larkin meant. Now that the truck was all
loaded, Eddie would dump us, and what could I do about it?

"Can you give us a ride back to town?" I said angrily.

"Hey, hold on there, partner! I've got to take off in the other
direction, but don't worry, there's a way around this problem. Why
don't you just make the delivery for me?"

"Wait a minute. You're just going to give me the keys to your
truck and let me drive off with it?"

"Why not? You're not planning on stealing it, are you?"

"Of course not, but . . ."

"I'm a pretty good judge of people. I don't figure you for a thief.
Besides it's not like she's worth very much. She's insured anyway.

Hell, you'd probably be doing me a favor if you stole her and I got the insurance money. Hey," he said suddenly when he saw the expression on my face, "that's a joke, Pete!"

"I don't even know where to take this stuff," I said, forcing myself to calm down.

"I'll give you a map. Tell you what, after you deliver the hay, you can use the truck to take the little girl home, long as you don't take too long. Have it back by what, Tuesday afternoon? That be long enough?"

Something was wrong here but I wasn't sure what and the more I thought about it, the more I didn't want to know. We were stranded here. It was take the truck or what? If I refused maybe he would drive us back to Lou's, but he might just tell us to walk. What would I do then? And what would we do when we got back to the highway? The truth was that I had no choice at all.

"Sure Eddie," I said after a slight pause. "That would be fine."

"Well, don't be so happy about it!"

"Sorry, you caught me by surprise. What do we have to do?"

"It's real simple. My customer has a ranch near Beatty. Just go west on 140 from Lakeview. He'll unload the hay, you get yourself a motel. I'll pay for it. Sunday morning you do what you have to do, then bring the truck back when you're done. Think you can handle that?"

"Sounds okay. I'll need directions to the ranch."

"Right, ahhh, look there's a note pad and a pen in the glovebox. Why don't you get them."

I opened the creaking door and felt around the dash. The glove compartment was an open indentation in the panel. It held a map, a three-by-four-inch note pad, and a BIC pen. I pulled out the pad and pen, got out of the truck and offered them to Eddie.

"That's okay, Pete, you'd better take this down. My handwriting's so bad, people say I ought to have been a doctor instead of a farmer." I pulled the pen and paper back and got ready to write down Eddie's directions.

"Okay, you go right at the end of the driveway, then left, then left again, then right on 299. Then north on 395 at Alturas all the way to Lakeview. Then west on 140 and keep going until you get about five miles west of Beatty. Watch for mile marker 291. At a point four miles west of the marker there's a one-lane road to your left, that's south. You go three-tenths of a mile down that road and stop. They'll meet you and unload the bales. That's all there is to it. Any questions?"

I looked up at Eddie. In the yellow glare of the naked bulb the bottoms of his eyes were black crescent shadows and his face glistened with an oily sheen.

"What am I looking for? A house? A barn?"

"It's their north pasture. They'll meet you there. No sense unloading it into the barn and then putting it back on their truck. They'll transfer the load then drop it off, a bale here, a bale there. It's about 120 miles. Let's say, what, three hours? Figure you take half an hour for dinner and another half an hour just to be sure, say four hours. It's about quarter to six. I'll call and tell them you'll be there between nine-thirty and ten."

"You want me to unload a truck full of hay at ten o'clock at night, in a rainstorm, on some back road in the middle of nowhere? That doesn't make any sense. Why can't we just do it tomorrow morning? It will be a heck of lot easier in the daylight. I mean, it's only a load of hay."

"Yeah, well, Pete, here's the problem. I told the guy he'd have it on Saturday. I made a contract. Now the customer, he's a pain in the butt, excuse my French. If I don't get it there by midnight then he makes a stink. The lawyers get into it. I don't want the problems. The contract says Saturday. As long as it's there by midnight, he can't complain."

"Sure," I thought. "Now tell me the one about the Tooth Fairy," but I didn't say it. Eddie handed me the keys. I belted Lisa into the passenger seat and walked around to the driver's side. I was just about to get in when Eddie called.

"Hey, wait a minute. Bet you thought I had forgotten my promise. Not me. A deal is a deal. Here's forty bucks. That'll cover the room and probably dinner too if you don't go to the Ritz." Eddie laughed harshly at the idea of Lisa and me and his beat-up truckload of hay pulling into some fancy restaurant. I smiled thinly and took the two twenties.

"Thanks Eddie," I said uneasily. "Don't worry. I'll take it easy with your truck."

"Yeah, sure, you do that. Remember, it's got to be delivered before midnight."

"I understand. Except for a stop for dinner we'll go straight there. I want to get this over as badly as you do." I got in, rolled up the window, and started the engine. Eddie stepped back a couple of feet, into the shadows at the side of the barn. I dropped the transmission into drive and as I slowly pulled out, Eddie smiled and gave me a cheery little wave.

"Now what have I gotten us into," I muttered under my breath, then I glanced over at Lisa. She was sitting primly in the passenger seat, staring fixedly through the windshield at the rain-darkened sky before us. I eased the truck through the doorway and into the droning storm.

# TWENTY-ONE

It was just after dinner when Carlos got the call.

"Carlos, Bob Jamison. I got a couple of hits on your picture."

"What?"

"Waitress at the coffee shop served them breakfast and the clerk at the thrift shop sold them a load of clothes."

"Them? The man and the little girl?"

"They fit your description all the way. They both changed into the new clothes in the restaurant bathrooms."

"What about the girl?"

"They say it's her. The clerk in the thrift shop wasn't positive, but the waitress was sure. She swears it was the kid in the flier. Still, you know how witnesses are."

"How was she? Was she all right? Was she frightened? Was she trying to get away?"

"No, just the opposite. Waitress said he took real good care of her. Said the little girl smiled at him and seemed happy enough. Not your typical kidnap victim, but you know about the Stockholm syndrome."

"Any leads on where they went? Are they still in town?"

"The clerk at the thrift shop said the guy helped the owner

move a load of furniture up to his Adin store. I've called the Adin number but I didn't get an answer. We've found out where he stays when he's up there. I thought you might want to talk to him yourself. His name is Salvatore Gianinni. Here's the number."

Carlos grabbed a scrap a paper and wrote down Bella's number in Adin. A moment later her phone was ringing. Bella answered and then put Sal on the line.

"Mr. Gianinni? This is Detective Carlos Ramirez of the Oakdale, Oregon Police Department calling. The Burney police gave me your number."

"The Burney police? What's happened? Was my store robbed?"

"No, nothing like that. We're following up on a report we received earlier today. We found a van abandoned near your store in Burney and the clerk told us that you might have given a ride to the driver."

"Pete? Are you looking for Pete?"

"Possibly. What's his full name?"

"His name—gee, I can't think, I'm so excited. I'm sure he didn't do anything wrong. He seemed like a nice guy."

"His name was Pete, Peter? Can you remember his last name?"

"Yeah, I'm trying to think. —You know how it is when you're trying to remember names. It'll come to me. Just give me a minute."

"What can you tell me about him? Where was he going?"

"Well, he was taking the little girl home. Oh, what was his name!"

"Taking the little girl home?"

"Yes, a sweet kid. Interested in astrology, she was. I told him that I couldn't take him all the way, but I got him a ride with one of my customers."

"Who was that?"

"McCray, Larkin McCray. He has a farm near Alturas. I've got his number down at the store. I could get it for you."

"That would be a big help Mr. Gianinni. You said this Mr. McCray gave the man, Peter, and the little girl a ride. Where was he heading?"

"Back home, up to Alturas."

"What time was this?"

"Oh, three, three-thirty this afternoon, something like that. What's Peter supposed to have done? He seemed like such a nice guy."

"As far as we know, Mr. Gianinni, he hasn't done anything. We just have some questions about the van he was driving. If I give you my office number could you call back with Mr. McCray's number?"

"Sure. Is fifteen minutes soon enough?"

"That would be great. As soon as you get that to me, I'll give him a call. Maybe he's putting them up for the night. Where did they say they were going?"

"You mean after they got to Alturas?"

"Yes."

"Peter said he was taking the little girl home, back to her family."

"Where was that?"

"Oregon? Yeah, that's it, Oregon. He said he was taking her back home to Oregon. What a minute, where did you say you were from?"

"I'm the Chief of Detectives for the Oakdale, Oregon Police Department."

"Now I understand. That's why you're looking for them. You were worried that he was late getting her home. I guess his van just broke down. I wouldn't worry. He seemed real determined. He won't let you down."

Carlos stared at the wall in front of him for a long moment, then, in a much softer voice, asked: "About the little girl, do you remember her name?"

"Oh, sure. Couldn't forget that. She said her name was Lisa."

Carlos concluded the conversation, hung up the phone, tried to figure out what was happening, and couldn't. It didn't make sense, any of it. A few minutes later the night dispatcher called in with Larkin McCray's home number. Carlos called it at once, but there was no answer. He called three more times over the next half hour, then got the Alturas PD to send out a car. A few minutes later they called back to say that the house was empty.

What did it mean? Lisa was kidnapped last spring and disappeared without a trace, then out of nowhere she shows up with some bum in a van with bullet holes in it. Now they're both hitchhiking back here. It couldn't really be her, could it? He didn't even want to hope.

Should he call Bill and Peggy, leave a message? No, better to wait until he knew more. No sense raising false hopes. They would be home late tomorrow. The odds were that the man and the little girl were with this Larkin McCray. By Sunday night he ought to have some answers. Hell, by Sunday night, maybe Lisa would . . . no, it wasn't safe to think that way.

The first thing was to get the DMV records on McCray's vehicle, then have every PD and sheriff's department between Adin and Oakdale be on the watch for it. There was only one highway they could take heading to Oregon. If McCray was anywhere on California 299 or U.S. 395 he would be stopped. Short of closing down an interstate highway there wasn't anything else Carlos could do. And they didn't have to go to that extreme. The deputies would find McCray somewhere between Adin and Oakdale by midnight, Carlos was sure of it.

# TWENTY-TWO

Jimmie entered his retrieve message code and heard Lou's call a little after five that Saturday afternoon. Tim Mathias had supplied Jimmie with a two-year-old red Dodge RAM pickup which Jimmie had immediately used to dump Eric's body where it was not likely to be found for a while. Devries then hit every gas station from Neubiber to the Alturas city limits. Now, in the gathering darkness, he turned around and drove back toward Canby and Lou's Cafe all the while keeping a careful watch for a blue Ford Ranger driving in the opposite direction.

When he got to Canby without spotting it, he turned around and drove north again. He knew Howard had to take 395 to the Oregon border so he grabbed a couple of burgers then passed through Alturas and staked out the highway from the country store parking lot at Davis Creek. The highway there was well lighted enough to be able to identify Eddie's Ford and yet remain unnoticed himself.

Jimmie knew that if Howard had had any inkling that Devries was looking for them he would swallow his pride and call the FBI. But Jimmie was sure Howard didn't suspect a thing.

# TWENTY-THREE

We headed east on 299 and entered Modoc County. The road rose gently up a long slope with Alturas perched about two-thirds of the way up, about 20 miles to the east. The old Chevy looked like a piece of junk but Eddie hadn't lied about one thing, it had a good motor. We had started out with a full tank of gas and the truck hummed along through the rain without missing a beat. That isn't to say I wanted to drive it one mile longer than I had to.

The front end shimmied, the brakes squealed at the slightest pressure, and the muffler had a pinhole in it. Add to that the weak, misaligned headlights, a worn right front tire, and spreading crack just to the left of the center of the windshield, and it was not something you wanted to pile the wife and kids into for a Sunday drive. But it did have lots of power and a seductive, deep-throated burble when I stepped on the gas, though part of that might have been due to the hole in the muffler.

Considering the state of the truck's steering and the darkness and the rain, it took us about forty minutes to reach Alturas. There are no Burger Kings there, no McDonald's, in fact no fast-food restaurants of any kind once you got east of Burney, a situation that encouraged a local capitalist to build a substitute.

I turned right off 299 at the 395 intersection and onto Alturas' four-lane main street. About two blocks down, on my left across from the three-story brownstone Elks Club and just beyond the Modoc High School stood something called "Mickies." The sign said: "Too Good To Be Fast Food, But It Is."

We pulled into Mickies at about half past six that Saturday night. While most people would consider Alturas a small town, to the farmers, ranchers, and sportsmen of Modoc County it was The City, and, except for Lakeview, Oregon, the biggest town for a hundred miles. And Lakeview was only about the same size. To find anything larger you would have to go to Redding to the southwest or Klamath Falls in Oregon to the north. Considered in that light, it wasn't surprising that Mickies was jammed that evening.

Mostly, it was filled with kids from thirteen to twenty. At first I was surprised. I couldn't imagine myself at sixteen asking a girl out for a date at a fast-food joint but then I thought about it for a moment. There was probably only one movie theater in town. Most of the places that had music or dancing would also serve alcohol. Other than sitting in the park, in February, in the rain, or taking your date back to your house to watch TV with your parents, probably a Matlock rerun, where else could you to go? Mickies would be the town social center by default, a situation that the management was happy to encourage.

So there we sat, one dirty, tired, confused businessman who felt considerably older than his thirty-seven years and his de facto ward, a brutalized, molested, terrified child whom, I was sure, did not and could not comprehend the maelstrom of events that had engulfed her. Across the aisle from us, six kids, three boys and three girls, laughed and giggled and traded French fries and, in their most boisterous moments, threatened to squirt each other with ketchup. The sheer innocence of it!

What would these kids make of Jimmie or Eric or Ken? There sat Lisa, primly eating her hamburger; her face did not betray any of the dismay or terror she had experienced. And she never, ever cried out loud. Could any of these laughing teen-agers have matched her courage? But then, I didn't know them. Perhaps they could.

I suddenly felt very old, a man ripped out of his time who no longer had a place in the world where he could feel at home. I looked again at Lisa and had an almost overwhelming urge to reach out to her, caress her face, place her in my lap and hold her close, to assure her that everything was going to be all right; to hold her until she cried all the pain from her heart, but I could not. She looked up and saw me staring at her.

"Peter," she said softly, "is something wrong?"

"No, swe—, no Lisa, everything's fine. I'm just tired, that's all." She stared at me for a moment longer, then turned back to her dinner. A few minutes later we finished eating and I was glad to go. As we were leaving, a chorus of laughter erupted from the teen-agers, then died suddenly, cut off in midsyllable as the thick glass door swung closed behind us. Full of fat and sugar and caffeine I pulled the battered truck out of the lot and back onto the highway.

About five miles east of Alturas, California 299 broke to the right and U.S. 395 continued straight on. We stayed with it and headed north. Even though 395 was a main road, on this rainy Saturday night there was practically no traffic. I guessed that if you stood by the side of the highway and counted cars you might come up with about twenty per hour, or about one car every three minutes.

The road was climbing again, winding through another canyon with the Pit River meandering along the narrow strip to the left of the highway. According to the map, the next town, more like a wide spot in the road, was Davis Creek, about 15 miles ahead. Another 15 miles beyond that was the village of Willow Ranch, then four more miles brought us to New Pine Creek a mile or so south of the California-Oregon border. We passed Davis Creek, the entire town consisting of the Davis Creek Merchandise Company grocery and liquor store. There was only one vehicle parked in the small lot in front of the market, a red pickup, and I paid it no mind. Sitting in that truck Jimmie was carefully watching the highway for a blue Ford Ranger and, luckily, not Eddie's beat-up old Chevy. With Lisa sitting too low to be seen in the dark and the rain he barely gave our gray Chevy a second glance.

We soon emerged into a flat tableland, over 4,000 feet above sea level. The night was completely black and I could make out nothing of the landscape beyond the windows of the truck. I knew that

Goose Lake, a huge alkali-salt lake was somewhere ahead and to our left, but I could see no evidence of it, or of anything else.

The rain continued in fits and spurts. The Chevy's windshield wipers had only two speeds: off and on. When they were in the off position a sudden squall would turn my view of the highway into a dim, yellow-gray blur. When on, the wipers smeared the droplets left and right, usually dragging two or three streaks behind them where nicks marred the blade.

To compensate, I drove in a peculiar oscillating rhythm: 50 or so miles per hour when the rain abated and about 20 when it started again. A few cars passed us, one or two at a speed that I thought little short of insanity, their taillights quickly disappearing into the storm-clouded night. Still, we made decent time until, finally, we were only a mile or two south of the Oregon border.

The rain had held off for the last ten minutes and my speed crept up to about 55. The highway hugged the right side of the valley in which Goose Lake was located, a valley that was now topped by impenetrable clouds which smothered the highway. I felt as if I was driving inside a sealed box. The yellow center line had been abraded by snow plows and logging trucks until it was little more than a gray smudge under the misaligned headlights. We rolled on through the night and closed in on New Pine Creek. Ahead the road curved gently to the left and rose through a cut in a low, rocky ridge. I could almost feel the Oregon border just beyond the reach of my high beams.

The first hint I had of an approaching car was the faint reflection of headlights from the rocks at the sides of the cleft just ahead of us. The indication was little more than a change in their color from pure obsidian to a slightly lighter charcoal gray. I stared at the crest in the highway trying to catch a glimpse of a glow in the air from the car's headlights. A few rain drops splattered the hood and windshield. Suddenly, a sheet of driving rain swept over the truck. I fumbled for the windshield wiper knob, glanced down at the dash just for an instant, then looked up to see a glare of high beams driving straight for us.

As much as I have relived that instant I can't be entirely sure of what really happened. I think that the other driver was also surprised by the squall and that he drifted over the center line, only a pale strip almost indistinct from the asphalt in the best of weather. The road rose on both sides of the cleft and curved slightly away from me. If I had wandered out of my lane, I would have headed for the shoulder while an error by the other driver would have taken him across the center and into our lane.

Maybe neither of us left our side of the road. Perhaps the rain-smeared windows and the loss of sight of the highway beyond the cut and the sudden glare of his headlights, and my momentary distraction while I reached for the wiper knob all combined to confuse me. Maybe I panicked without cause. I don't know.

All I can say is that I slammed on the Chevy's worn and squealing brakes and immediately locked up the right rear wheel, something that probably saved our lives. Certainly, if it had been the left rear wheel that had frozen we would have pivoted toward the center of the road and surely crashed head-on into the other car. Instead, we skidded to the right, onto the shoulder, barely clearing the rock wall, then we started down the grade on the far side, half on the pavement, half off.

The shoulder was soft and steeply sloping. Inexorably we veered off the highway and down toward the mud-lined ditch and, beyond it, a row of pines.

When I realized that the brakes had locked, I released the pedal for an instant then reapplied it, but it was too late. The passenger side wheels were already into the rain-soaked dirt. The resistance of the mud and brush dragged at the right side wheels and pulled us farther off the road. In an instant I had lost all control. The truck plunged forward, gouging deep ruts in the earth, then it slid into the roadside gully now swollen with a foot or more of rain. The cab angled sideways like a ship listing to starboard in heavy seas and we careened ahead still going 25 or 30 miles per hour.

Grasping the wheel with my left hand I reached over and placed my right arm across Lisa's chest to hold her in her seat. I still remember the sounds of our passage: the brief screech of the brakes immediately followed by the grinding hiss of our tires against the road; the squishing sound of the wheels tearing through sod and mud and all of it punctuated by the thuds and scrapes of bushes colliding with the bumper then catching on the undercarriage and being pulled out by their roots. Lastly, I recall the deep groaning rumble of metal being torn away as the truck's chassis scraped the top edge of the ditch like an earth mover leveling a high spot in a meadow that is about to become a parking lot.

I heard the muffler and the exhaust pipe and the tie rods and finally the front axle gouge through the rain-soaked soil and shear away. Then the frame caught the mud and beveled a new edge along the top of the gully. Lisa and I were thrown forward, straining against our seat belts. The noise and the pressure and the crazy flicker of the headlights against the cloud of fountaining brush and dirt and rain continued for two seconds, three, four, then, with one last convulsive jerk, the truck lurched to a stop halfway down the steep embankment, the top of the Chevy's roof almost level with the edge of the road. The Chevy's frame was buried in the mud, with earth and vegetation piled above the front bumper, almost up to the lights and the cab was canted at better than a thirty-degree angle.

My hand was still pressing Lisa back against her seat, I took a deep breath, released my hold, and turned to her.

"Lisa, are you all right? Are you hurt?" My voice sounded tight and thin in my ears. The truck lay tilted halfway on its side with only my seat belt holding me in place.

"Are we going to tip over?" she asked, her voice thick with fear.

"No, I think we're okay. Are you hurt?"

"I'm scared, Peter. I'm afraid we'll tip over and we'll be stuck in here and I'll never get home."

"Don't worry, sweetheart, I'm going to get us both out right now." I reached to my left and pushed against the driver's door. It resisted for a moment, frozen in place by the warp in the truck's frame but my lunges finally popped it free and, reluctantly, it opened. Now I had to figure out how to get out. If I let go of the door to release my seat belt, it would slam closed. If I closed the door, then released my belt I would slide out of my seat.

"Lisa," I said, forcing my voice to hold a steady tone, "I need you to reach over and release my seat belt when I tell you."

"Peter, I'm scared."

"I know you are, Lisa, but I've got the door open. I can get out if you can just reach my belt. Do you remember how to undo it?"

"Yes, Peter," she said quietly, fighting down her fear.

"Okay, I'm going to swing my legs out. As soon as I'm ready, I'll tell you and you push the button on the belt." I got my left leg up onto the doorsill and pressed my right foot against the panel to hold it open.

"Okay, press the button," I ordered. I heard Lisa twist in her seat and then the rattle of her small fingers trying to depress the mechanism. The clatter of the rain drummed against the roof of the cab. A moment later I heard a loud snap and the belt popped free. I lunged forward and tumbled out of the truck onto the rain-soaked earth. Behind me the door slammed shut.

"Peter! Peter, where are you? Peter, don't leave me!"

I struggled to my feet and the pouring rain washed the mud from my face. I grabbed the door handle and pulled it back but realized immediately that that would not work. I needed some way to hold it open while I pulled Lisa out.

"I'm fine, Lisa. I'll have you out in a minute."

I bent down and searched the ground in front of the truck. Miraculously, the headlights were still on. Buried in the mound of earth piled against the radiator I found part of a young sapling, perhaps an inch and a half in diameter. I yanked it free and returned to the cab. This time after I opened the door I jammed the wood between the base of the panel and the truck's frame near the hinge. The door sagged back a few inches slightly crushing the stem, then held. I leaned inside as far as I could reach.

"It's okay, Lisa. I can get you out now. Release your belt just like you did mine, then climb up to me." Without a second's hesitation, Lisa depressed the clasp then clambered over her seat, past the floor-mounted shift controls and up into my outstretched arms. I lifted her into the rain and hugged her close. She was shaking and held onto me with a fierce grip.

"It's all right, sweetie," I whispered into her ear. "Neither of us is hurt. Someone will be along to help us in a minute." As I said that I looked around. The road was deserted. There was no trace of the other driver. Had he even seen the accident? I doubted it. As soon as he passed through the cut he would have lost all sight of us as we disappeared into the storm.

I looked at the truck. It was pretty clear that it was a total loss.

The rope, or the tie-downs, one or the other, had given way and a line of broken hay bales trailed out behind us marking our path. Even those few bales remaining in the bed had been cut by their impact against the nylon line and had broken into two or three pieces. The baling wire had snapped like cheap string.

I shook my head. So much for Eddie's promise of on-time delivery. I looked at the hay one more time and was about to turn away when I noticed something peculiar. I thought I saw something glisten in the hay. The only illumination was the backscatter from the headlights, but there appeared to be spots of a different texture here and there in the back of the truck. I reached down and sifted through the remnants with my fingers. It didn't take me long to encounter a hard, plastic-wrapped object, shaped like a brick.

I picked it up and brought it close to my face. One sniff confirmed my suspicions. A kilo brick of marijuana. And not just one of them. Now that I knew what to look for, I saw several more. Each of the bales probably contained five or ten of them. Fifteen bales, a hundred and fifty bricks, 330 pounds of "grass." A pretty good shipment. Well, now I knew why Eddie had wanted me to make the delivery alone. If anything went wrong, he didn't want to be there. I don't think he was worried about a wreck. More likely he was afraid that his customers were cops or had ratted him out to the DEA.

Everything made sense now. Eddie said his handwriting was bad, so the directions were in my hand, not his. I would bet that his fingerprints were nowhere on the truck, but mine were. Of course he wasn't worried about me stealing it. It was probably already stolen, or else a friend of his using a phony name had bought it from some farmer for $1,000 in cash and it was untraceable.

Sure, if I was caught I could blame it all on Eddie and he could deny it. He could say that I had changed my mind about helping him or that his truck had broken down or that he called it off because his mother was sick. "No, officer, that's not my truck. I've never seen it before."

Maybe the cops wouldn't believe him but it would be my word against his, and I was the one driving the truck full of pot. Besides, even if Eddie was behind it, that didn't mean that we weren't in it together. Jesus, we had to get out of here before someone came along and tied me to the Chevy.

Lisa had taken what shelter she could between me and the side of the truck. I left her huddled there, grabbed my handkerchief and began wiping my prints from everything I remembered touching, first the driver's door latch and steering wheel, then I struggled back inside and wiped everything I could reach inside the cab: the seat belts, the windshield wiper knob, the gearshift, the inside door handles. Then I grabbed the nylon bag with our clothes in it.

Lastly, I left the cab, slid down the embankment and waded through knee-deep water to the passenger door where I wiped our prints from that handle as well. Thoroughly soaked and muddy to my thighs, I scrambled back up the bank. My last act was to reach inside and, using the handkerchief, depress the headlight control. We were immediately plunged back into the pitch-black night.

"Come on, Lisa, we have to get out of here," I said as I bent to pick her up.

"Why, is the truck going to catch fire?"

"No, but we have to get out of the rain. There's a town only about a mile down the road."

"Can't we stay here? Won't someone stop and help us?"

"It's kind of complicated," I said picking her up. Then, without thinking about it, I told her that same tired old cliché my mother used to tell me whenever there was a problem: "I'll explain later."

"Mom, why can't I go on the ski trip with the other guys?" "Mom, why don't we just get a new TV?" "Mom, why do you have to work so late?"

"I'll explain later."

How long had it taken me to figure out what she couldn't bring herself to say: "Peter, since your father died, we don't have enough money for ski trips or TVs, and I have to work as hard as I can just to put food on the table." When I was sixteen she married Bill Tamachek, the owner of the restaurant where she had worked her way up from hostess to manager. I kept asking her, "Why do you want to marry him? He's old, God, he must be almost fifty and he's going bald. There are lots of guys out there. My gym teacher's—."

She looked at me with that funny expression she always got when she was confronted by one of my inconvenient questions.

"Peter," she began, "Sometimes we have to do things. . . ."

"Mom, you don't have to marry him. You don't love him, do you?"

"Peter," she tried again, then took a deep breath and got that sad little smile that I saw more and more often after dad died.

"Peter, I've got to go to work. I'll explain later." Of course, she never did explain, not in so many words, but her actions explained for her, when I was old enough to understand them.

Two years after she married Bill Tamachek I got into UC Berkeley. Fours years later I was admitted to the Stanford MBA program. It took me a long time to make the connection. I was afflicted with such blind stupidity that I never seemed to realize that suddenly after marrying Bill there was enough money for me to have an apartment and to buy books and to have a car and to attend college and to go to graduate school.

My mother never did "explain later," not directly. She never said: "Peter, here is why I'm marrying Bill," but events explained things for her, my life explained, illuminated her motives for me, all for me—reasons that she was too embarrassed to put into words.

For a moment I considered being forthright with Lisa, not relying on my mother's ploy. "Lisa," I could say, "We have to run because the truck is full of drugs and they'll put me in jail if they catch me with it." "Drugs? Jail?" she would ask. "Will I go to jail? How will I get home if they take you to jail?" Was I insane? Of course I couldn't tell her that.

"Lisa, listen," I said finally when we were a couple of hundred yards away and the truck had already faded to a faint blob shrouded by the storm, "If we stay here, they'll ask all kinds of questions about the accident. It will take hours and hours and we'll have to fill out forms and reports. The police will come, and they love to write reports. The best thing we can do is just leave the truck there and find another ride so we can get you home as soon as possible."

"What about that man, Eddie? Won't he be mad we broke his truck?"

"Don't you worry about Eddie. I'll call him on the phone and explain it to him. He won't be mad. The insurance company will pay him for his truck. The important thing is that we don't let anyone know about the accident or they'll ask us lots of questions that we don't have time for. Okay?"

"Okay, Peter. Will it be long, before we get to town?" Lisa was too conditioned to complain, to tell me that she was wet and tired and afraid.

"No, Lisa, it won't be long. We'll be there in a few minutes." She shifted slightly and clung to my neck with renewed strength, her chin perched on my shoulder, facing behind us, her legs wrapped around my waist. We passed a sign embedded in the right shoulder of the road: "Wild Plum Winery—Stringer's Orchard—Estate Bottled," and behind a locked metal gate I could see the gray outline of a large slope-roofed building but no lights or any evidence of occupancy.

I thought back over all that had happened to me during the last two days and I felt as if I were Alice and had just fallen down the rabbit hole. On Thursday afternoon I was a millionaire heading out to conclude another one of hundreds of business deals, driving my fancy car, dressed in my Burberry suit. The worst problem in my sheltered life was a headache pounding at the base of my skull. Then I found Lisa, and I entered a world where events beyond my safe, comfortable existence could and did happen.

I remembered a "Star Trek" episode in which Mr. Spock was in command of the shuttle craft when it crashed on a primitive planet. At one point Spock complained to Dr. McCoy that in spite of the fact that he had made the logical decision each step of the way, things had just gone from bad to worse. "I know just how you feel, Mr. Spock," I thought to myself.

I shivered and increased my pace. The only part of my body that was warm was the portion of my chest where Lisa's tiny frame was pressed against me. I was reminded that night of how far a mile really is. Twice, I saw headlights in the distance but they turned off and the highway remained empty. Finally, soaking wet and shivering, we reached the edge of New Pine Creek. It was marked by an abandoned gas station, a closed discount liquor store, two more abandoned buildings, and finally the volunteer fire department, all dark and silent. I paused for a moment studying the scene before me. A hundred yards or so ahead I saw a few lights which marked the remainder of the village. Unsure of what lay behind those lights and what we would do when we got there I pushed off down the low slope just as another burst of rain engulfed us and dimmed the distant illumination to a low, blurry glow.

# TWENTY-FOUR

Jimmie had begun to wonder where things went wrong. He knew that the kidnapping business was dangerous but he had stayed in the background, handling the money and planning the snatches. If anyone got caught, it wouldn't be him. If anyone did talk, which, given his reputation, was unlikely, Jimmie would be long gone.

Grabbing Lisa had, initially, been a textbook operation. Eric stole an '87 Buick Regal in Portland, switched plates with an old, half-wrecked Buick they bought out of the want ads, "for parts," then had the stolen Regal, now with "clean" plates, repainted a dull chocolate brown. The car could no longer be traced back to Eric.

Jimmie liked working the small towns. Fewer cops with poorer training, fewer TV stations and reporters, less heat. You couldn't case the target very well, strangers were too visible, but a hit-and-run snatch was easier than in a big city. In two minutes you were out of town. One guy stays with the car which has the "cold" plates. The other guy puts the kid in the trunk of the backup car, turns around and drives back through town and heads off in the opposite direction.

Jimmie always picked up part of the cash in advance. The balance was paid through the middleman who found the buyer. Jimmie never met the freaks himself. The delivery was always done by Eric. Eric, that moron! He was supposed to have delivered Lisa to the buyer, Ken, in the backup car, another untraceable vehicle. But the engine wouldn't start so Eric took her to Ken in Eric's own van. His *own* van! Jimmie was glad Eric was dead. He was just too stupid to be allowed to live.

Jimmie had picked Oakdale because, though it was isolated, it straddled two major roads each of which connected with interstate highways. Also, it wasn't too far from the cabin Jimmie had rented (under a false name) near Burney. Nor was it too close.

"Go in and do it in the afternoon," Jimmie told them. "Late enough that the kids are out of school and playing on the street. Early enough so that the parents are still at work. Between four and five o'clock. Find a nice quiet street near the edge of town. Our guy wants a girl between five and eight. Don't stop for anything. Just grab her, get in the car and go. Get the backup car in place the night before. Don't set foot in that town in daylight before you grab her. We don't want anyone to see you there twice. Don't forget your gloves! If anything goes wrong, dump the kid and the car. I won't be around until the day after you deliver her to the customer."

And for once, except for bringing her to Ken's house in his own van, Eric had done what he was told. It had come off perfectly. Then Ken loses the kid! But that problem would be fixed soon. Jimmie wasn't going to jail for the rest of his life. He had decided, without much deliberation, that either Howard and the girl would both be finished, or he would be. Now all he needed to do was to find them somewhere between Canby and Oakdale. It shouldn't be that hard.

When Jimmie didn't spot the Ranger, he went back to his old tactics, checking gas stations, motel parking lots, restaurants. Methodically, he worked his way north from Alturas. He was sure it wouldn't take much longer to find them.

# TWENTY-FIVE

It was about eight-thirty or so when we straggled into the center of New Pine Creek. The town consisted of a market, a second-hand store, a real estate office, and a grange hall, all closed, the Hometown 101 Cafe, and the Lone Pine Bar & Grill, both noisily open, and Big Peg's Pizza Parlor, status uncertain.

Only a dim light glowed through Big Peg's red and orange leaded-glass windows. By now my various jolts and sprains had left me sore-footed and limping. Still clutching Lisa to my chest with one hand and the bag with our meager possessions in the other, I hobbled to the door then dropped the bag and pulled on the worn brass handle. It swung open easily. I smelled onions and garlic and stale beer on the rush of warm air that spilled into the night.

When Lisa and I limped in, the manager, probably the owner I decided, a beefy man of about thirty-five with short hair and a brown mustache, leaned over the counter and stared at us. No doubt he was wondering who would be wandering into his restaurant at this hour on a rainy Saturday night.

"Quite a storm," he said evenly as he watched water drip from my jacket and onto his floor.

"Sure is."

"Get you folks something?" he asked as he stared at me with hard gray eyes. There was a small dark blue tattoo of an anchor on the outside of his right arm, just above the elbow. A sickly blue rope encircled the shaft and trailed down below the prongs. Merchant Marine I figured, or maybe Navy. He was well and truly beached here in the California wilderness, I thought, stranded in front of a pizza oven at Big Peg's and, from his expression, not kindly disposed to ragged, rain-soaked travelers washed in by the storm. A Navy man should have had more sympathy for someone so clearly cast adrift. His expression made it pretty clear that I had better either order something quickly or turn around and head back into the night.

"Coffee. Do you have any hot chocolate?"

"No."

"Okay, one coffee and a milk."

"That'll be a buck seventy-five," he said not making any move to get the coffee pot. I pulled out a sodden pile of bills and peeled off two ones which he meticulously flattened then patted dry with a paper napkin before placing them in the cash register. He held the drawer open for a second then, reluctantly it seemed, extracted a quarter, dropped it on the counter, and turned his back on us to fill the order. Lisa stood huddled at my side, still shivering in spite of the heat radiating from the brick-lined pizza oven built into the wall behind the register.

"We close in twenty minutes," he said as he placed a cup of black coffee, an empty glass, and a waxed half-pint carton of homogenized milk on the counter next to the register. I handed Lisa the carton and picked up the coffee cup and the empty glass then turned and studied the tables scattered around the dimly lit room. We had our pick. They were all empty. I chose the one closest to the oven.

The manager bustled around cleaning up the grill, loading the dishwasher, and wiping down tables while I sipped my coffee and tried to figure out what to do next. They probably wouldn't find the truck until morning. We had that long to get out of town and across the state line. I used the pay phone and again called the Taylor home and again got only the broken machine. They must be out of town for the weekend, I decided.

I pulled a handful of napkins from the dispenser and wiped Lisa's face and sodden hair. I felt the counterman's gaze and looked up to see him watching me, clearly begrudging us the penny's worth of paper it would take to keep the water from dripping into Lisa's eyes. Yes, he was the owner all right. To hell with him! I stared back, our eyes locked while I pulled loose another handful of napkins. After a moment, he scowled then dropped his gaze and returned his attention to cleaning the counter-top.

I turned back to Lisa and succeeded in sponging off her face and ears and throat, an activity to which she submitted stoically. Just as I was finishing drying her off, the door opened and another customer trooped in out of the rain. He wore a long black trenchcoat and a brown fedora hat, an outfit that I thought out of place in this little town. Once inside he removed the hat and poured the water which had collected in its brim onto the tile floor. "Our sailor host won't like you doing that" I said to myself. As if on cue, the owner leaned past the register and appraised his new customer. The man was over sixty with frizzy gray-black hair and skin the color of Coca-Cola.

"I'm just getting ready to close up," the owner called.

"Surely there's enough heat in your oven to cook one more pizza," the old black man responded in a resonant voice.

"Reverend, it's going to take fifteen minutes to make you a pizza."

"By my watch, Roy, it's only a quarter 'til nine. That makes the timing perfect, I believe."

Roy let out a slow sigh and frowned. "I gotta close up at nine. How about if I make it to go?"

"I did not intend to eat it here," the Reverend said solemnly. Roy wasn't sure if he should take the Reverend's remark as an insult, but apparently he decided not to.

"You want the usual?"

"I would like a small pizza, pineapple, mushrooms, pepperoni, onions, Canadian bacon, and double Italian sausage with extra tomato sauce."

"Right, Reverend, the usual."

Roy moved up the counter past the register and began to assemble the pizza. The Reverend turned around, nodded to me, then saw Lisa and smiled.

"Hello, young lady," he said politely. "How are you doing this fine evening?"

"I'm all wet. And it's not a fine evening."

"That depends on your point of view," he said, smiling. "If you were a duck or a fish you might think it's a fine evening."

"I'm not a duck or a fish. I'm a human being and I think it's awful."

"I sense an interesting philosophical debate. Do you mind if I join you?" he asked looking at me.

"Not at all," I said promptly. At the very least the presence of another customer at our table would give us an excuse to stay here until the Reverend's pizza was ready. "I'm Peter and this is Lisa," I said politely, holding out my hand.

"Isaiah Williams," he answered, grasping my hand with his own. "And on this rock I will build my church."

"Excuse me?"

"When Christ met Peter, which means 'rock,' he named him the rock upon which he would build his church."

"The owner called you 'Reverend.' I see he knew what he was talking about."

"Purely an honorary title. I used to preach the Lord's Word before I retired and moved here to be near my sons. I help in their business now and then and do some volunteer work for the local congregation. My days of leading a flock are in the past."

"Where was your church, Reverend?"

"Where I was needed most. Where there was the Lord's work to be done. Most of the time I served Him in South Los Angeles. Fifteen years ago when my boys were at San Jose State I became the pastor at a small mission in the Tenderloin in San Francisco."

"That's a rough area," I said, a little surprised.

"All the more need for the Lord's Word and the Lord's help."

"In that part of town a minister may need more than the Lord's help," I suggested.

"As a great man once said, 'Meet trouble as a friend because you will see a lot of it and you may as well be on speaking terms with it.'"

"I didn't know they featured Oliver Wendell Holmes in Divinity School."

"I suspect that his work is not a central part of the curriculum," Isaiah said, laughing, "but I have found that a wider view than mere scripture is beneficial."

"You have an unusual taste in quotations for a man of the cloth."

"I find Holmes often appropriate. I've counseled quite a few lawyers in my time, and more than one judge." The Reverend stared at me a moment, assessing our woeful appearance, then continued, "I don't mean to pry, but if you are in trouble, if you need some help . . . ?"

"It's kind of complicated."

"And I take it that this young lady is part of that complication?"

I paused for a moment then took a sip of coffee and said nothing.

"Sometimes the most complicated problems are the ones most easily solved," Isaiah suggested.

"Unfortunately, Reverend, I have no knife with which to cut this particular Gordian knot."

"Peter, it's a pleasure talking with an educated man," the Reverend said smiling. He glanced briefly at my sports bag next to the table. "That hardly seems the luggage of a college graduate. Would I be correct in assuming that you have no plans for the evening?"

"That would be a safe bet."

"Have you eaten dinner?"

"Yes, yes we have."

"Are you sure? I can hardly eat an entire pineapple, mushroom, pepperoni, onion, Canadian bacon, and double Italian sausage pizza all by myself."

"Thank you, Reverend, but we really have eaten. Besides, that stuff will kill you."

"All the sooner then to rest in the arms of the Lord," Isaiah said smiling. "And where were you and Lisa planning on spending the night?"

"That's a little open right now. Is there a motel around here?"

"Thirteen miles up the highway. Do you have a car?"

"We were hitchhiking. Our ride dropped us off here. You see. . . ." but Isaiah held up his hand.

"Peter, don't say anything that will embarrass either of us later."

"Here's your pizza, Reverend," Roy called from behind the counter. "I'm closing up now, folks."

"My car's parked outside," the Reverend said, taking Lisa's hand.

"Your car . . . ?"

"You'll stay with me tonight, of course. I have a spare bed for Lisa and you can sleep on the couch."

"I, I don't know how to thank you," I mumbled as I stood and picked up our bag.

"No thanks are necessary. All of us need some help now and again."

The Reverend took Lisa's hand and helped her from her chair. Her sneakers made squishing sounds as she followed along behind him. Without thinking, I reached down and lifted her again into my arms. Lisa was exhausted and as soon as I had retrieved the bag and headed for the door, she laid her head on my shoulder.

Outside, the rain had stopped and I looked up to see a half moon and a handful of stars peeking through a tear in the clouds. The night breeze carried with it the scent of freshly turned earth and the faint tang of pine. Behind us, the glow in Big Peg's window vanished and except for the distant, half-echoing jangle of an electric guitar from the Lone Pine Bar, the town seemed vacant, asleep.

The Reverend led us to his car, a glittering steel heirloom. It was a 1956 Chevrolet Impala, with the classic three-tone paint job, rich blue roof, a white zigzag, lightning bolt shaped band across the middle of the doors, and light blue swath along the bottom for the length of the car.

"Three twenty-seven?" I asked as soon as we were inside.

"You know your cars," the Reverend said warmly. "Yes, it's the original engine, though it's been rebuilt a few times. I bought it used in '64 for nine hundred dollars."

"Powerglide too," I said nodding at the column-mounted automatic transmission lever. "You couldn't buy a '56 like this today for nine thousand dollars."

"How do you know it's a '56?"

"The taillights. The '55s had a square rear quarter with small vertical lights. The '57s had a light at the base of the vertical fin.

The '56s had a '55 kind of light, but bigger with an exposed bulb with the gas tank filler underneath. You can't mistake a '56."

"I wouldn't think you are old enough to remember the fifties."

"They made this car three years before I was born. By the time I got to high school everyone's dream was to get one of these and drop a 396 porcupine valve V-8 into it, add a 4.11 rear end, and a pair of Traction Masters to the rear suspension."

"That's like using Excaliber to trim a hedge," the Reverend said with a grimace.

"We were kids. What did we know?"

The Reverend slowly shook his head in dismay and pulled away from the curb then turned back south down 395. I opened my window a crack and each sound was surprisingly clear. I could hear the hiss of the tires against the damp pavement, the brief crackling snap as the Chevy's wheels encountered small puddles at the edge of the street. When we passed the Lone Pine Bar a burst of noise briefly engulfed us as a silhouette emerged from the doorway in a billow of smoke then turned and marched off into the shadows. The door swung closed and the babble of voices, the call of a fiddle, the echo of a plaintive female refrain, suddenly became muted and then vanished. The Reverend turned to the right, down toward the shore of Goose Lake. Above us the rent in the clouds widened and a thousand stars shone through.

# TWENTY-SIX

It was a small, neat house, set thirty yards back from Stateline Road and less than a mile from the shore of Goose Lake. A stand of birch and Chinese elm stood between the road and the front door but the view west, toward the lake, was unobstructed. Lisa was already asleep in my arms by the time we got there, and I carried her inside. The houses of older people living alone seem to me to fall into two groups: either extremely neat or very messy, the habits of a lifetime accentuated by the passage of the years. Inside the Reverend's home everything was in perfect order.

"Bring her in here," Isaiah said, leading the way to a small bedroom next to the kitchen. He made no attempt to keep his voice down. I suppose that people who have had children know that when kids get really tired nothing short of an earthquake will wake them. The bedroom was spartan, but clean. It contained a single bed covered with a brown-and-white comforter, a dresser, a night table, and a small lamp.

"Does she have clean pajamas?" the Reverend asked me as I laid Lisa on the bed. I realized that I had forgotten to buy her any when we did our shopping at the thrift store.

"No," I said, "I don't think I've got anything dry for her."

"I may have something that will fit her," Isaiah said and slipped out of the room. A moment later I heard a drawer open and close, then he reappeared fumbling with a small cardboard box.

"My grandson Richard's birthday is the week after next. His mother told me that he wanted a pair of X-Men pajamas. I special-ordered these from a store in Klamath Falls." The Reverend held the bold orange-and-yellow pajama tops over Lisa's chest.

"They look like they ought to fit," he said after a moment. "We'd better get her out of those wet clothes." He bent down, unzipped Lisa's jacket and rolled her first to one side then the other as he pulled her limp arms from the sleeves. After tossing the wind-breaker to the floor he gently lifted her into a sitting position.

"Hold her while I get her shirt off," he ordered.

I placed my hands at Lisa's sides, just above her hips and no-ticed that a ring four or five inches wide around the bottom her T-shirt was soaked. The Reverend stared at me and I realized that, of course, I had to hold her from inside her shirt so that he could remove it. Her skin was clammy and damp and the sodden fabric clung to the backs of my hands.

As the Reverend pulled the shirt up Lisa began to squirm and she twisted her arms against the movement of the cloth. I held her hips more tightly and Isaiah increased the tension until, finally, the shirt slipped over her head and pulled free. The Reverend had brought a towel along with the pajamas and carefully dried Lisa's torso and neck before slipping the boldly illustrated top over her head. He deftly maneuvered first her right arm and then her left into the sleeves. As soon as he finished, Lisa hugged her arms to her chest and the Reverend gently laid her back down on the bed. The only light in the room came from the small lamp on the night table next to the bed, and in its pale yellow glow Lisa looked even smaller and more fragile than usual. Isaiah undid the button and the zipper on her jeans.

"Lift her up," he said softly.

I grasped Lisa beneath each arm but when the Reverend began to pull down her pants Lisa started to squirm and make little noises deep in her throat. She crossed her legs and when the Reverend tried to loosen them she muttered, "No, no, no," in a small, sleep-filled voice.

"We've got to get her out of these wet clothes," Isaiah said. "Tell her to relax, that everything's all right." Lisa had twisted her arms across her chest and over my hands. Fighting the Reverend's efforts she tried to bring her knees up to her chest and to curl into a ball. In her sleep she fought against the liberties that she had been forced to endure while awake. How many times before had this happened? How many times had she been told to calm down, to do as she was instructed and take off her clothes? Now, if I repeated those orders, my voice would merge with those of all the other men in her nightmares. I could not have that. I would not allow her to think of me, to remember me, that way.

"Let her go," I told him.

"We've got to get her into dry clothes. Don't worry, I've done this a hundred times when my boys were small."

"No, let her go!"

The Reverend's head snapped up at the tone in my voice, and, after a moment's pause, he released Lisa's legs.

"Lisa, wake up!" I said loudly while shaking her shoulders. She mumbled something and twisted away from my grasp. "Lisa, it's time to wake up," I said again, more harshly. "Lisa—wake up!" She squirmed once more, then her eyes flew open. "Lisa, it's Peter," I said and let go of her shoulders. "Are you awake?" For a moment longer her eyes seemed wild and confused and I looked into the face of a terrified child, then the emotion fled, most of it, and she assumed the stoic expression that I had seen so many times before.

"What's wrong, Peter?" she asked quietly. "Do we have to leave now?"

"No, Lisa, everything's fine, except your clothes are wet and you have to change before you can go to sleep. The Reverend has a pair of clean pajamas for you and you need to put them on." I picked up the pajama bottoms and handed them to her. "I'll be right outside that door, just down the hallway. There's a bathroom next to your room. Do you need anything?"

"No, I'm fine." My little soldier had returned.

"Okay, remember, I'm right down the hallway if you need me. Good night, Lisa."

"Good night, Peter," she said quietly.

I stared at her for a moment and noticed again how small she seemed, and how hard she was trying to be strong. I took a step back, then reached down and hugged her tightly. "Good night, sweetheart," I whispered into her ear, then stood, turned off the light, and led the Reverend from the room.

"I'll get you a blanket," Isaiah said evenly when we returned to the living room. A few moments later he came back with a blanket and a pillow which he handed to me without comment. I sat down, removed my shoes, changed my T-shirt, and put on the other pair of pants that the sports bag had kept surprisingly dry. When I looked up a minute later the Reverend was still standing there, staring at me. I raised my arms in front of me, palms open, as if to ask, "What do you want me to say?" Isaiah walked over and sat next to me on the couch.

"What has happened to that child?" he asked in a low, even voice.

"I haven't asked her. Things, I'm afraid, that neither you nor I want to know."

"She's not your daughter." It wasn't a question.

"I have no children."

"Your niece? Stepchild?"

"No."

"What are you doing with a her? What's your relationship with her?"

"What was the Samaritan's relationship with the traveler?"

The Reverend stared at me oddly, trying, I think, to determine if I was mocking him. The fact was that all my strength had drained away and I felt like a hollow shell. I had no more energy for explanations, justifications. My arms dragged at my shoulders, my feet felt welded to the floor. My mind seemed to be in danger of detaching itself from my head and floating around the room, and strange thoughts entered my brain in peculiar flickers and bursts.

"Where did you find her?"

"In harm's way."

"And you're taking her home? To her parents?"

"I hope so."

"Then what?"

"Then they will kill the fatted calf," I said somehow pleased with the Biblical allusion.

"And after that?"

"And after that I will go home, and try to forget all of this."

"No, you won't," the Reverend said after a long hard look. I stared back at him. Won't go home? I wondered, or won't forget? He seemed to read my thoughts.

"You will forget nothing."

"I'm so tired, Reverend, that right now I feel like I barely remember my own name. In a month, this will seem like a dream to all of us." Isaiah shook his head.

"Get some sleep, Peter. Services are at nine-thirty tomorrow morning."

"Reverend, I appreciate everything you're doing for us, but . . ."

"How long has it been since you've been in the House of the Lord?"

I shook my head slightly. "Longer than I can remember."

"Then you're past due. It will do you good in ways beyond measure."

"Reverend, I've . . ."

"We will go to services at nine-thirty. Then we will have something to eat, and then I will take you and the child wherever you need to go."

"You don't know what you're getting yourself into," I said wearily, thinking of Jimmie, still alive out there somewhere.

"Have I ever? But that has not turned me aside from the Lord's work before and it will not do so now. If all those years in South Los Angeles did not turn my feet from the Path, I will not abandon it today. Go to sleep, Peter. I'll wake you at eight-thirty."

The Reverend smiled at me, then flicked off the light. I lay down and pulled the blanket over my shoulders. A pale bar of moonlight striped the edge of the floor and the bottom of the wall across from the couch. The only sounds were the hum of the refrigerator motor and the vagrant creaks and snaps of Isaiah's little frame house responding to the gusts of the night wind. I watched the bar of moonlight flicker once with the movement of a hanging branch then I fell suddenly and dreamlessly asleep.

Hours later I awakened disoriented and confused, lost in both time and space. I could see nothing beyond vague dark shapes, so faint that if I had been told that I was blind, I might have believed it. I twisted onto my back, then pulled myself to a sitting position. Slowly, I remembered that I was in the Reverend's living room, that it was early Sunday morning. I shook my head as if to clear it of the fog of sleep. The tiny light in my watch glowed at the press of a button but I could not make out the numbers. Something had wakened me and I strained my ears to catch a stray sound, a hint as to what it was that had dragged me back to wakefulness. Nothing.

I got up and walked toward the guest room and listened for the sound of Lisa's breathing. Standing in the doorway I could barely make out her form beneath the blanket. She was utterly silent. Had something happened to her? Had she stopped breathing?

"Lisa?" I whispered. "Lisa, are you asleep?"

For a heartbeat there was no response, then in a soft, breathy whisper, I heard her call, "Peter?"

I sat down next to her on the edge of the bed and she slid toward me and nestled her head against my waist.

"Are you sick? Are you catching a cold?"

"No."

"What's wrong? What woke you up?"

She was quiet for a moment then said, "I had a bad dream," in the voice that children use when they are scared but are trying not to show their fear.

"Do you want to tell me about it?"

Lisa cuddled closer to me and instinctively I took her hand. My presence seemed to make her feel safe, although I had done nothing but drag her from one dangerous situation into another, failing at each turn to do what I had promised. She grasped my fingers tightly and began to speak.

"I was home and they came for me again. It was that man, Eric, he ran right toward me. I shouted that we had to get away but Carla and Susan just laughed and went on playing. I tried to run but I couldn't get away no matter how fast I ran, I couldn't go anywhere. Then Eric got me and when he caught me I wasn't wearing any clothes and then Ken was standing there and I was in Ken's house and he didn't have any clothes on and—"

"It's all right, Lisa," I interrupted, afraid of what she was about to tell me. I didn't want her to explain what had been done to her, to relive her molestation. I'm no therapist. Maybe it's cathartic to talk about intensively painful events. Maybe it's not. There would be plenty of time later for professionals to answer that question. Not now.

"Those dreams are really scary, aren't they?"

"Peter, I'm afraid. What if it happens again?"

"What if what happens again?"

"What if that man, Jimmie, finds us and takes me back to Ken? I never want to go back to Ken!"

The room was so dark that I could not see Lisa's lips move as she spoke, could not see the tears glistening at the corners of her eyes, but I knew they were there. While she was only a pale shape under the blankets, the warmth of her tiny body clutching me, the pressure of her fingers squeezing my hand, the agonized words floating out of the darkness, made her, in some strange way, more of a real person to me than when she had been sitting primly in my car that morning as we drove to Porterville.

I don't have any children. Janet and I . . . Except for occasional contacts with a couple of nieces and nephews or the children of my friends, I am a man with no great familiarity with children.

I had heard people talk about their child's personality, sometimes their baby's personality and I could never see it. Children always seemed to me to be two-dimensional paintings in one or two primary colors. In that instant, in the darkness, I realized that until now Lisa had been to me more of a child in trouble, something broken to be fixed, than a real person about whom I had come to care more than I had thought was possible. I wasn't sure what I should say to comfort her, but I knew that I must say something.

"Lots of people think that dreams mean something, Lisa, but you know what? They don't. They don't mean anything at all."

"Then why do we have them?"

"No one knows for sure. Would you like to know what I think?"

"What?"

"I think that we store up all the bad stuff, all the things that frighten us and make us unhappy and we need a way to get rid of it, to throw it away. You know how we take all the empty ice cream cartons and carrot tops and chicken bones and put them into the garbage can, and we put the can out by the street and then they come and take it away and we don't have to keep it around anymore? I think that's what our dreams are. They're like putting the trash can out for the garbagemen to take away. Dreams are how we throw away all the bad stuff in our lives so that it won't hurt us anymore."

"You mean I'll never dream about Ken again?"

"Sometimes it takes a lot of dreams until the bad stuff is all gone, like when you have so much trash that it won't all fit into one bag. But you shouldn't be afraid of bad dreams, Lisa. When you have a bad dream, just remember that now more of the bad stuff is gone and it won't be in your head to hurt you anymore. When you have a bad dream, wake up and smile and be happy because you know that the garbageman has come and taken all that stuff away."

Was that the truth? I don't know. At that instant I was only interested in calming her fears, in settling her heart.

"Do you ever have bad dreams, Peter?" she asked. I thought I could hear a little less fear in her voice.

"Sure, everyone has them."

"Do they scare you?"

"Well, when I'm having the dream I may be upset, but as soon as I wake up, then I know everything is all right."

"Is there a way to know it's a dream when you're still asleep, so you won't be scared anymore?"

"Yes, but when you're asleep, you can't remember how to do it. Isn't that strange? When you wake up you see how silly the dream was, how things could never happen that way, and you think, 'Oh, that's obvious. It was only a dream,' but when you're asleep, you never seem to notice."

"How do I know I'm not dreaming now?"

Descartes had nothing on Lisa Taylor.

"Well, are you running and not going anywhere?"

"No."

"Are you dressed?"

"Yes."

"Are you in school and supposed to take a test and you can't remember anything you learned?"

"No."

"Then I'm pretty sure you're awake," I said laughing and I squeezed her hand.

"You're fooling me," Lisa said and giggled.

"Yes, I'm fooling you. You always know when you're really awake. You just do."

For just a moment I remembered my own recurring nightmare. I was thirteen and I was going to my Little League game and my dad was sitting in his chair. And I thought that was strange, because I remembered that he was dead, that a tanker truck had crunched his Corolla on the freeway, but there he was.

"Come on, Dad," I would say. "Throw a few pitches with me before the game." And dad would look up at me with this strange expression on his face and say, "No son, I can't. I've got to go back in a few minutes. I don't have much time left. I just want to sit here. Stay and talk with me."

And I would say, "I can't, Dad, I've got to practice. I'll see you after the game," and I would leave him there. But about two minutes later I would come back to the living room and the game would be over and he would be gone and I would think, "Of course, Dad's not here. He's dead. They killed him. And I forgot to say good-bye, and I forgot to tell him that I loved him." Then I would wake up and realize that it had been The Dream, again.

"Are you ready to go back to sleep now, Lisa?"

"Uh-huh," she said softly, then let go of my hand and put both her arms around me. I tried to gently disengage her but she would not release her grip.

"Lisa, let go. I've got to get some sleep too."

"Don't go, Peter, please. Please don't go."

I made one more attempt to free myself, but as soon as I removed her hand from one part of my T-shirt, she grabbed the fabric somewhere else. Finally, I slid down the bed and lay on my side on top of the covers next to her and Lisa snuggled her head between my shoulder and my chin. I draped my left arm over her blanket-wrapped form. It would only be a few more hours until dawn. When the darkness began to fade from the room, her night terrors would go with it and I would be able to return to the couch.

"Good night, Lisa," I whispered.

"Good night, Peter," she said, then after a moment's pause added, "I love you, Peter."

Those were words I had always had trouble saying to anyone, even to Janet. Emotions like that were discomforting, dangerous. I opened my eyes and stared into the darkness. A branch tapped at the roof. Lisa's face glowed with heat as it pressed into my chest. I remembered my nightmare.

"I love you, Lisa," I whispered as I closed my eyes but she was already asleep.

# TWENTY-SEVEN

The trail had gone cold. Larkin McCray was not to be found. He never returned home. Carlos wondered if his hitchhiker had killed him and then abandoned the truck somewhere. Had he decided to take the man and the little girl somewhere (Oakdale?) himself? A sweep along the route from Adin to the Oregon border by the Modoc County Sheriff's office had not spotted McCray's pickup.

Was it really Lisa Taylor? Lisa was a common enough name. Carlos didn't want to allow himself to believe it was her, but he did anyway. The Alturas PD would continue to check McCray's house. The Sheriff was watching the highway for him. If McCray's truck was spotted it would be stopped. The child would be too small to see clearly through a car window and Carlos had only the most general description of her companion. In the dark and the rain, nothing short of a roadblock had a chance of finding them, and they didn't have the resources, or the justification, yet, for measures like that.

Carlos didn't know what else to do, so he did the only thing possible. He waited for the phone to ring with the news that Larkin McCray had been found.

# TWENTY-EIGHT

Stiff and sore, I awoke lying atop the blankets on Lisa's bed, my body curled protectively around her. Daylight had begun to stream through the trees outside the window. According to my watch it was a little after seven. I slipped off the bed as quietly as I could and retrieved my bag from the living room. The bathroom next to Lisa's room had a shower and clean towels. I even found a half-full bottle of shampoo on the shelf next to the soap.

I caught a glimpse of my body in the mirror on the back of the door—blue-black bruises marked my stomach and chest where I had slammed against the seat and shoulder belts; my wrists and ankles bore red welts from Jimmie's nylon line; my chest and thighs carried a patchwork of seemingly random cuts, scrapes, and bruises suffered in my capture, interrogation, and the fight with Eric and Jimmie. The evidence of the blows to my head was covered by my hair, but I could still feel a knot where Jimmie's boot had hurled me into unconsciousness. I was sure that if I could see my back, I would find a livid bruise where Eric had kicked me.

I ran my hands over each injury feeling for damage beyond bruises and welts but found nothing that I could classify as more than superficial. All in all, I was in amazingly good shape. A few minutes later, after a shower and a shave, I was ready, again, to begin our journey. But first there was church.

The Reverend was up and dressed in a suit and tie when I returned to the living room. He stared at me for a long moment, appraising my T-shirt and jeans.

"Do I have something on backwards?" I asked as his stare continued.

"No, I was just guessing your size. You're what, five eleven, six feet? About one hundred and eighty pounds?"

"One eighty-five. Why?"

"I have another suit. Do you think you could wear a 42 regular?"

"Reverend, I appreciate the offer, but . . ."

"Sunday service deserves a Sunday suit. I'll get it." Isaiah disappeared for a moment and when he returned he was carrying a dark gray suitcoat that he held out to me. I didn't want to take anything more from the old man, but there was apparently no avoiding his generosity. Cautiously, I slipped on the coat. It was a little short in the sleeves and tight in the shoulders, but not terribly so. The Reverend was about my height but thinner and more wiry. While it didn't fit perfectly, it would pass.

"Excellent," Isaiah said, smiling. "Come into my room and let's see if the shirt fits as well."

A few minutes later I was dressed in the Reverend's charcoal gray suit, white shirt, black tie with little gray and red ovals, and his second pair of black oxford shoes which were half a size too small but which I could stand to wear for a couple of hours.

"Now if I only had a dress for the little girl," Isaiah mused as he appraised my newly attired form.

"I think she'll be fine the way she is," I told him.

By now Lisa was up and in the bathroom. I knocked on the door.

"Lisa, be sure and take a shower. Use the shampoo and wash your hair. Can you work the knobs okay?"

"Let me try," she called. I heard the shower start and then the sound of the spray varying in pitch.

"I can do it," she answered through the door a moment later.

"Okay. Then get washed up and dressed. The bag with your clothes in it is in your room. If you need anything else, call me."

"What would you like for breakfast?" Isaiah asked when I joined him in the kitchen.

"You don't have to. . . ."

"We can't go to church on an empty stomach!" he insisted.

When Lisa came out a few minutes later the Reverend was busy clattering pans and pulling plates and bowls from cupboards.

"I've run many a soup kitchen in my day," he said when he caught me staring. "Cooking is mostly a matter of efficient organization and having the right materials," he lectured as he depressed the toaster with one hand and pulled silverware from a drawer with the other. By nine-fifteen we had finished breakfast, had stacked the washed dishes in the drainboard, and were on our way to the church in the Reverend's classic Chevrolet.

The church was less than a mile away, on the eastern side of Main Street and a block down Pintail Lane. It was a simple structure, mostly one large room with a peaked roof but no steeple. A large wooden cross, highly polished and stained a rich mahogany brown was bolted to the front of the building above the double front doors. Located on a one-lane blacktop road the church sat amidst a neighborhood of small clapboard residences.

A few hundred yards away the town ended at the base of the cliff that formed the eastern side of the valley. To the left of the building toward the bottom of the hill was a gravel parking area that this morning held perhaps twenty cars. A sign on the front lawn proclaimed this to be the "United Christian Church, Everyone Welcome—Services at 9:30, Sunday School at 11:00."

It was a glorious morning. The only evidence of last night's storm was the puddles that filled the dips and hollows in the parking area and overflowed the shallow ruts next to the street. In the crystal clear air the mountain ridge fifteen or twenty miles to the west appeared almost at my feet. On the wind I could smell pine and wet earth and the faint odor of decaying leaves.

A few families, mostly those with young children, had already gathered in the flat area just outside the church's front door. The adults talked quietly among themselves while the children pulled at their collars and chased each other and bent to examine a particularly interesting leaf or stone. The Reverend led us up the walk. As we approached the front doors one or two more cars pulled into the lot. Almost all of the churchgoers seemed to be middle class or working class, the men dressed in Penny's sport coats and K-Mart ties. Burly shoulders and callused hands seemed to predominate. Most of the women wore dresses, generally heavy knit or woolen fabrics in dark colors. All were white except for two black couples at the entrance and they turned toward us as we reached the top of the walk.

"Peter, these are my boys, Matthew and Mark," Isaiah said proudly. "And, of course, Ellen and Genine," he added quickly, nodding to his sons' wives. "Everyone, this is Peter and Lisa," the Reverend said completing his introductions. Matthew and Mark seemed to be about my age, though possibly a little younger. Their familial resemblance was clear. Each had his father's wiry stature and I could see portions of his face in theirs, the wide-set eyes, the square chin. And they resembled each other. Not identical twins, but perhaps fraternal, or, if not twins then certainly born not more than a year apart.

Both of them studied me closely. Clearly they had recognized that I was wearing their father's suit. I suspected that this was not the first time that dad had brought some down-on-his-luck stray to Sunday services. I felt as if I could read his sons' minds: "Oh boy, Dad's found another one. How much of his social security check is this guy going to make off with?"

"I'm pleased to meet you," I said formally as we each exchanged handshakes. "Your father was kind enough to lend me his suit for the service."

"Dad's like that," Mark said coolly.

"Dad believes in helping people," Matthew added.

"He calls it casting bread upon the waters," Mark concluded. Twins, I thought, definitely. The conversation died at that point until Ellen noticed Lisa peeking out from behind me.

"Hello, Lisa," she said warmly and reached out to take her hand. Lisa gravely extended it for a formal little shake. "How old are you, dear?"

"I'm eight," she said, glancing at me briefly as if to ask, "That's right, isn't it?"

"I have a little boy who's just about your age. Richard will be eight next month."

"Where is he?" Lisa asked looking around.

"He's over there around the corner with his cousin, Robert." A family that likes alliteration, I said to myself. At that point the conversation ground to an awkward halt until Lisa looked pointedly at Ellen and said, "That's a pretty dress."

"Thank you, Lisa. This is my Sunday dress."

"I have a Sunday dress, but it's not here. I don't have any dresses here."

"Where is your Sunday dress, dear?"

"It's home. That's where Peter is taking me. He's taking me home, aren't you, Peter?"

"Right after church. We'll be there real soon," I said looking down and caressing her hair. When I looked up all of them were staring at me: the women's faces showed concern, their husbands', suspicion. "Who is this guy?" I felt them asking themselves. "What is he doing with that little girl? Is she a runaway? Is this some sort of confidence scheme?"

"It's a long story," I said, looking directly at Matthew in answer to the unasked questions.

"Don't you worry, Lisa. We'll have you home by dinner," the Reverend assured her.

"What are you talking about, Dad?" Matthew asked sharply.

"I'm driving Peter and Lisa home right after services."

"I don't think that's a good idea, Dad," Mark said.

"Dad, I don't think you should be taking any long trips," Matthew added.

"It's not that far. Besides, we need to get Lisa home."

"She'll get home, Dad," Mark responded. "You're always saying that the Lord will provide."

"The Lord has provided. He has provided me! This is His work and I am His instrument." Matthew and Mark looked at each other then Matthew turned back to his father.

"Where does the little girl live?"

"Oregon. Oakdale, Oregon, isn't that right, Peter?"

"Yes, Lisa remembers the address."

"Oregon? Dad that car of yours is forty years old. What if it breaks down?"

"My car is in perfect condition. It's a classic, isn't it Peter?" The boys' heads swiveled to regard me with a stony gaze.

"Yes, Reverend, it's a classic car. But, maybe your sons are right. There's probably a bus. . . ."

"Nonsense, I'm fine. My boys are just too careful. Comes from running those computers of theirs all day. I just have a little angina."

Suddenly Mark looked sharply at his father. "Dad, are you having chest pains?"

"No, of course not."

"You've stayed on your diet, haven't you, Dad?" Matthew asked. "You haven't been eating those pepperoni pizzas again, have you?"

"Why son, what a thing to say! Now, I didn't bring you boys up to be late for services. Let's go inside before Reverend Norton starts without us." Isaiah grasped Lisa's hand and led her to the door. Matthew and Mark paused a moment but their wives took their arms and steered them up the steps to where their sons had been playing and they all went inside. I followed meekly behind.

The little church was almost filled. Counting the children there were probably seventy or eighty people already seated. One pew in the middle on the left side was empty, apparently the family's normal seats. Isaiah let his sons take the empty bench and found seats for himself, Lisa, and me in the second to the last row on the right. The service began almost as soon as we sat down.

As a former altar boy I was not very familiar with Protestant services. Janet wasn't Catholic, but by the time we were married I was no longer religious either. I think that the last time I was in a church was our wedding day. From time to time after starting Orayis I had toyed with the idea that, like weddings, divorces should also be memorialized by a religious ceremony. You could invite the same people who had come to your wedding. The same minister could perform a little service formally dissolving the bonds that previously had joined you together. Each of you could then get on with your lives, after a symbolic, yet cathartic event, which would put a final period to your relationship, something that the piece of paper entitled Decree of Dissolution of Marriage which most people receive in the mail from their lawyer, together with his bill, does not accomplish.

The service was more or less what I expected: a few hymns, some announcements of church and local events, and a sermon. The topic was "Failure."

Failure is a normal part of life, the Reverend Norton contended. Everyone, at one time or another, fails. We fail as parents, as children, as spouses, as friends, as employees, and as Christians. It is because failure is not only common but inevitable that forgiveness is so important, he said.

The sin, he contended, is not failure, but failing to regret failure; not in making a mistake, but rather in not trying to avoid making a mistake. As Christians, he said, we must forgive failure. What is infinitely more difficult, he admitted, is to forgive a person who does not care whether they fail or not. It is the person who must be forgiven, not the act they committed. And to be forgiven, the individual must have sincere remorse.

I thought it was a very good sermon, but I was not sure that I was able to agree with it. If Ken tried to stop molesting little girls, but was too weak to do so, could I forgive him and simply say, "That's all right, Ken, better luck next time?" If a gang member who had already killed two or three people is released from the Youth Authority, and in spite of his desire to "go straight" gets mixed up with his old friends and kills a mother and her two children in a drive-by shooting, could I, should I, say, "I forgive you. After all, everyone makes mistakes"? No, I didn't think so, the Reverend Norton notwithstanding.

The service was over around ten-thirty and the minister greeted us as we left the church. Isaiah seemed to be very popular with the congregation and several people went out of their way to talk to him, to shake his hand, and inquire about his health. He politely introduced Lisa and myself to everyone, identifying us as his "new friends."

"Dad, we'll see you over at the house," Matthew said as the parking lot began to empty.

"I've made your favorite, Dad," Ellen told him.

"I'm sorry, Ellen. You know how I love your cooking, but we're taking Lisa home as soon as we change clothes."

Matthew and Mark looked at each other. "Here we go again," their expressions seemed to say. Mark let out a long sigh.

"We'll buy them a bus ticket, Dad. A hundred dollars should be enough, I guess," he said, and both brothers reached for their wallets.

"Have I raised you boys to be so rude! Every man deserves to be treated with dignity. This is an educated man. He's not asking for a handout. I offered to help him because I know the Lord's work when I see it."

"But . . ."

"Matthew, you know as well as I do that there's no bus through here today."

"We'll get them a room at the motel. Dad, don't look at me that way. It's only Christian charity."

"And is that bus going to take this little girl right to her door? It is not. The bus never leaves I-395. She needs to go up toward Silver Lake. No, no, no. The bus is a bad idea." Matthew and Mark stared at their father, their gaze a mixture of love and frustration. The Reverend looked back at them sternly, then, suddenly, broke into a smile. "Boys, I know you mean well, but I know the Path and the Way. I've heard the Word and I can never turn my back on it."

"But, Dad, that's pretty desolate country up there. If something should happen to you . . ."

"Matthew, if something happens to me today, then rejoice for me, for what better fate could I have than to go to His arms while doing His work."

The remaining members of the congregation paused to listen to Isaiah speak. His voice had increased in depth and his words were imbued with a driving resonance. I almost felt a "Praise the Lord" coming on. The man could preach! If he wanted to take over this church, he could have had the Reverend Norton parking the cars by the Sunday after next. And for an instant, he seemed about to walk that road, about to give a sermon right there at the church's front door. For just a moment his back straightened, his hands were raised, his eyes almost glowed, then he realized what he was doing and stopped, consciously. It was like watching the air leak from a balloon. A moment later he was just another old man in a dark blue suit.

I was never much for Religion with a capital "R"; I never had much respect for preachers. I thought they were mostly frauds and conmen, but not Isaiah Williams. No, not him. He was the genuine article.

He believed every word he said and he got his strength from the fact that he was absolutely certain that he was speaking the Truth. God and Right were real, concrete concepts to him. He believed in them with the same certainty that a physicist believes in $E = mc^2$. God and the Word were not a theory or a question or an issue to the Reverend. They were as real to him as the earth and the sky.

As far as he was concerned he had an obligation, a duty, to do Christ's work, a duty that was no less and little different than the dedication an Army officer with twenty years service would have to his men at the height of a battle. Isaiah would no more turn his back on what he believed was the Lord's work than that officer would throw down his gun and run away in the midst of an enemy attack. Such a thing was unthinkable. Isaiah's sons knew this. And it scared them more than they could tell him.

For a moment the boys looked at me, hoping that I would turn down the ride in favor of the money. But I could not do that. I had my own obligation, to Lisa. And besides, strictly speaking, the Reverend was not helping me; he was helping her. His duty was as clear to him as mine was to me. The other parishioners began to drift away again and in a moment we were alone in front of the church.

"Let's hear no more about this, please," Isaiah said in a concilia-tory tone. "Ellen, do you suppose that I could impose upon your hospitality for dinner instead of lunch?"

"Dad! You have to ask? Of course. Genine, you and Mark and Robert come too."

"I'll bring my scalloped potatoes and a blueberry pie," Genine volunteered.

"My favorite!" Isaiah said. "Genine, you are an angel. It's settled then, I will see you all for dinner. Boys?"

"Yes, Dad," Matthew said softly. "But, Dad, please drive care-fully. You know that car of yours doesn't have power brakes."

"And call me if you have any problems," Mark pleaded. "I'll be home all afternoon. I'll come and get you if it breaks down. You have my unlisted number with you?"

"If I have any problems, Mark, I will call you, and, yes, I have your number written on a card in my wallet, though why you think I can't remember a phone number that I've called a hundred times, I don't know. You boys seem to forget that I preached every Sunday for almost forty years and never once had to read my sermon. I'm not senile, you know."

"Now, Dad, when you're dealing with data, you always need a backup," Mark said firmly.

"Can't be too careful," Matthew added solemnly. What was it the Reverend had said? Something about his sons and their computers? Programmers? Designers? Yes, I could believe that. Lisa and I held back while everyone hugged Isaiah and then made their good-byes. Finally, we were alone and the Reverend led us back to his car.

"My boys worry too much," he told me as he started the engine. "They should have seen me in the Tenderloin with the crack dealers and the ladies who had lost their way." He paused and looked up at the deep blue sky, the pines lining the road, the mountains far to the east dusted with snow. "Such a wonderful day, praise the Lord," he said, momentarily filling the car with his melodic voice.

We returned to the Reverend's house and changed our clothes. I was glad to get out of his suit and shoes. At about eleven-fifteen we all trooped outside and drove back to the highway then north across the state line. The Reverend drove carefully, never going faster than 45-mph. In spite of his assurances to his sons of the car's roadworthiness, we all knew that it didn't have headrests or shoulder belts or air bags or side impact beams or crumple zones. While it did have power steering, the mechanicals were recirculating ball and socket, not the more accurate rack-and-pinion design. Combined with its manual brakes and a solid steel dashboard, it was not a "safe" car by current standards.

The road skirted the eastern shore of Goose Lake which extended almost all the way to Lakeview. To the right most of the trees disappeared from the slopes which were predominately brown and olive green under a cover of manzanita and sagebrush,

MY REAL NAME IS LISA

clump grass and junipers. Occasionally we passed small farms, all with barns full of hay. The idea that Eddie was going to truck hay into this area was on a par with carrying ice to Alaska.

Contrary to popular belief, all of Oregon is not drowned with rain and filled with trees. South-central Oregon, in fact, has extensive deserts and vast stretches of sand and sagebrush. The Cascade Mountains shelter huge areas from precipitation and the country south of U.S. 20 and west of 395 would serve well as the backdrop for any of John Wayne's westerns with locations like Alkali Dry Lake, Picture Rock, Fort Rock, and Fossil Lake. Goose Lake itself was devoid of boats, piers, water-skiers, fishermen, and fish. Only a peculiar variety of brine shrimp were able to survive in its salty waters. It was, in fact, the vast numbers of these shrimp that attracted the flocks of Canadian geese from which the lake derived its name.

It was a bit before noon when we pulled into Lakeview, "The Tallest Town In Oregon" a sign near the city limits proclaimed. It had a population in excess of 3,000 and was one of the biggest towns for a hundred miles.

Lakeview was situated at the head of a 25-mile-long valley with mountains both to the east and the west. About four miles south of town we finally passed the end of Goose Lake. It was spectacular country and on that bright, crisp late winter morning I was enjoying myself, my concerns over Eddie's wrecked truck and the fact that Jimmie was still on the loose receding now from my mind.

Just south of Lakeview Isaiah pulled into an ARCO station to fill up the tank and I got out to stretch my legs. There was little traffic on 395 and only one other car was near the pumps, a well-used '83 Pontiac Bonneville. Gray primer discolored its passenger door; the rear bumper was dented left of the center in a crash that also appeared to have damaged the left rear taillight which was bent out of true. The shattered plastic reflector had been replaced by a piece of red cellophane fastened with several strips of duct tape.

A thin, dark-haired man of twenty-five or so leaned against the front driver's fender and puffed on a cigarette. In contrast to his heavily oiled black hair, his skin was a pallid, marmoreal white.

"What kind a jerk would be smoking a cigarette next to working gas pumps?" I thought to myself. But it wasn't my job to tell him to stop.

"Billy Joe," a woman called from within the car, "I need a dollar for a can of pop."

"We don't need no damn pop," the man shouted back.

"Billy, Elaine is thirsty."

"So she's thirsty. I'd like to get me a nice steak right now, but you don't see me eatin' one, do ya?" Billy Joe took a deep drag on his cigarette and exhaled a cloud of blue-gray smoke. A moment later the passenger door opened with a rusty creak and a thin-faced brunette stepped out. She was in her early to mid-twenties with wide hips and heavy legs.

"Come on, honey," she called into the car. "Bring your brother with you." A moment later a little girl a year or so younger than Lisa emerged from the rear passenger door. In her arms she held a baby dressed in a yellow knit suit, maybe, six or eight months old.

"Where you think you're goin', missy," Billy Joe asked the child. His voice had a dangerous edge.

"No place, Daddy," she said timidly.

"This would be a good time to mind my own business and go to the men's room," I said to myself. I leaned into the Chevy and asked Lisa to come with me. Once she was inside the ladies' room I ordered her not to come out until I knocked on her door. With Jimmie still on the loose I was determined that she would not be out of my sight for one extra second until I could put her into her parents' arms. With her safely behind the locked door I used the men's facilities.

A few minutes later I knocked on her door and we walked along the side of the station, back toward the car. We had barely turned the corner from the restrooms when I heard Billy Joe's raised voice.

"You mind your own damn business, Boy, or you'll regret it!" He was talking to the Reverend. Lisa and I began to run and I heard Isaiah say, "Son, please put your anger aside. Wrath is the tool of the Devil." When we got closer I saw that the woman was hunched over the Pontiac's hood, crying into her hands. The little girl, Elaine, still held the baby and both huddled behind their mother's skirt.

"Reverend, what's going on?" I asked as soon as I got Lisa into the back seat and her door closed and locked.

"This old nigger your friend?" Billy Joe called. "You better teach him to stay out of other people's business if he knows what's good for him." Isaiah turned to me.

"The lady needed money for diapers and a soft drink. They argued and he hit her. We all fall prey to the Devil from time to time. I only want to help them." I looked again at the woman and saw a few drops of blood seep from between the ring and pinkie fingers on her right hand then trickle down to form a small scarlet puddle on the hood of the car.

"Reverend, it's okay. Let's just get back in the car. I don't think he's going to hit her again."

"Maybe I will and maybe I won't. She's my wife and what's between us is no business of yours." I put my hand on the Reverend's shoulder and gently pulled him a few feet back toward the Chevy.

"Sally, you stop your whimperin'," Billy Joe shouted suddenly. "Get yourself back in the car. We're gettin' out of here."

In my days in business I had employed, off and on, over a thousand people. From time to time I ran into men like Billy Joe: lazy, stupid, and mean—men who figured that all their problems were someone else's fault and who were always looking for that person so that they could make him pay.

The Billy Joes of the world were always the third or fourth guy in the lynch mob, men without even the leadership ability to take command of rabble. Guys like him loved being the center of attention, loved power. They terrorized their wives, their neighbors, their girlfriends, their kids.

Billy Joe was in his glory now, trying to give orders to the Reverend, pushing his wife around, causing a commotion with himself at its center. In a moment he'd be slapping his daughter and screaming at the gas station attendant. The best thing we could do would be to get away from him before he worked himself up to something more serious than bloodying his wife's nose.

"Billy Joe," Sally sniffled as she wiped her nose on a tissue, "what about little Tommy? We need to change his diaper."

"Jeez, do I have to tell you everything! Get one out of the trunk and let's get out of here."

"They're all gone, Billy Joe, remember?"

"You stupid bitch! Can't you do anything right?"

"Billy Joe, I told you back at. . . ."

"Just shut up, shut up! You get yourself into that store over there and get some."

"I need some money," she said in a frightened tone.

"I gave you twenty dollars yesterday. What the hell'd you do with it?"

"We had that pizza, last night, remember, and you wanted another pitcher of beer and . . ."

"You blamin' this on me? You throw our money away, you worthless bitch, and you blame it on me?"

"No, Billy Joe, I'm not blamin' it on you. It's just that I don't have any more money and . . ."

"Then I guess that you won't be buyin' any diapers or soda pop, will ya? You can just sit in the back with the baby and enjoy how he smells. Then maybe you'll be more careful with my hard-earned money the next time I give you any, if I decide to give you any."

"But Billy Joe . . ."

"Don't you talk back to me, bitch."

During this argument I had managed to pull Isaiah back to the passenger side of the Chevrolet. "Reverend," I said softly, "let's let them settle their own problems. We should get out of here while we can."

"The boy is troubled," Isaiah said.

"The boy *is* trouble, Reverend. I've paid for the gas. Now is the time for us to leave." Isaiah turned and looked once more at Billy Joe then nodded to me and walked forward around the front of the car and back to the driver's door. Lisa was safely in the back seat and I opened the passenger door and started to get in.

The Reverend reached the front of his car and began to walk through the gap between the Chevy's headlights and the Pontiac's rear bumper when he stopped, took his wallet from his pocket, extracted a ten-dollar bill and walked over to the passenger side of the Pontiac where Sally still stood whimpering and blowing her bloody nose.

"For diapers, for the baby," he said, handing her the money. Damn! He might as well have spit in Billy Joe's face and called him a trailerpark white-trash redneck. Here Billy Joe was feeling big and important and tough and in command, telling people what to do, putting his woman in her place, and then some guy, some old guy, some old black guy, gives his wife money for Billy's baby, money that Billy Joe himself doesn't have to give to her.

I started to get out of the car but I was too late.

"You stay away from her, Nigger!" Billy Joe shouted then ran around the front of the Pontiac toward Isaiah. "You keep your filthy nigger hands off my wife! I'll teach you to make up to a white woman!" he screamed. He shouldered Sally out of the way and let fly a roundhouse right at the Reverend's face. Isaiah just stood there. He didn't fight back. He didn't even put up his hands to defend himself. When the blow hit, Isaiah rocked back and fell against one of the pumps and then Billy Joe pulled back his left hand and threw a punch to Isaiah's stomach.

When the Reverend doubled up, Billy Joe laughed. "Hey," he thought, "this is going to be fun. I get to push Sally around and beat up an old nigger all in the same day." I thought about the story I had told Lisa about the gremlins on each of our shoulders, whispering into our ears, urging us on for good or ill. I thought about Reverend Norton's sermon on failure and forgiveness. I tried to understand Billy Joe, to forgive him. But I failed, completely.

Instead, I closed in on him from his left and sunk my left hand into the side of his stomach, just below his ribs. He was so surprised that he froze in place for an instant, his right hand pulled back for a blow that he would not land, then he dipped both hands to grab his stomach, which is what I was watching for. As soon as he lowered his arms I hit him again with my left, dead on his nose, hard. I felt bone crunch beneath my fist and almost instantly blood spurted from his face. Sally raced over and grabbed him before he could fall to the ground.

"You get him in the car and get him out of here, now!" I told her. "If he's here thirty seconds from now, I'm going to put him in the hospital." My voice surprised me. It was calm, even, almost matter of fact, but there was a nastiness, a meanness in my tone of which I was not proud. Sally nodded, dragged Billy Joe back to the Pontiac's passenger door and somehow got him inside. He was no help at all. He just huddled forward and pressed his hands to his face. Blood streamed down his chin while he cried, "My nose, my nose. He broke my nose."

"Yes, you worthless son of a bitch. You're lucky that's all I broke," I thought to myself. Sally slammed the passenger door, then stopped for a moment and looked back at the Reverend who now was sitting on the ground, glassy-eyed, with his back sprawled against one of the pumps.

"He gonna be all right?" she asked, fear clear in her voice.

"I hope so."

"Thank him for me, for the money," she said, nodding at Isaiah. "He's a decent man. It's," she fingered the ten-dollar bill, "more than any of Billy Joe's friends ever done for me."

"Sally!" Billy Joe screamed from within the car. "Get me home. I'm bleeding to death in here!" She looked at me sadly for an instant, an expression that seemed to say, "I know he's trash and that he doesn't love me, but I've got two kids and nowhere to go. What else can I do?"

"Woman's shelter—divorce—wage garnishment," I called to her. A moment later the Pontiac started and roared off in a cloud of blue smoke and screeching tires. I was already kneeling next to Isaiah.

He was conscious but had no strength at all. His eyes were glazed and staring straight ahead. His right hand clutched his chest.

"Where are your pills, Reverend, for your angina?" He feebly tried to move his left hand toward his coat pocket but failed. I reached in and felt a slim plastic vial. I pulled it out and almost broke a nail tearing off the childproof cap. I shook three pills into my palm and promptly dropped one of them before I was able to grasp a second one between my fingertips. I raised my hand to his lips and forced the pill into his mouth.

"Try to swallow, Isaiah. Try!"

I saw his lips make a feeble motion but I could not tell if he had been able to swallow the pill or not.

"We need an ambulance," I shouted to the attendant who had stayed as far from the trouble as possible but was now cautiously approaching. Finally, the boy, he couldn't have been more than eighteen, ran over to me.

"Call 911!" I yelled at him.

"I did. They're on their way. Did he stab him? I didn't hear a shot."

"Heart attack, I think," I said as I knelt back down. "Reverend, you hang on. The ambulance is on its way. It will be here any minute. You hang on now. Your boys will never forgive me if I let anything happen to you." He was still conscious and he smiled briefly, then grimaced in pain. I saw the Reverend's eyes shift and I looked up. Lisa was staring, terror-stricken, through the Chevy's windshield. I ran back to her and opened the door. She was as close to crying as I had ever seen her.

"Is he dying?" she asked suddenly, fighting to contain her tears.

"No, sweetheart, he's not dying. That man just knocked the wind out of him. The ambulance will be here in a second and they'll just put him in bed for the night. By tomorrow morning, he'll be fine. Listen, you just sit here for a minute and relax. I'm going to go back and keep the Reverend company until the doctor gets here. Don't worry, he'll be fine." Yes, it was a lie. He could be dying for all I knew. But I wasn't going to tell her that.

When I got back to him, the Reverend looked a lot worse. I laid him out flat on his back on the concrete then took off my jacket and bundled it under his head as a makeshift pillow. He looked at me, wheezed once, his breathing seemed to catch, and then he stopped breathing altogether. The attendant's eyes were big as saucers and his mouth had opened in a little "O," but I didn't have any time to worry about him. I started to administer CPR. I pinched Isaiah's nose, pulled his mouth open, and breathed into him, filling his lungs, forced him to exhale, then gave him another breath, then another.

I paused a moment and listened to his chest but I couldn't hear a heartbeat. I gripped my hands together the way I had been taught and struck his chest once, hard, just below the heart, then listened again. I heard a couple of faint uncoordinated rumbles, then a thud. The Reverend's body shivered as if caught in a sudden chill breeze, then I heard the tripwire sound of a rapidly beating heart. He wheezed again, then took a breath, inhaled noisily, and breathed once more.

I reached across him, grasped his left hand, placed my middle finger in the channel at the edge of his wrist about two inches below his thumb and was rewarded with the rhythmic throbbing of a beating heart. In the distance, I could hear the wail of an approaching siren.

"You're going to be all right, Isaiah," I said, laying the palm of my right hand against his cheek. "The ambulance is coming. It's almost here." I must have had a maniacal grin on my face because when I glanced up at the kid he shrank away from me. I looked down at the Reverend and saw his lips move. I put my head down, my ear close to his mouth.

"Take the car," he whispered.

"Take the car? No, we don't need to. The ambulance is almost here."

"Take the child home," he wheezed, and feebly tried to reach into his pocket to give me his keys.

"The only place I'm going is to the hospital with you."

"Before the police come," he whispered and struggled to sit up. I held him down and told him to rest, not to talk, to save his strength, but he would not be still. "Before the police get here, take the child home." His voice was no louder than the sound of a spring breeze through the blossoms of an apple tree.

"Okay, okay, Reverend. Whatever you say. Now don't move. Relax. I'll get the keys out of your pocket. Let me take your wallet too. I'll need to give your identification to the ambulance attendants." The Reverend finally stopped struggling. I slipped the car keys and his wallet into my pocket just as the ambulance pulled up.

"Heart attack," I told the paramedic who raced to Isaiah's side. "I did CPR when his heart stopped. Here are his pills." I handed her the vial. "I forced one into his mouth but I don't know if he swallowed it."

"Thanks," she said, shoving me aside. "We'll take it from here."

She started shouting orders, something about Lidocaine, other things, I don't remember. In a few moments they had him on a stretcher and into the ambulance. I jumped into the Chevy then started the car and followed the ambulance which was already retreating back the way it had come. I had no intention of leaving Isaiah until his sons arrived. I had lied again. I was getting good at it.

# TWENTY-NINE

---

Like most vacations, it was the shortest portions of the trip that seemed to take the most time. First there was the flight from Maui to Honolulu. Then the wait for the plane to Portland. Then the drive from Portland to Oakdale. It was after nine o'clock Pacific Time on Sunday night when Bill and Peggy Taylor finally arrived home. The house and yard looked the same. Had they only been gone ten days? Lisa's empty swing still hung from the leafless maple in the front yard.

Although it was only a little after six, Hawaiian time, both were exhausted. Within an hour they had opened their mail, unpacked, and gone to bed. The last thing Bill did was to check the answering machine, then turn it off. Tomorrow he would be back at work and Peggy would be addressing more fliers, making more phone calls. The first call would be to Carlos Ramirez though it was unlikely that anything important had occurred during their absence. He would have called them if he had any news.

# THIRTY

The clinic was about a mile away, west of the main street, F Street, down toward the valley floor on Collingswood just beyond Decker. It was a low building, barely more than an emergency room, an operating room, ten or fifteen patient rooms, and assorted broom closets, a waiting room, and a nurse's station, but it looked wonderful to me. I couldn't leave Lisa alone in the car so, reluctantly, I took her hand and together we ran inside not far behind the Reverend's gurney. I just caught a glimpse of him before he was wheeled through the treatment room door. For a moment, Lisa and I stood there and stared at the now-closed panel.

"Are you with that patient?" a voice behind me asked. I turned to find a stocky woman in her late forties clothed in nurse's whites and holding a clipboard.

"Yes, he's my friend. How is he?"

"I don't have that information. We need to have an admitting form filled out." She handed me the clipboard. "Please complete this and get it back to me right away." After a brief, insincere smile she turned back to her glassed-in office in the far corner of the waiting room. I led Lisa to a row of orange molded plastic chairs and looked at the form then picked up the cheap Write Brothers pen and started to work.

"Name:＿Isaiah Williams＿." "Occupation:＿retired＿." "Address:＿＿＿＿＿." I fished out the Reverend's wallet and filled in the answer. "Medical Insurance:＿Medicare＿." I found Isaiah's Social Security card and used the SS number as his Medicare policy number. When I was done I returned the clipboard to Ms. Emily Davis, according to her name tag.

"Mmmmm. Uh-huh. Yesssss—. Well, Mr. uh—?" she said, looking at me.

"Howard, Peter Howard."

"Yes, Mr. Howard, I take it that you are not one of Mr., ah, Williams, relatives?"

"No, we aren't related."

"I see. Now, does Mr. Williams have medical insurance?"

"Medicare."

"Yes, well, other than Medicare, does he have any medical insurance?"

"I don't know."

"Well, that presents us with a problem. We are a private facility and we only accept patients with medical insurance or with a proven means of paying for treatment."

"What's wrong with Medicare?"

"Unfortunately, Medicare, when it pays, if it pays, only covers about half of our normal charges. The Board of Directors has made a decision that we will no longer accept Medicare patients."

"What are you trying to tell me?"

"I'm very sorry, Mr. Howard . . ." she didn't sound the least bit sorry to me. She sounded pleased, as if she had foiled another deadbeat who had had the temerity to get sick and was planning to stick The South State Clinic with the bill. ". . . but we cannot treat Mr. Williams without proof of the ability to pay."

"I don't understand. He's in the emergency room right now. He's had a heart attack. What are you going to do with him, put him out on the curb?"

"The Lake District Hospital isn't far. It's a very good facility. As soon as Mr. Williams is stable, we'll put him in an ambulance and take him over there."

"The hell you will."

Emily's phony smile twisted into a frown. "I must ask you to not use that sort of language with me, Mr. Howard. We have rules here and it is my job to see that they are followed."

"If you move him now, you could kill him. He could die en route if his condition worsens. He could have a stroke or a cardiac arrest. He could suffer brain damage."

"Oh, I'm sure that won't happen, Mr. Howard," she said flippantly. "Our ambulance crews are very well trained and the ambulance carries any medication he may need," she finished, the plastic smile again plastered to her face.

"You don't know that. You're not a doctor. You're not even a nurse, in spite of that uniform you're wearing. You're just an administrator, a glorified bookkeeper."

"Mr. Howard, I do not appreciate your insulting behavior. Mr., ah, Williams will be transferred as soon as possible," she said sharply and began to turn away.

"Ms. Davis, just a moment. I am not only Mr. Williams' friend, I'm President of Orayis Corporation. Our attorneys are Madison, Lee, and Porter in Palo Alto, California. Here's my office address and phone number," I grabbed the ballpoint pen and wrote the information on the bottom of Isaiah's form then handed the clipboard back to her.

"You can go back to your office and call information in Santa Clara, California to verify that. You can also call the California State Bar Association office in San Francisco to confirm our firm's status as active members of the California bar." Emily stared at what I had written at the bottom of the clipboard and made a face as if she had just encountered a bad smell. No, lawyers were not very popular with hospital bureaucrats.

"Now, I'm going to tell you what will happen if you move the Reverend Isaiah Williams so much as five feet from that treatment room. My company's lawyers are going to associate the meanest, nastiest, most money-hungry, ambulance-chasing law firm in the State of Oregon and both the South State Clinic and Emily Davis personally will be joint defendants in the Reverend's suit, or if he dies, the suit brought by his two sons as his surviving heirs. The claims will be for medical malpractice, negligence, intentional infliction of emotional distress, and violation of the civil rights laws."

"You can't . . ."

"I'm not done. You see, if he has any complications, any injuries, any problems whatsoever, it will be our position that they were caused not by the heart attack, but by your transporting him to another hospital during a critical period in his care. If he dies or has a stroke or so much as gets a cold, you, personally, and this clinic of yours are going to be on the hook for it. Do you know why? Because you won't be able to prove which injuries were caused by the heart attack and what problems he incurred because you moved him, so you're going to be liable for the entire loss."

"Mr. Howard, if you think—"

"I'm not done. The Reverend is beloved by his neighbors in New Pine Creek. I'm going to have the entire congregation of the New Pine Creek United Christian Church come up here and testify about what a fine man he was and how strong and vital he was before your clinic destroyed his life because the Medicare money wasn't enough to satisfy your greed.

"No—" I said before she could speak, "I'm not done. The jury is going to be told how much money the doctors who own this clinic made last year, and I bet that it was more than $250,000 each. Ah, I see from your expression that it was a lot more. The jury is going to find out how much money they made and its members are going to be asked to consider two questions:

"One, how much money is enough? Does the Hippocratic oath of the doctors who own this place mean anything to them anymore? That oath will be read to the jury and they will be asked to consider how your bosses could still believe in it if they were willing to do this to a retired minister.

"Two, the jury will be asked to consider that if they let you get away with this, what will happen to them if some day they need emergency treatment and are unfortunate enough to be brought to this clinic. All I will need will be two or three people on the jury on Social Security, or close to it, and my friend is going to end up owning this place.

"Now, don't say anything. You just think about that and go back to your little office and call your boss and tell him that some guy is making trouble and threatening to sue them into the next decade if they throw out a black minister in the middle of a heart attack because the Medicare money isn't enough for them!"

"Well!—" Ms. Davis sputtered, then clamped her mouth shut, turned, and stormed off. I looked through the window and saw her hurriedly dialing the phone. Unless the managing partner-doctor was a complete idiot, I didn't think they were going to be sending Isaiah anywhere.

I turned away from the office's glass window and noticed that an older man sitting in one of the waiting room chairs was looking at me. When he caught my eye, he smiled, and then began to softly applaud. The five or six other people in the room, some suffering minor injuries, some relatives and friends of patients, joined in.

"Why were those people clapping?" Lisa asked me when I rejoined her. "Was it because you were fighting with that lady?"

"The lady . . ." I gritted my teeth at the use of the term, ". . . wanted to send Isaiah away because she thought he didn't have enough money to pay the doctor. I told her she couldn't do that and the people liked what I said." Lisa looked terribly worried.

"Can't we pay for him? How much money does the doctor want? Are they going to send him away?"

"No, Lisa, everything's fine. I convinced her that it would be the wrong thing to do. They aren't going to do anything to Isaiah. The doctors are helping the Reverend right now. I didn't mean to upset you. Everything is under control." She stared at me for a moment trying to figure out if I was just saying that to make her feel better. "Really, Lisa, believe me, the doctors are helping him right now and we're going to stay here until we know he's okay. All right?"

"Yes, Peter," she said hesitantly, then studied my face once more, decided that I was telling her the truth, and gave me a big smile.

"That's my girl!" I said and caressed her cheek. "Sweetie, look, you sit right here, don't go anywhere. I'm going over to that phone and call the Reverend's sons."

"Okay," she said pleasantly, then picked up an old *Life* magazine and began leafing through the pictures. I fished around in

Isaiah's wallet and found the card with Mark's home phone number and called him from the pay phone at the far side of the waiting room. The call was answered on the third ring.

"Mark, this is Peter Howard. I'm in Lakeview, at the South State Clinic. I don't know the—wait a minute, it's here on the pay phone—" and I read him the address. "Your dad tried to help some people at a gas station and one thing led to another and he's had a little heart attack. He's going to be fine. The ambulance got there right away and he's in with the doctors now. I managed to get one of his pills into his mouth as soon as it happened. But you and Matthew should get up here as soon as you can.—Mark? Mark, are you there?"

I heard Mark start to speak, then his voice faltered. "I'm here," he said, barely in control. "We'll be right there."

"Mark, listen to me! Take it easy. You're not going to do your dad any good if they bring you and Matthew in with broken necks from some car crash because you were driving like a maniac. It's the South State Clinic near Collingswood and Decker in Lakeview. Okay? He's going to be fine."

"I'm leaving right now," Mark said tersely, his voice a bit firmer, then the phone went dead. I walked back to where Lisa was sitting and we leafed through the magazine together. We started a game where each of us had to make up a story about one of the pictures. I picked a picture of a man in hipboots standing in a tree-lined river, a trout leaping from the water, bowing the man's rod.

I imagined that the man was a famous doctor who was on a fishing vacation after saving thousands of lives. He had just caught the fish to see if he could do it and he would let the fish go as soon as he took its picture and measured how big it was and wrote the fish's size down in a notebook he always carried so that he could show his friends what a wonderful fisherman he was.

Lisa chose a picture of a man chasing a cab on a crowded city street, his coat unbuttoned, his tie flying over his shoulder.

"What do you think that picture is about, Lisa?"

She stared at it for a moment, her lips compressed in concentration, then, suddenly, she smiled.

"He's a policeman!" she said proudly.

"Oh, like the policemen in the movies, the detectives?" I asked.

"Yes, a detective. He's chasing a bad man who is trying to get away from him. The bad man is in the car and the policeman is chasing him." Lisa's story was starting to make me uneasy, but I wasn't sure what to do.

"Maybe the man driving the car is a speeder, and he's driving too fast? Maybe the policeman wants to give him a ticket for driving so fast on a crowded street," I suggested.

"No. The bad man is in the back of the car. You can't see him, but that's where he is. The policeman knows he's a bad man and he's going to catch him and take him to jail and they are never ever going to let him out."

"Well, Lisa, that's a good thing. Bad men, criminals, ought to be put in jail. So we're all done with this picture. Do you want to do another one?"

"No! The bad man, he's really, really bad. He's got a little girl there in the car. She's trying to get away but he won't let her. He's holding her really, really tight. She's hitting him and kicking him and she's shouting, 'Let me go! Let me go!' but he won't. He and the man driving the car are trying to steal her. She's really afraid but the policeman is going to catch them. He's going to hit the bad men and knock them down. Then he's going to take the little girl home to her mommy and daddy and the bad men are going to go to jail and they'll never bother her again."

As Lisa spoke my eyes were fixed on the page. I couldn't bear to look at her; I didn't want to see the glitter in her eyes as she told her story. I just kept staring at the picture, at the cab pulling away, at the pedestrians oblivious to the man's frantic chase, at the man, the middle-aged white man about five feet eleven, six feet tall, with dark, medium-length hair, wearing a business suit and a dark tie, like me, like me when I first saw Lisa and chased after her and Ken; just like me.

I pulled Lisa into my lap and wrapped my arms around her and caressed her hair and hoped that no one saw the tears at the corners of my eyes, or, if they did, they thought they were for Isaiah. Lisa didn't say anything. She just curled up in my lap. But she didn't cry. That was more or less how Matthew and Mark found us when they arrived a few minutes later.

I turned as soon as I heard the door open. Both men were

dressed in designer jeans, one pair black, one blue, casual shirts, both with button-down collars, and sweaters, Mark's was gray, Matthew's white. And both of their faces were worried, both with that wide-eyed look of fear barely kept under control. Lisa had fallen into a dreamy half-sleep in my arms and I gently settled her in the chair next to me, then stood to greet them.

"How is he?" Matthew asked.

"What happened?" Mark said almost at the same time.

"I don't know how he is," I told them in a whisper so that Lisa would not hear. "He's been in there," I pointed to the treatment room, "about half an hour. I'm not a relative so they won't tell me anything." I didn't mention my altercation with Emily Davis.

"I'll try and find out," Matthew volunteered and he headed for Ms. Davis's office.

"Mark," I said, forcing him to turn back and look at me. "I'm sure he'll be all right. I got a pill into him right away. The paramedics were there in two minutes and they medicated him on the spot." Although Mark was standing in front of me, his eyes seemed to lose their focus, as if he was slipping into an alien landscape, far away, a country in which his father did not exist, in which he and Matthew had to go on alone. A place that I had journeyed to myself many years before.

I remember, clearly, my Aunt Margaret, my mom's sister, talking to me. My mother was crying, I could hear her in the bedroom. I didn't know what had happened. Why was Mom crying? If there was a problem, why wasn't Dad here to help her? Had something happened to Dad? Where was he? I kept asking Aunt Peggy, "What's wrong? Where's Dad?" And then she said what people always say: "Peter, there's been an accident. Your dad's been hurt."

"What happened? Can I see him?" Questions that she could not answer.

"Peter," she said, "It was a very bad accident. I'm sorry, but it doesn't look like your dad will be coming home." And that's when she began to fade out. She was there. I could see her but I wasn't looking at her, really, the way you don't look at the chair at the side of a room you're just walking through. It's just a shape at the edge of your vision and later you could not describe it or even remember what color it was if your life depended on it.

I kept thinking, "Dad's dead? Dad can't be dead. What about Mom? What about me? Where will we go? Will we have to move? Will I have to get a job? Who's going to go to Little League with me? Will I have to go to school tomorrow? What will I tell the other kids? Maybe Dad isn't dead after all. Maybe someone'll look around and figure out that they got the names mixed up and that it was somebody else's dad who died. Maybe my dad is still lying over there in the corner of the emergency room in a coma with the wrong name on his chart and he'll wake up and they'll call us and tell us he's alive and that it was all a big mistake.

"Maybe it will be like in the movies when they think someone is dead and they're ready to bury them and, suddenly, they notice that his finger is moving and they find out that he was just unconscious and that he's really alive after all."

All of that, and more, went through my mind while my Aunt Peggy was trying to talk to me. I heard her voice, but I didn't hear it; my mind was somewhere else. I thought I was listening to her, but I can't remember anything she said, like when you're really tired and trying to watch a TV show and you close your eyes during the commercial and you can hear the program and you think you're awake and that you're listening to it and then you notice that you have no idea what the story is about or how the characters got where they are and fifteen minutes has past and the show's almost over and you don't remember any of it.

That's where Mark was, I think, while I was trying to assure him that his dad would make it home, alive and well.

"Mark!" I said sharply. His head gave a slight quiver and I could tell I had him back. "Mark, listen to me! Your dad's going to be all right. I've been through this myself. He'll be fine."

Mark didn't say anything, but his chin nodded up and down in response to my assurances. I glanced over his shoulder and saw that Matthew had left Ms. Davis's window and was talking to the old man I had noticed sitting near the nurse's station. A moment later Matthew joined us. His stride was deliberate and he looked at me peculiarly, as if appraising some computer component or circuit board that he didn't quite recognize.

"What did they say?" Mark asked at once.

"They don't know. All she could tell me was that Dad was with the doctor. She said the doctor had a lot of experience, said that he had been a cardiac specialist in L.A. and that he came up here to get his kids away from the drugs and the gangs. She swears that he's the best heart man for five hundred miles." At this news Mark visibly relaxed, like someone who has been holding his breath and has finally let it go. Then Matthew looked back at me with that peculiar expression on his face.

"That nurse was awfully upset about Dad's medical coverage. At first I thought it was because he was black, but when I told her that Dad has AARP supplemental insurance, that it would cover all their charges, she got as sweet as could be. That's when she told me about Doctor Chang and what he did in Los Angeles."

"Well, these things are expensive," I said unconvincingly. Matthew just stared at me.

"That man over there, he said his name was Sam something, he told me that you got into a big fight with the nurse."

"What?" Mark said, immediately concerned. His dad's life was at stake and some drifter was giving the hospital a hard time?

"He told me that the nurse, that Ms. Davis, that she wanted to put Dad back in the ambulance and drive him over to another hospital." When he heard this, Mark's fist involuntarily clenched.

"He said you told her that you were the president of some big company and that if they moved Dad you were going to have your lawyers sue their pants off. He said you threatened to take every dime this hospital had if they didn't do their best for him. Is that true?"

"I just told her that it would be a big mistake to move Isaiah."

"He said you got pretty hot about it. He said that everybody in the waiting room heard you."

"I just told her that if they moved him, they'd get sued. The Reverend's going to be fine with or without me."

"Did you tell her you're the president of some high-tech company?"

"Yes."

"Is that true?"

"Yes."

Matthew took another look at my cheap cotton T-shirt and faded jeans. I could almost hear his thoughts: "Maybe he's mentally ill or a drunk. He's probably some lush who's lost his company and now is trying to get back on the wagon."

"Matthew, it's a long story," I said without being asked. "I didn't look like this last week. My company is in Santa Clara. I . . ." But I couldn't explain. I started thinking about Lisa and everything that had happened to her and the "policeman" who was going to save her from the bad men, and my words just caught in my throat.

"Something happened," I began again. "I," and I turned to look at Lisa where she was curled up in the plastic chair, "I found . . ." I said, not taking my eyes off her, and just stopped. Finally, I looked back at Matthew and Mark who were staring first at Lisa then at me with puzzled expressions. "I can't explain it right now," I said finally. "I can give you my office number. You can call there tomorrow if you want."

"No. That's not necessary. We don't need to call anyone." For the first time, I think they saw me as a normal person instead of some loser or con man who was out to take advantage of their father.

"Why don't we sit down," I said after an awkward silence. "It may take awhile. Oh, wait,—here—." I gave Matthew the Reverend's wallet. "I took this so that I could get his Medicare ID and your phone number. I guess you'd better have these too," I said, handing him the Chevy's keys.

Matthew took the wallet and slipped it into his pocket unopened. He played a moment with the car keys, looked at Lisa then handed them back to me.

"You'll need these," he said. "Dad said you need to take the little girl home. He trusted you. He'd want you to have the car. Bring it back when you're done." When I didn't move, Matthew forced the keys into my hand.

"It's what Dad would want," Mark said after a brief pause. "Dad didn't make too many mistakes about people. Take her home."

I squeezed the keys until the metal hurt my palm, but I didn't move. I don't know if I would have left right then or not. I was thinking about it, that's for sure. But I didn't get the chance to make that choice because just then a doctor in surgical greens came out of the treatment room, looked around, saw Matthew and Mark, and came over. He was of Asian ancestry, about five feet nine, black hair, glasses, maybe forty, forty-five years old.

"Mr. Williams?" he asked Matthew.

"I'm Matthew Williams. This is my brother, Mark. How's our dad? Is he going to be all right?"

"I'm Dr. Chang It's too soon to tell. He's had a moderately severe heart attack. I think we got to him in time, but it was close. We'll know in another eight to twelve hours if he'll make a full recovery. Were either of you with him when it happened?"

"I was there," I said.

"Tell me what happened. I need to know the timing, how long things took."

"It started when I was in the men's room. A man at the gas station apparently slapped his wife. The Reverend tried to help her. When I got there the husband was shouting at Isaiah, calling him names. I tried to get Reverend Williams back into the car but he wanted to help the woman. He gave her some money for diapers for her baby. The guy went nuts and hit him, twice, once in the face, then the second time in the stomach. I got him away from the Reverend, and . . ."

"How long did that take, after the first blow?"

"Ten, fifteen seconds. I think I broke the guy's nose. He quit pretty fast when that happened." The doctor started to take notes, making a list of the times involved.

"Fine, what happened next?"

"I got his pills out of his pocket. I pushed one into his mouth, but I don't think he was able to swallow it. That took another fifteen seconds." Dr. Chang wrote down "15 seconds."

"Don't worry about the pill," he said without looking up. "It's more effective if it dissolves under the tongue anyway."

"Let's see," I continued after a moment's pause. "Okay, then I laid him down and told him to relax. I yelled for the kid to call an ambulance and he said he already had. Maybe another ten seconds. Then the Reverend stopped breathing, and I administered CPR."

"What did you do?" Dr. Chang asked sharply.

"I breathed into him for four or five cycles, then when I couldn't hear his heart beating I hit him in the chest, just below the heart. I listened to his chest again and his heart had started up. That maybe took forty-five seconds, a minute, start to finish. Then he was breathing on his own. The ambulance got there within another thirty seconds. Less than a minute after they got there they were putting needles into him." As I spoke Dr. Chang completed his list of the times and now he totaled them, and seemed to relax. He actually gave us a thin smile.

"The timing looks good. There's a drug, Streptokinase, that prevents much of the damage sometimes caused by a heart attack but it must be given as soon as possible after the attack. The later it's given the less effective it is. I gave Mr. Williams the injection within two minutes of the time he was brought in. If these numbers are accurate, he got the medication less than ten minutes after the first symptoms—that's plenty of time for it to be highly effective. Of course, if you hadn't given him CPR, he never would have made it. You—excuse me, what's your name?"

"Peter Howard."

"Well, it's a good thing you took that CPR course, Mr. Howard, because there's no doubt in my mind that it saved his life. Mr. Williams," he continued, turning to Matthew, "I can't promise anything, of course, but I think we've got a good chance, a very good chance, that your father will come out of this all right. We won't know for sure for another eight to twelve hours. You might want to make arrangements to stay nearby. There's an Easy 7 Motel a block or so down Decker Street. A lot of our patients' family members use it for situations like this." Dr. Chang looked around him, back toward the treatment room. "Excuse me now, but I have to go," he said, his mind already on his next patient.

The boys stared at me then Mark tried to say something but I wouldn't let him. "It's okay," I said finally, "I just did what the Red Cross told me to. Anyone would have done the same thing." It was too much. It was all too much. My mind was numb and I felt emotionally exhausted. I sank back into my chair.

"Shouldn't you get going?" Matthew asked a few minutes later. I still had the Chevy's keys clutched in my hand. I opened my fingers and looked at them. I visualized myself carrying Lisa through the door and leaving the boys there in the waiting room. I saw her waking up, asking me how Isaiah was, and me lying to her again, telling her that he was fine when I really didn't know if he was alive or dead. I looked back at her, then again at the keys. I put them in my pocket.

"Not until your dad's out of the woods. Tomorrow. I'll take Lisa home tomorrow." The boys looked at me for a moment, not saying anything, then, almost in unison, all three of us looked down the hall toward the treatment room. I sat down, reached out and put my hand on Lisa's shoulder then laid my head back and closed my eyes.

There is a rhythm to time spent in hospital waiting rooms. First you sit and stare out the window; then you read magazines; then you nap; then you walk around the building, probably stopping in the cafeteria to get a cup of coffee; then you go back to the waiting room and do it all over again.

As an adult I could handle that sort of thing but after the first hour or so it was pretty tough on Lisa. Finally, around two-thirty we went down the street and rented a room at the motel Dr. Chang had mentioned. Lisa and I filled the afternoon walking around the town, window shopping and eating. I found a video store that would rent a TV/VCR combination along with the movie but because I had no identification and no credit cards I couldn't get one.

Around five o'clock we returned to the clinic and found Matthew and Mark still sitting in the waiting room. There had been no news. I decided to wait an hour or two longer then take Lisa back to the motel room where she could watch TV until it was time to go to bed. Earlier I had bought two children's books at a used bookstore we had found and Lisa settled primly in one of the chairs and began to read. I don't know why I felt so tired, I had done nothing strenuous that day, but I fell into a restless half slumber. I awoke slowly to the sound of Mark's voice.

"I don't know. I wasn't there. You'll have to ask Mr. Howard." At the mention of my name I opened my eyes and turned toward Mark. He was talking with a middle-aged woman and pointing at me. When she approached I stood up and rubbed my face to banish the remnants of my fitful sleep.

"Hello," she said, "I'm Sarah Banock. I'm the news director for Station KLKE, 870 AM. I heard about the incident at Bob's ARCO and I wanted to find out what had happened. I understand you were there."

Maybe it's because I was still half-asleep but the alarm bells that should have gone off didn't. I just stood there and stared at her and wondered how long this would take, not that I had anything else to do.

"Yes, but there isn't that much to tell."

"This is a small town, Mr. Howard and we're the only radio station this side of Silver Lake. My listeners are interested in local news. Could you describe what you saw?"

"I only met Reverend Williams yesterday. I was on a trip and my car broke down. I needed a ride and the Reverend volunteered to help me. We left New Pine Creek this morning after church services and the Reverend stopped for gas."

I rambled on, repeating pretty much what I had told Dr. Chang. Ms. Banock was holding a small tape machine with a built-in microphone and she recorded the story, asked me a couple of innocuous questions, thanked me, and left. I didn't think anything more about it. It didn't occur to me that the assault on a minister and his subsequent heart attack were, on a local scale, big news. Hell, the police hadn't even bothered to get my statement. But no one had told me that they had come to the clinic shortly after Lisa and I left and then had looked for me at the motel but in our wanderings around town they had been unable to find us, which I still don't understand because it isn't that big a town.

I wasn't listening to the radio, so I didn't hear Sarah Banock's six p.m. Sunday News Round-up where the Reverend's Battle With Death and my "heroic" intervention was the headline story. I sure didn't know that several other small southern Oregon and northern California radio stations had picked up the story, seen it as a symptom of senseless urban crime creeping into their quiet communities, and also featured it in their local news programs.

At that time Carlos Ramirez didn't know my last name, and the story didn't mention Lisa at all because I had been careful to keep her out it, so Carlos didn't make any connection between the

incident on the radio and the stranger and the little girl he was
looking for. For my part, I forgot about the whole thing the minute
Sarah Banock walked out the door. After all, I wasn't driving
around in a car listening to the radio, but Jimmie was. Jimmie was.

Sarah's report even included a line or two about the Reverend's
classic '56 Chevrolet not being damaged in the incident. So there I
was on Sunday afternoon, babbling into Sarah Banock's microphone, blithely unaware of the trouble I was getting Lisa and
myself into, again.

Lisa and I went to dinner and came back about seven-thirty
Sunday night. This time someone from the clinic called the police
and two huge uniformed officers arrived shortly thereafter and
asked me to repeat my story for the third time. I was careful not to
mention Lisa or how long I had known Isaiah. I didn't lie. I just
left out some details. They didn't even glance at Lisa where she sat
a couple of chairs away drawing on a piece of scrap paper with two
of Mark's numerous ballpoint pens.

Of course, the policemen's questions had a different goal than
those of Dr. Chang. "Did you get the license number of the other
car?" "Did you hear Billy Joe's last name?" "Can you give us a
better description of the suspect?" I got the feeling that the police
were considering charging Billy Joe with felony assault.

For myself, I would have liked to see him do some county time,
but I knew that the Reverend would not share that opinion. And, I
had to admit, by the time Billy Joe got done with four or five court
hearings, a plea bargain, a pre-sentence investigation and report, a
sentencing, and then was released early from an overcrowded jail,
most likely he would decide that he had beaten the system and
would come away from the whole mess more ready, rather than
less, to beat up somebody else.

Hell, he would be the center of attention in all of this. It would
make him feel important, especially after he got out and was able
to brag to all his buddies how he did time for "beating up a
nigger." On balance, I hoped that the cops never did find Billy Joe,
not that the Reverend would testify against him anyway.

The officers had barely finished taking my statement when Dr.
Chang appeared, smiling.

"He's going to be fine," he said when we crowded around him.

"When can we see him?" Matthew asked.

"He's pretty tired, but he's awake. You can see him now, but don't stay too long. He's down the hall, to the right, room 6." Lisa watched us talking with Dr. Chang and was out of her chair and at my side as soon as he told us that we could see Isaiah.

The old man looked small and frail with all the tubes and wires connected to him, but his face brightened when we came into the room. In spite of his many connections, the boys hugged their father, gingerly, and then I picked Lisa up and brought her to the bed where she also gave Isaiah an awkward embrace.

"How do you feel, Dad?" Matthew asked after a moment's silence.

"As President Reagan said after he was shot, 'I'd just as soon be in Philadelphia.' But I'm all right. Just a little tired."

"You gave us quite a scare, Dad," Mark told him.

"Now, Mark, you know that when it's my time, the Lord will take me and until then I will be here to do His work."

"Dad, it was Mr. Howard here who saved your life. If he hadn't been there, well, I don't want to think what would have happened."

"Mark, clearly the Lord put Mr. Howard there to help me because I still have some of His work left to do. But, Peter," he said looking at me, "you should have left already. Matthew, give Peter the keys to my car. He's got to take Lisa home."

"I gave him your keys hours ago, Dad. Mark and I knew that's what you would have wanted." At the news that his sons had tried to follow his wishes, the Reverend displayed a radiant smile.

"Thank you, boys, I'm proud of you. But, Peter, why are you still here?"

"We couldn't go until we knew you were all right, Isaiah."

"I'm fine, just fine. Now, you take that child home. Do you need any money? Matthew, please give Peter whatever he needs. I'll make it up to you later," Isaiah said, straining to sit up.

"Dad, don't worry about it. We'll take care of it. Look, it's getting late and the doctor said you need to get some rest. We'll be right outside if you need anything. We'll see you in the morning." The Reverend relaxed back against the pillows, visibly tired, and we trooped out of the room. A few minutes later I got Lisa to bed. I read a paperback for an hour or so then crawled into my own bed and fell almost instantly asleep. Tomorrow, Monday, I would get her home, at last.

# THIRTY-ONE

Our schedule the next morning did not go as anticipated. We were
going to be up at eight, have breakfast, be on the road by nine, and
I would have Lisa home sometime around ten-thirty. Had I kept to
that plan, Jimmie would have caught us at our motel for sure. But
as I was lying in bed and about to drift off to sleep it occurred to
me that at eleven o'clock on a Monday morning there might not be
anyone at home. Then what? Obviously, we would have to leave
earlier. As a result, I found myself waking up at half-hour intervals
starting at around four-thirty a.m. Finally, at about twenty to six, I
got up. We would leave as soon as Lisa was awake.

Yesterday afternoon, waiting for the doctors to finish with Isaiah,
I had called Willard and Peggy Taylor's home several more times
but all I got was that damn malfunctioning machine. In a strange
way I was just as glad that I had an excuse not to leave a message.
What would I have said? How could I have explained all this over
the phone? Should I call again this morning? No, I would have her
home soon enough.

"Is it time to go?" Lisa asked before my feet barely hit the floor.

"Almost. How do you feel? Do you want to sleep a little
longer?"

"No," Lisa said firmly. "I'm not tired."

"All right, then I'm going to shave and take a shower. When I'm done, you can use the bathroom. Okay?"

"Yes, Peter."

By six-fifteen we were washed, dressed, and packed, if you can call shoving a couple of pairs of dirty underwear into a sports bag "packing." It was about 40 miles or so to Oakdale. Given the state of the road and the Chevy's age, I figured it would take a little more than an hour to get there. By six-twenty we were out of town and headed north. Luckily, Jimmie didn't catch Sarah Banock's broadcast Sunday night. He was too busy checking all the motels, restaurants, and gas stations between Lakeview and Oakdale in his search for Eddie's blue Ford Ranger pickup truck. So he didn't hear the news report describing the heroic actions of one Peter Howard until a quarter to seven Monday morning, at which point he raced to the hospital to see if we were still there, still keeping a vigil at the Reverend's bedside.

When he didn't find us in the waiting room he politely asked if we were in the building and a helpful nurse told him the name of our motel. At about five to seven, he was knocking on the Easy 7 Motel manager's door to inquire if the "hero" he had heard about on the radio was staying there. A couple of minutes later, almost seven on the dot, he roared out of the motel's lot, turned north onto 395, and raced after us.

Our route took us through Warner Canyon, north on 395 through the Chandler Valley and on to Valley Falls. We got there just before seven, about the same time that Jimmie was knocking on the motel manager's door.

It was still dark at that time of the morning but the eastern horizon had begun to glow along the flanks of the ridge. The initial energy that I had felt an hour before had faded with the waning darkness and I decided that a little caffeine would be a good idea. I pulled into the only building in the "town," a gas station-grocery store-restaurant-drugstore combination housed in a neat frame building about a hundred yards from the point where Oregon State Highway 31 bears north and west away from 395's eastward path.

Lisa and I sat at the four-stool counter and I ordered coffee and a sweet roll for myself, milk and corn flakes for her. We were almost there, only about fifteen miles or so from Oakdale. While Lisa finished the last of her cereal I looked around the store. Outside, through the windows, I could see the sun clearing the edge of the mountains at the eastern side of the valley. Two golden eagles were circling, hunting the ground squirrels that thrived in the ever-present sagebrush.

From the lunch counter I could see shelves of Twinkies, coffee mugs, a small cabinet of jewelry, and numerous other items. I was sure that the store would also offer a complete line of aspirin, antihistamines, color film, and dental floss. Everything that the passing trucker or tourist might need.

Then I had an idea. In a few minutes, if my research was accurate, and if her parents had not moved away, and if Lisa had correctly remembered her name and address, and if . . . , and if . . . , I would have her home. And then I would leave. I probably would never see her again. Without warning, I felt an awful, sudden emptiness. I looked at Lisa as she primly and methodically captured the final three corn flakes, then set her spoon down neatly next to the bowl and looked up at me, and smiled. And smiled. After today I would never see that smile again. I needed something of her to take with me, to keep.

I found them on the far side of the last aisle on the shelf next to the alkaline batteries and pocket knives: a display of Kodak Fun-Saver disposable cameras, just point, shoot and then return the camera to the photo shop for one-hour developing. They had a FunSaver Weekend 35 with twenty-four pictures for $15.95 and a FunSaver 35 With Flash with twenty-seven exposures for $18.95. I thought about it for a second and decided that any pictures that I would be taking would be inside and that I might as well get the one with the flash. Even after the gasoline, meals, and the hotel I had over seventy dollars left. I paid for the camera and put it in the pocket of my jacket. It was about seven-fifteen when we pulled out of the lot and turned left onto Highway 31. We were almost there.

There was no traffic at this time of the year. The road to Oakdale hugged the south side of a huge, flat, sagebrush-covered valley that looked to be at least 20 miles wide and without a structure visible for as far as the eye could see. To my left, low, pine-covered foothills rose to form the valley's southern boundary. These hills were part of the Fremont National Forest and contained high meadows, groves of pine and Chinese elm, and miles of trout streams.

In July this road would have been busy with tourists and Winnebagos, but not in February. Today only one vehicle passed us in either direction, a red Dodge half-ton pickup, which went by like the proverbial bat out of hell. It roared by, screeched around a gentle bend a hundred yards down the road and momentarily disappeared from sight. Some local driving like a damn fool, I thought, and I dismissed him from my mind, until we rounded the same turn a moment later.

A hundred yards ahead of us the truck started to weave across both lanes of the deserted highway and the driver began, almost randomly, to apply the brakes. Was the man drunk? At this time of the morning? The truck's brake lights flashed again, longer this time, and blue smoke erupted from beneath both its rear wheels. Suddenly the pickup swerved more violently and for a moment I thought it was going to career off the road. At the last instant the driver managed to turn it back toward the center line and then he mashed the brakes again. The pickup went into a shallow slide, straightened, then began to skid again, inexorably, toward the right-hand shoulder.

Somehow the motorist managed to keep enough control to bring the vehicle almost to a stop before it finally lurched from the highway and slid to a dusty halt in the dirt and brush at the edge of the road.

I had slowed to stay behind the skidding vehicle and, as I drew near, through the truck's rear window I saw the driver's door begin to swing open then stop as the man suddenly slumped forward against the steering wheel. An instant later the truck's horn began to screech when his dead weight pressed against the button.

He was obviouly in serious trouble, having a heart attack, shot, snake bit, whatever. He must have been trying to reach Oakdale and a doctor when his strength failed. "Now what?" I asked myself. I couldn't just drive past and leave him out here. At least I could drag him into the back seat and take him to town with us. I pulled onto the shoulder and turned off the engine.

"Lisa, you stay here," I told her. "I think that man is sick. I'm going to see if I can help him." I patted her on the shoulder then jumped out of the Chevy and hurried around the back of the truck and up to the driver's door. All I could see was the back of the man's head as he sprawled over the steering wheel.

"Hello!" I shouted over the sound of the horn as I approached the front of the pickup. "Can you hear me?" I heard a muffled response that was little more than a groan. A second later I reached the cab and pulled open the driver's door.

If Jimmie said anything before he stabbed me, I didn't hear it. He just turned and lunged at me with a hunting knife as soon as I opened the driver's door. Slashing with his right hand, Jimmie's stroke ran from my left side to my right.

It's a strange sensation, being cut. At first you don't feel anything, just a slight burning followed by the wetness of your blood pouring out. I wondered why I wasn't killed there and then, a clean wound to my heart or across my throat. Maybe the awkwardness of rising up from behind the wheel, spinning in the driver's seat and jumping from the truck all in one motion had thrown Jimmie's timing a little off. Maybe I sensed something and pulled back a fraction of an inch just in time. I don't know.

I do remember trying to pull away. I remember the knife glittering as it lanced out and caught me just at the edge of my ribs near the middle of my chest. I remember the blade grinding against my bones and me trying to lean back, to dance away from the steel. I remember the knife cutting through my jacket and my flesh as if they were both made of paper. I remember the warm, sticky, wet feel of my blood pouring from the four-inch horizontal gash along my ribs.

Instinctively, I grabbed for the wound, and caught only a handful of blood as I backpeddled a couple of paces, somehow managing to remain on my feet. Jimmie had stumbled when he extended his arm at the end of the stroke but in an instant he was back on the balls of his feet and he lunged at me again. I kicked at him and missed. He waved his knife at me and swiped it at my leg the next time I tried to kick the blade out of his hand.

"Good," he said when my foot went wide and I almost fell. "I didn't want this to go too fast. I wanted you to see it coming, to feel it happen. I'm going to gut you like a fish. Then I'm going to sell that kid to the worst freak I can find. Here it comes!" he said and, almost laughing, he leaped at me once more.

I backpeddled, made it a couple of feet, caught my heel on a branch or a clump of weeds, and fell flat on my back into the shallow ditch that lined the side of the road. My arms were splayed out above and behind me. Frantically I sought some purchase that would bring me to my feet, but I only succeeded in reaching a sitting position and sliding my butt half a yard farther back until my spine ran into the shallow slope of the far side of the ditch.

Jimmie ran at me. My right hand encountered a small rock that I hurled at him with little effect. He paused for an instant, dodged to one side and the stone flew harmlessly past his head. By then I was already scrabbling for another rock. My fingers encountered one about the size of a flattened baseball, but it was half buried in the dirt. I felt a nail break as I struggled to free it from the soil. Jimmie was advancing again.

I saw his arm reach out and the point of his knife turn down. I saw his legs bend and tense for the leap that would land him on top of me, would drive the blade through my body with irresistible force. His knees flexed the last fraction of an inch and then, behind Jimmie, I heard Lisa scream. "Peter!"

Jimmie paused, just for an instant. He recognized Lisa's voice. Involuntarily, he looked over his shoulder. A small stone whizzed past his ear. He laughed and turned back to me.

Adrenalin does amazing things to the human body. It can leave you frozen in shock, your heart racing and your muscles locked, or it can make you move faster than you had ever thought possible. I was almost to my feet with the dirt-caked rock in my right hand when Jimmie turned toward me again. I strained to straighten up, to pull my arm back and throw the stone, but I knew that I was going to be too late. Suddenly, a second small stone bounced harmlessly off Jimmie's shoulder. He twisted toward Lisa and shouted angrily, "You're next, kid!"

As he turned back to me I lunged forward and threw the stone with all my failing strength. Jimmie was just about to spring, to finish me off, when his eyes went wide, his head started to duck and then my rock struck him solidly just above his hairline. The skin on Jimmie's forehead tore open and with only a brief muffled cry he collapsed into a boneless heap almost at my feet.

Bright red blood poured into his left eye socket and on down his cheek. He didn't even blink. Was he dead? I didn't know and I wasn't about to examine him to find out. But I couldn't leave him there. I couldn't take the chance that he would get away again.

I grabbed Lisa, staggered back to the Chevy, and collapsed inside, immediately staining the Reverend's seats with my blood. I started the engine and managed to pull the car past Jimmie's truck then I backed it up near his body. Lisa was paper white and shaking and breathing in little sobs. I left her in the car and lurched to the trunk. Jimmie had not moved and his blood now pooled in the dirt next to his cheek.

Fumbling, I opened the Chevy's trunk, put the keys in my pocket then made my way over to him. Carefully, I kicked the knife away then, forcing down my fear, I grabbed Jimmie under his arms and levered his head and shoulders up and into the Chevy's open trunk. My strength was fading and I struggled to finish before shock and loss of blood disabled me.

Gasping, I grabbed Jimmie's legs and pushed him, head first, deep into the trunk. When his head was as far as it would go, I twisted him sideways, doubled up his legs at the knees and some-how got all of him in there. I don't know how. I don't think I could do that again if you offered me ten thousand dollars. As I said, adrenalin can do amazing things.

Luckily, except for a green iron toolbox, the trunk had been empty. I didn't want Jimmie waking up and using a crowbar or something to spring the latch so I pushed the box out onto the ground before closing the lid. I had never felt such a surge of relief as when I heard the trunk's lock snap closed. And at that instant, the effects of the adrenalin disappeared and I thought that I was going to collapse on the spot.

The toolbox had hit the earth on its edge, sprung open and spilled its contents. A hammer, a pair of pliers, a small crowbar, a flashlight, a two-inch wide roll of masking tape, an X-acto blade, three screwdrivers, and an adjustable crescent wrench formed a tangled pile a foot behind the Chevy's rear bumper. I leaned on the trunk with my left hand and stared stupidly at the mound of screwdrivers and wrenches. For a moment I worried about losing the Reverend's tools. Insanity. I barely had the strength to stay on my feet leastwise the ability to bend down and pick them up. I would have to owe the Reverend a replacement set. Somehow I didn't think he would mind.

My blood continued to leak through my shirt, over my belt and onto the legs of my jeans. I took a deep, painful breath and looked down at the pile of tools one more time. Slowly, shakily, I reached down and retrieved the roll of masking tape. Using the car for support, I made my way back to the driver's door.

I lowered myself into the seat, my back to Lisa, my feet dangling outside, then unzipped my shredded jacket and tore open my shirt.

"Lisa, get me a piece of cloth from the sports bag," I called to her. "A shirt, underwear, anything. Hurry!"

I heard her sniffle and then, a second or two later, the sound of the zipper opening. Her little hand appeared at my right side. I grabbed the T-shirt she offered me and began to mop away the blood until the skin around the wound was momentarily dry. I ripped off a strip of tape about six inches long, wiped the shirt across the gash once more, then slapped the tape vertically over the center of the cut as I pulled the edges of the wound together. I repeated the process two more times until the cut was covered with tape. Then I applied two more strips horizontally in line with the gash. The tape quickly turned from beige to dark maroon and blood continued to seep through its seams, but a lot less freely then before.

I tucked the remnants of my shirt back into my blood-soaked pants. What a pointless act. Shock will do strange things to you. I swung my legs into the car and closed the door. It was thirty-one minutes after seven. I put the car into gear and then turned to Lisa. She was still shaking, her eyes round and frightened.

"Don't worry, Lisa. He can't hurt anyone any more."

"Are you going to die?" she asked, terrified.

"No, I'm not going to die. Haven't you ever seen the Western movies where the good guy gets shot and they think he's really, really hurt and when they get his shirt off and take a look they find that it's only a flesh wound?"

"What's a flesh wound?" she sniffled.

"That's when you bleed a lot but you aren't really hurt, when it's just a cut that looks a lot worse than it is. It's not even bleeding anymore. I put some tape on it like a big Band-Aid. Besides, we're almost home now."

Lisa's lip quivered and her hands were like ice.

"Look," I told her, pointing ahead of us down the highway. "Look over there. You see that bend in the road?"

"Uh-huh."

"Just around that bend, and then two or three more and then only a few miles after that is your home. We're almost there."

"Promise?"

"I promise." I pressed lightly on the accelerator and pulled back onto the highway. I hoped that I wasn't lying to her again.

# THIRTY-TWO

As we drove those last few miles I couldn't help wondering what disaster would occur next. Would the engine explode? Would a meteor blaze out of the sky and rip away one of our wheels? Did I really have the right Oakdale after all, although Jimmie's presence seemed to confirm that I did. And if so, did Lisa's parents still live there? Had they moved to China?

I had avoided asking Lisa how long ago she had been kidnapped. Children have a variable sense of time and the longer the period, the less reliable their interpretation. Often, six months and three years are both "a long time ago." As I drove those last miles, my mind was a whirl of such thoughts, questions, and uncertainties.

Oakdale appeared suddenly as I topped a low rise. In the near distance I saw the sprawl of stores along the main street and single-story commercial buildings and houses spreading out from the center of town. A hundred yards ahead the road dipped back down and I lost my perspective. A minute or two later we reached the outskirts of the town.

On the main street the Golden Eagle Coffee Shop was open and doing a good business but with my blood-caked clothes I didn't think that I wanted to wander in there to ask directions. Besides I didn't know if I had the strength to make it to the front counter and back again to the car. I could still feel blood trickling down my belly and into my pants.

I drove through the town and tried to find a pedestrian whom I could ask for directions. Finally, toward the far end of State Street I saw a boy about eleven or twelve years old delivering papers to the still-closed stores and offices. I pulled ahead of him, rolled down my window, and honked the horn. When he turned I waved at him and motioned for him to come over to the car. He paused for a moment and when he didn't recognize either me or the Chevy he walked his bike forward hesitantly and stopped six feet back from the driver's window. The children in this town had apparently been warned about strange men in unfamiliar vehicles.

"I need to find Avery Road," I told him. "Can you tell me where it is?" This was it. The answer to this question would tell me, at least, if I had the right Oakdale after all. If he just stared at me and said, "Avery Road? There's no street around here like that," I didn't know what I would do.

But the boy didn't speak. He just stared at me, his eyes wide in shock. I realized that I had gestured with my left hand which was painted with my blood. I didn't have the time or the strength to explain. "Son, where's Avery Road? It's really important."

The boy forced his eyes from my hand and studied my face which wasn't in much better condition. I had probably touched my cheek, scratched my temple, rubbed my nose in five or ten different unconscious ways, dappling my skin and hair with drabs and spots of blood.

"What happened to you?" he said in a voice part fear, part amazement. "Were you in a wreck or something?"

"I'm fine. I just need to find Avery Road. Is it around here?"

"Uh, sure. I live just around the corner from there. Okay, you go down here until you see the Texaco station, then you turn right for about a mile, then left on Cottonwood and keep going until you get to Avery."

I had found it! This was where she had lived. I tried to concentrate on the boy's directions but I was feeling increasingly light-headed. I repeated them back, but got confused. As we spoke the boy slowly moved closer to the car until now he was only a foot or two from the driver's door. He couldn't seem to take his eyes from my blood-stained hands and face, but he repeated his directions and this time I got them right.

I thanked him and started to turn away, and that seemed to break the spell. For the first time he looked past me, into the car, and saw Lisa. I didn't pay attention to him as I pulled away, but had I looked at him one more time I would have seen a look of confusion, then vast excitement cloud his features. I might even have seen his lips silently mouth her name. It was now about five minutes to eight.

As I drove toward the Texaco Station the boy, Donnie Wilson, jumped on his bike, his paper route forgotten, and tore off for his home. Taking a more direct route than the one he had given me, racing through alleys, across back lots, he managed to reach his house, around the corner and two houses down from 749 Avery Road, barely a minute after I finally arrived at our destination.

It was a white frame house set to the right of a two-car garage. The front yard sported two large, now leafless maple trees from one of which hung a homemade swing that wobbled, empty, in the light morning breeze. Brass numbers, "749", were affixed to the face of the waist-high gate that opened onto a concrete walk.

"Is that your house, Lisa?" I asked her. She stared out the window and studied the building for a long second or two.

"Yes," she said, nodding her head. Is it her house or does it just look like the house she remembers from God knows how long ago? I wondered. I couldn't help thinking that after so many false starts, so many disappointments, that this might be just one more false hope, one more dead end.

I opened the door and was surprised at how difficult I found it to stand. My legs felt boneless. Supporting myself on the car and leaving bloody handprints across the Chevy's fender and hood, I limped around to Lisa's door. I got it open and she slipped out. I looked down at her, wiped my fingers on one of the few remaining unstained portions of my shirt, and took her hand in mine. Together we moved up the walk and mounted the two steps to the front door.

The front door's hinges were to my left and when we reached

the top of the steps I pulled Lisa to my right side, beyond the right edge of the doorway, to a place where she would be out of the sight of whomever opened the door. I could not shake the feeling that, in spite of everything, this might be the wrong house, the wrong city, (couldn't there be two Avery Roads as well as two Oakdales?), that some relative or a tenant or new owner might be the one to open the door, that Lisa, her memory faded or her will overcome by hope, might race into that stranger's arms only to find that the lady was not her mother after all. I know it sounds overly cautious, silly even, but if I was wrong to have those fears it would only delay reuniting Lisa with her parents for a few seconds, and if I was right, then I might save her from more pain.

"Sweetheart," I said, bending over, close to her. "I'm not completely certain that this is the right house. I want you to stand there and let me make sure that the people who live here really are your parents. I don't want us to get all excited if I've made another mistake. Okay?"

"Yes, Peter," she said softly, and I realized in that instant that if I had asked her to walk through fire for me, or to take on Satan himself, that Lisa would have done it with no more response than a placid, "Yes, Peter." In fact, she had already done that for me when, unasked, she had thrown those rocks at Jimmie and saved my life.

I rang the bell and leaned against the door frame. It was almost exactly eight a.m. I heard footsteps approaching and a muted, "Who's that at this time of the morning?" then another voice asking, "Do you suppose it's Carlos?" A moment later the door opened and a man in his early thirties, dressed in a white shirt, looked out at me and his mouth opened in shock at the sight of my blood-soaked clothes.

"Oh, my God!" he shouted, then ordered, "Come in, come in!"

"What is it?" A woman called. "What's happ—" she started to say then she got to the door and saw me. The man reached forward to help me inside, but I pulled my arm back, out of his grasp.

"No, no," I said. "That's not why I'm here." I made an effort to stand up straight and I placed myself in the center of the doorway.

"Are you Willard Taylor?" I asked him formally. The question, the fact that I was not some crash victim who had stumbled to his door but someone who was looking specifically for him, frightened him. He nodded hesitantly.

"Bill Taylor? Bill Taylor?" I persisted.

"Yes. What is it? What do you want?"

When I spoke Taylor's name I saw his wife shrink back and grasp her husband's arm. "Why has this man, covered in blood, come to our door, looking for my husband?" she asked herself. I turned my gaze to her.

"Margaret Taylor? Peggy Taylor?" I asked.

"Yes," she said, visibly frightened. "Who are you? What's this about?" I could hear more than fear in her voice. She and her husband were, for an instant, frozen in time, and they knew, I'm certain, that this was about Lisa. I took a deep breath and the pain in my side billowed then it and my weakness suddenly vanished.

"Is this," I said my eyes brimming so that I could barely see. My voice faltered and I began again. As I spoke I turned to my right, bent down, picked Lisa up, lifted her to shoulder height and held her out at arm's length in front of me, out to them.

"Is this your little girl?"

Both, as one, shouted, "Lisa!" and pulled her from my grasp. Peggy clutched Lisa to her chest and Bill hugged them both.

Behind us, at the corner of Cottonwood and Avery, Donnie Wilson watched Lisa being embraced by her parents' then turned and rode full speed back to his own home.

I fell back against the doorway and took in great lungfuls of air, for when Lisa left my arms my strength fled with her and I became an empty shell. My chest began to throb and I wasn't sure how much longer I could remain on my feet. I closed my eyes for a moment, and when I opened them I saw Bill Taylor turning from his wife and reaching for me.

"Take my arm, here," he ordered. "I'll call an ambulance. Come inside."

"The police," I demanded. "You have to call the police." Jimmie was still in the trunk. Maybe he had awakened by now. Could he get out? I leaned on Bill and, as he led me into the house, I noticed that I was leaving bloody stains on his clean white shirt.

"I have to wash my hands," I told him firmly.

"It's fine," he said, meaning his ruined shirt. "It doesn't matter."

"I have to wash my hands," I insisted. I wasn't thinking very clearly at that moment, but it was suddenly important that I wash away the blood. Reluctantly, Bill Taylor led me through the living room to the kitchen and I washed my hands and face with dishwashing liquid and dried them with paper towels. With great satisfaction I watched the rusty brown stains swirl down the drain as I lathered and rinsed. While I washed, he called the police.

I felt a bulge in my jacket pocket. I still had the camera I had bought in Valley Falls. I ran my fingers through my hair. My comb had disappeared. I checked to make sure that my hands were free of blood. I hobbled back into the living room where Lisa was cradled in her mother's arms. "Could you do me a favor?" I asked, holding up the camera. "Could I take a picture of the three of you?" They must have thought me a lunatic, deranged. Some stranger, covered in blood, returns their missing daughter, and then pulls a camera from his pocket and wants to take their picture! But at that moment they would deny me nothing. Bill and Peggy sat together and cradled Lisa across their laps, holding her securely in their arms. I don't know if I can describe their expressions, but I will try.

Lisa, Lisa smiled beautifully, angelically. All her problems were solved, all her prayers answered. It was a smile like none I had ever seen before, and will probably never see again.

Bill and Peggy's expressions were different from each others, yet both the same. Tears stained their faces and their eyes glittered. Their mouths formed smiles, almost—expressions of equal parts heartbreak and vast relief. It was the smile of a person who has been told that he has almost died, but that the operation was, after all, a success. Through the viewfinder I could see deep crimson patches of my blood clearly outlined against the fluorescent white of Bill Taylor's shirt.

All in all, it was a picture that might have graced the cover of *Life* magazine and had it done so, anyone who saw it would have paused to stare, to try to imagine the events that could have contorted human faces with such conflicting emotions.

The camera clicked and then clicked again as I took several more shots. I prevailed on Peggy to take a picture of Bill and me with Lisa, then Bill took a picture of Peggy, Lisa, and me. Finally, I asked them to take a picture of Lisa and me together.

We sat there, Lisa in my lap, heedless of the spreading stain that had soaked through my jacket and now was marking the back of her shirt. We both looked straight ahead, into the camera, and smiled on command. After we heard the shutter click, I turned to Lisa, almost for the last time, I thought.

"You see, sweetheart," I whispered to her, "I told you I would get you home. I promised you that everything would be all right." And as I said that I was overcome by a most peculiar emotion of mingled joy and an aching sense of loss, because I knew that she was not mine and that I had just given her away and that I would miss her more than I could have imagined I could miss anyone or anything.

And as I thought that and stared into her eyes, Lisa looked back at me with an expression that I had never encountered before, not from Janet, not that I could remember from my father or my mother, an expression, I am convinced, that is only possible from the very young, a look of pure and unconditional love. At that moment, I heard the shutter click on the last frame. Outside, coming closer, a siren wailed. God, I was getting tired of that sound.

# THIRTY-THREE

As soon as Donnie Wilson saw the Taylors' door open and Lisa scooped into her parents' arms he raced back to his house, burst through the front door, and began shouting at the top of his not-insubstantial twelve-year-old lungs:

"Mom! Dad! Lisa's home! Lisa's home!"

While Donnie's parents considered him to be a responsible boy, they had heard these sorts of alarms before. They had experienced his flying saucer phase: "It's a UFO! I saw it right over Miller's ranch!", and his "America's Most Wanted" phase: "I saw him at Talbot's, the ax murderer who was on TV last night!" and so they didn't get too excited when he ran into the living room and proclaimed Lisa Taylor's return.

"Slow down, Donnie," his father, Fred Wilson, said calmly. "What's this all about?"

"I saw her, Dad, Lisa Taylor. She was in this guy's car down on State Street. He asked me for directions and he was all covered in blood. It was her!"

"Hold on, Donnie. Let me get this straight. A man covered in blood had Lisa Taylor in his car down on State Street?"

"That's right, Dad. He looked awful, like he'd been in a wreck or something."

"Donnie, are you sure you aren't exaggerating? Maybe he cut his hand with a bread knife or something. It's been almost a year since Lisa was kidnapped. Maybe this man had his daughter in the car and she just looked like Lisa."

"Dad! It was Lisa Taylor. He even asked me where she lived."

"Wait a minute! He asked you where Lisa Taylor lived?"

"No, he asked me how to find Avery Road. He said it was very important that he find Avery Road." By this time Harriet Wilson had come down from the bedroom and was standing next to her husband. Fred Wilson fixed his son with a firm stare.

"Donnie, this is very important. How sure are you that this little girl looked like Lisa Taylor?"

"Dad, that's what I'm trying to tell you. She didn't look like Lisa Taylor. It was Lisa Taylor. Anyway, I saw him take her home."

"What?"

"I saw him. I took the shortcut through the back lot and I got to the corner right after he got to the Taylor's door. There was a lot of shouting and crying and they grabbed Lisa and then they all went inside."

"Donnie, if you're making this up . . . !" But Fred Wilson knew he wasn't, knew his son was not that kind of kid. Fred and Harriet looked at each other then both ran out the door and down the street toward the '56 Chevy parked in front of the Taylor house, the Chevy with reddish-brown handprints still wet on its fenders and hood and with a sticky puddle of blood congealing in the middle of the driver's seat.

Fred was afraid to ring the bell, to intrude on his neighbors' privacy, but he had to know. Guiltily, he crossed the lawn and peeked through the front window and saw Lisa and Bill and Peggy huddled on the couch. Fred stared for a moment not quite able to believe that this miracle had happened and then he ran back to his wife.

"It's her!" Fred said struggling to control his emotions when he rejoined his family.

"That's what I told you!" Donnie reminded them, but Fred was no longer paying much attention to his son. He was too busy trying to figure out what they should do next.

"Harriet, call everyone you can think of," he suggested a moment later. "And tell each of them to call somebody else."

"What are you going to do?"

"Donnie and I are going into town. We've got to get Earl Scheinberg to open up the store."

Harriet headed for the Taylors' neighbors at number 747 while Fred and Donnie ran back to their home and climbed into Fred's Ford Explorer. In a couple of minutes they were pulling up in front of the Golden Eagle Coffee Shop, now at the height of the breakfast rush. At almost that same instant, Bill Taylor was dialing the police.

When Nancy Stern answered the phone with her usual "Oakdale Police Department," Bill Taylor found that he was almost unable to speak. Finally, when he managed to tell Nancy that he needed to talk to Carlos Ramirez, right away. She didn't recognize his congested voice and asked who she could say was calling. Bill tried to give her his name, started to explain that he was calling about Lisa, that it was an emergency, but found he could barely speak.

Nancy Stern found Carlos in the squad room, talking with the Chief and one of the uniformed officers, Mike Coleman, about the sudden rash of stolen cars, all two of them. The three men looked up when Nancy ran into the room. She hadn't started out running. At first she just put Bill Taylor on hold and walked quickly to the little swinging gate which led from the front desk to the station's public area. Once through the gate she quickened her pace, intending only to walk rapidly to the squad room, but she couldn't stop thinking about Bill Taylor and how he had sounded, and she found herself running down the hallway, grabbing the door jam and swinging herself, still racing, into the room. Before she even got to the doorway, she was shouting:

"Detective! Carlos!"

So, when Nancy passed through the door, Carlos Ramirez was already looking up, his coffee and his stolen cars all but forgotten.

"Detective," she shouted, "It's Bill Taylor on line two. He says it's urgent! He says it's about Lisa." Instantly, Carlos reached for his phone, but Nancy was still talking.

"Detective, he's crying!"

Ramirez's hand froze for a moment above the phone, then grabbed the receiver.

"Bill, this is Carlos. What's happened?" He listened for a moment then interrupted, "Bill, Bill, slow down! Wait! There's a man in your house, bleeding on your carpet? Wait! Nancy, get an ambulance over to Bill Taylor's place right away— Okay, Bill, I've got an ambulance coming. What's happened?"

After a moment of silence Ramirez's eyes seemed to lose their focus and his knuckles turned white as he tightened his grip on the phone.

"He found Lisa?" he said softly, not looking at Nancy or Mark or Mike Coleman, though all three of them were staring at him.

"Where? When?" There was another long pause as Ramirez listened while Bill Taylor labored to get his words out in coherent sentences. Suddenly, Carlos sat straight up and stared down at the phone's mouthpiece as if he would be able to see through it and into Taylor's living room if he only concentrated hard enough.

"Yes, yes, I would," he said then paused, five seconds, ten, then blinked his eyes rapidly and said gently.

"Hello, Lisa. How are you? Yes, your Daddy told me about your friend. The doctor is already on his way. We'll be right there. I'll see you in a couple of minutes." Ramirez held the phone next to his ear for a second or so longer, then dropped it to the desk.

"She's alive!" he shouted when he raised his eyes and saw the expressions on the faces around him. "Some guy bleeding, covered in blood, just brought her home! Nancy, we're going to need crowd control! Get everyone you can out to the Taylor place right now. And call the clinic. Have them get on the radio to the ambulance. Make sure they know that this guy just brought Lisa Taylor home. Tell them to do whatever it takes but to get there fast. And make sure they have some plasma and a surgeon standing by."

Ramirez had already gotten to his feet and was almost to the squad room door by the time he'd finished giving his instructions.

"I'm coming with you," the Chief said running after him.

"Me too," Coleman called to their already retreating forms.

\* \* \*

A block away, Fred and Donnie Wilson had entered the Golden Eagle Coffee Shop and located Earl Scheinberg, the current owner of Talbot's Drugstore, as he worked on his breakfast of waffles and scrambled eggs.

"Earl, we've got to get into your store!" Fred told him as he began to pull Earl from his stool.

"Fred, what are you doing? You know I open at nine-thirty."

"Now Earl! We can't wait. It's an emergency!"

"Oh my God, what is it? Is somebody hurt? What do you need?" Earl asked as he pushed his plate away and began to stand.

"Yellow ribbon. We need all the yellow ribbon you've got, right away."

"Fred, have you gone nuts!" Earl said harshly, already beginning to sit back down. "What kind of an emergency requires my entire ribbon supply, I'd like to know."

"It's Lisa Taylor, Mr. Scheinberg," Donnie blurted out. "She's come home." Earl froze, halfway onto his stool and looked first at Donnie, then at Fred. All conversation in the restaurant had ceased.

"It's true, Earl," Fred told him. "Some guy, cut up real bad, brought her home a few minutes ago. I saw her myself."

"Dear God!" Earl shouted. "What are we waiting for?" And the three of them, followed by everyone else in the place except the owner raced out the door and across the street. Jim Mason paused long enough to pick up a Magic Marker and make up a sign from a piece of cardboard that he cut from a potato chip carton:

**Lisa Taylor Found Alive & Well Brought Home.**
**Gone To Talbot's For Yellow Ribbon.**
**—Closed—**

He Scotch-taped the sign to the inside of the glass portion of the front door then locked the door behind him and ran across the street to join the rest of his customers.

\* \* \*

When Carlos Ramirez arrived at 749 Avery Road about twenty neighbors had already gathered on the lawn and street in front of the house. The ambulance had not yet arrived. The three officers sprinted up to the front door and Carlos anxiously rang the bell. Bill Taylor opened it and let them in. After a few words of greeting they hurried into the living room.

I was still sitting on the couch. All the energy and determination that I had possessed only a few minutes before had evaporated and just lifting my head, just holding my eyes open was becoming a struggle. But I had one more task to perform. Detective Ramirez hugged Lisa and then came over to me. He had seen plenty of wounded people in his years on the LAPD.

"What happened? Were you shot?"

"Knife. It's not that bad. I taped it up in the car. I'm just a little tired."

"Okay, don't worry. The ambulance is on its way. We've got a doctor standing by. You'll be fine," he said but there was something about his eyes that told me that he wasn't quite so sure.

"The man who did this—"

"Don't worry about that now. We'll get your statement later. Just take it easy."

"No! This is important. Help me up." I struggled to stand but Ramirez put a hand on my shoulder to hold me down, just as I had done to Isaiah. "You've got to help me get to the door. Help me!" I begged him. Ramirez stared at me a moment and realized that I was determined to show him something and he slipped his arm around my shoulders and pulled me to my feet. Together, Ramirez on the one side, Bill Taylor on the other, they half carried me to the front door. At my insistence, Carlos opened it.

"That car out there, the '56 Chevy. Do you see it?" They stared at me, confused. Of course they saw it. What was I getting at? I freed my right arm from Carlos's grip and pulled the Reverend's keys from my pocket. I grabbed Carlos's hand, put the keys into his palm and forced his fingers closed, pressing them tightly around the keys.

"In the trunk," I said nodding toward the car. "The man who kidnapped Lisa and stabbed me. I knocked him out and locked him in the truck. Be careful! I didn't search him. He might have a gun. He had one before. Please," I pleaded, "Be careful!"

The officers looked from me to the car. Ramirez held up the keys as if he had never seen anything quite like them before. And then his expression changed: determination, anger, hunger appeared on his face.

At that moment two more patrol cars arrived and Carlos and Mark Powell and Mike Coleman propped me against the wall next to the door and raced outside. The new officers were instructed to get the crowd back, across the street, far away from the Chevy. Carlos and Powell took up positions to the left rear and right rear of the trunk while Coleman was given the keys. They agreed that he would release the lock, throw up the lid, then fall to the ground out of the way.

Bill Taylor heard me tell Carlos that the man who had stolen his daughter was right outside. Rigid, his eyes fired with hate, he rooted himself in the doorway next to me and stared at the scene on the front lawn. Lisa and her mother came over too, though Bill didn't realize that Lisa was standing behind him and Peggy didn't know what was going on, just that Bill and I were looking out of the doorway and that the police had hurried outside.

Carlos and Mark pulled out their guns. Mark's was a Beretta 92; Carlos's a going-away present from his friends on the LAPD, a Glock seventeen-shot, 9-mm double-action automatic. Coleman got into position and, at a nodded signal from Carlos, twisted the key and threw open the trunk. Jimmie's body was turned now, back and butt facing the officers, head and hands out of sight.

"This is the police," Ramirez shouted. "You're under arrest for kidnapping and attempted murder. Come out slowly! Keep your hands in plain sight. If you make any suspicious movements we will shoot you." Jimmie did not move. "You in the car!" Carlos repeated. "This is the police! You're under arrest. Come out of the trunk and keep your hands in plain sight and you won't be hurt."

For another heartbeat or two nothing happened. Was Jimmie still unconscious? Then he moved. First his right foot, then his left. Slowly he rolled onto his back and dropped his feet out of the trunk and dangled them over the bumper. His right hand was visible but his left grasped his side inside his coat. Carefully,

Jimmie maneuvered himself into a sitting position, but was hunched over so that you could only see his knees and shoulders and the top of his head. Finally he slid his butt off the edge of the trunk and planted his feet on the ground.

Now he stood, still hunched over at the waist like a man who has been sucker punched and is trying to hold the pain in his stomach. Both his hands were inside his jacket and out of sight.

"Turn around, put your hands over your head and get down on your knees!" Carlos ordered. "NOW!"

Jimmie began to turn as if about to comply, then in one swift motion he pulled his right hand from beneath his coat. A dark, black, metal object was clenched in his fist and he swung it in a smooth arc toward Carlos Ramirez.

"GUN!" Coleman shouted and a split second later, Carlos and Powell both fired. I've heard a thousand times about incidents where people say that time slows down, about people who experience extraordinary events and claim it all happened as if under water. As trite as that sounds, that's what this was like to me.

Each of the shots was separate, distinct. The first one hit Jimmie in the left shoulder and passed cleanly through. His body jerked but other than that he didn't even seem to notice the bullet's impact. He just spun his revolver a little farther in its arc and pulled the trigger. His shot went several feet wide of Carlos to the left.

Then Powell fired, then Carlos fired, then Coleman fired. Bang! Bang! Bang! A slow, methodical rhythm. And with each shot Jimmie jerked, and blood and bone and gibbets of flesh spurted from his body, and still he would not fall. It was as if the force of the bullets themselves held him upright.

At first Bill Taylor was pleased that the man who had sold his daughter into slavery was suffering, until the blood sprayed from Jimmie's back at the impact of the second bullet. Then the third shot hit, and then the fourth. Bill Taylor, a decent man, could not take pleasure in the carnage that he witnessed. Horrified, he began to turn away, but behind him, Lisa still watched.

She had seen so much, but had witnessed nothing like this. Piece by piece, shot by shot, the jerking, jumping half dead on its feet mannequin that had once been Jimmie Devries was torn and shredded and ripped apart.

Bang! Lisa's eyes grew wider. Bang! Her mouth opened in horror. Bang! Her throat tried to emit a silent scream, but still she watched. Bang! A great spray of blood and tissue flew from Jimmie's side. Bang! A horrible, tortured cry slipped from her throat. Bang! Bang! Bang! Bang! Bang! She threw her arms around her father's legs and screamed "NO!" with all her strength. Sobbing, she buried her face in the folds of his pants and for the first time she allowed herself to cry aloud.

I stood there, watching her, knowing that this carnage had reopened her wounds but that now, at last with Jimmie's death, they might be able to heal. I listened to her tears, reached out to caress her hair, then, just as my fingers touched her, my feet seemed to lose their purchase on the ground and I floated away soundlessly into a formless gray fog.

# THIRTY-FOUR

I slept for six hours, woke up, had a late lunch, then an hour later I was asleep again. It was Tuesday morning before they finally let me out of the Urgent Care Clinic, weak and sore but more or less all right. The doctor had stitched up my chest (it turned out that it was only a flesh wound), filled me full of antibiotics, washed and cleaned my various cuts and scrapes, and gave me a tetanus shot for good measure. I would not be running the Bay To Breakers Race for the next few weeks but at least I was again walking under my own power. Then the real discomfort began. It was time to fill out the police reports.

Because Lisa had been taken across state lines, this was a Federal crime and two FBI agents had already arrived. I figured that the simplest thing to do was to tell the story right from the beginning. "Why didn't you just call the police as soon as you found her?" they kept asking me. All I could say was what I had told Larkin McCray, that everything that I did had seemed like a good idea at the time.

They were very interested in Ken's identity but I thought we would not be able to find him. Later, when I led them back to Jimmie's cabin near Burney they found my business card with

Ken's license number written on the back still in the trash. Ken was arrested that evening. Lisa and I will be testifying against him some time this decade, given the structure of our criminal court system. The good news was that Ken could not make his million-dollar bail and so is awaiting trial in the Federal lockup on Terminal Island, Washington.

They never did find Ray, the man I had hit with the lamp at the Belair Motel. (When I got home I sent George a check for a hundred dollars to cover the broken lamp and the smashed door. All things considered, I figured I owed it to him.)

Eric's remains, on the other hand, were discovered by a couple of hikers a few hundred yards off Highway 299 about ten miles west of Burney. There was a Coroner's inquest but after the FBI agents submitted a copy of their report and Carlos Ramirez drove down to testify on my behalf it was quickly decided that Eric's death was a clear case of self-defense.

I was a little worried about the pickup truck full of marijuana but the officers merely listened to that part of my story without seeming to make any notes and they never mentioned the incident again. Neither did I.

I called the Reverend when I got out of the hospital and told him that I would bring his car back in a few days. I managed to find an auto detailer who was able to clean it and even get the blood out of the seatcovers. I told Isaiah that I had lost his toolbox but that I would replace it with a new one. I think he figured out that I might be omitting a few details from my story but he was too much of a gentleman to say so.

I was offered more gifts than I can remember. My blood-soaked clothes were replaced. I was given a plane ticket from Redding to San Francisco, plus I got enough offers of free meals to feed me for a year.

Of course, I called my office and they were frantic. It turned out that the Highway Patrol had found my Lexus abandoned where its tire had gone flat and no one knew if I had been kidnapped or was alive or dead. One of my employees arranged to have his son go down to the CHP impound lot and drive it back to Santa Clara. I assured my secretary that I was fine and I told her to cancel and reschedule all my appointments for the rest of the week and that I would try to get in on Thursday or Friday to go through my mail and to return telephone calls.

I had dinner with Lisa and her parents on Tuesday night. Carlos drove me over and it looked as if a Hallmark warehouse had exploded—there were yellow ribbons everywhere, on the houses, on the street signs, on the branches of trees, and where they ran out of ribbon they had used yarn, tape, even twine festooned with yellow Post-It notes. I don't know how much Lisa understood what these ribbons meant but everyone else in town did; it was a celebration of their joy as much as hers.

It was a strange dinner, at first. Initially, we were all kind of stiff, afraid to say the wrong thing or mention anything that might upset Lisa, but she was so happy to be home that eventually we loosened up and had a nice time. I actually got Lisa to laugh twice. I told her that I had talked to Isaiah on the phone and that he was doing great. They were going to have him out of the hospital in a day or so. Then she asked if we could visit him sometime. He apparently had told her that his birthday was in mid-August, only a few days after hers, and since he didn't live that far away, she wanted to know if we could go to his party. Who was "we"?

I felt as if I was intruding into Bill and Peggy's family. Lisa was their daughter, not mine. How could I be anything more to her than a reminder of the pain that she had suffered? But, to my surprise, her parents seemed to think that a joint birthday party with Isaiah was a fine idea. Would the Reverend have room for some additional guests? Would his sons mind if we invited ourselves? Did I think I could get away from my business and come on up for the celebration? August was a few months away. I decided to see if they still felt this way later, after things had a chance to get back to normal.

I left town on Wednesday morning. Bill and Peggy saw me off. Bill insisted on telling me that whatever he had was mine, that he could never repay me for what I had done for Lisa, but that if I ever needed anything, anything at all, all I had to do was ask and, somehow, he would get it for me. I tried to explain to him that I felt that the debt was the other way around. Then he asked me again if I would come back this summer for Lisa's and the Reverend's joint birthday party. I told him that I would let him know.

When it was time to leave I took Lisa aside to say good-bye. I told her that she had to forget everything that had happened to her and to go on with her life and not to let the Jimmies of this world hurt her, and other stuff like that, much of which she probably did not really understand and which I felt like an old fool saying, even as the words were leaving my mouth. Then she surprised me.

"I'll do what you asked me," she said.

"What I asked you? What was that?"

"To help someone someday, just the way you helped me. I won't forget." I looked at her, tried to say what was in my heart, but I couldn't. I just hugged her and whispered to her, "I love you, Lisa." And then it was time to go. As Carlos drove me away, I watched her wave to me until she disappeared from my sight.

Oh yes, I developed the film and I sent one set of prints to Bill and one to Carlos. I had a custom lab blow up the picture of Lisa, Bill, and Peggy to 11 by 14 inches and then had it matted and custom framed. I paid them extra to do it right away. I brought it to my office on Friday morning when I returned to work. Had only one week gone by? I rushed past the receptionist and went straight to my office where I removed the wrapping paper and hung the framed photograph on the wall to the right of my door. I had just finished putting it up and was going through a week's worth of mail, when Rick Barnes came in.

"Peter, what the hell's going on?" he demanded.

"And good morning to you, Rick."

"Peter, there are messages out there for you from the FBI, something about scheduling your testimony? Your car was discovered abandoned near Tulare. Tulare, for God's sake! You look like you've been in a war. Peter, what's happened?" I looked at Rick and tried to explain.

"There was this little girl. . . . Rick, last Thursday, a week ago, when I was going to meet Baumbach I stopped for some aspirin. I found this child, this little girl, and she had, she had, this man had . . ." and I couldn't say anymore. I turned away, took a deep breath, blinked, and turned back from the window.

"I can't explain this yet, Rick," I finally told him. "Not yet. Maybe I'll write it all down, write it down and give it to you so that you can read it. Maybe it will make more sense that way."

275

And that's what I've done. I've written this all down here, but now I don't know if I will ever show it to Rick or any of the people who were not directly involved. But I think I'll let the Reverend read it. Somehow I feel that he'll understand it best. His birthday is next month and I'm going to the party. They're going to hold it in Oakdale. I've already typed up invitations for Larkin McCray and Sal Gianinni and Bella. I figured they would like to know how this all turned out.

Bill tells me that the town has been looking for the right occasion to celebrate Lisa's return. An old-fashioned Barbecue Birthday Party with the Reverend and me and Lisa as the guests of honor has everyone pretty excited. Bill said he figures we'll probably do nothing but eat and drink and dance for about two or three days. I'm looking forward to it. Actually, I can't wait.

When Rick, reluctantly, turned to leave my office, he saw the picture I had just hung and he stopped. It's that kind of photo, and only someone who is dead inside could pass it without staring.

"What's this?" he asked in amazement.

"That's the best picture I've ever taken. I put it there so that I can look at it every day."

"Who are these people? You said something about a little girl. Is that her? Who is she?"

I looked up at Rick and told him the only thing that I have been able to tell anyone about what happened that week: I pointed to the photo, to the smiling child cradled lovingly and securely in her parents' arms, and said:

"Her name is Lisa."

# THIRTY-FIVE

August in the high prairie was hotter than Peter had anticipated and sweat soon began to seep beneath his shirt and dribble down his sides and back. In honor of the occasion, Lisa and Isaiah's long-awaited birthday party, he had bought a new Burberry suit and a Nordstrom custom-fitted shirt and tie. On the phone two weeks before Carlos had said something about Peter being the "guest of honor." While Peter thought that designation was inappropriate, he had done more things wrong than right, if that's how people felt then he should at least dress the part. But the suit didn't last an hour after his arrival.

There was small airport, really little more than an unmanned asphalt strip, just east of town, and Peter landed there around ten that Saturday morning, his longest solo flight to date. His plane was a Cessna 210, the most powerful single-engine craft the company had ever produced. Peter had bought it as soon as he finished his training and received his license.

He hadn't planned on becoming a private pilot but he got to thinking about Oakdale, how far away it was, and how awkward it would be to fly commercially to Klamath Falls then have to rent a car and drive to town. Besides, maybe it was time for him to try something new, to expand his horizons. There were lots of places he could go in his own plane. He could afford it. The quarterly interest on the appreciation on his NowSoft stock covered the cost of the Cessna.

Bill and Peggy Taylor and Lisa were waiting for him at the end of the runway and after a tearful reunion they bundled him and his baggage into their Voyager and headed back to town. By the time they reached State Street, Peter was already sweating heavily and he left his coat in the van. Fifteen minutes later his tie joined it there.

State Street had been blocked to traffic and now was filled with picnic tables shaded by large beach umbrellas, a temporary bandstand draped with flags and bunting, coolers full of soft drinks and beer, and at least ten different barbecue grills spewing smoke scented with the fragrance of steaks and hot dogs and chicken and fresh Pacific Coast salmon.

Around noon a parade of three cars arrived from New Pine Creek with Isaiah's '56 Chevy in the lead. The Reverend and Matthew rode in the Chevy while Mark and his family and Matthew's wife and children and half a delicatessen worth of pies, salads, and casseroles filled the other two cars.

The afternoon passed in a blur of eating, drinking, volleyball, baseball, horseshoes, gossiping, tall stories, and then more eating and drinking.

Peter lost track of the number of times he was asked to re-tell his story. Sal told all who would listen that Peter's heroism was obvious to anyone who knew his birthdate and anything about astrology. Larkin McCray not only attended but brought his daughter, her husband, and his two grandchildren all the way from Crescent City. He insisted that after dinner he would teach Peter to dance, country style, which Howard took as more of a threat than a promise. Bill Taylor seemed particularly interested in Peter's new hobby—did Peter enjoy flying? Could he take time away from his business now and then? Did Peter have any plans for Thanksgiving or Christmas? Could he fly up for the holidays?

Late in the day, buffet tables were set up and food prepared for the scheduled eight o'clock banquet. Two bands were ready to begin alternating their play beginning at nine-thirty and continuing as long as anyone was still on their feet. Finally in the golden light of the early summer evening Peter was called to the bandstand to say a few words. At first he felt as if he couldn't string two coherent sentences together, then he focused on Lisa, standing between her parents just a few feet before him, and he began to speak as if he was talking only to her.

He apologized for all of the mistakes he had made, all of the risks to which he had exposed her, told her that he had tried to do the best he could and admitted that it was only through her courage and good luck or fate or, as he looked down on Isaiah's smiling face, divine intervention, that they were all here today, safe and sound. Then he told her that he loved her. Then he sat down.

Peter left late Sunday afternoon with firm promises to come back soon. It turned out that the Oasis Project managed to ship on time after all and by Thanksgiving Peter found that he had the time for a quick flight up to Oregon. And somehow, his Christmas schedule seemed to resolve itself the same way.

The next spring, when he flew up for the award of Lisa's team's second place soccer trophy it seemed foolishly inconvenient to keep pestering Bill and Peggy to drive him around town so he bought a used Explorer and rented a garage in which to keep it from Earl at the drugstore. True, he didn't really need a four-wheel drive, but Bill and Carlos had been talking to him about this trout stream. . . .

Next summer, Lisa's birthday party was more restrained, a more private affair, but it gave Peter and Lisa the chance to talk about things, her friends, school, other details of her life, and he started thinking about what she might want to do when she grew up. Peter had gone to grad school at Stanford and he began to wonder if it was too early to start working to get her accepted there. The tuition wouldn't be a problem. Not the way NowSoft was going. And then? Then she would have her whole life ahead of her. Peter's musing was interrupted by a shout from the front yard then the sound of Lisa giggling.

"You're too big!" Bill shouted, laughing. "I'm getting tired. We need to get someone else out here to push you for a while."

"Peter! Peter," Lisa called. "Can you push me on the swing?"

"Coming, sweetheart," Peter shouted as he rose and trotted happily toward the front door. "I'll be right there."